LOST & found

A NOVEL

D1468897

NICOLE WILLIAMS

Cover Design by Sarah Hansen of Okay Creations
Editing by Cassie Cox
Formatting by JT Formatting

For my Dad
Thank you for being such a strong and silent protector in
my life, and for setting the bar for what a man can and
should be.

CHAPTER one

THERE ARE LOW points, and there are *low* points. This—rattling down an endless stretch of interstate in a Greyhound bus toward the middle of farm-country-nowhere a week after barely graduating high school—was my *low* point.

I didn't understand why "barely" graduating high school was indicative of how I would do in art school in the fall—high school was designed to torture teenagers, not teach them—but Mom thought otherwise.

If the art school in Seattle I wanted to attend didn't cost a fortune and a half, I wouldn't have given a damn what Mom thought. She was on the road so much I was lucky to see her one day a week. Even on that one day, she was usually in and out so quickly you would have thought my brand of "freak" was contagious. I didn't understand why a woman who had ignoring her one and only spawn down to a science was putting her foot down when it came to funding my future.

I'd been accepted into the art school I'd been dreaming about since I'd given the proverbial finger to Home Economics in eighth grade and taken Art 101 instead. I'd never been so excited about anything in my life. But that didn't matter to Mom. She wouldn't foot the bill for school unless I convinced her I could step up to life's plate and prove myself a responsible member of society, unlike the drain to it she was convinced I was.

So where, in all the possible places, could I prove myself to dear, suddenly-concerned, checkbook-holding mom?

Willow Springs Ranch, smack in the middle of Hickville, USA.

That's right. A ranch.

I'd never been on one, but I didn't need to in order to know ranches and Rowen Sterling should stay on opposite ends of the universe. I was a city girl who'd never been around anything four-legged other than dogs or cats. I believed wide open spaces and starry nights were over-rated and only idealized so the country music industry could stay afloat. I thought rural was synonymous with hell.

I was the *lucky* girl who'd be spending my entire summer up to my knees in "rural."

I wasn't sure *how* I'd do it, and I sure as hell didn't *want* to do it, but I had to. Three months in hell was worth four years of art school. My life had never been easy, so I knew I could handle whatever waited for me at Willow Springs. A long time ago, I'd learned I was good at "hand-ling" life. I didn't excel at it, and I certainly didn't thrive at it, but I could handle life and everything it had thrown at me.

My secret? I'd simply accepted that life was pain.

There wasn't a rhyme or a reason to the universe and those who occupied it. We were here. Some of us for long durations and some of us for not so long, but the one thing we humans could depend on from life was pain.

Accepting that had somehow made living easier. I'd

2

stopped looking for happiness and, in so doing, wasn't living in a steady state of let-down anymore. I didn't let myself hope either. That was the real poison that put the vacant expression in so many people's eyes.

I accepted.

That was the only reason I was about to hop off the Greyhound bus in western Montana. I'd accepted that if I wanted to go to art school, I'd have to pay a pain price to get there.

After twelve hours on the road, everyone practically bolted out of their seats the moment the bus came to a stop. Even though "Big Sky Montana" wasn't anything to bound out of a bus toward, it was more appealing than hanging back in the recirculated air that had gotten especially rank the last hundred miles. The middle-aged guy who'd snored his way through the whole trip leapt out into the aisle without a look or word my way. After shouldering my purse, I tucked my hair back into my hoodie and slid the purse strap over my head.

I took a few steps toward the aisle and waited for someone to let me into the line. I was sitting in one of the first few rows. Surely the entire bus wouldn't have to off-load before I got to. Part of my strategy for getting a seat in the front of the bus was so I could sneak off at the earliest opportunity.

As the line of bodies continued by me, it became obvious I would be the last one off. I wasn't invisible to the other passengers. They just *treated* me like I was. I was familiar with that act.

Moms steering cartfuls of kids and groceries through the store would shoot me sideways glances like they expected me to roll my sleeve up and shoot up right there in the middle of the cereal aisle. When I'd passed my peers in the hall, they narrowed their eyes because I had the audacity to take up space on the planet.

People had never ignored me, but they wished they could. They wished people like me would just disappear or fall off the face of the earth so they wouldn't be reminded their little lives were so fake and full of shit.

As one guy about my age passed me, his attempt to ignore me faltered. Giving me a quick once-over, he shook his head and mouthed *Yikes* before he went on his Abercrombie-wearing, cheerleader-screwing way. I was tempted to give his back the bird, but for once, I controlled myself. Besides, that was nothing new. I lived that at least a dozen times a day back in the lowest form of purgatory known as high school.

I'd worn so many different labels I lost count. People liked to label things; it made them feel like the world made some sense. Like, if I was one thing, they were the other. I guess that made people feel better about themselves. If they focused on how screwed up I was, they could pretend they weren't just as screwed up.

I'd been labeled a goth, an emo, a druggie, a loser, and my personal favorite only because it showed just how ignorant people were: a freak.

I'd been called a million and a half other colorful names, but those were the most popular. However, labeling me a goth or an emo was just an insult to actual goths and emos. I didn't want a label; I didn't want to fit into a certain crowd. I was who I was, wore what I wore, and did what I did because that was who I was. Or at least the person I'd convinced myself I was.

I wasn't overly mysterious like a goth or exceptionally sad like an emo. I'd done drugs, but I'd never wandered into first period stoned off my ass like the hardcore druggies. I wasn't sure "loser" fit either, since I was a conscientious objector to all things that made conventional "winners" and "losers" out of people. So maybe out of all of those labels, the one that fit me best was freak.

A few more people shuffled by, and their attempts and immediate failures to ignore me confirmed I did freak well. As I fell in line behind the second to last person, my belief that people basically blew went up a few conviction levels.

Montana was bit warmer than Portland; that was the first thing I noticed as I stepped off the bus. The next thing? It already smelled like cow shit. Not overwhelmingly so, but that pungent tinge was in the air, along with the sweet note of grass and the not-so-sweet note of a sucky summer to come.

I almost sighed. I came so close.

But I didn't.

I didn't sigh anymore. Sighing showed disappointment, but I didn't hope anymore . . . thus eliminating disappointment from my life.

But I came pretty darn close when I examined the landscape. I'd been right. Wide open spaces, no building in sight taller than two floors, and nothing remotely resembled something I was familiar with.

"This must be your bag, young lady," the Greyhound employee said as he held out my bag.

"Why would you assume that?" I snapped, ignoring the man's overdone smile. "Because it's as dark and dilapidated as my clothing?"

That overdone smile fell quicker than my GPA in

middle school. Apparently Montana and I were already off to a rocky start.

"Ehhh . . . no," the man said, clearly flustered. "It's the last bag in here."

I glanced at the storage compartments. Empty.

Well, crap.

"Oh." I took my bag from him. "Sorry about that."

"I meant no offense." The man dusted his hands off on his pants before closing up the compartment doors.

"Me, either," I said as I headed away from the bus. "It just comes naturally, unfortunately."

My bag had to weigh almost as much as I did. I wasn't exactly a light packer, and sporting a black hoodie in the heat of a Montana summer day while attempting to haul my huge bag was my bad. I didn't make it far before giving up my one-woman trek toward the parking lot. Tossing my beast of a bag on the ground, I plopped down on it. I couldn't tear out of that hoodie fast enough.

I was supposed to meet one of the ranch hands from Willow Springs in the parking lot. I couldn't remember his name, just that it began with a J and was one hundred and ten percent a cowboy name. I was supposed to link up with some total stranger, after driving across a couple state lines on a Greyhound bus . . . and that was the first step toward proving my responsibility to my mother?

Yeah, that was fucked up.

Tilting my head back, I searched the sky, half expecting buzzards to be circling.

Man, even the sky was different. Too big and too blue. Where I came from, the sky was gray on most days, and on the rare day the cloud cover did shift, the sky was never quite blue. Almost as if it couldn't let go of the gray consuming it more days than not.

I was just about to close my eyes for a quick siesta and let Mr. Ranch-Hand-With-A-Gritty-Cowboy-Name wait when a figure passed by me.

On a typical day, I was passed by hundreds, if not thousands of people. Passed by, passed over, passed *something*, so I don't know why that particular figure caught my attention. Leaning up, I shielded my eyes from the sun and watched the "figure" I couldn't ignore. After a second, I understood why.

The guy was wearing positively the tightest, most painted-on jeans I'd ever seen a guy slide into. And my generation thought guys sporting skinny jeans was socially acceptable.

However, that cowboy, in what I could only assume were a pair of faded Wranglers, had just secured the sash and crown in the Tightest Pants in the Universe title.

"Excuse me, sir?" Tight Pant Boy tapped the shoulder of the employee I'd snapped at. He waited for the employee to turn around and acknowledge him before continuing.

"Yes?" the employee said, shaking Cowboy's hand when he extended it.

"Is this the bus that came up from Portland?" Cowboy Tight Pants glanced up at the windows like he was looking for someone.

"Sure is. Last passenger just got off a few minutes ago."

The cowboy's back was to me, although his *back* wasn't exactly what I zeroed in on. My attention had nothing to do with ogling, lusting, or wanting to run my hands all over it . . . I just couldn't wrap my mind around how those stitches were holding strong with pants two sizes too small cupping those butt cheeks.

"Was there a young woman on board? A girl about my age?"

"There were lots of young women on board, son," the employee replied, doing a better job of masking his sarcasm than I would have. "Do you have a description? Maybe a name?"

"I think she's blond, maybe strawberry blond," he began, tilting his head to the side. "Petite, I'm guessing . . . I don't know. I've only seen a picture of her that's ten years old."

My stomach fell a little.

"I've got her name right here," the cowboy said, sliding a piece of paper out of his front pocket. I didn't need to hear him say it. I already knew the name scratched down on that scrap of paper. "Rowen. Her name's Rowen Sterling."

My subconscious couldn't decide what to curse first, so it mixed, matched, and uttered a *Shuk* and a *Fuit.*

When my mom had told me I'd get a ride to Willow Springs with a ranch hand whose name I'd forgotten, I pictured a scratching, spitting, old-timer like the town sheriff in one of those old westerns. Not some young, fit man adhering to the tighter-the-better policy in jeans selection.

I had yet to see his face, but from what I'd seen of his back, I already knew what to expect. And if I was a typical eighteen-year-old girl who liked typical teenage girl things, I'm sure I'd be panting for the opportunity to catch a ride with Cowboy Montana in what I guessed was a big diesel truck with four tires on the back. I'd heard what that kind of truck was called, but I couldn't remember. Where I came from, people didn't need six tires because four did the job just fine.

Catching myself right before I let out a long sigh, I stood and made my way over. No sense in stalling.

Stopping a few feet behind the vacuum-sealed ass, I cleared my throat. "Looking for Rowen Sterling?"

Cowboy turned my direction. "Yeah. You know her?"

I gave a shrug. "Kind of."

"Do you know where she is?"

"Yeah," I replied, trying to get a look at his face. Between his huge-ass cowboy hat and the position of the sun, his whole face was shaded. He could have been the thing of female fantasies. He just as easily could have been eyeless and toothless.

After a few more seconds of quiet—I guessed he was waiting for me to add something—he shifted. "Could you tell me where she is then, please?"

I glanced at the photo in his hand. He'd been right. It was almost ten years old to the day. Taken at my ninth birthday party. I was wearing the biggest, pinkest, most god-awful princess dress ever created, and I was blond and beaming.

I was none of those things anymore. His reaction ought to be fun to witness.

"She's about two feet in front of you," I said, thankful I couldn't see his face. Whether it was a ten or a zero or somewhere in between, I didn't want to witness the shock and the cringe bound to come.

When someone compared the young girl in the picture to the older girl that was me present day, a cringe seemed the standard response.

What I didn't expect him to do was remove his hat and extend his hand. "Hey, Rowan." He flashed a smile that almost made me flinch. I hadn't been smiled at like that when meeting a stranger in a long time. "I'm Jesse. It's nice to meet you."

Jesse. That's right. The cowboy J name that had slipped my mind was the name that I was certain I'd never forget again. Not because his eyes were the same color as the sky, or because his light hair sort of cascaded down his forehead like it knew just where to fall, or because of the dimples drilled deep into his cheeks from the continued smile. Nope, the reason I'd remember Jesse's name from that day forward was because of the way he looked at me. He didn't study me like I was something different and scary. He looked at me like I was a human being, no different from himself, and yet unique just the same.

It was . . . staggering. It made me feel all light and floaty. For a girl who liked to keep her feet firmly on the ground and who, as a policy, didn't do "floaty," the whole sensation was a tad overwhelming.

After I'd left his hand hanging in the air like the staggered idiot I was, he dropped it back to his side and lifted his other hand, still holding the picture, toward my face. Studying the picture, then my face, his smile stretched higher. "Yep. You're Rowan Sterling all right," he said with certainty. As though he could see past my dyed dark hair, eyebrow ring, dark lipstick, and my inky black combat boots to find the little girl I'd once been. "Do you have a suitcase or anything?" His voice, like his smile, was warm and welcoming. In fact, if I had to pick two words to describe Jesse, those would be the ones: warm and welcoming.

10

And attractive. There was no denying that. Even to a girl like me, who most people probably assumed would prefer Dracula's company to a warm-blooded, all-American, sexy-as-all-hell boy.

Reminding myself I wasn't here to admire the male scenery, I hitched my thumb over my shoulder. "That black bag that looks as if I've stashed a dead body in it is mine," I said, cursing myself. A girl like me shouldn't talk about dead bodies stuffed in a bag. People wouldn't assume I was joking.

"Well, if you don't mind, could we get going?" Jesse asked, sliding that bucket-sized hat of his back into place before heading toward my abandoned bag. "I've got about two dozen fence poles to dig and set before dinnertime."

"Sounds like a killer time," I said. "Is fence pole maintenance a regular sort of thing on a ranch?"

"That depends how you define 'regular.' If thirty to forty every few days does, then yeah, I suppose fence pole maintenance is a regular sort of thing on a ranch."

"I thought you were a ranch hand," I said as we paused in front of my monster-sized bag. "Sounds more like you're a ranch bitch." I couldn't quite hide my smile, and it was a totally failed effort when Jesse laughed.

Damn, that laugh. Just hearing a few notes of it seemed to change my whole outlook. Not a total one-eighty, of course, but maybe a half of a percent. If someone like Jesse could laugh like that, the world couldn't completely blow.

"Yeah, I suppose ranch bitch is a more fitting title, come to think of it," Jesse said as he grabbed my bag and heaved it over his shoulder. From the way he'd just man-handled that thing, you'd have thought it was filled with feathers. When Alexander, my mom's boyfriend-of-the-month—a Grade A Douche by my standards—wrangled the bag into the trunk, I was fairly certain he'd have to meet with a chiropractor twice a week for the next year.

"Man, Rowen," he said, lifting the bag like he was trying to guess the weight. "From the weight of this sucker, I believe you could have a dead body zipped inside."

"Consider yourself warned," I said as we made our way into the parking lot. "Don't piss me off, or you'll wind up in a black travel bag."

Another couple notes of laughter rolled out of him. Two genuine laughs in less than a minute. Surely that had to break some sort of record.

"Thanks for the heads up." Jesse made his way around a truck that had been seeing better days for the entire twenty-first century before tossing my bag into the bed.

"What is this thing?"

"It's a truck," Jesse said slowly, giving me an odd look.

"It was a truck thirty years ago," I said, examining it again. The thing couldn't be street legal. "This is a corpse on wheels."

"What? No way," he replied, sounding a little offended. "This is Old Bessie." He tapped the truck as he made his way to the passenger's side. Opening the door, he stepped aside, obviously waiting for me to climb in.

I wasn't sure what to be more disturbed by: that he'd named his truck Old Bessie or that he'd opened a car door for me. I didn't think guys actually did that outside of movies and books. The door opening, that is. I'd known plenty of guys who'd named their cars, but none had named them Old Bessie.

When I stood in a frozen stupor, Jesse cleared his throat. "Not what you were expecting?" He admired his truck as if he could see no wrong. I suppose if you were cool with your vehicle having more dents and dings than there were stars in the Milky Way galaxy, or if you didn't mind the car being new when your parents first got their licenses, there was nothing "wrong" with it.

"Jesse, I didn't have any expectations when I came here," I said. "Least of all expectations about the truck of the guy picking me up from the bus station."

"Then climb on in," he said, motioning me inside, "and let Old Bessie redefine some non-expectations for you."

I bit my cheek and tried not to smile. It didn't matter what I threw at the guy; I couldn't shake that darn sunny attitude of his. Worst of all, I was afraid it might be contagious. "Just so I'm prepared . . . Are all cowboys like you?" I asked, stepping up into Old Bessie.

Jesse stepped between the door and me before I could close it. His body took up almost the entire door frame. "There's *no* other cowboy like me," he said with a half smile.

I had to swallow before I could respond. "I suppose 'Old Bessie' should have alerted me to that."

He had no other reply than that half smile of his becoming a whole one before moving out of my way. My door was closing at the same time his opened.

"Miss me?" he teased, shifting in his seat until he got comfortable.

"Like a tumor," I shot back.

Jesse chuckled, shaking his head. "Rowen Sterling: Putting the wise back in wiseass. I think I've found a kindred spirit."

Before I knew what was happening, I was laughing. *Laughing.* I'd been under the impression I'd forgotten how, but whether I'd remembered or Jesse had taught me a new kind, I was unmistakably laughing.

"So, other than hauling dead bodies around and being a wiseass, who is Rowen Sterling?" he asked before the truck fired to life. It was a good thing he'd completed his question first because Old Bessie's engine firing up was damn near a sonic boom.

"I think you're breaking noise ordinances in the next state over," I shouted above the noise, but he didn't hear me. By the time we were out of the parking lot, the engine had quieted a few decibels so my brain wasn't vibrating into my skull any longer.

"So?" he said over the engine. "Rowen Sterling life story? Bible-sized biography?"

He wouldn't let that go. Too bad I didn't sigh any-more because I could have used one about then. "How about I give you the one-word story that sums it all up?"

"Wiseass?" he said, his eyes gleaming at me.

I smirked at him. "Complicated," I stated, rummaging through my purse. "Very complicated."Locating my cell, I slid it out to check the reception. At least I still had some out in Middle-Of-Nowhere-Ville. "There. That was two words. What more could you possibly want to know?"

"We're all very complicated, Rowen. Sorry, you don't corner the market on very complicated" he said, shifting in his seat. Probably because his jeans were five sizes too small and cutting off the circulation to his junk.

"So there's a whole bunch more I'd like to know about you."

Dammit. Cowboy Jesse was a closet philosopher. I hadn't seen that one coming.

"You'd *like* to know," I said, rolling down my window. Not only because it was hot but because Jesse's all-man scent was getting to me. What he did or didn't smell like shouldn't get to me.

"I've been around long enough to know no man or God can get a woman to open up if she doesn't want to." Jesse rolled his window down, too. "I'd like to know, but I don't need to know. We have a right to keep our secrets."

My brow quirked. "Spoken like a person who knows what it's like to keep some."

Not a second passed before he replied. "We all have secrets, Rowen. Every last person on the planet. And you know what else? We all experience the same kinds of things. We just go through them at different times and to different degrees." Jesse paused as he rolled up to a stop sign. Checking both ways, he turned down a dirt road that looked like it went on for a hundred miles. "If we were to just accept we're not so different from each other, we wouldn't feel so alone."

There was only about an entire world more to Jesse than a pair of tight jeans. "What are you doing digging fence posts when you can arrive at those kinds of ideas and put them into easy-to-understand words?" I asked, peering over at Jesse. He peered over at me. "Get yourself a few certifications to frame and put up on the wall, and you could make a killing preaching this kind of stuff to all the head-cases out there. The money my mom alone spent on her shrink last year could keep a person living upper-middle class."

Jesse shook his head once. "I think I'll stick with what I'm doing. I'd rather dig fence posts than dig too far inside of some people's heads, you know?"

"Oh, believe me, I know," I replied, looking at the landscape passing by. Other than a house or a farm dotted throughout, there was a whole lot of nothing.

Nothing except for blue sky and green grass. So much color. I almost wished I'd picked up some watercolor paints before coming out here. I usually worked with charcoal or pencil since it was easy to take with me and, back in Portland, most of the landscape was some shade of graphite. Here, though . . . I could put some watercolors to good use.

"So what about you, Jesse? What's your life story? What's your Bible-sized biography?" I asked, utilizing my favorite conversation weapon: dodging the topic and turning it around.

"I'll give you more than the one-word reply I got from you, but I'm not going to give you everything because then what kind of incentive would you have for opening up to me?"

My brows came together. "Why would you holding back stuff about yourself be an incentive for me to tell you more about myself?"

"Because what I do tell you, and what you learn about me, will be so darn intriguing you're going to want more. You're going to *need* more." I could tell from his tone he was teasing, but I rolled my eyes anyways. "You won't be able to settle with just knowing eighty percent of me. You'll want the whole one hundred and ten percent."

"Cocky much?" I muttered, hanging my arm out the

window like Jesse was. I opened my hand and splayed my fingers to feel the wind rushing through them.

"Only when a pretty girl is sitting next to me and trying her hardest to pretend I'm the most irritating thing in the world," he replied, staring at the road and smiling.

That statement confirmed it: Jesse had a screw loose. I wasn't pretty, not by any definition of the word. Edgy, yes. Mysterious, maybe. But pretty? Fuck, no.

"So you open up to me if I open up to you?" I said, trying to sum it up.

Jesse gave a shrug. "Pretty much."

"Sorry to break it to you, Cowboy, but there's a serious flaw in your little plan there."

"Oh, yeah?" Jesse replied, turning down *another* dirt road that looked like it went on forever. "What serious flaw?"

"Assuming I *want* to open up to you." That was one giant-sized beast of a flaw.

He slid his hat off and dropped it on the dashboard. That mop of blond hair fell back into its perfectly imperfect style. "We all want to open up to someone, Rowen. The hard part is finding someone we trust enough to open up to. That person we're not afraid to let into the darkest parts of our world."

By that point in the conversation, I wasn't as shocked when that little gem came from his mouth. He seemed full of them.

"And you think you're the person I'll trust enough to open up to?" I said, pulling my arm back inside the truck to cross my arms.

Jesse lifted his shoulder. "Only time will tell."

I'd been in some strange situations in my eighteen

years of life, seen some crazy shit, but that. . . having the deepest kind of deep conversation with a Montana cowboy I'd met fifteen minutes earlier at a Greyhound station had to rate in the top ten.

"Do you ever just do casual conversation?" I asked, hoping he answered with a yes or that Willow Springs was less than a minute away.

"Once in a blue moon," he replied.

I pursed my lips to keep from smirking. I'd never heard the blue moon reference come out of the mouth of someone who didn't qualify for the senior citizen discount.

"Since it's still light out, let's just assume that to-night, the moon's going to be blue," I said. "It's casual conversation time for the rest of the ride."

"Fair enough. What do you want to talk casually about?"

I rolled my eyes. "If it's easier, we could just not talk."

"Nah, that's definitely not easier for me. I like to talk. I like to talk so much, sometimes I find myself carrying on one-sided conversations with the cattle," he said, as Old Bessie hit a pot hole that made me bounce a good foot in the air. Apparently modern conveniences like paved and maintained roads were not so "modern" or "convenient" out here. "I'm a pretty good listener, too. You know, if you ever have anything you want to *open* up about."

I groaned and contemplated shoving his arm. I didn't though because, judging from the size of his arms and knowing those arms could lift my bag like it was a two-pound dumbbell, my weakling shove wouldn't even register.

"How about a little harmless Q and A?" Jesse

suggested. "You ask me a question. I ask you one. Round and round we go until we get to Willow Springs."

I was opening my mouth when Jesse cut back in.

"Don't worry. We'll keep the questions as impersonal as possible." Studying my face for a moment, he quirked a brow. "That work for you, Miss Very Complicated?"

Only because I was already exhausted from going back and forth with him did I nod.

Jesse smiled like he'd just pulled off a solid victory. "Ladies first."

I rolled my fingers over my arm. I wanted to ask Jesse a bunch of questions; at least a dozen fired off in my mind. But only one made its way through my vocal chords. "Why in the hell do you wear such tight jeans?"

Jesse's face flattened for a second before it lined from the laugh bursting from his mouth. "I thought we said nothing personal," he managed to get out around his laughter.

"Eh . . . is that a personal question?" It didn't seem like one to me.

"Yes," he said, his laughter dimming. "And no. But I'll answer it anyways."

"How very *open* of you," I tossed back.

"Ignoring that wiseass comment . . ." he said, giving me a look. "I wear tight jeans because I'm on a horse at least a few hours every day. Tighter jeans mean less chaffing. Your first lesson in Ranch Survival 101? Avoid any and all forms of chaffing."

"Noted." I nodded once and tapped my head. "Your turn."

"I wasn't done answering your question yet." He gave me a look that suggested that should have been obvious.

"Carry on," I said with a wave of my hand.

"I wear tight jeans because when I'm out in the fields, I don't want anything crawling or slithering past my knees. I knew a guy who wore a baggy pair of jeans one day when he was setting a fence, and let's just say his wife has been a very unsatisfied woman for the past six years."

"Yikes." Just the thought of a snake, a spider, or some other creepy-crawler heading up my leg was enough to make me want to invest in a pair of tight-as-tight-could-be jeans.

"And last but nowhere near least, I wear tight jeans because I like the way the girls' heads turn when I walk by." His eyes twinkled. They goddamned twinkled.

Groaning again, that time I did lean over and give him a half-hearted shove. "They're only looking because they've been taking bets on when those things are going to bust a seam."

"Ah, please," he said, pursing his lips. "Don't pretend you weren't checking my butt out when I walked by you earlier. I felt like my ass was about to catch on fire from your unblinking, laser eyes."

I wasn't much of a blusher, but I might have just felt the heat of one surfacing. I wasn't sure if it had more to do with being caught or the image of Jesse's backside flashing through my mind again.

"Are you going to ask your question, or are you going to go on and on about your love affair with your back-side?" I tried to glare at him. It wasn't working.

He raised a hand in surrender, but those dimples of his stayed drilled deep into his cheeks. "Sticking with the whole personal attire thing . . ." he said, glancing at me. "Do you have a thing against color or do you just really love black?"

It was clear from Jesse's tone and expression that there was nothing antagonistic about his question. Just genuine curiosity.

"No," I answered, moving in my seat. "Color has a thing against me."

I felt Jesse's eyes on me, waiting for me to say something else,—explain just what the hell I meant—but he could wait for the rest of eternity before he'd get any more out of me.

"And you said I'm the philosophical one?" he said after a while.

"Yep, that's what I said." I sat up and stared out the window. "Now that was two questions, so I get two before you get to ask me another."

"Wha . . .?" he said before it registered. Jesse sighed. "Just for future reference, rhetorical questions don't count in this little question game."

"A question's a question," I stated, all matter-of-fact.

Jesse sighed again. Louder that time. "I didn't take you for the question rule police."

"And I didn't take you as the question rule corrupt." I continued to stare out the side window so he wouldn't see the smile twitching at my lips.

Jesse chuckled. "Fine. You win. Besides, I learned years ago that to start an argument with a woman is to lose an argument." Before I could praise him with a *Smart Man* comment, he continued. "We're getting close to Willow Springs. You better hurry and ask your *two* questions."

Looking at him, I took a guess before asking, "How old are you?"

"Nineteen."

Not bad. I'd guessed twenty, so I'd been pretty darn close.

"Next," he prompted, turning down yet another dirt road. It had two tall logs on either side of the road with a rusted metal sign hanging from the top that read *Willow Springs Ranch*.

Home not-so sweet home. For the next three months.

Just shoot me now.

CHAPTER two

Jesse was persistent, and the road leading into Willow Springs was never-ending. That's the only reason I agreed to continue our twisted game of question and answer.

"Okay, okay," I said, finally giving in. "This is a big one. In fact, it's so big, our future friendship hangs in the balance."

"That's a bit melodramatic," he said, slowing the truck down a bit. Maybe he wasn't ready for our question game to be over. "But I hear you city girls have a flare for the dramatic."

I narrowed my eyes. "And I hear you country boys have a flare for some good, old-fashioned bigotry. But I like to give a person the benefit of the doubt before I make assumptions about them being a bigoted asshole."

"Or a melodramatic diva?" he added, grinning like the devil. Before I could snap back, his wicked expression flattened. "Anytime today with that big, pivotal question, Non-Melodramatic-Rowen."

"Okay, Non-Bigoted-Asshole-Jesse,"—now I was the one smiling wickedly—"do you, have you ever, or do you in the future plan to . . ." I drew it out a few more moments for "melodramatic" flare, " . . . listen to country music?"

Jesse's eyes flickered to Old Bessie's newer CD player, then to me. He moved fast, but I moved faster.

His hand had barely left the steering wheel before I hit the eject button and snatched the CD that popped out of the player.

"Johnny Cash?!" I shouted. "Shit, this is worse than I thought. You don't just listen to country. You listen to prehistoric country." Pinching it with my fingers, I held it out for him. "Take it. Just take it. Before it burns me."

"No, of course not. You're not melodramatic," Jesse said under his breath as he took the CD spawned in hell away from me.

"You can call me melodramatic when it comes to country music," I replied. "In fact, I'm almost certain the term 'melodramatic' was invented in response to the birth of country music. That was, as the song goes, the day the music died." I was lukewarm about most things in life, reserving my passion for a rare few. Country music, and the eardrums it damaged both near and far, was one of those rare few.

Then, fast as I'd moved removing it, Jesse popped that CD back into the player and twisted the volume dial until it could twist no farther. Before I could ear-muff my ears with my hands, music exploded. Some dude with a deep, Elvis-esque voice started going off about walking and lines.

"Not funny, Jesse!" I hollered above the music, dropped a hand from my ear, and chanced the inner ear damage the hellfire music would cause in order to try to wrestle his hand away.

"It's pretty darn funny from where I'm sitting," he shouted, welding his hand over the CD player so I couldn't budge it. The harder I tried, the harder he laughed.

Just as I contemplated throwing myself out of the

24

truck to be free of the whole walking lines shit, the most welcome/unwelcome sight I'd ever seen came into view: a white, two-story farm house, complete with a freshly painted, big red barn beside it.

"Oh, thank sweet baby Jesus." I gave up my hand war with Jesse to grab the door handle. Once was one time too many when it came to riding in Old Bessie with Johnny Cash on full blast.

Right before we rolled to a stop in front of the house, Jesse mercifully turned the music off. But the damage had been done.

I would never be the same after that. Never.

"Do me a favor, will ya?" I said, shoving open the door.

"If it involves snapping in half or burning my favorite CD . . . sorry. No can do," he replied, his own door creaking open.

"Next time I need a ride, don't offer. I'd rather run, walk, or bloody crawl twenty miles than listen to that shit-for-music for another twenty seconds." Once I was out of Old Bessie, I turned to look at him. His hat was back in place, and he studied me again with that same knowing smile. "Capiche?" I added, pretending like staring at Jesse staring at me didn't make my knees feel a bit out of whack.

"I don't speak melodramatic city girl talk, but how about if I promise to not force Mr. Cash on you again if you need another ride from me?" He slid out of his seat without taking his eyes off of me, and he slammed the door closed. Both dimples were buried in his cheeks. "Just please, promise you won't do anything to my favorite CD? It would break my heart."

"Even if I tried, that sucker is so chock-full of black voodoo magic it would take a dozen witches to destroy it," I replied, arching a brow at him, which only made his smile go higher.

Jesse was just opening his mouth when a screen door screeched open behind me.

"If you aren't the spitting image of your mom," the woman coming down the porch steps said, smiling at me like I could have been her long-lost daughter.

I felt my face pinch together. Not because the woman looked like a modern version of the women on Little House on the Prairie, but because she'd said I looked like my mom. No one said that because we had no similarities. On the exterior or the interior.

"Rowen Sterling, it is so good to finally meet you," she said, and just as I extended my hand to her, she wrapped her arms around me and pulled me into a solid hug. "I'm Mrs. Walker, but if you know what's good for you, you'll call me Rose." Giving me a final squeeze, she lowered her arms. "My mother-in-law is Mrs. Walker."

"Okay, Rose," I said. "I think I can manage that." Especially since the only time I called people Mr. or Mrs. was when it involved a hefty dose of sarcasm.

She tucked a few curls of hair that had escaped her ponytail behind her ear. "We're all so glad you're here. When your mom called and asked if you could spend the summer with us, I don't think I gave her a chance to finish her sentence before I said yes."

Rose and my mom had grown up together back in Portland. Mom went off to college, and Rose went off to Willow Springs after marrying Mr. Walker, whose first name I'd also forgotten. Examining the warmth and sim-

26

plicity that was Rose Walker made me wonder how, in our universe or the next, my mom and her were childhood best friends.

If two people could get more opposite, I hadn't seen it. Mom was tall, platinum blond (thanks to her stylist), believed makeup wasn't only a tool but essential to every-day life, and didn't wear an article of clothing that wasn't expensive and in season. Rose was shorter, had dark brown hair, didn't wear a smudge of makeup from what I could tell, and her flower-print dress looked like it could have been homemade.

From what I knew, mom and Rose didn't keep in touch all that often, but every year, we got a Christmas card from Willow Springs Ranch. They had to be good enough friends that mom would entrust her only child to a family a couple of states away.

When I thought of my mom and Rose, the phrase "oil and vinegar" came to mind.

"Thanks for having me," I said, reminding myself to be gracious. Rose didn't have anything to do with Mom's nutso idea to send me off to Ranch Responsibility School for the summer.

"Are you kidding me? A chance to have another woman on a ranch overrun with men who think a decent conversation consists of a half a dozen words?" Rose patted my arm. "Thank *you* for having us."

Either she was high on the latest and greatest mood-enhancing pharmaceutical, or she was just plain high on life. There was no arguing she was high on something.

Behind us, Jesse cleared his throat. I hadn't forgotten he was there. It seemed, I couldn't.

"I'm going to run Rowen's bag up to her room. Then

I've got to get back to work on that fence." He pulled the giant-sized bag out of the truck bed in one seamless move, and he flashed that dimpled smile at me as he passed by.

"Have fun with those fence posts," I said, meeting his smile with an overdone one of my own.

"Oh, I will," he said, continuing up toward the front door. "I'll think of you and your excellent taste in music the whole time."

Rose watched Jesse disappear through the screen door. When her gaze shifted back to me, noticing that my eyes had also watched Jesse's entire journey, she gave me a knowing kind of smile. "He's a good looking kid, isn't he?"

I bit the inside of my cheek to give myself a moment to recover. "I suppose," I started, giving a small shrug. "If you're into that whole Brad Pitt in *Legends of the Fall* thing. Which I'm not." That was true. I never went for the blond-haired, blue-eyed, sexy-shmexy, boy-next-door-to-the-tenth-power guy. I went for the dark-haired, pale, lanky, brooding type. "I was more team bear-that-tried-to-kill-Brad-Pitt-in-the-end."

Rose didn't bat an eye. Instead, she laughed an honest to goodness one as she weaved her elbow through mine. "My," she said, leading me up the front steps, "the ride from the bus station must have been interesting."

"Interesting is a good word for it," I said, taking a closer look at the farm house. Even for all my doom and gloom preferences, I kind of dug the place.

It was old, from the intricate, beveled windows to the way the wrap-around porch creaked when we walked over it, but it had been well preserved. The front door was cobalt blue to match the shutters, and there was a porch swing on either side of the door because one just wasn't enough, I guess.

It was a house that was "lived in." It had history, and I could only imagine the number of stories and moments that had been shared inside its walls.

"I imagine after your day, you'll have just enough energy left to take a bath and crawl into bed." Rose swung the screen door open and waved me inside. "So I'll send a dinner plate up to your room later if you like. Tomorrow, after you've had a good night's sleep, we can settle you into the routine here at Willow Springs."

After she'd said the word, my muscles almost ached for a bath. "That sounds great."

"But I'm afraid three young ladies are very eager to meet you before you escape," Rose said as she led me into a living room with robin egg blue walls and white crown molding. A few antique looking pieces of furniture were mixed in with a few more contemporary pieces. It was a mish-mash of decor, a designer's worst nightmare, but somehow, it worked. I'd barely taken five steps inside the room, and I already felt comfortable enough to plop down on the floral couch and kick my feet up on the distressed coffee table.

"This is really nice," I said truthfully. Everything about the room, from the bold use of color to the window of walls, was a stark contrast to my room back in Portland. My walls were a deep aubergine purple, the ceiling, too, and I kept the lone window covered with a black-out curtain. I liked to keep the light out—except for when I was drawing or painting—while Rose preferred to let the light in.

Before I could get too deep down that thinking well,

three figures hovering off to the side caught my attention.

"These lovely, eager girls are my daughters," Rose said, waving at the three girls looking at me without blinking.

"Hey," I said awkwardly, flashing them just as awkward a wave. I wasn't sure how much my mom had told Rose about my life and the "mess" (Mom's term, not mine) I'd made of it. From the looks of it, those girls either knew everything and were wide-eyed in terror or knew nothing and were under the impression I was as cool as chocolate ice cream.

"I'll make the formal introductions since everyone seems a little tongue-tied," Rose said, giving her daughters a confused look. "This is Lily." Rose motioned at the tallest girl, a clone of her mom right down to the flowery dress and the long, dark hair and eyes. "She's sixteen, and if she goes missing, the first place to look for her is hiding in the barn loft devouring her latest book."

Lily smiled shyly at me before dropping her eyes. Quiet, a little awkward, and liked to hide away from the rest of the world whenever she got the chance . . . I liked her already.

"This is Hyacinth." Rose moved on to the next girl who was yet another clone. "She's thirteen and every bit of thirteen." Rose lifted her brows and gave her daughter an equally maternal and amused smile.

Hyacinth gave me a smile and a wave. She had none of the pissed-off-at-the-whole-world attitude I'd possessed at thirteen, but I guessed Rose's and my definition of a teenager were a wee bit different.

"And the little one is Clementine. She's seven." Rose bit her lip as she inspected her youngest daughter dolled up in head-to-toe princess garb. Even though the whole princess thing was pretty much my arch nemesis, I had to give the girl credit. She was going to be the best damn princess she could be.

"Mom," Clementine said, sighing in exasperation, "I'm not little."

Rose lifted her hands in apology. "You're right. Forgive me, Your Highness." Nudging me, Rose cleared her throat. "This is Clementine. She's my big girl."

Clementine rolled her shoulders back and gave a small nod, obviously appeased. "How do you do?" she said formally, capping it off with the best curtsy I'd ever seen.

"Nice to meet you, Your Highness." I gave her my own sucky attempt at a curtsy. Clementine, no big surprise, was yet another mini-clone of Rose.

"And I know you already know, but just to make the introductions formal, this is Rowen," Rose said, glancing from her daughters to me. "My girls have been crossing off the days on their calendars since they learned you were coming. We don't get female company out here very often. Especially female company from a big city."

I suddenly became very aware of myself. My outfit, my eyebrow ring, my dark lips. What a disappointment I must have been. No doubt those girls were looking forward to some chic, trendy girl plucked straight from the pages of Cosmo, not a troubled girl who lived dark like it was a religion.

Oh, well. It wasn't the first or the hundredth time I'd disappointed someone. I cleared my throat and tried to forget about it.

"Rose," I said, pointing at her. "Lily." I pointed at the

one still diverting her eyes. "Hyacinth." My finger moved to the next sister, who was still smiling at me, before ending on the littlest "big" girl of the bunch. "And *Clementine*?" They must have run out of flower names by the time she came along.

"My husband wasn't too big on the names Peony or Iris, so we compromised and went with a name just as sweet and delicate as the rest of ours," Rose answered. Clementine stood a couple of inches taller.

"It's nice to meet you all," I said, really needing that bath and bed. The crack-of-dawn wake up, the twelve hours of nose rot, the ride in Old Bessie with the cowboy I already both loved and hated, and meeting the mini-Rose clones who were overwhelming me with a skewed version of hero worship . . . I was spent.

"Let me show you up to your room," Rose said, steering me out of the living room. "You and the girls have plenty of time to get to know each other this summer."

We were almost out of the living room when something caught my attention. I came to an abrupt stop. So abrupt, Rose continued all the way into the hallway before she noticed I wasn't with her anymore.

"Rowen?"

I didn't reply. All my attention was concentrated on the mantle where four framed portraits highlighted four smiling faces: three dark-haired girls I'd just been introduced to . . . and one light-haired boy smiling that dimpled smile. He was in the same sort of outfit he'd worn earlier: a snug white tee, tighter than tight jeans, a simple belt, cowboy boots, and that light straw cowboy hat. Leaning into the side of Old Bessie, his eyes twinkled behind the glass of that frame like they had at me.

"What is it?" Rose asked with a hint of concern as she made her way back to me. Taking a look at what my eyes were bored into, she gave me a gentle nudge. "He's a good looking kid, isn't he?" Even if I wanted to agree or disagree, that was beside the point.

"Why do you have a picture of Jesse on your mantle?" I asked, my voice a couple notes higher. "Next to the pictures of your daughters?" I didn't really need the confirmation, because my thought process had already traveled from A to B to arrive at C.

"Jesse's our son, silly," she said, giving a small laugh. "Didn't he mention that?"

Great. Cowboy Infuriating Jesse wasn't just a ranch hand; he was the ranch owner's son. He didn't only work here, he lived here. He'd grown up here. Which meant . . .

He had a room somewhere inside the suddenly small-seeming farmhouse. Somewhere, he took a shower at the end of a long day before crawling between his sheets and falling asleep. For all I knew, his room could be a piece of drywall apart from mine. I wasn't sure if the knowledge of Jesse buck naked a room away or the possibility of waking up to Johnny Cash blasting every morning unsettled me more.

"Shit."It slipped out before I could catch it. Covering my mouth with my hand, I shot Rose an apologetic look. "Sorry about that." I looked over her shoulder at the girls doing such an overdone job at playing ignorant to what I'd said, I knew they weren't.

"It's all right," she said. "Lord knows with the men we have working around here, they've heard worse."

I felt better knowing I hadn't just introduced the Walker girls to a new four letter word, but I felt nothing better about Jesse being a Walker. "So Jesse's your son?" I guess hearing it once just wasn't enough to convince me. Really, other than the country attire and warm personality, he had no physical similarities to tie him to his mom and sisters. Maybe Mr. Walker was tall, built, and blond like Jesse.

"He's our son," she said, smiling affectionately at Jesse's photo. "At least on the days he remembers to pick up his wet towels from the bathroom floor."

Super. After she mentioned Jesse and wet towels, my mind went to him all wet and soapy in the shower.

"Are you surprised?" Rose asked, looking from his photo to me.

"Maybe a little," I said, at the point where I was ready to forfeit the bath and just head straight to bed. I needed to put the day on pause before it got any more trippy.

"Well, now you know." Rose patted my arm before heading back into the hall. I followed her because if I stared at that picture for another second, I wasn't sure I'd be able to look away. "Jesse's a hard worker, a good son, and an even better person. If you ever need something, Jesse will be the first in line to help you out."

I felt a twinge of pain hearing the way Rose talked about her son and watching the affection on her face. No one had ever talked about me that way, like I was so close to perfect the imperfections were washed away.

I followed Rose up the staircase to the second floor. The hall walls were painted a Tuscan gold, and on the outside of each door, a letter made out of heated and formed horseshoes swung from a piece of rope. An L and an H hung from the first doors we passed. Then a C.

I swallowed and felt my stomach coil as we approached the next door. I blew out a rush of air when Rose stopped. No letter swung from it. So I had Clementine beside me and Lily across the hall and down. My room was the last room at the end of the hall. Wherever Jesse's room was, I could sleep easy knowing it wasn't anywhere near mine.

I wasn't sure whether to be happy or disappointed.

Rose opened the door. "This will be your room for the summer. It's not much, but if you think of anything else you need, just let me or Neil know—"

"It's great," I interrupted, stepping inside the room. "Really. It's great. I wasn't sure what to expect when I came here today. I was half expecting I'd be sleeping out in the barn."

"Why ever would you think that?" she asked, lingering in the doorway. "You're our guest here. We're happy to have you, Rowen, and I don't know how you big city people do it, but we certainly don't put our guests out in the barn." A smile pulled at the corners of her mouth. "At least not on the first stay."

"I might be a guest to you, but my mom thinks of me more as an inmate out here— fulfilling a sentence."

"Oh, honey," Rose said through a sigh. "I know your mom would rather die than show her emotions most days, but I'm as certain as I love my own children that she loves hers, too." She drew me into a tight hug. I was thankful she couldn't see my face because I knew my eyes were a little glassy. I felt the familiar burn. I might not have cried in years, but I still remembered how it felt.

I wasn't sure if I was approaching the cry zone because we were talking about my mom and her inability to show any positive emotion, or because in a half hour,

Rose had shown me more affection and maternal concern than my mother had in five years. Whatever the reason, I wasn't ready to break my dry spell.

Guessing I needed or wanted to be alone, Rose gave me one final squeeze before heading for the door. "Neil and I are down on the first floor if you need anything, but I guarantee if you knocked on any of my daughter's doors, they would cut off their ponytail for an excuse to chat with you. So don't hesitate to ask one of us if you need something. Okay?" She started to close the door but stopped and waited for my reply.

"Okay." I nodded, wondering if when I woke up, the Walker family I'd met today would still be the same. Despite resembling something all too idealistic for my pessimistic outlook, I found myself almost hoping nothing would change. "Thanks again for having me."

"Thank you for having us," she said with a wink before closing the door noiselessly.

I exhaled. I'd done it. I'd made it across Oregon, some of Washington and Idaho, and into Montana. I'd survived the Greyhound system. I'd met the Walkers, and really, I couldn't imagine a better family to be "enslaved" to for the summer. Sure, they seemed like hard working, dawn-to-dusk people, but they also seemed fair and good. I'd survived introductions, and I had some time to myself to unpack and unwind.

I clomped across the room in my combat boots before realizing my feet had been in them for over twelve hours. I kicked them off and wiggled my toes. My black "body bag" was placed on the foot of the bed and almost meticulously centered. The reminder that Jesse had been inside my room only a few minutes ago, lowering my bag onto that bed . . . Well, it did things to my stomach and my body that no red-blooded cowboy should do to my stomach and body.

Jesse had just been in here . . .

That explained why the room still smelled like him. Kind of soapy, kind of earthy, and kind of like some other scent I couldn't quite put my finger on. Something familiar, but only vaguely so.

Musky? Leathery? I couldn't quite pinpoint it.

What the . . .

What the hell was I doing? Contemplating the undertone scent of some tight-pant wearing guy I'd just met? I had to remind myself I was not a boy-crazy, stars-aligned sucker a few times before heading over to my bag. If a fury of unpacking couldn't do the job of removing Jesse from my mind, I just might have to soak in a tub for a while because there was no way, in my wound up state, I could fall asleep.

After unzipping my bag, I headed over to the simple wood dresser across from the bed. I slid open the first couple of drawers to confirm they were empty before heading back to my bag, scooping up an armload of clothes, and dropping it into the top drawer. I repeated the process until my bag was empty and the top four drawers were filled to capacity. I had more drawers than clothes, so I never got around to opening the bottom drawer. I slowed down and took my time when I got to my art supplies. I stacked my box of charcoal on top of my sketchbook and centered them on top of the dresser.

Okay. Unpacking complete. What next?

I stared at the double-sized bed for a moment. It matched the dresser and nightstand: dark cherry wood, a simple, no-nonsense design. However, what covered the bed was anything but simple. One of the brightest, most colorful quilts in existence blanketed the mattress. It had lots of blue and green squares, some patterned, some textured, and the rest of the squares ranged in color from chocolate brown to scarlet to pale yellow. From the looks of it, the quilt had been washed hundreds of times, but other than the fading and obvious wear to the fabric, it was pristine. There were no rips or dangling threads.

Great. I was admiring an ancient quilt.

Yet another *What the . . .* moment.

Someone needed a bath, and fast. Snatching my shower bag from the dresser, I had to rummage around the drawers before I could wrestle out a pair of my pajamas. After opening the bedroom door, I scanned the hallway before hurrying toward the bathroom. It was across from Clementine's bedroom and it was empty, which was probably an unlikely thing in a family of three girls. I heard some commotion downstairs and guessed everyone was probably about to sit down for dinner. A family like the Walkers probably still did that sort of thing: sit-down dinners complete with conversation and home-cooked food.

Once I'd tucked myself away inside the bathroom, I cranked on the tub faucet and tested the water. In an old house like theirs, I expected the water to take a half hour to get hot, but it was warm almost right away. After taking my time undressing, I dumped in a capful of lilac bubble bath I found hanging out in a basket beside the claw-foot tub, made sure there was an available and clean towel nearby, and eased my way into the steaming bath.

Before long, all thoughts of a J named cowboy had

drifted away. Along with the rest of any and all thoughts of everything else.

I don't know how long I was passed out in the tub, but it was long enough for the water to get chilly. I had to blink a few times to clear my head before I remembered where I was and whose bathtub I was in.

Just when I remembered I was at the Walkers, turning into a popsicle in their claw-foot tub, I heard footsteps down the hall. They got closer and had the distinct tap-clack sound of a pair of boots. At Willow Springs Ranch, it could only mean cowboy boots.

I sucked in a breath, afraid to make a sound. I didn't need to see the owner of those boots tap-clacking closer to know who wore them. I could . . . *feel* him.

Damn. For once, I was on the same wavelength as the rest of my polo-shirt and jean-skirt wearing peers: I was certifiable.

I didn't have a chance to wonder at how messed up the wiring in my head was because those tap-clacking boots came to a sudden stop. Right outside the goddamned bathroom door I was naked in a tub behind.

What should I do? Yell at him to get lost? Leap out and cinch that towel around me as fast as I could? Make an appointment with the nearest clinical psychologist to have my head examined?

All were tempting solutions, especially the last gem, but what did I do instead?

I scooted down in the tub, clamped my lips shut, and hoped he'd keep moving.

After a good ten seconds of cowering inside a cold bath not even daring to take a breath, the boot steps re-started down the rest of the hall, down the stairs, and who knows from there.

"Real smooth, Rowen," I said under my breath, thumping the drain release lever with my big toe. "What were you worried he was going to do? Break down the door, tear off his clothes, and make hot, passionate cowboy love to you?"

After verbally flogging myself a little longer, I shrugged into my old sweats and warned my subconscious, who obviously had a closet fantasy for rough and rugged types, that if she didn't behave, I'd medicate her into obedience.

I stalled for a few more minutes by tidying up the bathroom a bit before twisting the doorknob open. I scanned the hall, up and down, twice before literally tiptoeing down the hall. Despite it being almost dark outside, a bunch of noise was still coming from the first floor.

I didn't notice the plate sealed up with plastic wrap until I was a few steps from my bedroom door. It looked to be some slab of beef, accompanied by au gratin potatoes, green beans, and a dinner roll, complete with a knife and fork on top of the plastic wrap. Resting on top of the silverware was a folded piece of paper.

I gazed down the hall again, half expecting to see Jesse leaning against the wall and watching me with that smile of his. I exhaled when I found it still empty. I grabbed the plate and note and ducked inside my room, trying to close the door as noiselessly as Rose. Apparently she had the gift, or years of experience, because that darn door creaked and groaned so loudly I worried the entire house would hear it.

After setting the plate on top of the dresser with my shower bag, I leaned into the door for support and opened the note. My heart raced before I read one word.

My turn to ask a question.

I swallowed. I hadn't realized our game of question and answer would go on past the truck ride. If Jesse assumed it would carry on the rest of the summer, I was in trouble. Opening up wasn't exactly a strong point for me.

Shaking it off, or at least trying, I finished reading the note:

Are you seeing anyone? And before you get all literal on me, you know what I mean. Do you have a boyfriend?

So much for keeping the questions in the non-personal realm. Only because I knew if I didn't write my answer down right away, I never would, I went over to my purse to dig a pen out. I didn't stop to wonder why Jesse wanted to know if I was seeing someone. I didn't pause to wonder what he'd think when he read my answer. I had all night to overanalyze the hell out of his question. Right then, I just needed to get my response down on paper.

Uncapping the pen with my teeth, I scribbled down my reply.

No. I'm not seeing anyone at this very moment, but that's not to say that might change the next moment.

Flipping the note around, I scribbled down my question because it was my turn:

My turn. Are you seeing someone? And before you get

all vague on me, you know what I mean. A special girl, boy, or cow in your life?

After inhaling the dinner roll, I slipped the piece of paper underneath my door. I knew he'd come back to check for it. Then I finally crawled into bed.

I'd finally fallen asleep before I heard those boots make their return journey.

CHAPTER three

I ignored the first knock on my door. It was still dark, and I was so sleep confused, maybe I'd imagined the knock. I'd almost convinced myself of that when another knock sounded; it was a bit louder.

"Rowen?" came a soft, girl's voice. One of the older sisters, though I couldn't make out who.

"Yeah?"

"Mom told me to come and wake you up."

I didn't know what time it was, but I didn't need to. It was dark outside. It wasn't time to get up unless there was an emergency.

"Why?" I asked, sitting up on my elbows in bed.

"It's breakfast time," she said. "If you need to use the bathroom, it's free. We're all done using it."

Before I could reply, assuming I could work up a reply in the midst of my shock, whichever sister had roused me in the middle of the night for breakfast started heading back down the hall.

Reaching in the general vicinity of the nightstand, I fumbled around until I found my cell phone. My eyes bulged when I saw the time. Four fifteen a.m. I usually went to bed at that hour; I'd never once gotten up so early.

Was it some kind of sick prank? In my world, it

might have been, but in the Walkers' world, I knew it wasn't. From the breakfast smells creeping into my bedroom, I guessed breakfast was just minutes away.

I groaned as I sat up. After crawling into bed, I hadn't fallen asleep as fast as I thought I would. I don't know when I fell asleep exactly, but the last time I'd checked my phone, it was a little past midnight. My mind couldn't stop over and under-analyzing Jesse's question. Did he ask if I was with someone because he was curious? Did he ask because he wanted to ask me out? Did he ask because he wanted me to think he wanted to ask me out? Or did he ask just because he knew I'd be up half the night over-thinking the hell out of it?

From what I knew of Jesse, the last option was the most likely.

On top of the overanalyzing, the scent I found waiting for me when I crawled under the blankets kept me up too. That Jesse smell that clung to the air inside the room was about a hundred times more potent when I crawled into bed. It was like he'd laid down on my bed after dropping my bag off and rolled around on the sheets, quilt, and pillows. Trying to fall asleep while every inhalation seemed as if my nose was pressed into his neck, while trying to figure out some cryptic question, was not easy.

As evidenced by how difficult it was for me to crawl out of bed. I took about a minute to throw the covers off, then another minute before I could swing my legs over the side. By then, there was just enough of a sliver of sunrise to cast a gentle glow throughout the room so I didn't need to turn on the bedside light.

Putting one foot in front of the other, I made it to the dresser. I pulled out the first couple of things my hands fell on. A few minutes later, I opened the door and immediately inspected the ground where I'd slid my reply to Jesse. It was gone. Either he'd come back for it, one of his sisters wound up with it, or a little mouse ran off with it. I decided to do something out-of-character and think positively. The right person had wound up with it. Whoever that was . . .

While I lumbered down the hall, I plaited my mass of hair into a side braid. I made a quick stop over in the bathroom to apply a couple coats of mascara, slick on some dark lipstick, and pop in my dark contacts. Normally, I didn't leave my bedroom without a full face of makeup, but I didn't want to press my luck. It had been a while since my wake-up call, and I didn't want Rose to have to come looking for me.

As I clomped down the stairs in my staple combat boots, I already smelled breakfast, and not the poured-into-a-bowl-with-a-little-milk kind. It was the kind of breakfast that sizzled in skillets.

Even though I hadn't had the whole tour of the Walkers' place, the kitchen was easy enough to find. If my nose couldn't have found its way there, my ears could have. Voices that were way too perky for so early in the morning jabbered about something.

I paused inside the doorway of the kitchen and waited. Rose and the three girls scurried around the large kitchen like someone was cracking a whip behind them. One dug around in the fridge, another scrambled a ginormous skillet of eggs, Rose filled a pitcher with orange juice, and Clementine set the longest table I'd ever seen. I did a quick count of the place settings. Twenty. They must be, literally, feeding the entire village.

Everyone was so busy with their tasks no one noticed me right away. Toeing the linoleum, I cleared my throat.

"Good morning," I said, even though that time was generally more *good night* for me.

"Rowen!" Rose called out as she handed the pitcher of juice off to Lily. "How did you sleep last night?"

If I went with the truth, her next question might have to do with what had kept me up. Since admitting to Rose her son was responsible for keeping my mind reeling last night, I decided to answer with a simple, "Good."

"You got the dinner plate I sent Jesse up with?" she asked, making her way to me. Today she was wearing a sleeveless, button-down blouse, jeans, boots, and some ornate silver and turquoise jewelry.

"Oh, I got it." Along with a vexing little note with a vexing little question. "Looks like you're about to feed an army. What can I do to help?" I was there to work, Rose and I both knew that, but maybe if I made it seem like I was offering, working would seem less like indentured servitude.

"What, this little breakfast?" she replied, lifting a shoulder. "Around here, this is an everyday, three times a day, sort of thing. When it gets real interesting is when we host a meal with the hands and their families or significant others. Now *that,* that's feeding an army. This is just a simple breakfast."

My mouth fell open a bit. "You do this every day?"

"Six months out of the year, three meals a day," Rose replied. "The other six months we only cook for our family and maybe a couple others."

Insane.

"Every day as in Monday to Friday, right?" Fifteen

meals for twenty people a week? There had to be some sort of international award for that.

Rose laughed. "Honey, the day cattle only need tending to Monday to Friday is the day I'm booking a vacation to Hawaii."

Oh my God. They did it seven days a week. Every single day. Breakfast. Lunch. Dinner. My mouth dropped a bit further.

"Do you have a magic wand or something?" I asked because, really. How could four women, well, one woman and three girls, prepare three *hot* meals a day, seven days a week, for twenty people if some kind of magic wasn't involved?

"I wish. I live by a philosophy that's served me well for over two decades of ranch life—organized chaos," she said with a wink. "That's our marching theme around here."

Emphasis on the chaos part.

"Got it," I said, practically wincing as Hyacinth diced up a potato like she had mad ninja skills. I kept waiting for the bloody top of a finger to roll onto the floor. "I'm not the best cook in the world, and it's better I don't handle anything sharp, but I'm pretty sure I can set a table without breaking anything or pour drinks without spilling. Better not give me anything hot in case I spill it on somebody"—super, I was rambling on like an idiot—"but just point me where you want me, and I'll do my best not to turn your breakfast into *disorganized* chaos."

"Mom!" Clementine shouted. "They're coming!"

"Plate up the food, girls, and go ahead and get it out on the table," Rose said, all calm and cool. "I've got to talk with Rowen for just a couple minutes." Placing her arm behind my back, Rose steered me through the kitchen, entryway, and living room. We wound up across the house in what looked to be a mini-Laundromat. Four washers, four dryers, an arsenal of detergent, stain remover, and dryer sheets, and an island in the center of the room that I guessed was for folding or sorting or something.

"Please don't take this the wrong way, Rowen, because I like you. I really, really like you, and despite my own blah attire, I'm a supporter of women having the right to wear whatever the heck they want to," Rose began, keeping her arm tight around my back the whole time. "Just not when I've got a dozen young men coming and going out of my kitchen several times a day. These are good boys we have working for us, but they're still boys who don't always do their thinking with their brains," Rose said, followed up by an exaggerated clearing of her throat.

I, along with every woman in existence, knew exactly what she meant.

Glancing down at my outfit, I suddenly felt self-conscious. "You don't like the way I dress?" I asked, though it should have been more of a statement. Most people didn't like the way I dressed. Despite everyone advocating uniqueness and marching to the beat of your own drum, that only went so far.

"Are you kidding me?" Rose said, raising her brows. "I love the way you dress. I love that you know who you are and aren't afraid to show it." Man, did I have Rose fooled. "But I also know a fair share of those guys are going to love it, too. Love it in the inappropriate way." Her eyes fell to the hem of my plaid, pleated skirt. It was short. Short even by a call girl's standards. I had an opaque pair of black tights on below it, but I'd cut and slashed them, so just as much skin showed as was covered.

"Oh," I said, fingering the hem of my skirt. "I guess I didn't think about that."

"Don't you worry about it, Rowen. I'm not here to tell you how or how not to dress. If this is what you wear, that's great." Rose ran her hand up and down me, making her silver and turquoise bracelets jingle. "But Neil and I are also responsible for your safety and well-being while you're here. I've got a household to run, and I can't be worrying at every meal that one of those guys out there will try to sweet-talk you into his bed at night." Rose paused. Tucking her hand under my chin, she lifted it until I looked at her. "Do you understand, Rowen? I want to respect who you are, and I need to look after you. If this is how you dress every day and will continue to dress while you're here, that's just fine. There's always plenty of laundry and household chores that need doing every day that would keep you out of the guys' sight."

"I understand." I suddenly felt very aware of the hoop pierced through my eyebrow and my shirt's low neckline. "Thank you for respecting me enough to not order me to go change." When I'd started dressing differently and wearing my hair and makeup darker than other girls, Mom went so far as to hold me down and remove what I was wearing, one piece at a time. A lot of good that had done. "But even if I wanted to, what you see is what I packed. I can't remember the last time I bought a pair of denim-colored jeans."

"Then let's do this today. I'll have you manning the laundry room, and if you decide you just can't imagine doing another load of laundry come tomorrow, we can figure out a way to get you some boring blue jeans. Then you can rotate through the chores like me and the girls do. Whatever you want to do, I'm good with it."

As Rose started for the door, I said, "That's right. You're good with chaos."

"So long as it's organized," she added, lifting her finger.

"See you later then. I'll try not to break your laundry room."

"I'll check in with you after breakfast to see how you're doing. You can get started with the clothes in that cart." She pointed at a cart, an actual cart the size of a couch, filled to the brim with clothing. For the third time that morning, my mouth dropped open. "Oh, and Rowen . . ."

"Yeah?" I managed after pulling my jaw off the ground.

"I really do like the way you dress. If I had your figure and your courage, I'd wear the same thing."

"What are you talking about?" I said, taking a good look at her. "You've got a great figure, and any woman brave enough to cook twenty-one meals a week for twenty people has a heck of a lot more courage than me."

Rose waved her hand dismissively. "I used to have a great figure. That was before having kids." She patted her stomach like it was anything but flat.

"For a woman who's given birth to four . . . *four*," I emphasized, "babies, you look amazing."

Rose's face fell for a moment, just barely, but I took note. That warm smile of hers lit up her face again before she waved and closed the door behind her.

I DIDN'T CARE if I had to wear overalls, pig tails, and rename myself Peggy Sue for the rest of the summer. I would do it to avoid spending another all day stint in the laundry room I was quite certain would haunt my nightmares for years to come.

That one ranch could keep four washers and four dryers in non-stop rotation didn't seem possible, but after being up to my elbows in suds and sheets, I discovered just how possible it was. If I never saw another white undershirt in my life, I'd be good to go. Really.

I'd barely made it through the small vehicle-sized cart of laundry before the girls walked in with another full cart of sheets and towels. Willow Springs didn't only provide meals for the ranch hands; they provided living quarters in some bunkhouse I had yet to see and, as I'd gained first-hand knowledge of, laundry service. The girls all took a break from their chores to help me fold the first four loads, and if speed folding was a competitive sport, each one would have a first place ribbon. They were still shy, casting a few sideways glances my way, but Clementine actually braved a few words. With a concerned face, she inspected my tights before offering to let me borrow a pair of her tights if I wanted. Hers didn't have any rips or tears.

I thanked her for the offer and said I'd have to get back with her.

After another eight hours stuffed inside that torture chamber, I didn't care if her tights were pale pink and dotted with cutsie white bows. I needed out of here. I had to figure out a way to get some "ranch appropriate" duds unless I wanted to spend another day in laundry hell. I had no clue how far away the nearest store was, but I didn't care if I had no other way to get there than on foot. I would whistle every step of the way.

Rose had brought me breakfast and lunch and check-ed on me a few times in between. I guessed dinner was getting close because the room filled up with food smells again. I wasn't sure how much longer I'd be in here, but the new dirty laundry arrivals had stopped coming a few hours ago, so maybe . . .

I was folding my last pile of clothes when a sock fell off the side of the island. I'd dropped as much laundry as I'd folded.

Blowing out a breath, I kneeled and crawled around the side of the island. I'd just snagged the escapee sock when the door to the laundry room flew open. But it wasn't Rose.

Nope. Definitely not Rose.

Jesse tossed his hat onto the island before tugging his shirt free of his jeans. They were just as tight as the ones he'd worn yesterday. I was ready to bolt up and demand to know what the hell he thought he was doing stripping in front of me when he pulled the dirty, damp shirt from his body and tossed it into one of the laundry carts.

He didn't know I was there. I wasn't exactly making my presence known by staying motionless in my hiding spot. I might have been on all fours on the floor of a laundry slash torture room, but right then, I had the best damn view in the house.

Making his way over to the utility sink, Jesse cranked on the water before leaning down and splashing his face and hair. Hello, fine, fine ass. How I'd missed you.

He turned off the water and grabbed a towel hanging over the edge of the sink. As Jesse straightened up, my eyes shifted from the denim suctioning that backside up the seam of his back.

Hot damn, did that man have more than his fair share of muscles. As my eyes explored his back, lingering on the shadowed groves and highlighted peaks, I had the nearly uncontrollable urge to touch him. To feel him. To scroll my finger through the lines making up Jesse Walker.

My heartbeat picked up, along with my breathing, and the space below my navel started firing to life in a familiar way.

What the hell?

Was I about to get off in a laundry room spying on the back of some cowboy I'd known for all of a day and a half?

After Jesse finished drying his face, he tossed the towel into the cart, too. Okay, he was done. He'd removed his filthy shirt, washed up, and he could get out of here so I could get back to taking full breaths again.

That was when he unfastened his belt buckle and moved for his fly.

Ah, hell.

"Stop!" I shouted right as his thumbs hitched beneath the waist of his jeans. If I had to watch the rest of the Jesse Walker strip tease, I would moan the alphabet.

Jesse spun around. His look of surprise fell when he saw me peeking my head around the side of the island.

My gaze shifted from his face down. And I thought his back had been worthy of building the pyramids all over again. The wide chest, flowing down to his tapered waist, trailing down to his . . .

The undone belt buckle and button of his jeans did not make it easy to not think about certain pieces of anatomy I really shouldn't be thinking about when he looked at me like that.

"Are you spying on me?" Those sky blue eyes sparkled as he took a few steps my way.

I forced myself to close my eyes because I seemed incapable of looking away from his general navel area. Those deeply grooved muscles angling their way to his . . . *ahem* . . . weren't making it any easier for me to not think about *it*.

"No," I replied, my voice three notes too high. "I was looking for some stupid sock I dropped, minding my own business, when you burst in and started taking your clothes off." In addition to my voice being a few notes too high, it was also a few notches too loud.

"And you decided to stay silent and hidden for the entire time I was stripping and washing because . . .?" he asked, but he wasn't really asking. That smirk of his gave away that he knew exactly what I'd been doing. When I didn't answer, his smirk grew more pronounced. "Because you were enjoying the free show." Not a smidgeon of doubt.

My eyes snapped open, and I forced them, upon penalty of plucking them out, to stay north of his neck. Not that Jesse's face calmed my heartbeat, but at least my lady business wasn't about to bust something.

"Not even," I said, narrowing my eyes at him. "I was waiting patiently for you to be on your merry way."

"Sure you were."

"Sure I wasn't doing whatever you so egotistically think I was doing," I snapped back.

"Whatever, Rowen. You were checking me out so hardcore your face is still red." Jesse took a few more steps my way. Crouching down beside me, his smirk shifted into a smile. "Mind if I join you down here?"

"Yes, as a matter of fact, I do," I lied. "Besides, I don't think there's enough room for your big head and bigger ego down here."

He leaned his arms onto the tops of his legs, making his shoulders roll forward. So much for keeping my eyes in the safe zone.

"Not to mention my big muscles," he replied in that tone that was as infuriating as him smirking at me. To drive the point home, the muscles spanning his chest popped a bit more to the surface.

My throat went dry.

"If you're going to hover a foot in front of me, put on a damn shirt or something." I wrote off playing it cool because I'd failed miserably. Jesse knew exactly what he was doing to me, and from the look on his face, he was enjoying the way I was unraveling.

"If I put on a shirt, will you do something for me?" His eyes, for the first time since he'd kneeled beside me, shifted from my face. They skied down the plane of my back and bend of my legs. His eyes went a shade darker before he clamped them closed. "Could you sit up? Or, better yet, stand up?" When his eyes reopened, one side of his face lined when he found me in the same position. On my hands and knees. With a short skirt on and my ass practically hanging in the air.

I don't know if I'd ever sat up so quickly in my life.

"Sorry," I mumbled, skimming my hands down the front of my skirt before standing. I didn't know what the big deal was. It wasn't the first short skirt I'd ever worn, and I'm sure it wasn't the first time I'd been in an inappropriate position wearing one, but Jesse had a way of making me more self-conscious about it. He made everything a bit more intimate.

"I guess I see why Mom's got you hiding out back here." He flashed me a wink as he popped up beside me. "And no need to apologize." He grabbed a white undershirt from the top of the pile and tugged it over his head. "I wasn't complaining."

I rolled my eyes and gently punched him in the stomach. Yep. It was as hard as it looked.

"And here I thought you cowboys were supposed to be gentlemen."

Jesse lifted an eyebrow. "Emphasis on the *men*." He was tucking his shirt into his pants when he paused. "Whoa. This is the whitest, most wrinkle-free undershirt I've ever slipped into."

I patted the stack of shirts and pants on the counter that I'd taken a bit more care with. The clothes labeled with a JW on the inside tags. "I might have bleached your shirts and ironed them after."

"You . . . *ironed* . . . my shirts?"

He looked and sounded a little shocked. All I could do was nod.

"Why?"

Exactly. Why? Why had I taken such care with Jesse's clothes? My immediate answer scared me, so I decided it was time for a conversation change. "By the way, thank you for mentioning you're not just a ranch hand at Willow Springs, but you're the owner's son."

"You didn't ask," he said, tucking his shirt into his pants before buttoning and buckling his pants back up. It was a relief. And yet, it wasn't.

With Jesse properly covered again, I had an easier

time keeping my eyes on his. "Are we back to that whole question and answer thing? Because I don't think the fact that you're a Walker is something I should have to waste a question on. That should be common knowledge. A freebie, or something."

"A freebie?" he repeated, like he was unfamiliar with the idea.

"Yes, a freebie. Things like last names, pedigree, shoe size, et cetera, et cetera, shouldn't have to be revealed through this sick game of Q and A you forced me into. Some pieces of information should qualify as freebies." Crossing my arms, I leveled him with a look. "Things like your last name being Walker."

He crossed his arms, too. "I didn't realize this was a rule to the game I made up. My bad. It won't happen again." He was amused. By me or the conversation or who knows what, but I could tell from the way only one of his dimples was on display. "And you expect me to believe you would or will give me any freebies in the getting-to-know-you department? Because really, Rowen. I've seen brahma bulls that open up easier than you."

I knew that was true. I had a million issues, the most apparent one being my inability to open up to others, but hearing it from Jesse still hurt like hell. In a little over twenty-four hours, he had figured that out about me.

Only because I felt a little belligerent did I snap back when I should have shut my mouth and gotten back to folding. "Oh, really? Two ton bulls who can't talk, have kiwi-sized brains, and basically want to kill you if you come within ten feet of them open up better than I do?" I stepped into him, trying to get into his face. I stepped back when I realized just how close that put me to his mouth.

"What do you want to know then, Cowboy? What are you so certain I've been hiding from you? What could someone like you possibly want to know about someone like me?"

The words spilled from his mouth like he'd only been waiting for me to ask. "Why are you here?"

That was quite possibly the easiest hard question to answer.

"I want to go to art school in the fall," I said, hoping that answer would appease him. Knowing it wouldn't.

"And what does Willow Springs have to do with art school in the fall?" He searched my face like he expected the answers to be there if he looked close enough.

I inhaled slowly to give myself a chance to put together my answer. "The school I want to go to is expensive. My mom only agreed to fund it if I came and worked here this summer." I did an internal cartwheel; honest, yet vague. Just the way I preferred my answers.

"Why would your mom only agree to pay for school if you worked the summer here?" Jesse asked with genuine curiosity. He leaned into the island and waited for my response.

"Your dad and mom didn't tell you why I was coming here?" I found that hard to believe.

He shrugged his shoulders. "They told the girls and me that the daughter of one of Mom's old friends was coming to spend the summer with us. There weren't any additional details."

"They didn't tell you why?" If it wasn't for the innocence of Jesse's expression, that would have been utterly impossible to believe.

"No," he said with another shrug. "And I didn't ask."

I didn't know what was worse: assuming Jesse knew what a bad egg I was all along, or realizing I'd have to tell him face-to-face.

Either way, I was about to find out.

"I'm here because I mess up, Jesse. I mess up a lot. So much my own mom has pretty much written me off as a lost cause. I'm a failure at pretty much everything—I barely graduated high school—and, for whatever reason, she chose Willow Springs as the place I could redeem myself and prove to her I'm not the piece of shit failure she thinks I am." The words came out strong, but I felt anything but. Admitting that to Jesse, a person I wanted to like me, I *really* wanted to like me, made me feel weak and vulnerable.

Jesse's expression didn't change. His eyes didn't leave mine. Nothing I said ruffled him. "Rowen," he said, moving his hand toward mine like he wanted to grab it. At the last moment, he pulled back. "I've known you a solid day and a half, and I would swear on my life that you're not a lost cause. Or a failure."

I opened my mouth to interrupt.

"Or a piece of shit failure," he said, making air quotes with one hand. "So why are you *really* here?"

Just like that, he'd moved past the whole Rowen-Sterling-Is-A-Waste-Of-Space topic. Apparently it was settled in his mind I was not the person my mom, ninety-nine percent of other people I'd come in contact with, and myself, as of late, thought I was. The only thing that mattered to him was why I was there.

"Because I don't have any other option," I whispered, looking away from him at last. Our conversation in the laundry room had gone about five levels too personal for my taste.

"Bullshit," he said instantly.

That brought my attention right back to him. "Excuse me?"

"That's not the reason you're here," he stated. "You don't have any other options? Please." He made a face and shook his head once. "Ever heard of a little thing called financial aid? How about a summer job waiting tables at one of those big city coffee shops? Oh yeah, and let's not forget about scholarships."

I didn't like what he was getting at. I liked even less the way it made me rethink a bunch of things. Narrowing my eyes, I met his. "I. Didn't. Have. Another. Option."

"Bull. Shit." Apparently, that was Jesse's new favorite word. Appropriate given he spent the majority of his days up to his knees in it. "You've got as many options as the rest of us. You're just choosing to ignore them for some reason."

I'd had enough. Enough laundry room, enough Jesse, enough crippling conversation. "You're right," I seethed. "There is 'some reason' I'm here. Good for you for figuring it out. Discovery of the decade." I clapped at him. "What other scintillating tidbits do you have for us?"

Again, Jesse's expression didn't change. Nothing I said or did seemed to unnerve him. "Just one more thing," he began, looking so hard into my eyes I half expected his stare to go right through me. "The reason you're pushing me away, and the reason you've probably pushed everyone else away, is also the reason you're here." Stepping into me, Jesse's eyes dropped with what I guessed was sadness. "You think you deserve this. You think you deserve to be alone and suffer. You've convinced yourself you're so worthless that you've gone to the extreme to punish yourself. You think you deserve a life of misery."

Yeah, I was going to cry. Big, ugly tears I really didn't want him to witness. Instead of letting myself open up that way, I did what I did best. Stepping away from him, I lowered my eyes. "Get out," I said, my voice shaking. "And leave me alone."

Jesse sighed, then followed the first part of my directions. After the laundry room door closed behind him, I almost got down on my hands and knees to pray to whoever and whatever that he wouldn't follow the last part of my directions.

CHAPTER four

If a brain could shrivel up and die from too much contemplation, mine was dangerously close to living out the rest of its days as a pruney, gray raisin. I wasn't sure how much time had passed since Jesse dropped that bomb on me, but I couldn't stop thinking about what he'd said. How had a teenage guy figured out what I worked hard to ignore? All in the span of a couple of conversations?

I came up empty in the answer department. What was almost as frustrating as having no answers was worrying about what those answers might be. Was I just that transparent? Had everything I'd done to build the eighteen-year-old girl equivalent of the Berlin Wall been nothing more than a house of cards? Was Jesse Walker the most perceptive human being to have ever walked the face of the earth? Was he psychic?

I felt a migraine forming when the door to the laundry room opened a while later.

"Oh, honey. Have you been in here the whole time?" Rose asked, inspecting the room. Her eyes widened. "When I assigned you laundry room duty, I didn't expect you to clean the actual room top to bottom."

I dumped the bucket of soapy water into the sink and shrugged. "I finished up with the laundry a couple of hours ago," I guessed. The concept of time had escaped me after

Jesse left. "Sorry. I still had some energy, so I figured I'd keep going."

Rose chuckled. "I doubt this room has been this clean since the day it was built a hundred years ago."

I slid the bucket back beneath the sink, finally feeling tired. It had taken about thirty loads of laundry, a hardcore cleaning of an entire room, and a loaded conversation with Jesse, but exhaustion finally creeped into my veins.

"Don't tell my mom I know how to clean. It'll ruin her whole world outlook."

Rose took a few steps inside the room, looking around it like she didn't recognize it. "Speaking of your mom . . ." Nothing good could come of that opening line. "I just got off the phone with her. I guess she hasn't heard back from you since you got in yesterday, and she was worried."

That's because I hit "ignore" every time one of her calls came in. "I doubt that was worry, Rose. It was probably irritation. Or annoyance. Or something more along the Rowen-is-hopeless line."

Rose stopped in front of the island and leaned her hip into it the way Jesse had. In fact, I saw a lot of Jesse's mannerisms in Rose. Like mother, like son. "No, it was worry. Concern. After thirty years of knowing your mom, at least give me a little credit that I've almost got her figured out. Your mom might act a certain way and say certain things, but she keeps her intentions hidden between the lines." Rose paused and looked at me pointedly. "Sound like anyone else you know?"

Damn. If Jesse wasn't shoving my repressed issues into my face, it was Rose. What did a girl need to do to catch a break? I had issues. I didn't like to talk about them.

I didn't like to *think* about them. End of story.

"Is there anything else you need tonight?" I asked, worrying over a stack of shirts on the island to distract myself. I noticed a JW written in black pen on the tag. Dammit. Did I even gravitate to his clean laundry?

The skin between Rose's brows came together. She opened her mouth to say something, then closed it. Shaking her head, her face ironed out. "No, I think you've done more than your fair share of work today. In fact, I'd say you earned yourself a day off tomorrow." Her voice was back in all its Rose warmth. "Go into town and check out the sights. Relax. Unwind. You have my blessing."

The sights? Jesse and I'd driven through what I guessed Rose was referring to as the "town," but it was more like a one horse village still stuck in the 1800s. It was so non-descript, I'd already forgotten its name.

"Did you tell my mom you were giving me tomorrow off?"

"No," she answered. "That's between me and you. Your mom wanted you here so you could 'prove' yourself." Rose's eyes almost performed a full-on eye roll. Impressive. "From the moment you stepped foot at Willow Springs, you've proven yourself, Rowen."

I shifted and eyed the exit. The conversation was taking another turn toward the uncomfortable.

"Listen, I don't know what you've done, or what your mom *thinks* you've done, to deserve spending your whole summer where I'd guess is the last place you'd want to spend your summer. And you know what?" She didn't wait for me to reply. "I don't care. Every morning we get a chance to be different. A chance to change. A chance to be better. Your past is your past. Leave it there. Get on with the future part, honey."

The laundry room was either the mecca of pure genius or utter insanity. After what Jesse and his mom had said, I couldn't quite decide. What was it about the Walkers and their need to have deep, meaningful conversations? Apparently they'd missed the memo about the rise in casual conversation.

"I drank a lot. I skipped class a lot more," I started, the words coming out of me before I knew they were coming. "I messed around with guys. I did drugs." Rose's gaze didn't shift once. "I ran away from home. Twice. I got arrested. Twice. I tried hurting myself so many times I can't remember how many."

After that, I shut my mouth. Not that it really mattered. I'd said more than enough, but at least she knew who I was and what she was dealing with. If Mom had decided to leave out the gory details, Rose knew now. I wasn't just one of those kids off on the outside; I was off all the way through.

"So now you know why I'm here. This summer is my chance to convince her I'm more than a liability." I crossed my arms, trying to hold myself together. "But here's what I can't figure out. Why would you want me here in the first place?"

"Oh, sweetie," she said, a little breathless. "Get over here." She opened her arms and motioned me into them.

I went after a moment's pause.

Rose folded me tightly against her, and I wondered if I'd ever been given such a fierce hug. "You're here because you're supposed to be. There's nowhere else you should be right now. As God is my witness, I'm a hundred percent sure of that." She sounded like she had a huge lump in her throat. That made two of us. "But you're wrong about one thing. This summer isn't your chance to prove yourself to your mom." Leaning back just far enough my face was in front of hers, Rose's eyes locked on mine. "This summer is your chance to prove yourself to *you.*"

Holy brain overload. So much was being said, even more was being meant. I needed some time alone to figure that out before any more pearls of wisdom got dropped on me.

"I'd better get to bed then," I said, managing a smile. "I'm going to have my work cut out for me if I'm supposed to be proving myself to me." There was a brain bender if I'd ever heard one. "Thanks for everything, Rose. You're pretty cool, despite being my mom's childhood best friend."

She laughed and let me out of her arms. "You know what they say. Opposites attract," she said, her voice loaded with inflection. "Keeps things interesting."

When I thought about my polar opposite, a tall, grinning cowboy with a rosy outlook and a fine ass popped to mind.

I had to shake my head to get Jesse out of there. There was so much wrong about fantasizing about the son of the woman standing in front of me, I was sure there was a special place in hell for people who did it. I started heading for the door.

"So what do you think? Gonna take tomorrow off?"

I paused in the doorway. "Nah. I think I'd better earn my keep."

"You're really up for another full day of laundry duty?" Rose's voice was full of disbelief. Rightly so.

"About that . . ." I turned to face her. "Are you still okay with me working around the rest of the place if I wear something less . . ." I glanced down at my clothing, trying to paraphrase it, "intense?"

Rose nodded. "More than okay with it. You want to hang with me and the girls tomorrow?"

"Um, yeah," I began, fiddling with the hem of my skirt. "I just don't . . . I don't exactly have . . ."

"Why don't you stop by Lily's room before you head to bed?" she said, saving me. "She'd be happy to loan you a few of her things until we can get into town to get you some new clothes. You two have to be pretty close in size."

"Really?" I said. "You don't think she'd mind?"

"I know she wouldn't."

Why? Why would a teenage girl not mind another teenage girl who was basically a stranger knocking on her door and asking to borrow some clothes? Oh yeah, because the Walkers were the damn nicest people I'd been around. Something was in the well water out at Willow Springs.

"Okay," I said with a wave. "I'll see you in the morning. I mean, I'll see you at the crack of dawn." I smiled at Rose as I left the laundry room behind.

"Tomorrow morning. Brand new chance. The first day of whatever life you want to have for yourself." Rose called after me, "Wake up wisely."

The first floor was quiet as I headed for the stairs. No sounds other than the ticking of the old grandfather clock in the foyer and the chorus of crickets coming through the cracked open windows. The kitchen lights were turned off, along with most of the other lights, except for one small lamp glowing in the living room window. Rose had told me earlier they always kept that one light glowing to remind them that when the night is at its darkest, there's always a promise of dawn to come.

Yeah. I wasn't living with just the nicest family in existence; they were probably descendants of Aristotle.

I still hadn't met Neil, Rose's husband, but if Willow Springs kept him as busy as Rose, it wasn't a big surprise I hadn't bumped into Jesse's dad. Especially since all I'd been bumping into was washing machines and dryers.

Before traipsing up the stairs, I took one more look around. He wasn't here.

Maybe he didn't live here anymore. He was nineteen after all. Maybe he lived some place else and only worked there. Maybe he stayed back in the bunkhouse with the rest of the ranch hands.

When I realized I was spending way too much time contemplating where Jesse laid his head at night, I gave myself a mental slap and bolted down the hall toward Lily's room.

The door was halfway open, but I still felt the need to knock.

"Entrez-vous," was the sing-song reply.

"Hey, Lily," I greeted, stepping inside her room. It was almost identical to the one I was staying in except the walls were a minty green instead of tan.

"Oh . . . hey, Rowen," she said, spinning in her desk chair. "I thought you were mom."

"Am I interrupting you? I can come back later." I hitched my thumb at the door and stepped toward it. She had a couple books spread over the desk and a pencil behind her ear.

"No, an interruption was exactly what I needed. If I have to conjugate one more French verb, I'm going to go voulez-vous crazy."

"French verbs?" I wrinkled my nose. "It's summer break. Why are you doing anything that resembles homework?"

"I'm one of those unfortunate few who goes to school year round," she said, not sounding the least bit devastated.

"Why?" I'd known the summer school kids—I'd been one of them—and Lily didn't fit the profile.

"Mom home schools us, so other than Sundays, a week in the winter, and a week in the summer, the Walker kids are in 'class' every day. Except for Jesse. He graduated last summer from Willow Springs High." Lily smiled at me in a girlish way. That, combined with the side braids and makeup-free face, made her seem a few years younger.

"What are you going to do after you graduate?" I asked, obviously not understanding the way it worked out there. Everything seemed a little backward compared to where I came from, yet it also made some sense.

"I want to go to one of the state schools and work on getting my veterinary medicine degree," she said, her eyes glowing. "Specializing in large animal."

"I imagine that profession is in high demand out here." I was impressed. The girl had goals and didn't look the least bit concerned she wouldn't achieve them.

She bobbed her head. "Willow Springs alone could keep me employed full-time. I grew up with so many cattle and horses I feel like I'm already halfway to becoming a vet."

"I bet you are."

Her smile grew. "How was your day? Do you never want to see another bottle of laundry detergent for the rest of your life?"

"For the rest of this life and my next," I said. "That's actually kind of the reason I wanted to talk with you."

Lily sat up in her seat. "Do you want me to give you a hand tomorrow? I'm sure mom wouldn't mind once I get my other chores—"

I lifted my hand. "Thank you, but I was actually wondering if I could borrow some clothes? I can't spend another day in that place."

Lily hopped out of her chair. "I totally don't blame you, and of course you can borrow some clothes. What do you need?" She slid her closet door open and swept her arms through its contents.

"Whatever you think I need," I said, peering inside the closet. "I'm officially in unchartered territory." I ran my eyes down my body. "Obviously."

Sorting through a few pairs of jeans, Lily pulled a couple of the newer looking ones off their hangers. "These ought to work," she said and slid a few T-shirts free. "Here you go. Will these be all right?" She handed me the heap of clothing and waited.

"These will work great," I said, studying the shirts and jeans in my arms. I couldn't remember the last time I'd worn sky blue, the color of one of the shirts she'd handed me. Sky blue. The color of a certain pair of eyes who saw too much when they looked at me.

I gave my head a shake. "Thanks, Lily. You're pretty great, you know that?"

From her expression, I couldn't have given her a

bigger compliment.

"I'll let you get back to your homework." I flashed her a smile before heading for the door with my Willow Springs-approved borrowed wardrobe.

"Rowen?"

I stopped and looked over my shoulder.

"Did that hurt when you had it done?" Lily asked, glancing at my eyebrow.

"A little. But I've experienced a lot worse."

Lily gave me a nod and a smile. "I wish I could be more like you. You're so confident in who you are."

I had to look away from her eyes full of admiration. "I don't know who I am, Lily. I'm just really good at pretending." Then, because I couldn't say or hear another "deep" word, I darted out of her room.

Hyacinth and Clementine must have also been busy with homework because the hall was quiet. After shutting myself inside my room, I dropped my armful of clothes on the foot of my bed and wandered to the window. It was warm up there, and if the old house had air-conditioning, it certainly wasn't on.

As soon as I whooshed the window open, I understood why. The days might have been warm, but the nights were almost chilly. Fresh, cool air flooded the room, and in less than a minute, the hot air was gone. I headed over to the dresser, grabbed my sketchbook and pencil, and wandered back to the window. A few minutes of losing myself on a blank white page sounded like just the way to end the day.

As I lowered my pencil to the paper, my eyes shifted to the barn, where a warm, yellow light flooded from its open doors. The pencil dropped from my fingers.

Jesse stood in the bed of his old truck, parked just outside the wide doors, heaving huge bags of something onto the barn floor. The white shirt he'd slipped into in the laundry room wasn't clean anymore. I started to understand why the washing machines ran non-stop at Willow Springs.

The bed of his truck was stacked high and wide with bags about the same size as me. Jesse lifted each one, threw it over his shoulder, and walked it to the tailgate as he had my bag. Like those bags were filled with packing popcorn. Farm work obviously gave a person superhuman strength and, from what I'd witnessed earlier from my spy spot on the laundry room floor, superhuman muscles as well. He wasn't even breathing heavily.

Yeah, the way my heart started hammering in my chest and the way my whole body went all tingly was pretty much the opposite of winding down.

Jesse had just tossed another bag onto the ground when he froze. His whole body went wire straight right before he started to twist around.

"Crap," I hissed, dropping to the floor as fast as gravity allowed me. He knew I'd been watching him . . . *spying* on him. He knew.

Jesse was as hardwired to me as I was to him and, right then, that scared me more than anything else. I didn't like letting people get close. I didn't want them to see past the smoke and mirrors.

I stayed cowered down on the floor for so long, I fell asleep there. My dreams that night, as always, were in black and white.

CHAPTER five

Another soft rapping on the door. Another groan from me. I sensed a routine forming.

"Rowen?" Lily's voice was just as timid as it had been yesterday morning. And by morning, I mean butt crack of dawn. "Rise and shine time."

I groaned and attempted to peel myself from the floor. The carpet was practically pasted to my cheek. "I will rise, but I do not shine," I croaked as I stood. "Even if I did, I sure as heck wouldn't this early."

Lily laughed a few soft notes. "I'll see you downstairs."

"Yay," I said with a hefty dose of sarcasm. Before shuffling over to the dresser, I took a quick peek out the window. Jesse and his truck were long gone, and the barn was dark. After peeling out of the clothes I'd slept in, I grabbed the first jeans and shirt my hands touched. Lily was a couple inches shorter than me and a rail, so the jeans were tight—Jesse's jeans tight—and the tee fit kind of snugly, too. At least I'd have more than Maytag and Whirlpool to keep me company. Wearing tight, uncomfortable country digs was worth it.

I was sure my black boots looked ridiculous with the rest of my get-up, but the other shoes I'd brought would have looked even weirder. A quick mirror check revealed I was a mess. A hot, crazy-haired one. Not wasting any time, I undid my braid from yesterday, tore a brush through my unruly hair, then re-braided it. I wiped away the smears of what was left from yesterday, but I didn't apply any more makeup. It was too early, I was too tired, and I doubted if Midnight Scarlet lipstick paired well with a simple, sky blue tee.

Great. I had on *that* tee. Talk about a Freudian slip . . .

I flipped off my reflection before leaving the room. A peek inside each of the girls' rooms showed them empty, beds made, and no clothes dotting the carpet. I was less and less surprised by that sort of things when it came to the Walkers.

When I rounded the corner into the kitchen, I found it much the same as it had been yesterday morning. Rose and the girls were all busy prepping something for breakfast, zipping around the room like little worker bees.

When Rose spun away from the fridge, she smiled when she took me in. "I think we just put a little bit of country in this girl," she said, setting a couple cartons of eggs on the counter.

I made a non-committal motion with my hand. "Here I am. Put me to work." The girls stopped what they were doing to check me out, too. They weren't as good at hiding their surprise.

I gave Lily a *What do you think?* look, and she flashed me a thumbs up. She was infinitely more sure about the way I looked than I was.

"Have you ever made pancakes before, Rowen?" Rose asked, waving me over with a spatula.

"Not exactly," I said, eyeing the frying pan suspiciously. "But I've eaten my fair share."

"Then that qualifies you. Come on over," she said, stepping aside to give me the front and center position. "Clementine already mixed the batter up, so all you need to do is pour it onto the griddle, flip them, and throw them onto the platter."

Clementine waved at me from where she was whipping up something else. A seven-year-old was kicking my ass in the home economics department. I wasn't sure whether to be proud of myself or ashamed.

"Do you have a diagram or directions I can follow?" I asked as Rose handed me the spatula ceremoniously. "Because this is not going to be pretty."

Holding up her finger, she turned to the griddle. "Ladle. Scoop." She grabbed the ladle and scooped out a full serving of batter. "Pour." The batter sizzled as it hit the griddle surface. "Repeat." She was pouring another ladleful, then four more, before I blinked. "Flip." She flicked the spatula in my hand, patted my cheek, then went back to her eggs. "Ladle. Scoop. Pour. Repeat. Flip."

"Burn," I said, studying the six pancakes as though they were a puzzle. "Fail."

As I was about to *attempt* to flip a pancake, Hyacinth shouldered up beside me. She smiled as she nudged me. "Wait until tiny bubbles surface around the outside before you flip them."

It wasn't even dawn, and I'd already learned something new.

"Thanks," I replied, matching her smile before she got back to work pulling plates out of a cabinet. They used plates? Real plates they had to wash? Along with air conditioning, paper plates must not have made their way to the Walkers' corner of the world yet.

I turned my attention back to the pancakes, watching them so intently I don't think I blinked once. The second those bubbles started popping to the surface, I wielded my spatula and flipped the first pancake.

It was a proud moment. Not only had I managed to flip it without getting batter all over the place, the cooked side was a perfect golden brown. If that was all there was to cooking, I had it down. No problem.

I repeated the process with the other five; all were a beautiful golden brown. As soon as I let myself get a little cocky, like I was the modern day Betty Crocker, the kitchen door to the porch flew open. Goosebumps trailed up my spine. I hadn't yet turned my head, but I was as sure the person who'd just stepped into the kitchen was Jesse as I was sure the air in the kitchen had gotten a little thin.

"First one to breakfast," Lily said in a teasing voice. "Big surprise."

"It's not my fault the rest of the guys like to sleep in 'til the last possible minute. I've been up for an hour checking the new calves, and I'm hungry. I'm a growing boy." I willed myself to stare at the pancakes. I willed myself to not let his voice get to me. I willed myself to be unaffected by his presence.

I wasn't very willful.

My body twisted around of its own accord, and my eyes locked on his at the same time his locked on mine.

Jesse. Smile. Dimples. Jeans. Hat.

I grabbed the edge of the counter to keep from wavering.

"Look at you," he said, hanging his hat on one of the pegs sticking out of the wall. I guessed they were for hanging hats. Lots of hats. He headed my way, rumpling

Clementine's hair as he walked by her. Toward me. Where I braced myself against a countertop to keep from passing out. "Country looks good on you, Rowen." Jesse ran his eyes down me before stopping a few feet in front of me. When he glanced down at my shoes, his smile pulled higher. He was in his standard blood-cutting-off jeans, boots, and hat, but he had on a tan Carhartt jacket over yet another clean white tee. How many of those things did he go through in a day?

"And silence might look good on you if you ever gave it a try," I threw back, right before I realized four other people were in the room. Four women who had stopped what they were doing to watch the two of us with rapt interest.

Catching Rose's stare, I shrugged. "Your son likes to talk. He *really* likes to talk," I added, remembering all the things he'd said in the past few days. The frequency of his words wasn't really the issue; it was the power behind them.

Rose studied the two of us for another moment, almost like she was trying to put her finger on something, before getting back to cracking eggs into a skillet. "Breakfast in five, girls. Get movin'."

Just like that, Jesse's sisters' attention moved from us back to breakfast.

"How are those pancakes coming along?" Jesse asked, leaning closer to inspect the skillet.

"Swimmingly," I replied, checking them. No bubbles yet.

He moved a little closer. So close, I could tell he'd recently taken a shower. He still smelled like soap and shampoo. "You really do look nice, you know," he said, his voice quieter.

I huffed. "Really? Because you seemed to be a pretty big fan of that outfit I wore yesterday." My mind flashed with the memory of him catching me checking him out.

"That was pretty great, you're right." His eyes told me he was reliving the memory of me on all fours. "But this look appeals to me in a different way."

I did a quick check of the kitchen to make sure no one was paying us any attention. "In what way?"

"In a quid pro quo kind of way."

I rolled my eyes. Apparently someone had gotten an A in Willow Springs English. "Why's that?"

"Because every time you make fun of how tightly my jeans hug my backside, I can throw the same thing right back at you."

I didn't need to look to confirm he was inspecting my backside. Lily's borrowed jeans suddenly seemed to be squeezing the hell out of my ass.

"Don't you have some cows to milk or something?" I elbowed his stomach. Yep, it was just as hard as it'd been last night.

Jesse laughed and shook his head. "We're not a dairy farm here, Rowen. We're a beef ranch."

Sorry, I didn't speak hick. His chuckling unsettled me in a couple different ways.

"Then maybe you could go unload another truckload of ginormous bags." A clamp for my mouth would have so come in handy.

"So that *was* you spying on me again last night," he said, his voice so damn confident. "I knew someone was watching me, and I figured it was you."

I glared at those six pancakes. Still no bubbles. "And

why would you figure it was me?"

"Well, you know," he said.

"No, I don't know."

He leaned his hip into the counter. "Given your track record of spying on me."

"For Pete's sake," I said, tempted to dump the bowl of batter over his head. "I wasn't spying on you in the laundry room. I was *hiding* from you."

"You were hiding from me?" He crossed his arms.

I nodded.

"And what about last night when you were watching me from your window? Were you hiding from me then?" My hands actually moved for the batter bowl.

"I had 911 on standby in case you keeled over from a heart attack lifting one of those suckers," I snapped back. "It was my civic duty. Now, if you're done harassing me for one morning, I've got some pancakes to attend to."

Jesse glanced at the pancakes, and he looked like he was about to bust up laughing before he caught himself. "I'm done harassing you for one morning. But do you think it'd be all right if I offered a heartfelt apology?"

Say what?

I studied his face to see if it was some kind of trick to get me to continue battling it out with him, but his expression was flat. His eyes clear.

"Proceed," I said with a wave of my magic spatula.

Jesse sucked in a breath before proceeding. "I'm sorry for what I said last night. I had no right to stick my nose into your business and start making assumptions about your life." His words flowed with such ease it seemed he'd rehearsed them. "I've only known you a couple of days. That's not long at all. I don't know you well enough to pretend like I know you and your problems. But I want to know you. I want to know your problems. That is . . . if you want to know me."

One corner of my mouth pulled up. Luckily, it was on the side he couldn't see. Jesse could make one hell of an apology. I had to give him that.

But I couldn't let him off so easily.

"Why do you want to know me better?" I said, checking the outlet to make sure the griddle was still plugged in because those suckers were not bubbling. "So you can tease me more specifically? So you can expose my weakness and take advantage of it?"

Jesse moved a step closer. I felt his upper half against my side. I grabbed the ledge of the counter again. "So when I ask you on a date, I'll know where to take you to really impress you." His mouth was so close to my ear I felt the warmth of his breath.

I whipped my head around to meet his eyes. Damn. He was dead serious. His gaze drifted to my mouth right as the kitchen door flew open again.

"Save some of the food for us, Jesse!" a man's voice ordered good-naturedly as a staggered line of men in hats and boots streamed into the kitchen.

Jesse stepped away from me, but he didn't look away. Before turning toward the table, he tilted his chin at me. "Check those pancakes. I think they're smoking." His dimples set into his cheeks. "What can I say? I have that effect on things."

I was ready to glare at him when that burnt smell entered my nose. A quick inspection of the griddle revealed that my lovely golden pancakes were, indeed, smoking.

"Shoot," I said, unsure how I managed to censor myself in the midst of my first attempt at breakfast going up in flames. Or, up in smoke. "They never bubbled!" I fumbled with the spatula and tried to slide it under the center pancakes.

Even through the hustle and bustle of the rest of the ranch hands making their way into the room, I heard Jesse's amused chuckle from back at the table.

"They don't bubble once you flip them over, silly," Lily said, appearing out of nowhere. Grabbing the spatula, she had all of those pancakes off the griddle faster than I could have removed one of them.

"Then how do you know when they're done?" I asked, grimacing when I saw the damage. One side was golden brown, and the other side was a crispy char black.

Lily dropped a pat of butter onto the griddle, swirled it around, then poured six more pancakes. "You just get a feel for it. Through a lot of trial and error." Her eyes dropped to the ruined pancakes, and she smiled.

"Story of my life," I muttered. "The trial and error part. I still haven't experienced the whole get-a-feel-for-it part yet."

"Tomorrow's another day," she replied, focusing on the pancakes. "Dream big."

I lifted my brows. Was that what I thought it was? A note of smartass in sweet Lily Walker's vocab? I didn't realize that characteristic ran in anyone in the family other than Jesse.

"Why don't you pour the coffee?" Lily suggested. "Carefully."

"No guarantees." I made my way over to the coffee pot and hoped I didn't spill hot coffee on some poor cowboy's crotch.

In a minute's time, the kitchen had filled up with more cowboys than I could count. The couple dozen pegs sticking out of the wall were almost all filled with different kinds and colors of cowboy hats. Apparently wearing your hat to Rose Walker's table wasn't tolerated. The guys milling about the room were as varied as their hats. Tall, short. Slim, stocky. Young, old. Light skinned, dark skinned. It was the most varied group of cowboys I'd ever seen.

Well, it was really the first group of cowboys I'd ever seen.

However, one characteristic joined them all together. They all drank coffee. And a lot of it. Before Rose and the girls had finished setting all the breakfast goods on the table, I'd gone through three full pots of coffee. I understood why Rose prepared a few gallons of it in advance.

Jesse introduced me to everyone as I milled my way around, and everyone greeted me with a tip of their head and some sort of greeting followed by *ma'am*. By the time everyone had full plates, I felt as comfortable as I could around a couple dozen ranch hands, and I knew that was thanks to Jesse and his easy introductions. He was a member of the club, and he saw to it I became one right off the bat.

It was nice to be included. It was nice to feel a part of something.

It was the first time I'd had that in a while.

"More coffee?" I asked, stopping behind Jesse. His cup was still half full.

He twisted in his seat, a smile already on his face. "Please," he said, handing me his cup. My fingers grazed his when I took the cup, and if I'd ever felt a more intimate touch, I couldn't recall it. God. One finger graze and my heart thrummed like it was about to take off.

As I poured, Jesse's eyes shifted to mine and they didn't look away. Mine didn't either, or . . . they couldn't. When Jesse Walker looked at me that way, it was all I could do to look back and stay upright.

"Coffee," he said suddenly, glancing at his cup.

My eyebrows came together.

"Overflowing." He smirked at the cup so I really couldn't peel my eyes away.

A few chuckles sounded around us.

"Pooling on the floor." When Jesse reached for his napkin, I finally caught up.

Gauging from the size of the puddle, coffee had been spilling over the side of the cup for longer than a second or two.

"Shit," I said, righting the coffee pot immediately. Setting it on the table, I grabbed a stack of napkins before kneeling beside Jesse. "I mean . . . shoot."

"Nah," he said, wiping up the sea of coffee in one long sweep. "You mean shit. This is definitely a mess worthy of a shit, not a shoot."

I smiled at the floor as I wiped up the last of the coffee. "At least it didn't end up in your lap."

"I'm counting my blessings as we speak." His hair fell over his forehead, moving in ways that made me want to run my fingers through it as he continued to scrub the floor. His hair was really much too nice to stay hidden beneath a cowboy hat all day. "So . . . have you decided?"

"Decided on what?"

"If you're going to let me take you out some time. You know, a date? Something other than kneeling on a floor and cleaning up coffee?" Jesse's gaze stayed on the spot where the coffee had been. Almost like he was suddenly shy.

I cleared my throat and looked around. Everyone was too busy eating to pay us any attention. "Well, you didn't really ask me," I said. "And you haven't really given me much time to think about what you didn't really ask me."

Jesse scooped up the wet napkins and tossed them into the garbage can at the end of the kitchen without standing. He inhaled a long breath before locking his eyes on mine. "Rowen Sterling," he said, his voice strong, "can I take you on a date sometime?"

I knew I should try, but I couldn't keep my face from lighting up. "I don't know. Can you?" I teased.

He sighed. "May I? May I take you on a date some-time?"

"Because you don't have a girlfriend—"

"Or a boyfriend. Or a cattlefriend," he mumbled, giving me a look. Good. So he remembered my question.

"And because you're kind of cute," I continued, "and because you're not afraid to get down and dirty," I stared pointedly at where he kneeled beside me, "I promise I'll think about going on a date with you. Sometime."

If Jesse's expression could get more relieved, I couldn't envision it. "I've never been so excited for *some-time*."

I heard the kitchen door open behind us, but I didn't pay it any attention. That was, until a shiny, black pair of cowboy boots stepped right next to me.

"No need to get down on your hands and knees on my account."

Jesse went rigid the instant he heard the guy's voice.

My eyes moved up those black boots, to his hub cap-sized silver belt buckle stamped with a man riding a bull, and ending on his black, felt hat. His skin was almost as fair as mine, and his eyes were so dark it was hard to distinguish the pupil from the iris. Lanky, dark, and sinister. That guy, minus the hick wear, was just my type.

When Jesse shifted beside me and all two hundred pounds of bronzy, brawn, and blond of him stood, my heart thundered in my chest again. Maybe my type had changed. Or was changing. Or was in transition. It was all very confusing.

Mr. Dark and Sinister's mouth curved up on one side as those dark eyes took me in. "Not that you don't look great down there, but let me give you a hand," he said, extending his hand toward me. If the expression on his face didn't say it all, his tone did.

Jesse pivoted in front of him, lowering his hand toward me. I took it without stopping to think. It was natural. Easy. Effortless. When Jesse reached out for me, I reached back.

"Who's your new friend, Jess?" the other guy asked, stepping around the tower of man in front of me.

If it was possible, Jesse's body tensed even more. I wasn't sure if Jesse kept his mouth sealed shut because he plain just didn't want to talk to the other guy or he didn't want to introduce us. Either way, he obviously wouldn't make the introductions, and the other guy obviously wouldn't move until the introductions were made.

Taking matters into my own hands, I crossed my arms and leveled the other guy with a no nonsense look. "I'm Rowen."

Jesse's eyes closed.

Dark and Sinister Boy's eyes went a shade darker. "Rowen . . .?"

"*Miss* Rowen to you," I said, lifting a brow. "And a first name's all you're getting because you have to *earn* a last name."

"Does this guy know it?" he replied, hitching his thumb Jesse's direction.

"Yeah. He does."

"So you'll give Jesse Walker your last name, but you won't tell me," he said, resting his thumbs on his belt buckle. "Why's that?"

"He earned it." I glanced at Jesse from the corner of my eyes. He watched me so carefully it was like he was worried I was about to be snatched away in the blink of an eye.

"Garth," he said, extending his hand. I let it hang there. "And because you're the finest thing I've seen in a while, you've earned yourself a last name." Jesse's hands curled into fists. "Black. Garth Black."

From his jeans to his boots to his eyes . . . to his entire demeanor, he personified his last name perfectly.

When Garth realized I wouldn't shake his hand anytime this century, he dropped it. His eyes slid from me to Jesse. They went a shade darker.

"Long time no see, old pal," he said.

Jesse blew a rush of air from his nose. "What are you doing here, Black?"

"Well, it certainly isn't to worship at your feet like the rest of this damn town. And it sure isn't to make a heartfelt apology."

Storm clouds rolled through those sky blue eyes of Jesse's. "Spit it out," he said, his jaw clenching. "What the hell are you doing on my property?"

If it wasn't so hot inside the kitchen, chills would have crawled up my spine from the ice in Jesse's voice. Those two had history. That was as obvious as their mutual hatred. What that history was and where that hate came from was the mystery. As much as I loved a good mystery, now was neither the time nor place to get to the bottom of it. For the most part, the rest of the guys sitting around the table were consumed with stuffing their mouths, but I caught Rose and Lily throwing us a few sideways looks.

"Your dad hired me on," Garth replied. "I'm going to be helping out this summer."

"How long are you going to last this time?" Jesse replied, angling in front of him. Toe to toe, Jesse had him by a couple of inches even with Garth's hat still on. "Two weeks? Maybe three?" He shook his head. "Commitment isn't really your thing."

"No, it certainly isn't," Garth said with that wicked half smile of his. "Commitment's boring. Predictable. It sucks the life out of a person." He ran his eyes down Jesse intentionally. "Commitment's more your thing."

Whatever had happened between them ran deeper than an everyday disagreement. Judging from the looks in their eyes whenever they looked at each other, if murder was legal, they wouldn't have hesitated.

"You boys catching up?" A middle-aged man stepped up to the three of us and clapped one hand over Jesse's shoulder and another over Garth's.

"We sure are, Mr. Walker," Garth replied, his eyes gleaming.

Ah. So there was the Mr. Walker I'd heard so much

about but was starting to believe was the man hiding behind the curtains. He was on the short side and had brown hair and eyes like the rest of his family minus one. How had Rose and Neil created the blond Viking god beside me? DNA was a funny thing.

"I thought we were all hired up for the summer," Jesse said to his dad.

"We were. Right up until Phil Jepson decided his old body couldn't take another summer at Willow Springs. He let me know he was leaving yesterday morning, and when I ran into town last night to pick up some supplies, guess who I ran into?"

"Since Garth Black is standing in front of me, I don't think I need to guess," was Jesse's clipped response.

"Since you boys go so far back, and Garth promised me he was committed to finishing out the entire summer, unlike last summer," Neil quirked a brow at Garth, "I decided to give him a second chance." Neil's gaze shifted to me, and he smiled. "We're big fans of second chances around here."

"Second chances, sure," Jesse said, staring down Garth. "Seventh chances, not so much."

Neil gave his son an odd look before extending his hand toward me. "Rowen Sterling, it's nice to finally meet you. Sorry it didn't happen sooner. A couple thousand head of cattle have a way of eating up a person's day *and* night."

I matched his smile and shook his hand. As with Rose, I liked Neil immediately. "I can imagine."

"We're glad to have you here, Rowen," he said. "How's your first day going in the kitchen?"

Jesse shot me a wry smile which I pretended to

ignore.

"I crispified a batch of pancakes and spilled some coffee," I answered, lifting the empty pot in my hand. "Could have been worse."

Neil chuckled. "I have a feeling you'll keep things exciting around here," he said, before heading to the last empty seat at the head of the table.

"Me, too," Garth added, giving me an expectant look.

"Take a seat, Garth," Jesse said, more of an order than a request.

"That's all right," Garth replied, refusing to look at Jesse. He looked at me so intently, I stepped back. "I want to get to know Rowen better."

"Give it a rest, Garth," Jesse said. "Rowen's smart. Smart enough to know to stay away from guys like you."

Garth clucked his tongue. "You know who wasn't smart enough to stay away from me?"

Jesse's face went from tan to red in about two seconds flat.

Time for an intervention.

"You two know each other, eh?" I said, asking what was quite possibly the stupidest question of the year. There was no doubt those two knew each other.

"We were best friends," Garth answered.

I don't think I would have been more surprised if I'd just been crowned Miss America.

"*Were*," Jesse said under his breath.

"We used to share everything." Garth was pushing Jesse's buttons. That was obvious from the way his smile slid a little higher when Jesse's face went another shade redder.

"*Used* to."

"I don't know, Jesse," Garth said, polishing his belt buckle with his thumb. "I seem to recall us sharing something recently."

When I was certain Jesse would lunge at Garth, Hyacinth slid up beside the three of us, looking oblivious. She tapped Jesse on the shoulder. "Josie's on the phone."

"Take a message." Jesse's voice was ice, but his face was still on fire.

"Again?" Hyacinth replied before Jesse leveled her with a look. "Fine." She sighed as she left. "I'll take a message. *Another* message."

"Say hello to Josie for me, will ya?" Garth called after Hyacinth. "It's been a while."

Hyacinth waved her response and continued on.

"Just how long's it been, Jesse? I forget." Garth stroked his chin.

"Who's Josie?" I asked Jesse.

But Garth answered. "Jesse's girlfriend." Garth's eyes darkened and he flexed his hips.

Moving so fast he was a blur, Jesse shoved Garth so hard in the chest Garth stumbled across half of the room.

"Jesse!" Neil bolted out of his seat and squared himself in front of his son before Garth got there. "What the hell is going on here?"

Jesse's chest rose and fell hard. His eyes were as dark and narrowed as I'd ever seen them. They never left Garth, who had recovered from the shove and was scowling at Jesse. I half expected him to curl his finger in welcome so they could finish what they'd started.

When Jesse stayed silent and seething, Neil looked over his shoulder at Garth. "Well? Someone better speak up, or I'll have you both on laundry duty the rest of the month."

Garth adjusted his shirt where Jesse's shove had rumpled it. "Just a miscommunication, Mr. Walker."

Neil studied Garth for a minute before turning back to his son. "Jesse?"

After another minute of Jesse looking as if he was attempting to kill Garth with his stare, he backed away and headed for the back door. "What Garth said. A miscommunication." The screen door slammed shut behind him, and then he was gone.

Neil, along with the rest of the kitchen who'd seen what had happened, watched the door where Jesse had disappeared. They studied it as though it made no sense. A few moments later, Neil headed back for his seat. Passing Garth, he said, "That's not to happen in my house again, young man. You got it?" Neil waited for Garth to nod his acknowledgement. "I don't care who starts it or what it's about, I will not tolerate fighting on my ranch."

Done with that, Neil dropped back down in his chair and dove into his eggs. Everyone else did the same.

I just stood there, trying to figure out what had just happened. Jesse had almost gone full-on Hulk in front of me. He'd become a person I didn't recognize. He'd looked ready to strangle another person for two dozen witnesses to see.

It was a series of messed up things. But the most messed up thing I couldn't get out of my head were those two words from Garth's mouth: *Jesse's girlfriend.*

Jesse had a girlfriend. He'd just asked me out on a date. The phrase *What the hell?* came to mind.

"Hey," Lily nudged up beside you. "You okay?"

The answer was a firm, resounding *no,* so I went with

a half-hearted shrug.

"What was that about? The last time I saw Jesse angry was when I took a black Sharpie to his cowboy hat when I was in preschool."

So his surge of anger was as out-of-character as I suspected. Whatever bad blood flowed between him and Garth ran deep.

"I don't know," I answered. "Testosterone overload? Those tight jeans were cutting the blood off to their brains? Men as a whole are reverting back to their monkey origins?" I could go on, but right then, I wanted to forget the whole thing and get through the rest of breakfast. "I don't know, but I do know one thing—it's a waste of time trying to figure out the male brain since most of them are lacking one."

Lily laughed softly. "I've had my suspicions the whole time."

"That's because you're a smart girl." I retrieved the empty coffee pot and headed to refill it. Almost all of the cups I'd filled less than five minutes ago were empty. Cowboys drank more coffee than beings of a mortal quality should be able to handle.

A couple minutes later, everyone had settled back into their breakfasts, and I made sure to stay busy. I was like a squirrel in fall, bustling about the kitchen, moving from one task to the next seamlessly. Against all odds, I managed not to spill, break, or drop anything else. I started to wonder if my body had been invaded by some alien being, and then my gaze landed on Garth. He sat at the table, ignoring his meal, ignoring everyone else . . . except me. His eyes followed me with the kind of intensity that made it hard to determine if I was the predator or the prey.

As soon as my eyes met his, that dark smile of his moved into place. I tripped over my own feet. Thankfully I wasn't carrying anything or it would have been a goner.

After that, I didn't look at Garth again, but I still felt his eyes on me. Every move I made, I was aware of him watching me.

By the end of breakfast, I was certain of what I was to him: the prey.

It excited me as much as it alarmed me.

For all the prep and work that went into it, the actual consumption of breakfast was a quick deal. In addition to be champion coffee chuggers, cowboys could pound down some serious grub. We're talking a half dozen pancakes, a slab of ham, and a plate-sized portion of scrambled eggs each. What would have taken me a year to get through had just been consumed there that morning.

Once we'd all eaten, the table was cleared, the dishes washed, and everything laid out for lunch, Rose set us free. Well, kind of free. The girls had school work to get to. I gave them a sympathetic smile as they headed into the living room with their pencils and calculators.

Since I had yet to explore any more of Willow Springs than the house, I decided to head outside for a little fresh air. I grabbed my sketchbook and favorite pencil just in case I found anything I just had to draw, tucked them inside of my oversized purse, and headed outside. The weather had taken a turn and the early morning air had enough of a chill I wished I had my trusty black hoodie.

The giant red barn loomed in front of me like it could swallow me whole. When the reminder of the big reveal at breakfast raced to the forefront of my mind again, I kind of wished it would. A bunch of guys had lied to me about their relationship status. More guys than I could count. That wasn't what I was upset about. The lies I'd come to expect. What I was upset about was that I hadn't expected it from Jesse. I'd lowered my guard around him because my subconscious had been fooled into believing he was different. Jesse Walker, golden cowboy whose dimples alone could unnerve a girl, couldn't possibly be hiding a girlfriend like the rest of them.

But he had been. The whole time. In all our conversations, our flirty banter, our asinine question game, and when he'd asked me out . . . never once had a certain Josie come up. Even though I'd only known Jesse a few days, his betrayal cut deeply.

I wandered into the barn and tried to push all thoughts of betrayal, girlfriends, and Jesse Walker out of my mind. I was done pretending there might or ever could be something special between us.

The barn was as huge from the inside as it was from the outside. It had a grassy, tangy smell right between pleasant and offensive. I couldn't decide. As I passed a stack of bags taller and wider than I was, I saw what Jesse had been heaving out of his truck: feed grain.

The barn had a never ending number of stalls, an unbelievably tall tower of hay bales, and only about a million different tools, buckets, hoses, and thingamajigs hanging on the walls. The only tool I was familiar with was the row of shovels. Everything else I would have been at a loss with.

I was almost to the end of the barn when a wheel barrow bounced out of the last stall on the right. Followed by a certain cowboy I really wasn't in the mood to see. His trademark dark smile and predatory eyes went into posit-ion as soon as he noticed me.

"Well, if this isn't the damn pleasantest surprise I've had all week," Garth said, parking the wheelbarrow outside the stall before walking my way. Actually, it was more of a saunter. Garth Black had a serious saunter as unapologetic as the way he stared at me.

Damn, the guy was so my type everything inside me tightened in anticipation. At the same time, I also knew "my type" had gotten me a whole lotta nowhere in the past.

"It *is* a surprise," I said, crossing my arms.

The skin between his brows came together. He was thrown by my lack of warm welcome. Cocky bastard. I wanted to ignore him that much more.

"You don't like me," he guessed, stopping a few feet in front of me. His black hat was tilted low on his fore-head, making his eyes dark as onyx.

I lifted a shoulder. "I just met you. Not liking you would assume I've actually spent time thinking about you. Which I haven't." I wondered if that ever present curl to Garth's mouth could be ironed out.

"You're about as good a liar as you are pretending you're not attracted to me."

My mouth almost dropped. He wasn't just a cocky bastard. He was the cockiest bastard to have ever saunter-ed the earth.

"Are you always this full of yourself or just today?"

Garth's smile curled higher. "Always."

Of course he was. "And where does this full-of-one-self attitude come from?" I asked, crossing my arms tighter.

"Experience."

Garth infuriated me, but a thrill of excitement rushed through me at the same time. I didn't know what it was about that kind of guy, who thought they were next in line to rule the world, that appealed to me, but the desire ran deep. So deep I doubted I could root it out even if I wanted to. Which, while Garth held me with his stare and smile, I didn't want to.

But I had enough experience with that kind of guy to know one didn't keep their attention by falling into their traps on the first day. They craved the chase, the antici-pation of the kill. Guys like Garth were the ultimate predator.

"You know, I don't live all that far from here if you're ever bored and looking for something to do," he said, resting his hands on his belt buckle.

I huffed. "You mean if I'm ever looking for some*one* to do?"

"That depends on your answer to that."

I really regretted my decision to explore the grounds, especially with the way Garth's thumb made those slow circles over that belt buckle of his. I wasn't sure if he did it to draw my attention to his junk, or he just liked having a hand as close to it as was acceptable in public, but it definitely had something to do with the junk.

"My answer is no," I said. "Any day. Every day. It will be no."

Garth's twisted smile didn't falter. "It's always no until it's yes. And I've never met a no I couldn't turn into a yes."

"Well, you're looking at your first no that's going to stay a no." *Oh, and by the way, that ego of yours is sucking the air right out of the room.*

He slid his hat off and lowered it at his side. His hair was as dark as his eyes, maybe a shade darker, but still not as dark as his smile. I'd never met a person who so exactly fit their last name. His eyes flashed, and at that moment, I was fairly certain if he sauntered up to me, grabbed me in his arms and kissed me deep and hard, I would have kissed him back. And he knew it.

"We'll see," he said with a wink.

I gave myself an imaginary slap to the face and waited to reply until I was sure I wouldn't come off sounding like a befuddled schoolgirl. It took longer than I thought.

"I'm going to leave you to your cow shit," I curled my nose at the wheelbarrow, "and ego. Not enough room for anything else with that head of yours in here." I was halfway down the barn when Garth spoke up.

"Going after Jesse?"

I bristled and stopped in my tracks. "No. I'm planning on staying as far away from Jesse as Willow Springs will allow."

"Glad to hear it. I know the outcome to a girl like you chasing after a guy like Jesse Walker. And it isn't a pretty one."

I closed my eyes. I knew that. Even with a girlfriend he'd lied to me about, Jesse was still ten levels above me on the dating scale. Nothing I'd done or would do could ever be worthy of the likes of Jesse, even on his worst day, which, after today, may have been it.

I was heading for the entrance when Garth spoke up again. "What are you doing Saturday night?"

I paused. I knew better than to answer, but I couldn't

stop myself. "Nothing."

"Ever been to a rodeo?"

I almost snapped back *Does it look like I have?* when I remembered I wasn't in my usual attire. As far as I knew, Garth didn't know anything about me except what he'd seen after he arrived that morning.

When I didn't reply, I heard him move closer. "You want to come watch me at one?" There wasn't one note of doubt in his question.

Twisting around, I narrowed my eyes. "Does it look like I do?" The question was rhetorical, but Garth didn't take it that way.

"Yeah," he answered. "It sure does."

I hated it like I couldn't have hated anything more, but he was right.

CHAPTER six

I never knew being surrounded by a couple of hot guys would be such a chore. After that week, I knew better.

The day in and day out chores at Willow Springs kept me busy from dawn to dusk, but it didn't seem to matter how busy I was or looked. Almost every time I turned around, I ran into Garth. Or Jesse. I literally couldn't escape them.

With Garth, I rolled my eyes, threw something snarky at him, and was back on my merry chore way. He still looked at me like he was just waiting for me to trip his trap, but I knew guys like him. I'd dated legions of them. His mysterious aura combined with his troubled vibe might have scared off other girls, but not me. Troubled and mysterious was my Kryptonite. My Achilles' heel. My weak spot. My specialty.

With Jesse, it was harder. Infinitely so. Bumping into him around the ranch wasn't so easy to shrug off because whenever I came within a foot of Jesse, my body went on high alert. Every molecule zinged to life. I tried to brush it off, like being around him didn't undo me, but I doubted I did a very good job.

He'd tried to corner me that same day, to explain the whole Josie thing, but I basically told him enough had been explained and to leave me alone. He did.

And he didn't.

Just when I was sure Jesse had forgotten my name, I'd find him watching me in the middle of lunch. As soon as I'd look his way, his gaze would shift.

After a few days, though, I didn't catch Jesse staring at me once. He'd taken my advice after all.

It was Saturday night, and the ranch was quiet. Other than the cattle mooing, the crickets chirping, the noise coming from the ranch hand bunkhouse, and the washing machines whirring a floor below me. So, yeah. Quiet wasn't the right word for it, but it was as quiet as Willow Springs ever could be.

It was rodeo night, and I guessed around those parts, that was a big deal. Like Texas football big deal. Most everyone had already headed out. Rose had stopped by my room to see if I wanted to go and needed a ride. I told her I wasn't sure if I was going yet and that I was sure I could find a ride if I decided to go. I didn't like telling Rose a white lie, two of them at that, but I didn't want to take the chance of finding myself crammed next to Jesse in the family Suburban.

From the sounds of it, the rodeo fairgrounds weren't far away. I'd hoofed it plenty of times in my life.

I watched the Walkers' Suburban head down the driveway before grabbing my purse and heading down-stairs. I checked my phone and found the same missed calls I'd been missing all week. Not that I was missing much.

Mom had blown up my phone ever since I got to Willow Springs. I'd never answered one of her calls. She'd even left a few voicemails. I didn't listen to them. She called Rose and left messages with her asking I give her a call back. I never did.

Mom was the reason I was at Willow Springs. It wasn't that I didn't like it there. I just felt as if she'd written me off and went with the easiest way to deal with me as she could. When it came to me, Mom was a pro at identifying the avenues that required minimal time and effort on her part. Basically, I'd been a houseplant for the past eighteen years. I was given just enough water and sun to keep me alive, but nothing more. Willow Springs was a classic example. Instead of trying to get to the bottom of why her daughter was floundering through life, she sent me off to ranch boot camp to "prove" myself worthy of art school.

There was so much messed up about that it made my head spin.

It made my head spin so much, I walked as fast as my legs could move. The weather had been cool the past week, and that night was no exception. Thankfully I'd pulled on my hoodie before leaving. Even at my power walk of a pace, my mostly bare legs were on the threshold of goosebumps.

About an hour later, the fairgrounds were in view. From the sounds of it, I guessed the rodeo happenings had started. The noise was as impressive as any concert I'd ever been to, but the sounds were different. Instead of screams and wails, there were a lot of hee-haws and whistling.

After weaving through a caravan of shiny, big trucks, I made my way up to the entrance.

"Hey, hun," the middle-aged ticket lady said, trying to make her inspection of me casual. "Just one?" She reached for the ticket roll to tear one off.

"Um, Garth Black was supposed to leave a ticket up here for me," I said. "One ticket for Rowen Sterling." Garth told me a couple of days ago he got a few free tickets as a perk to competing, and he'd leave one for me at the ticket counter.

From the frown on the lady's face as she shuffled through a few envelopes in a drawer, I guessed that ticket wasn't waiting for me.

"Hmm," she said, pulling one of those envelopes free. "I don't have one here from Garth Black, but I do have one with your name on it." She flipped the envelope over so I could see my name scribbled down on it.

My eyebrows came together. "Are you sure that isn't from Garth?"

"Honey, trust me, I'm sure." She pulled the ticket out of the envelope and slid it across the counter toward me.

"Because he pretty much looks like the rest of the guys here. Big hat, big belt buckle, big ego . . . that sort of thing."

"Garth Black may look like the rest of the cowboys out there, but the boy who left you this ticket is something else altogether." My throat was already going dry when she said, "Jesse Walker left you this ticket."

"Are you sure?" I tried not to look too flustered.

She chuckled a few notes. "Yeah, I'm sure. When Jesse Walker comes smiling up to your booth, that's not the kind of thing a girl forgets."

I knew the feeling.

"Okay." I took the ticket. "Thanks."

As I headed into the grandstand area, I tried not to over think the ticket issue. Garth said he'd leave me one and he didn't. Jesse never said he'd leave me one and he did. I had one big *Why?* to both of those statements and no answers.

In fact, I wasn't sure I wanted the *Whys* answered.

The grandstand was even bigger than it'd looked from outside. Row upon row of metal bleachers crept up and around the dirt arena, and they were packed to capacity with bodies. A sea of cowboy and cowgirl hats swayed and bobbed in waves. It was an impressive sight. And it was noisy. So much so, I almost wished I had a pair of earplugs handy. A nose-plug would have been useful, too, because the place had that familiar barn smell that leaned more toward the offensive side. That might have been because I walked right past one of the big corrals where a bunch of frothing at the mouth and pawing at the ground bulls were stored. Damn. Someone had to have a death wish to attempt riding one of those things.

I hurried by the bulls and glanced at my ticket. It looked like most of the grandstand area was general seating, but my ticket had a seat number listed. So it wasn't a cheap seat. Jesse had forked out a little dough to get a good seat at an event that seemed a notch above barbaric for the girl who'd barely known the front of a horse from the back of a horse a week ago.

I still wasn't sure how I felt about the whole idea.

When I saw where my seat was, an aisle seat without any familiar faces close by, I decided to be grateful for it.

Until I settled into my seat and did a quick scan of the surrounding seats. Jesse was, in fact, close by, although not close enough he'd noticed me. He was about ten rows back and over and surrounded by a mini-harem of peaches-and-cream girls.

They ranged from cute to pretty. One could even be classified as drop dead gorgeous. Dark hair, light hair, red hair, tall, short, brown eyes, blue eyes . . . They were as different as one girl to the next could be, but they shared one similarity: their clear eyes and sweet smiles. Every single last one of the half dozen of them had it, and it wasn't the contrived kind of sweet either. It was the real deal.

I only knew that because I'd seen every kind of impostor, fabricated kind of sweet out there, so when the real deal came around, it was as clear as the sky was blue.

I couldn't dislike them, even if I wanted to, which I did because they had Jesse's attention and I didn't. They were sitting next to him, and I wasn't. As much as I wanted to deny the way I felt about Jesse, I couldn't ignore it. My feelings for him were instinctual, as automatic as blinking my eyes.

Jesse Walker had worked his way inside of my impenetrable walls, and I didn't know how to shove him out. I wasn't sure how he'd gotten there in the first place. I wasn't even sure if I wanted him out.

So much confusion over some guy. I'd officially become my worst nightmare.

If I was being honest with myself, since that seemed to be a new pattern for me, I was confused about more than one guy. As mysterious as Garth liked to come across, he was less of a mystery to me than Jesse was. A guy like Garth had easy to decipher motivations, especially since I was so experienced with his type. They liked to keep people at arm's length, although they preferred the term "mysterious." They liked the chase, the immediate reward post-chase, and then they were out. Clean, permanent breaks. Basically, I was the female version.

However, the Jesses of the world were impossible to understand. A good guy was foreign territory to me. I didn't understand his motives, or his goals, or anything really. I needed to know what to expect so I could maintain control of my world. Getting what I expected from Garth was better than not having a clue what I'd get from Jesse. I'd take a broken heart I knew was coming over one I didn't see coming from a mile away any day of the week.

I had control over so little in my life that I had to make calculated decisions to keep what control I did have.

Jesse was a big, fat question mark I couldn't risk.

I'd gotten so lost in my thoughts, I forgot what I'd been staring at the entire time.

Or *who* I'd been staring at.

As soon as I pulled myself out of my head, I noticed Jesse's eyes were locked onto mine. Those sky blue eyes of his that made my stomach about drop to the ground when they looked at me that way.

He waved and smiled.

Oh, God. Please say he didn't notice me the whole five minutes I was think-staring at him.

Since I didn't get a divine answer, I decided to wave and try to smile back. The girls around Jesse stopped their chatter and took notice of who he was waving at. Then, surprising the hell out of me, every last one of them smiled and waved. Some took a little longer, I guess they were trying to move past my clothing or piercings, but they all waved. The drop-dead gorgeous one was the last, but after her gaze moved from Jesse to me a couple of times, she joined in.

The way people did things around there was so different. Almost entirely different. Back in Portland, when a stranger made eye contact with you, you dug your mace out of your purse. Here though, you smiled, waved, and invited said stranger over for steak and potatoes. Even a cynic like myself had to admit it was kind of refreshing.

Jesse said something to the girls, stood, and side-stepped his way down the row. His eyes stayed on mine, but I couldn't help but notice every single set of female eyes shifting as he passed by them. I suppose if that ass was half a foot in front of my face, my gaze would have dropped for a while, too.

He wore what he wore everyday: tight jeans, snug tee, belt, boots, and hat. Everyone else seemed to be a bit more dressed up. Like watching a bunch of dudes and livestock stomp around in the dirt was worth getting decked out for. I liked that Jesse was who he was every day. He didn't have the need to be somebody else, rodeo or not. He was just Jesse.

Well, he was *all* Jesse.

He bounded down the aisle, his smile getting a little bigger with each step. I reminded myself I was upset with him. He had a girlfriend, probably one of those six still pining after him with Bambi eyes. Even though he hadn't told an outright lie, he'd lied by omission.

Thou shalt not ask a girl out if thou hast a girlfriend.

That was the eleventh commandment.

"You made it." Jesse stopped at the end of my seat and kneeled beside me in the center of the aisle. I'd forgotten how nice those eyes were to look into. It'd been so long since I'd let myself. My heart was already racing, and he'd said three words.

"Thanks for the ticket." After ignoring him for almost

a whole week, those words felt like something of a defeat.

They also felt like a victory.

"I wasn't sure you'd show up, but I wanted to make sure you had a good seat if you did."

"Why wouldn't I show up?" I asked, like I hadn't been hmmhaw'ing over it all week.

"Because I was here." Jesse shifted closer to let someone pass him. He didn't move his arm sharing my armrest once the couple passed.

He has a girlfriend. One named Josie. It was sad how I had to remind myself every two seconds.

"So is Garth," I said. "He's competing in something tonight. Something that has to do with one of those devil creatures over there." I pointed toward the far end of the arena where the bulls paced around in their corral.

"Garth Black," he said with a sigh. His expression shadowed for a moment before it cleared. "Have you been seeing a lot of each other?"

"About five seconds more than I've seen you this week. You know how it is. If you're not working, you're sleeping. This is the first R and R"—I made air quotes—"I've had in a week."

"There's a reason we're kept so busy, you know?" Jesse said, his smile recovered.

"What's that?"

He leaned in closer. So close I smelled the soap on his skin. "To keep us out of trouble." He laughed a few low notes, and I couldn't not join in.

"It's working." Even if I'd wanted to get into trouble, which was my M.O., I didn't have enough time or energy. I wondered why they didn't parole criminals at ranches.

Jesse's attention shifted to the arena when the M.C.

announced the next event: bull riding. At least I knew the official term for it.

"Don't you compete?" I asked while Jesse watched the arena.

"I used to. Up until I was ten or eleven, I competed in team calf roping."

Judging that the term "bull riding" perfectly described the event taking place, I made an educated guess on what calf roping entailed.

"Why did you quit?" I guessed there was some tragic reason behind it. One he probably wouldn't open up about.

"I didn't quit, Rowen," he replied as his eyes latched back onto mine. "It's what I do every single day. I just don't need some shiny belt buckle to prove I can rope a calf from twenty yards."

I peaked an eyebrow. "My . . . Either you're rather full of your calf roping abilities or you're really just that good. Which one is it?"

"I'm all right," he said with a small shrug.

"Which means you're the best there is," I said under my breath.

His smile pulled higher. "The point is, even if I wanted to rodeo, there isn't time for it, and at the end of each day, I feel like I've competed in my own personal rodeo. It's not as novel when it's your life."

"So why are you here?"

"Because in case you haven't noticed, there's not a whole heck of a lot to do around here," he said, counting the reasons off on his fingers. "Two, because rodeo night is like a family reunion. You don't miss it unless you want everyone else talking about you. And three . . . I had to swoop in and save the day in case Garth Black forgot to leave that ticket he promised you."

My eyes narrowed a bit at him. I wasn't sure if it was because of his number three, or if because I knew number four was that posse of pretty girls still batting their eyes at him from ten rows back.

"Why don't you like Garth?" I asked, wanting to get to the bottom of it.

Jesse's shoulders rose and fell slowly. Then those eyes of his flashed with something I couldn't make out. Whatever it was made me shift in my seat though. "Why do you?"

Answering a question with a question was a familiar defense mechanism. I was its number one fan. "I'm not sure I do yet."

Jesse's whole body visibly relaxed. "That's good, Rowen, and I know I'm probably the last person you want to believe when it comes to Garth, but you should steer clear of him. Really. I wouldn't tell you that if I didn't mean it."

Jesse's voice and expression held so much sincerity. I didn't doubt what he said was what he believed, but I wasn't so sure he was in a position to warn me off guys that were no good for me. I knew what was no good for me, and I was staring at him.

"Says the guy who asked me out and winds up having a girlfriend." That I didn't say under my breath.

His eyes didn't leave mine. "And if you would have given me two minutes to explain everything to you, like I tried a hundred times this past week, you'd be feeling pretty silly making that accusation right about now."

"The only reason I'd feel silly is because I almost said yes to you." Those words were out of my mouth before I could stop them.

Jesse's eyes widened. "Wait. You were?" His fore-head lined. "You were going to say yes?"

"No!" I snapped, my voice an octave too high. He gave me a look and waited. "No, I wasn't." His look got more pronounced. "I don't know. And now we'll never know, so it doesn't matter anyways."

"It matters to me." His voice was soft and almost silent.

Why was I having this conversation? I avoided those kinds of heart-to-hearts the way I steered clear of baby pink in my wardrobe.

"If you don't drop the whole girlfriend, date, did-I-didn't-I conversation right now," I lifted a finger and leveled him with my own look, "I will hop up in my seat and scream 'OBAMA RULES' at the top of my lungs."

That got Jesse's attention. As it should have. I didn't need to see the voting cards of the thousands in attendance to know I'd be strung up and left for dead for saying something like that.

There was so much red in the room I could barely breathe.

"You're funny, Rowen. You know that?" was Jesse's amused reply. "And by the way, I voted for Obama. I would have the first time, too, if I was old enough to vote."

I rolled my eyes. Of course he did. The red-blooded cowboy through and through voted for the blue as blue can be Democratic president. The ironies just never ended in Nowhere, Montana.

"You're such a dichotomy, Jesse Walker." I tapped the front of his hat so it covered his eyes.

"Whoa. Was that just a 'dichotomy' you just dropped

on me?" The hat still covered the top half of his face, but his smile and those damn dimples were visible. "How can a girl who supposedly barely passed high school drop vocab like that and think she's got us all fooled?"

I hated having him next to me as much as I loved it. As far as my relationship with Jesse went, that was pretty much par for course. "You know, you hovering in the middle of the aisle is creating a fire hazard." Since it didn't look like he would do it, I tilted his hat back into place. His eyes were just as amused as the rest of his face. "So why don't you get back to your harem and leave me alone?"

"Nah. They're good without me," he said, glancing back at his empty seat. "And I've left you alone enough this week." His voice was full of intention. He'd left me alone, *somewhat*, like I'd asked, but apparently he was done with "alone time."

I groaned and tried to elbow him. He dodged it easily and chuckled. "How did you get here?" he asked, thankfully shifting the conversation back into the acceptable range.

"Would you believe me if I told you I hijacked your horse?"

"Nope. No, I wouldn't," he said. "Sunny only lets me ride him. Not once in ten years has he let another soul on his back."

"Your horse must be partial to the depraved," I muttered.

"Maybe. But then he would have let you hijack him like you mentioned."

"I took Old Bessie." I focused on the arena so he wouldn't see my smile.

"Ha! I'd believe you charmed Sunny before you climbed into Old Bessie—*willingly*—and drove her here."

I couldn't slip a single thing past Jesse. "I walked."

"*Sure* you did."

I lifted my eyebrows.

"What? Really? You walked?" he said in disbelief. "It's, like, five miles from Willow Springs to the fairground."

I lifted a shoulder.

"You walked?" he repeated again, like it was inconceivable.

"Yes, I walked. You know, one foot in front of the other? Arms swinging gently at the sides?" I said dryly. "I've been doing it for a while now. Almost seventeen years. I'm pretty good at it."

"I sure have missed that attitude of yours this week," he said in such a way I wasn't sure if he was being a smartass or serious.

Before I could reply with my own smartass comment, a gate inside the arena flew open and a bull the size of a tank busted out of it. As if that wasn't frightening enough, a guy was on top of it holding on to the bucking and twisting animal with only one hand. I'd thought the sport was insane based on the name alone, but watching it in real life, I thought insane was thoroughly inadequate.

"What the hell is this?" I asked, utterly stunned.

It didn't seem possible a creature that stocky and large could move and jump the way it was. Something having to do with the laws of gravity. How the dude on top could stay upright seemed like yet another slap in the face of physics.

"Some people call it bull riding. Other people call it a

death wish," Jesse replied as a buzzer went off. The guy on top of the bull leapt off and tumbled to the ground. A couple of guys dressed like clowns clapped and moved to get the bull's attention while the rider righted himself and sprinted for the exit.

The sport just got odder by the moment. Not to mention scarier. Anything where clowns were involved amped the scary factor up a few levels.

"Have you ever done that?" I asked, still in shock. I didn't know what I'd just seen, but I'd never forget it.

"Nope. I'm one of those crazy people that likes the use of all their body parts."

"After just watching that, you are not the crazy one." Another guy was getting ready at the gates, but I couldn't watch another ride yet. Garth wasn't up, so I looked back at Jesse. He was back to smiling at me.

I gave up and smiled right back. It was that infectious.

When I caught sight of the person who'd stopped behind him, my smile died on the spot.

She was even prettier up close.

"Hey, Jess, I'm heading out," the drop-dead girl from ten rows back said, resting her hand on his shoulder. Then she smiled at me, and as much as I wanted to dislike her because she had her hand on him and had a special nickname for him, I couldn't. Girls didn't normally smile warmly at me. Girls didn't even smile coolly at me.

"Oh, okay," he said, rising. "Are the rest of the girls taking off with you?"

"No, they're going to hang out and see about either getting your attention back or some other poor, unsuspecting cowboys'."

"Sounds terrifying," Jesse replied. "Thanks for the

heads up."

"So," the girl said, looking between Jesse and me, "are you going to introduce us anytime soon, or have you forgotten your manners altogether?"

Jesse's forehead creased. "Uh, yeah. Sorry. This is Rowen. She's—"

"Helping out at Willow Springs," the girl finished as she continued to smile at me. "I've already heard a lot about you. It's nice to finally meet you, Rowen."

I didn't know who'd been talking about me or what had been said, but it made me nervous that the girl with a sweet smile had already "heard a lot about me." In the past, whenever anyone had heard anything about me . . . Let's just say it wasn't for being on the honor roll.

However, I did my best to think positive. "Thanks. It's nice to meet you . . ." I stared at Jesse and waited, but he looked like he'd suddenly been struck mute. Finally, I elbowed him and gave him an *anytime today* look.

"Rowen," he said, before clearing his throat, "this is Josie."

Of course she was.

Jesse couldn't have looked more uncomfortable if he'd wanted to. I don't think I could have felt any more awkward. And I don't think Josie could have looked more oblivious.

So what did I do when the girlfriend of the guy I liked smiled at me like she didn't know me from Adam?

I kept my smile plastered in place and glued my hands to the armrests so they wouldn't misbehave. "Nice to meet you, Josie." I sounded as contrived as I'd feared I would.

"You know, if you're ever looking for some place to

escape to, my parents' place isn't all that far from Willow Springs," Josie said. "You could come hang out anytime."

Just what I wanted to do: hang out with Jesse's girlfriend. As friendly as she was being to me, I knew she didn't have a clue about the thing between Jesse and me. No girl could be that gracious to the girl who'd almost become "the other woman." No girl could smile at the girl who had a thing for her boyfriend. Whatever that "thing" was, I didn't know, but it was most certainly a thing. A serious thing.

A serious thing I was trying to eviscerate.

"Thanks, Josie. That sounds great, but the Walkers keep me pretty busy." In the body and the head. When I wasn't up to my elbows in scrambled eggs, my mind scrambled about over two boys.

"I can imagine. But if you do ever find yourself with nothing to do on a free night, give me a ring." She shoved at Jesse lightly. "This guy's got my number."

Yeah, I figured that.

Jesse stayed silent the entire time Josie and I chatted. In fact, he was so still he could have been a statue. It wasn't quite the caught-with-my-pants-around-my-ankles expression I'd seen a few too many times, but it was close. Jesse knew he was treading on thin ice with his girlfriend and the mistress-that-could-have-been talking it up like old friends.

"I'm out of here before it turns into a blood bath out there." Josie gave an exaggerated shudder at the arena where the last rider had just been thrown a good ten feet from the bull. He'd landed in a way that wasn't natural. "Nice to meet you, Rowen."

I nodded and reminded myself to be nice before

replying, "You too, Josie."

She nudged Jesse again—the girl really liked nudging him. Not that I could blame her. What I'd felt of Jesse's body, I'd want to nudge up on it, too. "I'll see you later, okay?"

Naked in bed later.

"Are you by yourself?" Jesse spoke up finally.

"I came with a couple of the girls, but like I said, they wanted to stay and hang."

"Let me walk you to your truck," he said. "I don't want you in a dark parking lot by yourself."

Josie beamed. I'm talking full on I-just-won-the-sash-and-crown beaming. "That would be nice." She waved at me as she continued on down the steps.

"Are you going to be here when I get back?" Jesse asked me, not quite able to look me in the eyes.

Guessing that whole, smooth "I'll walk you to your truck" routine was so he could have a quick roll in the bed of it with her, I slouched down in my seat and looked away. "Probably not."

I felt Jesse's eyes on me, studying me, and then he sighed. "Okay, we'll talk later. But if I don't catch up with you first, make sure you find my parents for a ride home. Do not, and I repeat, do not walk home alone. Not safe and not smart. Okay?"

I rolled my eyes. Romeo had a Juliet waiting for him a few stairs down. "Bye-bye, Jesse." I flicked a wave at him and hoped he'd take the message that I was done talking.

After a few more seconds, he did take that message. I couldn't help it. My eyes shifted back to him as he lumbered down the rest of the stairs toward another girl.

CHAPTER seven

I needed something to get my mind off of Jesse. I needed to forget about the way he made me feel. I needed to forget the way he'd just followed after his girlfriend, his female equal. Not just in the looks department, but in the everything-else department.

I didn't have the looks, the friendly aura, the sweet smile, and I sure as hell didn't have the not-a-care-in-the-world outlook. In fact, what Jesse and Josie were, I was the opposite. I doubted I could get any more opposite if I tried.

I needed something to make me forget.

Or someone.

Lucky for me, I caught sight of Garth's black felt hat bouncing above the gate. Sitting on top of one of those bulls.

My stomach barely had time to drop before the gate swung open, and out charged, I kid you not, the biggest bull of them all. He was the Zeus of the bulls, and dammit if he wasn't out there proving it.

Garth's body bounced and flailed about like a rag doll's as Zeus kicked his back legs a few times before spinning. The bull had barely made a full revolution before Garth flew off. Well, it was more like ejecting. Everything about it was violent: the way his arms and legs grabbed at the air, the way his face looked, and the way his body slammed into the dirt. Nothing about this sport wasn't brutal. Gentle was checked at the gates.

The bull stopped spinning as soon as Garth had been bucked off. He stood for a minute, his entire body heaving, as he and Garth seemed to have some kind of stare down. Just when I couldn't decide who would be the first to charge, those crazy-ass clowns intervened and got the bull moving toward the open gate at the end of the arena.

The crowd applauded when Garth stood, but that only seemed to make him angrier. I'd seen plenty of shades of pissed, and Garth's expression definitely made the top ten list. Stomping over to where his hat had landed, he dusted it off before settling it low onto his forehead.

Without so much as a wave or even a look of acknowledgement into the crowd that was still clapping for him, Garth powered out of the dirt arena.

I'd known zilch about bull riding coming into the rodeo, but I'd picked up enough to know his ride hadn't made it to the buzzer. I wasn't sure if that meant he received a reduced score or no score, but either way, I knew he wouldn't leave with a shiny, new belt buckle.

I knew what failing was like. If I was an expert at anything, it was failing. I wasn't sure if Garth wanted to see anyone right away, but it wouldn't hurt to try. I'd seen enough bull riding for one night, and I certainly didn't want to be in that seat when Jesse came back with a flushed face and a satisfied smile. No, thank you.

I was out of my seat and down the stairs in a flash. I didn't know exactly where he'd be, but I headed in the direction of a bunch of cowboy hats bobbing above the gate on the opposite side of the arena. I was pretty sure one of those black ones had to be his.

I got a few curious looks as I wove toward the pack of cowboys with numbers on their backs. Maybe I was heading into an "off limits" area, but since no one stopped me, I kept going.

Ducking under a rope, I headed for a familiar back. Sporting his signature color on everything from his boots to his chaps, his body was still rigid, but he had a beer in his hands. All had to be somewhat well in the universe.

There was a good-sized crowd around Garth, all about the same age and sipping on their own beers, likely commiserating the woes of bull riding, when I stopped a few feet behind him.

"I don't know who looked more pissed off out there," I said. "You or the bull."

Garth twisted around. He had a serious scowl on his face. That was, until he took one look at me. His eyes skimmed up and down me once, then repeated. When his eyes finished on mine, they were ice. "This is a rodeo, sweetheart. Not the circus." His voice was just as icy.

I flinched. At least on the inside. It took everything inside of me to keep from wincing on the outside. "Excuse me, Garth I-can't-stay-on-a-bull-for-longer-than-two-seconds Black? And thanks for remembering to leave me a ticket, asshole." I was about to spin away and get the hell out of there when a single chuckle rolled out of him.

"Rowen?" he said, like he couldn't have been any-more dumbfounded. "Holy shit. I knew you were troubled, I just didn't think *this* troubled." He waved his hands up and down my way and shook his head. "I might be able to overlook the hot mess if you're as freaky in bed as you dress."

He wasn't saying anything I hadn't heard before, but he'd taken me by surprise. I was always on guard for those kinds of cruel words and nasty names, but I'd let that wall fall sometime recently. Each of his words hit me in a sore spot. Each of them would leave a permanent scar. That was why I didn't let my walls down. Not even for a second because the moment I did, I was reminded why I'd built them in the first place.

Making sure those walls were back in place before I replied, I glared at him. "I knew you were a poser, I just didn't realize how much of one until I saw that sorry excuse for a ride out there." He might have known where I hid my emotional underbelly, but I guessed where he hid his, too. Rodeo. Winning. Proving he wasn't a failure. Proving to himself and to everyone else.

From the expression darkening his face, I knew I'd hit the right spot. "Why don't you get the hell out of here?" he said before pointing for the exit. "You're confusing every-one." He cupped his hand over his mouth and shouted, "No, people! It's not Halloween! It's just our resident freak who's really letting that freak flag fly tonight!"

Shit. That would have done some damage if those trusty walls of mine weren't back up. I'd known from the start Garth was one of those troubled, angry souls, but I never guessed he was the cruel, downright nasty type.

Dropping his hand, he took a sip of his beer. That predatory look in his eyes returned. "You know, when teachers told us not to be afraid to be who we are, you really shouldn't have listened."

The rest of the guys around him chuckled. A few tried to hide their amusement, but the majority didn't. I hated being laughed at. I hated being seen as a joke. I hated feeling the way I did then. I turned to rush for the exit, when a body plowed past me.

"Shut the hell up, Garth." Jesse squared himself a foot in front of Garth and very intentionally looked down at him.

"And what makes you think I'd listen to anything you say?" Garth replied, his voice and expression lazy and unimpressed.

Jesse's fists clenched and unclenched. "Because I know, and you know, I'd have no problem shutting you up if you don't want to do this the easy way."

Those words, or that warning, hung in the air for a moment. The rest of the guys around Garth stepped back a few feet. Maybe to give those two space to duke it out if it came to that, or maybe just because they feared the quivering mass of muscle that was Jesse Walker. Whatever the reason, those guys were ten times smarter than Garth Black. He just stood there, staring back at Jesse and taking swigs of his beer.

"Go ahead," Garth said after a solid minute of their silent stare down. "She's all yours tonight. I'll take my turn later." Glancing my way with a look of disgust, he shook his head. "It's not exactly like she's shiny and new."

"What did you just say?" Jesse fumed, stepping into Garth. They would have been nose to nose if they were the same height. "What did you say, you little piece of shit?"

It was the first time I'd heard Jesse curse with real emotion. Other than that time in the kitchen, which seemed like the kiddie pool in comparison to what was going down, I hadn't seen Jesse's lid about to fly off.

I had turned him into a seething, cursing, crazed man. I'd been the one to make him lose his cool. Sure, what

Garth had said and did really set him off, but my being there, being the target of Garth's words and being who I was, had set the fire to the flame raging in front of me.

I wasn't sure if I'd ever had a less proud moment.

I'd screwed up enough. I'd done what Rowen Sterling did best and made a shit-storm of everything. Enough for one night. Before the guys said another word, I spun around and rushed the hell away. Maybe once I was gone, they could forgive, forget, shake hands, and share a couple of beers. That's what guys did, right?

Once I was outside the fairgrounds, in the dark and quiet, I felt comfortable. Like I could breathe again. As much as I'd tried to fight it, the dark and quiet was home to me. The only place I felt accepted.

The air was a bit cooler than when I'd arrived, but by the time I'd speed walked a few hundred feet down the road, my body was so warm I rolled up the sleeves of my hoodie. I made a note to remember a flashlight the next time I planned on walking at night. Out in the sticks, there weren't such things as street lights. If not for the clear sky and almost full moon, I would have been lost in no time.

The crickets were really chirping, and for the first time since arriving at Willow Springs, I found the sound soothing. I'd kept my windows shut for the past week because those little buggers made a lot of noise, and for a city girl used to being serenaded by car horns and sirens, trying to fall asleep to a cricket chorus was like trying to fall asleep with a fog horn going off a few inches from my ear.

But I'd grown to like the crickets. In one week's time, I'd been converted.

The country was slowly making its way inside me.

First the people out there who, other than Garth Black, had to have some of the biggest hearts on the planet, and the crickets. I had a feeling I was on a slippery slope.

I was maybe a mile down the road and a million miles down my thought-path when I heard a car approaching. Well, a truck approaching.

The driver dimmed the headlights as they approached. The truck wasn't familiar to me, so I knew I should probably duck into the field and run, but if the person inside that truck wanted to catch me, they were close enough running wouldn't matter. Plus, I could qualify as the world's slowest runner. The clodhopper boots didn't help.

The driver's window whirred down, and a sweet smile greeted me. "If Jesse knew you were out here walking all by yourself, he would bust something," Josie said, slowing the truck to keep pace with me.

"He doesn't know, and he doesn't need to know," I replied. "So no need to worry about Jesse busting anything." My eyes drifted automatically to the bed of her truck, and my stomach twisted. "And didn't you leave a while ago?"

"I did. Until I realized I'd left my purse behind."

You left your boyfriend behind, too I almost added.

"Hop on in," she said with a tilt of her head. "I'll give you a ride. Willow Springs is on my way."

I thought about that for all of a second. I still had a few miles left to go, I was exhausted physically and emotionally, and I knew the rodeo was close to finishing. Jesse and the Walkers would drive down the road soon, and they would pull over the instant they saw me. I didn't want to be pressed up against Jesse in a car any more than

I did earlier.

"Are you sure?" I asked, already crossing toward the truck.

"Sure as sure can be," she replied.

Josie's truck was nice. It was shiny red, and even though it didn't seem to have a lift on it, I had to jump to get into the passenger seat.

"Thanks," I said as I snapped my buckle into place. "I wasn't really thinking when I walked to the rodeo tonight. I guess it slipped my mind I'd have to make a return trip, too." I glanced down at my boots. I might have ticked off some miles in my day, but ten miles in the span of an evening was a bit ambitious. I already felt a couple blisters on my heels.

"Lord knows I've done plenty of things I didn't really think about either," she replied as she hit the gas. The truck was one of those loud ones, too. "Things way worse than not wearing the right shoes to walk in." It was dark inside the cab, but Josie's face visibly shadowed.

Miss Peaches and Cream had secrets, too. She'd made mistakes she regretted. I knew everyone did in theory, but sometimes that theory didn't seem to apply to people like Josie.

"Yeah. Me, too." There was a whole encyclopedia-sized record of the screw ups and mistakes I'd made in a mere eighteen years of living.

Another few seconds of silence ticked off before Josie's face cleared. That smile that seemed as perman-ently embedded on her face as Jesse's was on his re-formed. As much as I wanted to dislike her, I couldn't. "Do you have a boyfriend?" she asked.

I huffed. "Hell, no."

"Why not?"

Might as well be honest with the girl. "I've been with so many pieces of shit, I've lost count. That's why."

Josie peered over at me. "Sometimes a girl needs to be with a piece of shit—"

"Or fifty," I muttered.

"—so she recognizes when one who isn't comes along." She lifted her shoulders. "The more experience you have with P.O.S., the better equipped you are to identify one who isn't."

I nodded as I wondered what those words would look like tattooed across my forehead. It could change a lot of girls' lives.

"So what did you think of the rodeo?" Josie moved from one topic to the next so quickly I was about to get whiplash.

It sucked ass.

"It was . . . interesting," I settled on. Interesting was a versatile word and my go-to when I didn't want to admit the truth.

"Yeah, I'd imagine it's pretty barbaric seeming if you weren't raised on rodeo," she said.

There were definitely barbaric low points, but they had nothing to do with the actual rodeo.

I shrugged my reply.

"Are you going to the big summer dance and barbe-cue next week?"

"Since this is the first I'm hearing of it, I don't think so." After that night, I would make staying away from the cowboy masses a top priority.

"You've got to go. Everyone's invited. There's a ton of good food, some good, old country music,"—I cringed at the "good" part of country music—"cute cowboys, and a really good time. Come. You can hang out with me and the girls. If you don't want to drive over in the Walker caravan, I could pick you up. Or Jesse could give you a ride in Old Bessie. Although that's an experience I'm sure you can live without."

"Unfortunately, Old Bessie and I are already acquainted," I said. "But you're right. That was an experience I could have done without." The Old Bessie part, not so much the Jesse part.

"You've been in Jesse's truck?"

I didn't miss the subtle nuance there. It was Old Bessie before she learned I'd been a passenger in her boyfriend's truck. Then it became Jesse's truck.

"Eh, yeah," I said, wondering if it was too early in the ride to stick my foot in my mouth. "Just one time though. When he picked me up at the bus station. I haven't ridden in it since. I haven't even seen it." Jesse in the bed of his truck that night outside the barn jumped to mind. I'd been a cowboy-stalking Peeping Tom that night. Probably not something I should admit to her. "I mean, I haven't seen his truck *running*, with him in it, since first day."

Oh, dear God. Strike me mute before I said anything else. Maybe that was why I pushed people away: It was a defense mechanism to keep myself from going on like a blubbering idiot.

Josie gave me a curious look, but that was it. "No big surprise since Old Bessie isn't a big fan of running. At least not consistently." She laughed, and I couldn't help but join in. If I couldn't laugh about something like Jesse's truck, there was no hope for me.

"So? Are you going to come?" she asked once we'd

stopped giggling like a couple of girls.

"I'll think about it," I said, grabbing the handle above the window and hanging on for dear life as Josie took a right turn at forty miles per hour. And I'd thought Jesse drove like a maniac. Apparently speed limits and road rules didn't apply to country kids.

"What's there to think about?" she asked as the bed of her truck fishtailed when she punched the gas coming out of the turn. "Music. Barbeque. Dancing. Cute boys in tight jeans. There is nothing about that line up that needs thinking about."

I agreed with at least one of the four things there.

"Yeah . . . well,"—I bit my lip and decided how much to say—"I don't think I'd fit in very well at that kind of thing." That summed it up without going into too many details.

"Says who?" she said instantly.

"Garth," I admitted.

I couldn't tell if Josie was cringing or shuddering, but if someone could dislike Garth Black as much as I did after tonight, it was Josie. The fact that we weren't fans of the same guy made me feel some sort of sisterhood with her. Like we were sisters in boy tastes. The more I thought about that, the truer it was. We didn't just dislike the same guy; we both liked the same guy.

"What did that asshole do, say, or ruin?" Her voice took on a certain chill. I wouldn't have guessed Josie had the word "asshole" in her repertoire. We really did share some kind of sisterhood.

"Just some asshole thing . . ." I started. "About me being a freak. Or dressing like one. I don't really know. Or care." I lied. I usually didn't care about the constant name-calling, but when it came to Garth—a guy I thought liked me—the names cut me more than usual.

"I'm going to tell you something, Rowen, and I want you to really hear me out. Okay?" Damn. Her hands were almost shaking over the steering wheel. "Don't let a guy like Garth Black ruin your summer. And don't let him ruin your life. Guys like that, people past the point of saving, have only one goal—to take as many others down with them as they can. And they're good at it."

I certainly hadn't expected to get a sermon from Josie on the evil ways of Garth Black when I'd jumped into her truck, but I was kinda digging it.

"Okay, Rowen? Steer clear of Garth, and if he gives you a hard time, let Jesse know. He'll take care of it." She looked over at me and lifted her eyebrows. She was obviously waiting for a response.

"O. Kay," I said dramatically, giving her a salute. After what he's said, I'd dodge Garth as much as Willow Springs would allow. Speaking of Willow Springs . . .

We pulled into the driveway. The house was dark except for the porch lights and that lone lamp shining in the window. We'd beat the Walkers home, so all I had to do was rush upstairs and lock myself in my room before they got back. I wasn't in the mood to recap the night, and I really wasn't in the mood to see Jesse.

"Thanks again for the ride, Josie," I said before leaping out of the truck.

"Anytime." She inspected the Walkers' house. When her eyes drifted up to my second floor bedroom window, her expression fell. I only hoped it wasn't because she was clairvoyant and knew I'd checked her guy out from that window. "If I don't see you before, I expect to see you at that dance or else I'll come and drag you there."

It was a full week away. An eternity. So I shrugged and said, "I'll make sure to wear my non-freak wear."

"Wear whatever the hell you want," she replied.

Flashing her a wave, I closed the door and headed up the porch. The girl reversed out of the driveway as fast as she drove forward down it.

Once I was inside, I was up the stairs and in my room as fast as my booted and blistered feet could carry me. It was late, I was tired, and all I wanted to do was get into bed and put the day in the delete folder. But first, I needed pajamas.

Unfortunately, I hadn't listened to Rose when she'd reminded me to bring my laundry down. In the midst of the sunrise-to-sunset work, doing one more chore at the end of the day just hadn't been a priority. As I pawed through my drawers, unable to find one article of clothing that could work as sleepwear, I realized I should have made personal laundry duty a priority.

Live and learn.

Desperate, I slid open the bottom drawer. I knew it would be empty—the top drawers had enough space to hold my clothes—but I had to check.

And the heavens opened and rained down pajama shirts.

It wasn't mine, but one folded white undershirt was in the back corner of the drawer. I pulled it out and gave it a whiff. It was fresh.

I lifted it and let it unfold in front of me. Clean, too.

My pajama dilemma was solved.

Sliding out of my freak-wear, according to Garth Black, I slipped into the white tee. It went down to my knees, and I was pretty sure I could fit two more Rowens inside of it, but I wasn't complaining.

I couldn't crawl into bed fast enough, and after a couple of minutes, I was out.

I FELL ASLEEP fast no problem. The *staying* asleep, not so much. I didn't know what time it was, but it was still dark and the house was quiet. Sneaking a peek at my phone, I saw it was just past midnight. I'd barely slept for two whole hours, and from the way I felt, I doubted I could fall asleep again anytime soon.

I threw the covers off and headed for the window. Maybe the crickets would lull me back to sleep.

A rush of cool air burst inside my room, instantly filling it with the scent of grass and the sound of those crickets. I stood at the window and breathed in a few slow breaths. The Walkers' Suburban was in its usual spot, and from the looks of the bunkhouse, everyone was asleep. Except for me.

I crawled back into bed, closed my eyes, and tried to fall back asleep. *Try* being the operative word. I was about two minutes into failing to sleep when strange, creaking sounds started outside my window. Not even a second later, something crawled inside said window.

Well, *someone* crawled inside.

Instead of screaming bloody murder, I rolled across the bed, grabbed one of my boots, and took aim. The boot circled through the air and couldn't have landed in a better spot: right in the side of the person's face.

The dark shadow huffed in surprise, or maybe pain, and rose to a full stand. I'd picked a Goliath-sized monster to pick a fight with. Not my finest moment.

I was just readying those vocal chords for what I should have done instead of reaching for my boot when the figure came closer.

"Good aim." The voice was so familiar I didn't need a light to identify who stood in my room. But I still switched the bedside lamp on.

"Jesse!" I managed to shriek quietly since three sleeping girls were close by. "What the hell?"

"Quick question," he said, lifting his finger while he rubbed the spot where I'd clocked him with his other hand.

"What?" I said, wondering what in the world Jesse Walker was doing in my room after midnight.

"Are you planning on throwing anything else at me?"

"Not as long as you don't scare the living shit out of me again," I said, finally calm enough to give him more than a quick look.

My eyes almost popped out of my head.

He was in his pajamas, too: a pair of navy blue sweats cut off at the knees, along with . . . absolutely nothing else. No shirt, no shoes, no hat. It was the least cowboy-fied I'd ever seen Jesse, and even though he was sexy six ways to Sunday in his cowboy gear, this look was hard to beat.

Probably had something to do with all of the tanned, muscled flesh on display.

"Rowen? Is something wrong?" He sounded like he was about to start snapping his fingers in front of my face. "Because your eyes are doing something kind of crazy right now."

That's because you're practically naked and were descended from gods.

I almost had to slap my face to clear my dazed

131

expression. "Other than you leaping into my room in the middle of the night? No, nothing's wrong." I had to look away or I was sure my eyes would go crossed. My eyes landed on the window. "And how in the hell did you get in here?" I rushed to the window. Yep, just how I'd remembered its location before Superman soared in: two stories up, *straight* up. No roofline, trellis, or ladder to climb. Nothing other than siding. So if he didn't have Superman DNA, it was Spiderman DNA.

Jesse appeared beside me and stuck his head out the window with me. His shoulder rubbed against mine. The innocent graze practically undid me. "You're looking in the wrong direction," he said, tilting his head up. I did the same.

All I saw was the outline of the roof and another window set right below where the roofline came together. I'd never noticed it before. It was a bit smaller than my window, but a light shone from it, too. Jesse Walker had been sleeping ten feet above me the whole time.

"Holy shit."

"You guessed how I did it yet?" he asked eagerly. Thankfully, he'd guessed my shock had to do with how he'd gotten from point A to point my B.edroom. I suppose I was still in some shock about that whole feat, but most of it was focused on the fact he'd been right above my sleeping head the whole time.

"I'm guessing it had something to do with lunacy," I replied. I really had no logical explanation for how he'd scaled down almost ten feet without the aid of a rope or a ladder or pixie dust.

Jesse nudged me with that arm I was ever so aware of running down the length of mine. "Maybe a little bit of lunacy, but a whole lot of skill, too. But, come on. Aren't you at least going to make a guess as to how I did it?"

I opened my mouth.

"Something *not* having to do with lunacy, maybe?" he interjected.

Okay, I could do this. Pushing all lunacy, superhero DNA, and miracles aside, I tried to put it together. Jesse's window to my window. Nothing but a whole lot of white cedar siding and one cobblestone chimney a couple feet to the side . . .

"Oh, dear God." I felt my stomach drop as I scanned the chimney. It ran from the ground up past the rooftop. Right by my window, right by Jesse's. "Please tell me you didn't—"

"Climb down the side of the chimney?" He studied the chimney with me and grinned. "Yeah. I did."

If he lost a foot or hand hold, he would have fallen a good twenty feet. There weren't any sharp projectiles or concrete landings below, but still. Best case scenario was some broken bones and internal bleeding. Worst case was a one way ticket to the hereafter.

"And the bull riders are supposed to have some kind of death wish?"

Jesse chuckled. "I've done it dozens of times, and the nice thing about the chimney is that it's predictable. You don't have to wonder which way it's going to spin, or how high it's going to buck."

"Ha. Ha," I said humorlessly. I saw very little humor in the situation. Sure, Jesse was standing beside me, talking to me, rubbing his fine, next-to-naked body against mine, but if he needed to see me so badly, why didn't he just come through my door?

"Why in the world did you do that?" I couldn't stare out the window any longer. In fact, I'd never stare out of it the same way again.

"Because I needed to talk to you, and I didn't get to finish what I needed to say tonight," he said, ducking back into the room. "I've been trying to talk to you all darn week, but you've been dodging me like a calf on branding day."

I pursed my lips to keep from laughing. He was being serious, and I didn't want to hurt his feelings, but really? Like a calf on branding day? I'd most certainly never heard that before and doubted I ever would again outside of Willow Springs.

"This whole week, your window's been closed, so when I heard it finally open, I decided to make my move. Because, Rowen, I need to talk to you whether you want to talk back or not. I need to explain a couple of things. I might have gone about this the wrong way by bursting through your window at night, but you didn't really leave me another choice."

I kept pursing my lips together. Jesse all flustered and rambling was adorable and appealing on so many levels, but he'd misunderstood my question.

"Not *Why?* as in why did you need to see me so badly, but *Why?* as in why didn't you just knock on my door?" I plopped down on the edge of my bed and tried really hard to keep my eyes on his. When his hands moved to his hips, that feat became next to impossible.

"Because you wouldn't have answered and because I didn't want to worry about waking my sisters. And because I didn't want to worry about answering their questions as to what I was doing knocking on your door at night. And because I could climb that chimney blind-folded. And because I was really hoping to impress you with my mad chimney climbing skills." Jesse's dimples emerged. My throat went dry. "So, are you impressed?"

Men and their need to impress. Looking from him to the window, back to him, I said, "Consider me sufficiently impressed."

His dimples drilled a little deeper with his smile. "I'd say my work here is done, except it's really only started." The skin between his eyebrows came together as he studied my big nightshirt.

Two and two came together right as his face ironed out. "Nice shirt," he said, looking a little smug.

"At least I'm wearing one," I said, giving him the briefest once-over I could manage.

"I was out of fresh shirts," he said, lifting his shoulders. "You're lucky I wasn't out of fresh shorts."

Yeah, that burn in my throat? It was from the flames erupting in my stomach.

"No, you're lucky," I said. "I've heard cobblestone chaffing is really uncomfortable."

"I'll take your word for it," he said, followed by a chuckle. "But, really. Next time you want to borrow one of my shirts, all you have to do is ask me. You don't have to steal it when I'm not looking."

I could tell from his face he was teasing, but I wasn't in a teasing mood. "I didn't steal it. It was in one of the drawers in my dresser. The–"

"Bottom one," Jesse finished my thought.

My suspicion that Jesse was clairvoyant seemed more and more likely. "How did you know that?"

"Because that's where I kept them." He shrugged and

crossed his arms. I loved when he crossed his arms. I loved it even more when he was shirtless. "I must have left one behind."

"Left one behind? Are you in the habit of leaving your things in random dresser drawers throughout the house?"

"Nope, but I try to make it a habit to leave my things in *my* dresser drawers."

"*Your* dresser drawer?" I repeated slowly, grabbing the comforter to cover my legs. The shirt had seemed large before, but having Jesse look at me that way made me feel all kinds of exposed.

"Well, yeah." He spread his arms and did a spin. "This is my room."

"Come again?" I knew I hadn't heard him wrong, but I wished I had.

"This has been my room from day one. My dresser, my nightstand,"—his smile curved higher on one side as he examined the space around me—"my bed. And my blankets." He took a few steps toward *his* bed and *his* blankets, and I felt like a thousand butterflies had been set loose in my stomach from the way he looked at me.

"Why did you move out?" I asked.

"Because you were coming," he replied matter-of-factly. "I know from growing up with three sisters that a girl's bedroom needs to be within arm's reach of a bathroom, and this room stays a heck of a lot cooler than the attic in the summertime."

I finally understood why I couldn't escape Jesse's scent or presence even when I was locked in my bedroom. I'd been sleeping on the same mattress he had. I'd been snuggled beneath the same old quilt he had. We'd shared a bed the whole time without even touching each other.

"You just picked up and moved into the attic because I was coming?" I said, sounding as dumbfounded as I felt.

He nodded.

"But you didn't even know me."

His forehead wrinkled, and he gave me a curious look. "I didn't have to. You needed a room. I had one. And the attic was empty."

"You make it sound so easy," I said, shaking my head. I doubted I'd ever figure out the goodness that moved inside of Jesse Walker. It was the kind that didn't quite make sense in our world.

"It *is* easy, Rowen," he said. "Besides, look at how it all worked out. You're sleeping on my bed, wearing my undershirt, and haven't thrown me out the window for jumping inside of it unexpectedly in the middle of the night. I'm not exactly on the losing side of this arrangement."

He was trying to make less of a big deal out of something that was a very big deal. If I had to move into the attic because some random stranger was coming for the summer, gracious was the last thing I would have been.

"Thank you," I said, having nothing else to offer. "That was a pretty cool thing to do."

He waved it off like it was nothing, and he approached the bed. "Please. When I get to move back in, I can sleep all warm and happy every night knowing you were in my bed for a whole summer." Very slowly, he took a seat next to me on the edge of the mattress. He was so on the edge of the mattress, he could have fallen right off. And now, Jesse and I were sharing a bed in the literal sense.

If it was possible, my heartbeat sped up some more.

"That's totally worth spending a summer in the attic," he said, glancing between me and the mattress with a smile. His eyes locked on mine, and with him so close, I could make out every speck of gold in those blue eyes of his. "Whoa." His head tilted to the side. "Your eyes are blue."

My face lined with confusion until I remembered Jesse had never seen me without my contacts in. Since I only took them out at bedtime and promptly replaced them after waking up, no one else at Willow Springs had either.

"I wear contacts," I said as he continued to examine my eyes with an intensity I felt was about to make me combust.

"Oh, are you near or farsighted?"

"Neither."

"Then why do you wear contacts?"

"They're color contacts," I said, wondering why Jesse had to be so observant. Of course I would be attracted to the one guy in the world so observant he probably remembered the color of the shirt I wore yesterday.

"But your eyes were so dark before. I couldn't tell if they were dark brown or black."

My shoulders rolled forward. I'd never had to explain it before. The few people who knew the actual color of my eyes didn't ask why I wore dark color contacts; it just sort of made sense with the rest of me. "I like dark," I said, wrapping the comforter tighter around me.

"I've noticed." He hitched a leg up onto the bed and twisted to face me. Could someone, please, for the love of God, find the man a shirt? The whole encounter couldn't be healthy for a girl's heart. "It seems that preference for dark, or . . . *black* applies to your taste in guys, too." Jesse tried to mask it, but the bitter note in his voice was obvious. "I'm hoping after tonight and what that guy did and said, you'll change your mind."

Just like that, I was reminded of a rather large something standing between Jesse and me. Someone who kept me from running my hands and lips all over him the way I wanted to.

"And I hope you'll change your mind the next time you come talk all sweet and make flirty looks at me when your girlfriend's a few rows behind us." I'd never been very good at censoring myself, and that wasn't the moment to change.

"Ah, perfect segue," he said, looking . . . was that . . . *relief?*

"Perfect segue? Come again?"

"Josie isn't my girlfriend."

"Jesse?" I made a face. "I think you're mistaking me for one of those girls cool with believing whatever you tell her."

He smirked at me. "It's the truth. Josie and I aren't together."

"Does she know that?" I asked. I knew what smitten looked like, and Josie had it just as bad, if not worse, as me.

"Yes." He nodded so strongly his mess of hair fell over his forehead. "We broke up over six months ago."

Wow. That was a serious case of WTF whiplash. "Wait." I lifted my hands up. "You and Josie aren't together anymore?"

"Isn't that what I've been saying?"

I lifted an eyebrow and waited.

"No," he said. "I am not with Josie. She is not with me. I'm not seeing anyone."

How had I been so convinced otherwise then? Oh, yeah. "Then why did Garth . . ?"

"Because Garth likes to create controversy everywhere he goes," Jesse said, his jaw tightening.

Create controversy everywhere he goes . . . yep, that pretty much hit the Garth nail on the head.

"Then why didn't you tell me?"

"I tried. And I tried. And I tried again. You wouldn't let me." He stared at me pointedly. "You remember any of that?"

I bit my lip and felt two inches tall. "Maybe a little bit."

Jesse laughed and nudged my leg with his. His bare skin against my bare skin. I almost shuddered.

"How long were you two together?" I asked.

"Just over two years."

"Why did you break up?" Even a possible reason was beyond me. The kind of girl Josie was matched the kind of guy Jesse was spot on.

Jesse stayed silent for a few seconds, playing with the corner of the quilt, then cleared his throat. "We just couldn't be together anymore."

How wonderfully detailed. "Anything else you want to add? Maybe the actual reason you couldn't be together anymore?" I was prying, I knew that, but I didn't back off. When it came to Jesse and Josie, I wanted that whole relationship tied up in a neat little bow.

"That's not really my story to tell," he said, shifting on the bed. "I promised Josie I'd never tell anybody, so the only way you'd be able to find out is from her."

I recognized that flash of pain on his face. Betrayal.

"She broke your trust." I felt a strange sense of protectiveness for Jesse. Josie had hurt him, betrayed him, and Jesse was the one person in the world I could say with absolute certainty didn't deserve it.

"Well, yeah," he said. Meeting my eyes seemed to be difficult for him suddenly. "But that wasn't the main reason we broke up." My nose wrinkled. That seemed like the "main" reason to end any relationship. Trust was a deal breaker. I should know. It had ruined every one of my relationships singlehandedly.

Jesse continued, "Everyone talks about how important trust is, and even though I agree, I'm not going to cut someone loose because they break my trust." Just the fact he could say that meant people hadn't broken his trust all that often. "We're all going to break a person's trust. That's inevitable. As long as it doesn't become a habit, I can forgive someone on a trust issue." Jesse paused and looked as defeated as I imagined he could look. "I just couldn't move past what happened. I knew I never would be able to, so it ended."

I wanted to reach out and remove the pain I saw so clearly on his face, but I didn't know how. So I scooted closer and hesitantly placed my hand over his. His skin was warm, and almost immediately, Jesse's shoulders relaxed.

"Are you glad it ended?" I asked.

"I wasn't. Not for a while. Josie and I'd been together for a long time. She knew things about me no one else knew, and I knew things about her no one knew, but now I'm better with it."

"Why's that?" My hand took on some of his heat. I

felt it going deep and spreading up my arm.

"I took it one day at a time until I could move on," Jesse replied, then he smiled down at the blankets. "And then I met this other girl."

Knife through the heart. So that's what it felt like.

"Another girl is always the cure for a guy to get over another girl," I said, working to keep my voice level. "They say that after a break up, a woman mourns and a man moves on. Looks like *they* are right."

The corners of his mouth twitched. Amusement? Irritation? "Josie and I broke up six months ago, and I haven't been on a single date since. I wouldn't consider that a rebound move-on."

"So why haven't you gone out with said 'this other girl'? Because you and I both know based on your looks alone, you could land any girl you want." I said, taking another good look at his "looks". Almost painful so close up. "That's not even taking your personality into account." Because really, as good looking as Jesse was, his persona-lity was just as attractive.

"Wait. Did you just say you think I'm hot? On the outside *and* the inside?" When he looked up at me, I could better make out that expression. Amusement.

That's why I didn't just lay it all out there. Because people could respond to my gut spilling with amusement.

I moved my hand from Jesse's. "I'm not going to answer that until you answer my question. Why haven't you asked her out?"

"I've tried, but she's kind of dodged the idea," he said, cracking his neck. "She's been avoiding me."

"You had the attention of every female in attendance tonight, and you expect me to believe this girl is avoiding you?" I said, letting my sarcasm loose. "Who would avoid you?"

When Jesse's eyes slid back to mine, with a look in them that would have dropped me if I hadn't been sitting, I knew. And then I realized how dense I was at times.

"Don't answer that," I said, unsure if I should scoot closer or as far away from him as I could. I was torn. Half of me wanted to follow that desire I had for him, and the other half wanted me to stay away from him because I knew I'd eventually do what I did best and make a huge mess of things.

"Why not?" he said, making the decision for me and scooting closer. "Why don't you want to know that I like you, Rowen? Why don't you want me to tell you I'm so damn attracted to you, I almost don't trust myself to be alone with you like we are right now? Why don't you want to know that I care about you so much, I wanted to rip Garth Black's throat out tonight for saying those things?" Jesse paused just long enough to take a breath. "Why?"

I wasn't living my life right now. This wasn't Rowen Sterling's life. Guys like Jesse didn't say those kinds of things to me. They didn't look at me the way he was now. No guy said or felt those kinds of things for me, because I wasn't the kind of girl who deserved to be adored. Or cherished. Or whatever it was that Jesse was expressing.

I wanted to be that girl that deserved the way he was looking at me. I wanted to be that girl that deserved *him* . . . but I wasn't that girl. Not yet. Maybe never. I wasn't sure. Willow Springs brought something out in me, almost like it was drawing out the poison inside of me and filling in the empty places with purpose. It was too early to be sure, but something was happening. Something big.

I couldn't look away from him even when I tried. "Jesse, why do you like me?" It made no sense to me. None at all.

His hand settled along my jawline. Slowly lifting my head until I looked straight at him, his eyes blazed. "Why do you think I shouldn't?"

That question rocked my world. Or upended it, more accurately. I had the first part of the answer to his question: I didn't deserve him. But the second part, the why I didn't deserve him, I came up empty on. Since I knew he was waiting for an answer, I'd just have to give him the best one I had.

"For a whole bunch of reasons—"

"That aren't valid," he interrupted, shaking his head.

"They're valid to me," I shot back, knowing I needed to put some space between us. So what did I do? I pressed my cheek harder into his large hand.

"They aren't to me, and if you don't mind picking this conversation up later on, there's something I've really been wanting to do." His voice went lower, even a bit rougher.

"What's that?" I asked needlessly. What he wanted to do was pretty obvious from the desire in his eyes as he studied my mouth.

Jesse scooted closer. So close, more of my body touched some part of his than didn't. His hand framing my face slid back around to my neck. His thumb skimmed the skin just under the collar of my shirt, causing my skin to erupt in goosebumps. Jesse's touch was powerful stuff, I'd known that from the first day I'd shook hands with him, but having his hands touch and caress me in gentle, intimate ways made the power of his touch difficult to

144

bear.

His other hand went to the small of my back right before his head tilted and he closed the last few inches of space between us. A smile was still on his lips when his mouth pressed into mine. It was so damn tender and gentle, I would have turned into a pile of mush if I was capable of it. Then, as quickly as it had dropped to mine, his mouth drifted away.

I could have cried from the separation.

"That's what," he whispered against my lips.

That was a good answer. Both the verbal and non-verbal.

"That's all?" I said with just enough inflection.

"No." He pressed closer to me. "No, that's not all."

When his mouth covered mine again, it wasn't so still and soft. It may have started out that way for the shortest moment, but before my eyes closed, Jesse's lips polished and sucked at mine like nothing I'd yet experienced. In addition to his other forms of divinity, the man was a kissing God.

His hand on my neck kneaded the muscles at the base of it as his thumb continued to skim lazy lines just under my collar. The hand on my lower back, remarkably, stayed where it was. Instead of grabbing the hem of my shirt to tug it over my head, instead of skimming under in search of my chest, his hand stayed in place. Holding onto me like I grounded him. Or like he grounded me. With the way he was kissing me, I couldn't be sure.

It was positively the best kiss I'd ever had the privilege of being on the other end of, but my body craved more. My inner thighs were squeezed so tightly together, they started to tremble, and I knew the rest of my body wasn't far behind.

I rose in place and shifted until I swung my leg over Jesse's lap. When I lowered myself over him, his grip tightened and his breathing picked up. Never, in even my most fantastical dreams, had I ever had the courage to imagine that one day I'd straddle Jesse Walker while we kissed like it was the only thing keeping us alive. Never once. Yet here I was. Living it.

When Jesse's lips dropped to my neck, I tilted my head back and pressed harder against him. I didn't stop pressing closer until I felt his chest thumping hard against mine. I didn't stop until I felt his breathing pick up yet again. I didn't stop until he was fitted so hard between my legs I knew if I were to slide up or down, I'd come undone instantly.

So instead, I ran my hands up his wide arms and didn't stop until they were combing and tugging through his hair. What I wanted to touch more, his hair or his body, had been a toss-up before. After doing both, I could confidently say neither had let me down. The debate was still out on which I preferred to touch though.

Moving my hands down the base of his neck, I continued toward the center of his back, tracing the deep seam that ran into his shorts. Jesse sighed against my neck when my hands repeated the motion. I didn't know how he could sigh because I was one slide away from screaming out. Waking the house would be a really bad thing. For them and for us.

As soon as Jesse's lips left my neck, my hands clutched the hem of my shirt and started sliding it up my stomach. I appreciated the whole gentleman thing he was keeping with, but the clothing was really starting to get in the way of things.

"Whoa," Jesse said suddenly, his voice strained. "Easy, tiger. I'm about to go into cardiac arrest with your shirt *on*." Jesse's hands fitted over mine and moved them back down into my lap, shifting the shirt down at the same time. "Let's leave it where it is, okay?"

If I woke up tomorrow speaking a different language, I don't think I would have been more confused. "You don't want to go any farther?" My voice was just as breathless as his. "You just want to kiss?" Surely I was misunderstanding something. As good as the kissing was, and believe me, it was the kind of thing people wrote songs about, even *I* wanted to go farther. My body felt like it needed to. It was programmed to do so.

"Well, I'd like to go farther, *one day*, but right now, I'm pretty damn happy just kissing you." Jesse's grin reappeared right before he pressed a soft kiss into my lips. "Although I wouldn't say we're 'just kissing.'" Another soft kiss, slightly longer. "Would you?"

I shivered in his arms. "Whatever we're doing, Jesse," I said, still tasting him on my lips, "whatever this is . . . it's definitely not 'just kissing.'"

When his mouth covered mine again, it stayed there. When our mouths opened at the same time, my tongue touched his, and I realized there was nothing better than what we were doing. We were exploring each other, bit by tiny bit, and we were enjoying each and every touch and moment. It wasn't what I was used to, not even close, but as our mouths, hands, and bodies tangled together, it seemed I was getting used to something new.

When I let myself just enjoy the moment and get over anticipating the next thing, I found "just" kissing a rather pleasurable experience. Especially when Jesse was doing the kissing. I'd kissed a lot of guys, but his kisses were a whole different thing. In fact, just kissing Jesse was more intimate than any sex I'd had with someone else. If I added all of those encounters up, their total wouldn't have even come close to the intimacy I felt with Jesse's mouth on mine. I'd never known a guy happy to just kiss and hold me close to him. Not since I was in the sixth grade.

Then again, I'd never known Jesse Walker until that summer.

CHAPTER eight

Jesse must have slipped out of my bed and either back up the side of the chimney or out my bedroom door sometime before I woke up. It was a good thing he had, too, because a rapping on the other side of my door woke me up, followed by the youngest Walker bursting into my room before I invited her. Clementine, though, was always invited. Just as long as her big brother wasn't sleeping next to me.

"Mornin', Rowen!" she greeted, skipping into the room with her braids bouncing up and down. She saw I was still in bed and sleepy eyed. "Were you still asleep?"

I nodded and yawned. "Yep. I didn't sleep very well last night." After the night I'd had with Jesse, I didn't care how little sleep I got or how tired I was. Last night was worth it. After making out to the point both our lips and hands were practically rubbed raw, he nestled beside me in bed, wrapped those strong arms around me, and we fell asleep together. Fully clothed. Even though we didn't have sex, I'd never fallen asleep more satisfied and content in my whole life.

"You've got a silly smile on your face," Clementine said, giggling as she pointed at me.

I was still smiling. That's how great last night had been.

"Did you need something, squirt? Or were you just making sure I was awake?" I threw the covers off and headed for the dresser. I was about to open the first drawer when I remembered my dilemma from last night: I didn't have any clean clothes.

That would make today challenging, if not impossible. I couldn't very well whisk about the kitchen and the chicken coop in nothing but a white, oversized tee.

"Could I borrow that pretty purple scarf you wore last night?" she asked, coming up beside me and grabbing my hand. "Purple is the color of royalty, so if I'm wearing purple, everyone will know to bow when I walk by."

The purple scarf was perhaps the only thing clean in my room. I grabbed it off the dresser and kneeled down beside Clementine. "Of course you can borrow it," I said, winding it around her neck. "And if anyone doesn't bow when you walk by, just wave your flamingo croquet mallet and say, 'Off with his head.'"

Clementine's face squished up on one side. The kid had no idea what I was talking about. She knew fairy tale princesses, but not *Alice in Wonderland*. I'd been the other way around at her age. Finally, she giggled again when I tickled her neck after tying the scarf into a pretty bow.

"You're weird, Rowen," she said, smiling up at me.

"Believe me. I know." I patted her head, turned her around, and led her toward the door. I couldn't solve my no-clean-clothing situation with a little girl bouncing a-round the room. "You know what? That scarf looks so good on you, I'm giving it to you. Okay?"

"What? Really?" If a seven-year-old could look more thrilled, I hadn't seen it.

"Really, really," I said as we got to the doorway. A

gift bag with a black and white polka-dot ribbon tying the handles together sat just outside. "What's this?"

Clementine shrugged. "I saw Jesse put it there early this morning when I was going to the bathroom. Then he walked away all quiet and quick."

So Jesse had snuck out of my room, snuck back to drop the bag off, then snuck off to somewhere else. Not to mention when he'd snuck into my room last night. He'd done a lot of sneaking in twelve hours.

Once Clementine was bouncing down the stairs, I grabbed the bag and hurried back inside my room. I didn't get presents often. Mom had resorted to pulling out her wallet and handing me a couple hundred dollar bills at breakfast on my birthday since I'd become a teenager. I wanted to take my time untying the ribbon and pulling out the tissue paper.

The moment my fingers tugged on one end of that ribbon though, that bow was untied and the tissue paper was flying. I could have cried when I saw what was inside.

Clothes. New with the tags on them and in my size. A few pairs of jeans that, knowing Jesse, would still hug my butt but hopefully not as bad as Lily's had. A few tees in different colors, two airy button-up shirts with those pretty, pearly button snaps, and a pair of boots at the very bottom of the bag. Again, they were in my size, a Western style that wasn't overt about it, and chocolate brown and lavender colored. They were functional for life on the ranch, but still round-toed, didn't have a heel, and mid-calf like my trusty combat boots.

My clothing problem was miraculously solved by a man. Go figure.

Rose had offered all week to take me into town to

pick out some new clothes, but I'd put it off and borrowed Lily's since the only spare time we'd had was last night, and I didn't want Rose to miss the rodeo because she was helping me pick out clothes.

I was just about to tug a shirt over my head when a white folded note nestled in the tornado of tissue paper caught my attention. I'd been in such a hurry, I'd missed it. I grabbed it and opened it up.

I picked these up for you last week, but since I was scared you'd bite my head off if I did anything but stay silent and avoid eye contact, they've hung out with me in the attic. You know, that place right above you? Where I sleep? Sometimes naked?

My throat went dry when I visualized that. My legs went weak when I thought of me joining him in that naked state.

That was a joke. Kind of . . . Anyways, you needed some clothes, I wanted to help, problem solved. And while I've got your undivided attention . . . You remember that date I asked you about last week that you were about to say yes to before someone I shall not name really messed that up? Yeah, well, since you got me to sleep with you last night, I think the least you owe me is a date. Tonight? 8ish? You. Me. Food. Sound okay?

P.S. You can still kick serious ass in these boots.

I read the note once more. It made me laugh. As much as I wanted to read it again, I smelled breakfast. That meant I was running late.

I changed into a pair of jeans which, as suspected, hugged my butt but not as badly as Lily's had, slipped into the olive green button-down shirt, and slid into the boots. Everything fit. The boots fit my feet so well, my old ones were in danger of becoming my second favorites.

After ripping a brush through my hair, I rushed down the hall. My lips felt chapped, no big surprise there, so I made a layover in the bathroom to slick on some lip balm.

Voices buzzed in the kitchen already, which meant I wasn't only late, I was really late. As soon as I skidded into the kitchen, my eyes locked onto his and his onto mine. Jesse was already seated at the table with the rest of the hands, eating breakfast. After finishing the bite of food in his mouth, a grin spread across his face as he took me in decked out in my new clothes.

"Wowza! Don't you look fabulous," Rose said when she pulled her head out of the fridge.

"She sure does," Jesse added, his grin stretching wider. The rest of the hands, along with Neil, turned and took a quick look. A few nods, a couple smiles, then they got back to their breakfast.

"Thank you," I replied to Rose before glancing back at Jesse. I don't think he'd blinked yet. "And thank *you*." I hoped he'd pick up on the subtle inflection because I couldn't just walk across the kitchen, kiss him full on the lips, and thank him for the clothes the way I wanted to. I wasn't sure how his family would take it. I was still trying to figure us out for myself, so whatever Jesse and I had, we'd have to keep it quiet until we figured out just what *it* was.

"Sorry I'm late," I said as I rushed over to the coffee

pot. That was my area of expertise. I ground, made, and poured the coffee. After that first day, I hadn't spilled any. Occasionally, I'd be brave enough to whip up the pancake mix or scramble the eggs, but manning the coffee was the safest bet.

"That's all right, hun," she said, waving it off. "Clem said you had a tough time sleeping last night. You could have slept in, you know?"

Clementine waved at me from where she flipped pancakes on the griddle while standing on a step stool. Her purple scarf was proudly on display.

"What kept you up? Mind, body, or both?" Rose asked as I grabbed the coffee pot.

I couldn't look her in the eyes when I answered, "Both." I promptly spun around and whisked toward the table.

I felt one set of eyes on me. So intently, I remembered the way he'd kissed me last night. It made me remember the words he'd said to me.

Reliving last night when I had hot coffee in my hands wasn't a good idea. I stopped beside Neil and lifted the pot. "Refill?" It was a rhetorical question. Not once in the past week had Neil turned down a coffee refill.

"Please," he said with a nod. "Did you end up going to the rodeo last night, Rowen? We didn't see you there, but it was packed as usual."

"Yeah, I went." I focused on pouring coffee into his cup. I did a quick scan of the table and was relieved to see a certain seat empty. I wasn't quite ready to see Garth Black yet.

"What did you think?" he asked, turning in his seat toward me. "This was your first rodeo, right? I bet it left quite an impression."

"It certainly left an impression," I replied as I set his cup back down in front of him.

"Well, good. I'm glad you could make it," he said as I moved on to the next cup that needed topped off. "Did you do anything especially fun afterward?"

From across the table, someone started choking.

The guy sitting next to Jesse hammered his back a few times while Jesse took a few sips of water. "Geez, Jesse. Try chewing your food before you swallow it. Basic stuff here, buddy."

Jesse lifted his eyebrows in acknowledgement, took another sip of water, and glanced my way.

I shot him a thumbs up and made a face. He shot me back a smirk.

"I just went back up to my bedroom and stayed there all night." I continued to make the coffee rounds. Jesse picked his fork back up and dove into his breakfast, but his eyes shifted my way every few seconds. So much for playing it subtle.

"Sounds like an uneventful night," Neil said.

"Perfectly uneventful," I replied.

Jesse shook his head and grinned into his plate.

The pot was empty a few cups later. After a detour to refill, I headed back to the table. En route, Jesse lifted his full cup of coffee and took a drink. He didn't stop until the cup was empty. He swung it from the handle with his finger and winked at me.

If he kept that up, the entire ranch would know something was going on between us.

"Refill?" I stopped beside him and held out my hand. I was likely imagining it, but his eyes twinkled a bit more this morning.

"I thought you'd never ask," he replied as he handed me his cup. His hand grazed mine purposefully, and in that briefest of grazes, my heart picked up speed.

"Did you have trouble sleeping last night, too?" I asked innocently as I poured his coffee. No one was paying us any attention, but just in case . . .

"Maybe a little." He twisted in his seat and gave me a not-so-innocent smile. "Once I did fall asleep, I slept great. Best sleep of my life even."

I was one more flirty innuendo away from a blush. It took a lot to make me blush, and I really didn't want to do it right here for all of these guys to witness.

"Did you have a tough time getting to sleep last night, too, son?" Neil spoke up. I almost jumped out of my skin. I didn't think anyone could hear us above the din of conversations roaming around the room.

"Yeah, I did, Dad," Jesse replied in a collected voice. Like he hadn't just gone from talking in code with me about last night to discussing sleep with his dad a second later.

"You know, I did, too," Neil said. "I kept hearing a bunch of creaking around and odd noises last night."

It would have been my turn to choke if I had anything in my mouth.

"This house is older than you are, Dad. It creaks and makes odd noises all the time," Jesse said with a shrug while he soaked up some hamburger gravy with a biscuit.

"Thanks for the age reminder, Jesse. Always something I love to be reminded of. But these were odd-*er* sounds." *That's probably because your son climbed down a chimney, hurled himself into my room, and made out with me in ways that are probably illegal in this county.* "Anyways, I'm sure it was nothing, but it looks like a few of us are going to be getting by on nothing more than caffeine and grit today."

Jesse lifted his cup and took a sip. "Looks like it."

I sighed with relief as I reached for the next empty cup. Breakfast was almost over, Jesse and I had dodged a few danger zones, and I'd managed to keep from kissing him the way I wanted to as soon as I walked in and saw him.

Maybe we could keep things on the D.L. until we figured them out and were ready to go public.

That was when Clementine shouted from across the room, "Rowen? Why were you wearing Jesse's shirt this morning?"

Jesse's fork clattered to his plate. The empty coffee cup in my hand clattered to the floor.

CHAPTER nine

The Walkers had believed me. They'd believed my explanation as to why I'd been wearing Jesse's shirt. Of course, I told them the truth—I didn't have any clean pajamas and found it buried in the back of the dresser drawer—but I'd found adults were unappeasably suspicious when it came to teens. Especially when it came to the topic of sleeping around.

For example, if I'd woken up wearing some guy's shirt at home, my mom would have just assumed we'd done the deed. She wouldn't have asked for an explanation because she didn't need one.

Neil and Rose, on the other hand, gave Jesse and me a curious look after Clementine's announcement. I gave them a simple explanation, they nodded, then they got on with the morning. They trusted me. They believed me—they believed *in* me.

It had been a while since anyone had trusted or believed in me, and I didn't want to do anything to betray them. Even if that meant Jesse and I had to admit what was going on between us sooner rather than later. I didn't want to lie to them.

I knew the idea of their perfect son linking up with someone like me, with a less-than-perfect past, might make them uncomfortable, but the Walkers were quite possibly the most understanding and forgiving people out there. If anyone would give me the thumbs up to date their son, it would be them.

After I'd put a few loads of my clothes into the dryers, I wandered back into the kitchen. The guys were moving the cattle to a different pasture and wouldn't come in for lunch, so we'd packed a sack lunch type meal, and I would drive it out to them in a few minutes.

Rose was stacking the sandwiches into a big cooler when I walked into the kitchen.

"Clean clothes are a mere dryer session away," I said, walking over to help her.

"You know, my dear, you can always ask me or one of the girls if you need some pajamas," she said as I started laying bottles of water into the cooler. "No need to go into the bowels of Jesse's dresser in search of an old, smelly shirt."

I almost corrected her. It wasn't old and smelly. In fact, I'd take a shirt of Jesse's any night over the finest, silkiest pajamas out there. "Okay, thanks. It wasn't so bad, really."

We were quiet for a few moments as we continued to load up the cooler for an army of ranch hands. The cooler was so big, I wasn't sure Rose and I could move it on our own.

"Your mom called again," she said slowly.

The chill Zen I'd managed to achieve at Willow Springs flew out the window. It always did when someone brought up the topic of my mom. Rose generally tried not to mention her, but she was in a tough spot. Since I'd refused to take any of my mom's calls, my mom had moved on to Rose. Rose was the intermediary between Mom and me, and that wasn't a role I'd wish on my worst enemy.

"She said she still hasn't been able to get ahold of you," Rose said diplomatically. *That's because I've hit ignore every time she's called.* "And that you haven't returned her messages."

"I don't have anything to say to her, Rose. Her ultimatum included me working hard out here and not stepping a toe out of line. She didn't say anything about pretending we have this great mother-daughter relationship where we check in with each other every day." My voice was rising. It always did when I started down the rabbit hole that was my mom and me. "But I'm sorry you're in the middle of this. I'll give her a call so she'll leave you alone." *I'll just make sure to call when I know she's at work so I can leave her a message and not have to talk to her directly.*

"You do whatever you think is best, Rowen. I'm a big girl, and I've been dealing with your mom's drama for decades now. I'm an expert in drama dealing with that woman." Rose placed the last few sandwiches on top of the pile and closed the fridge. "She's seeing some new guy, I guess. She said she wanted to bring him out here to meet everyone and have dinner."

So much was wrong with those couple of sentences I glanced around, half expecting the apocalypse.

"She's always seeing a new guy. There's never not been a new guy in my mom's life." I couldn't think of a single instance when her boyfriend lasted longer than two months. As old as she was, that meant she'd dated so many guys, if you laid them down in a straight line, they'd circle the earth once. At least once.

Rose shrugged. "She sounded pretty serious about this one. Just the fact that she wanted to make the journey with him out here to meet you made me stop and make sure the sky wasn't falling."

"The only reason she wants to bring him out here is because she probably wants to break up with him. She knows seeing her freak of a daughter will be enough to send him running. It's worked before. Makes it easier on her if they just run away screaming." I leaned into the counter and looked out the window. I didn't want Mom there. Willow Springs was my special place. A place where I didn't have to walk on egg shells around her. A place where some "new guy" didn't take automatic priority over her flesh and blood. I didn't want to taint what small sliver of peace I'd found with the wars and battles that would surely come if we were under the same roof.

"Please stop calling yourself that, Rowen," Rose said in as firm a voice as I'd ever heard her use. "You're no more a freak than I am. You're just as much a freak as I am, too. Don't let some ignorant name you've heard directed your way define you. You define you." She pressed her finger into my face. "Stop playing the victim and live your life."

I think if she'd just slapped me across the face, I wouldn't have been as shocked. Rose was such a calm soul that seeing her so fired up was a bit unnerving.

"Those are some powerful words," I said slowly.

"That's because they're true." Rose looked at me and waited. She wouldn't let me out of the kitchen until she'd pounded it into me.

"I'll think them over." I reached for the handle of the cooler. Uncomfortable conversations were something I tried to avoid at all costs.

"Promise you will."

To argue would have been pointless. Rose may be small, but she was mighty. "I promise."

"Good," she said, and her whole body relaxed. "Now,"—she grabbed the other handle—"let's get this thing loaded up before those boys keel over from starvation."

"Yeah, we wouldn't want them to kill a cow and start roasting it over a fire."

"No, we wouldn't," Rose said around a chuckle.

Rose and I managed to wrangle that cooler out of the kitchen, out the back door, and down the stairs before we had to set it down and take a break. Last week, I couldn't have helped carry that thing five feet. Just went to show how strong one got working around a ranch. I also knew my muscles weren't the only things getting stronger.

Everything about me was getting stronger.

"What car do you want to take?" Rose asked. Her breathing wasn't even labored like mine. "The Suburban or Neil's truck?"

I studied them and made a face. The family Suburban was almost as long as a school bus, and Neil's truck was an extended cab monster truck. Then another vehicle caught my attention.

"Why don't I take Old Bessie?" I said. "It's the only one I think I have a decent shot of seeing over the steering wheel without having to prop a phone book under my butt."

Rose studied the truck with me and gave a good

laugh. "Old Bessie it is then. Jesse would be happy to know someone on this ranch other than him isn't too embarrassed to drive it."

We lifted the cooler again and headed for Old Bessie. "I didn't say I wasn't embarrassed to drive that thing. I'm just choosing the lesser of two embarrassing options." Rose lowered the tailgate, and we swung the cooler up into the bed. I grunted like it weighed a ton. Rose smiled like it was light as a feather. "Drive Old Bessie or sit propped up on a phone book . . ." I lifted both hands and weighed the options. "Kind of a tough call."

"Well, enjoy the ride and make sure to wash your hands when you're done driving that thing. Lord only knows what could be growing in it." Rose lifted the tailgate and wiped her hands off on her pants. "You got your phone in case you get turned around?"

I patted my jeans' pocket.

"You shouldn't have a problem. Just follow that windy dirt road until you see a bunch of cattle and guys on horseback."

"I think I can handle that." I came around the truck and opened the car door. It made a whiny, screeching sound. I leapt up into the driver's seat and found I could see over the steering wheel. Barely, but I could. "Oops. I need keys."

"They're in the ignition," Rose said.

Yep. Sure enough. I guess no one would want to steal Old Bessie anyways. Turning them over, the engine fired to life. When I say fired, I mean I expected a real life, raging fire to erupt from the hood.

"See you later. If I'm not back in a few hours, send the search party." I waved at Rose before closing the door and heading out of the driveway.

Surprisingly, Old Bessie drove fairly smoothly for a truck in its condition. And that truck had something no other truck had: Jesse's smell overpowering the cab.

I was about a couple miles down the bumpy dirt road when I reached for the CD player. I hit play without thinking, and that Johnny Cash character Jesse was such a fan of started singing in that deep, dark voice of his about rings and fires.

Actually, it was pretty good. It could have been badass good if the country twang about it could be removed. The lyrics were like poetry, and Johnny Cash's voice was like nothing I'd heard before. When the CD moved on to the next song, I realized that, in a little over a week, I'd gone from hating-with-a-capital-H country music to tolerating, and maybe, just maybe, appreciating it.

What. In. The. Hell. was happening to me?

I didn't know yet, but I did know the changes taking place inside and outside of me were good ones. They were changes to be proud of, so I would just keep keeping on. I didn't need to have all the answers to my questions yet.

After a few more miles, I found what I was looking for. Even from a good football field length away, I made out which of the guys on horseback was Jesse. The white tee and straw hat were a dead giveaway, but it wasn't just that. It was almost like I was . . . pulled to him. Almost like he was what my eyes were trained to find. Man, it was a cheesy thing to think, but Jesse was the only one I saw out there.

The cattle were stopped and grazing in the large field, and the riders just trotted around them, checking them over. A few of the hands must have noticed the truck because one shouted over at Jesse on the far end of the field. Everyone glanced over before steering their horses toward the truck. Those cowboys took their mealtimes seriously.

I parked Old Bessie under a large shade tree and jumped out. I checked my cell phone and, no big surprise, there was no reception In-the-Middle-of-Nowhere. If I'd gotten lost, Rose wouldn't have been a simple phone call away.

Most of the guys' horses trotted over. Jesse's horse galloped. If nothing said "obvious" like a smiling guy riding his horse balls-to-the-walls toward an equally smiling girl, I didn't know what did.

When he and his horse were so close I could make out the color of the horse's eyes, Jesse pulled back on the reins. His horse came to an immediate stop. So immediate, a cloud of dust erupted from his hooves.

I smirked up at Jesse. The rest of the guys weren't even close. "Hungry?" I asked, shielding my eyes as I looked up at him. Jesse made "cowboy" look good like no other, but him on a horse . . . I couldn't imagine anything sexier.

He flashed me a knowing smile. "Like you wouldn't believe. Especially after seeing you pull up in my sweet ride." He winked before swinging his leg around and dismounting. He came toward me, horse in tow, and didn't stop until his body was almost against mine.

"I missed you today," he said as his eyes scanned my face. "I missed touching you." Jesse's hand dropped to my hip, and the breath I'd been holding rushed out. "I missed talking to you."

My eyes closed for a moment when his thumb drew circles into my side. Jesse's touch was hard to explain, but that didn't mean I enjoyed it any less. When my eyes reopened, I noticed a few bobbing heads over Jesse's shoulder getting closer.

"Cowboys on the horizon," I said before stepping back. Jesse's hand fell from my side, but I still felt it there. I swung around the truck and opened the tailgate before taking the cooler lid off. I heard Jesse's footsteps and his horse's hoofsteps follow me.

"Are you embarrassed to be seen with me?" I could tell from his tone he was teasing, but it was a delicate topic for me.

"No," I replied instantly. "I'm embarrassed for *you* to be seen with *me*."

Jesse's eyebrows came together. "Well, that makes a whole lot of no sense."

"It makes a whole hell of a lot of sense," I said, giving his chest a gentle shove, "and you know it."

He studied me for another moment with a furrowed brow before his expression cleared. "What are you doing right now?"

I swung my arms toward the cooler. "Serving lunch."

"These guys know how to reach in and grab a few sandwiches," Jesse said, tilting his head back at the guys dismounting behind him. "So it looks like you're on break."

"And what do you have planned for my break?" I crossed my arms. "You want to hide behind the tree and make out the rest of the afternoon?"

Jesse's dimples made their appearance. "That sounds nice. *Really* nice," he said, smiling at the tree behind me.

"But I was thinking I could take you for a ride."

"Oh, really?" I crossed my arms tighter.

Jesse lifted the reins in his hand. "A *horse* ride," he said in an amused tone. "But if you've got another idea, I think I could be persuaded."

I cleared my throat and tried to ignore the thick band tightening around my stomach. "A horseback ride sounds nice."

"It doesn't sound all that nice now that you've got me thinking of something else."

That comment earned him a soft elbow to his hard stomach. I walked around the side of his horse and wondered about how to go about it. Jesse made it seem so easy. His movements were seamless whenever he got on or off of a horse.

Inspecting the saddle and all its gadgetry, it didn't look anything close to easy or seamless.

"Wait," Jesse said, coming up behind me. "Don't try to get up on Sunny unless I'm already in the saddle."

Even if I wanted to, I couldn't have. I might as well have tried to climb Everest.

"So this is Sunny?"

"This is Sunny boy," Jesse answered, patting the giant horse's muscled neck.

Sunny was white with big, black patches scattered over him. His mane and tail were streaked black and white, and he had one blue eye and one brown. He was beautiful in a very . . . odd type of way.

Jesse stepped in front of Sunny and ran his palm down the horse's face. "Hey, boy, this is Rowen. We're going to go for a little ride and I want you to be a good boy. She's special to me." His eyes shifted to mine when he said the last part.

Special? *Special*? No one had called me special once in my entire life. At least not in the way Jesse had meant it.

Sunny's big head flicked into the air a few times before Jesse came back toward me. In yet another seamless move, Jesse swung up on Sunny before I even noticed his foot was in the stirrup. He held his hand out and waited.

"Come on, Rowen. You'll be fine. Besides, if he didn't like you, you couldn't be as close to him as you are now." Jesse reached his hand toward me again.

I glanced over at the truck. The guys were already tossing around sandwiches and water bottles. A few of them looked as though they'd already finished their first ones. Lunch was served. Time to live a little.

I took Jesse's hand, and his fingers wove through mine. "My life and limbs are in your hands, Cowboy," I said.

Jesse chuckled. "Put your left foot in the stirrup."

I inhaled and followed his instructions.

He chuckled louder. "Your other left."

I was off to a great start. I did, contrary to appearances, know left from right. Dropping my right foot back down, I tried again.

"Okay, good. Now just step up, keep your weight in the stirrup, and swing your right leg up and over Sunny."

"I'm sure it's nowhere near as easy as you make it sound," I said, gripping onto his hand like it was a life ring.

"It's not," he said. "It's easier."

I narrowed my eyes at him which only made his smile widen. I felt everyone's eyes on me. I was sure I was quite the spectacle. After blowing out a breath, I tightened my hold on Jesse's hand and got after it.

Jesse's bicep flexed as he curled his arm up, and once I found myself magically on top of Sunny, I knew it had more to do with his effort than my own.

"You did it," Jesse said, looking over his shoulder at me.

"Don't sound so surprised," I said as I shifted in the saddle. The thing was really only made for one backside, but I couldn't exactly complain. The front of my body was pressed tight into the back of his. The apex of my legs was pressed into that perfect butt of his, and when Jesse shifted in the saddle, I suddenly became *very* aware of the spot below my belly button.

"You want to back out of this adventure?" he asked, sounding like even if I wanted to, he wouldn't let me.

"I think it's a little late for that," I replied, feeling every eye on me. I hoped no one could hear the way my heart pounded, or noticed the pick up in my breathing. I'd never felt like such an open book before. Usually I controlled my emotions and the physical reactions accompanying them, but with Jesse, I could do neither. The way I felt about him wouldn't allow me to hide it.

"Wrap your arms around me and hold on tight," he said, grabbing one of my arms to wind around his torso. We hadn't taken one step and I already loved horseback riding. "And don't forget to enjoy the ride."

I wound my other arm around Jesse's middle and clasped my hands together. "If I had a dollar for every time a guy gave me that line . . ."

It took a moment for that to sink in since Jesse's head wasn't as sick and twisted as mine, but he shook his head and laughed when it did. "I will gladly take you for any and every kind of ride you'll let me, Rowen."

Before my stomach had a chance to bottom out, Jesse clucked his tongue, and Sunny lunged forward.

The ride was surprisingly smooth, and I could, literally, feel the wind breaking over my face. Jesse held the reins in one hand and covered mine where they were locked together around his stomach with the other.

Riding through a grassy green field at a breakneck pace while wrapped around Jesse Walker's body on a warm summer afternoon was the closest I'd come to perfection. It was the closest by a long shot.

I didn't do perfect. I didn't believe in it and, up until right then, I hadn't wanted it either.

My whole life was shifting, like I was experiencing my own personal earthquake. I felt the plates shifting and rearranging below the surface. I felt the fire and heat molding and shaping them. I felt change, whether I wanted it or not. It was happening, and I might as well embrace it.

So while my instinct was to push someone away if they tried getting too close, I rested my head on Jesse's back and breathed in as much of him as I could. It was a powerful moment and over much too soon.

Jesse pulled back on the reins a few minutes later as we approached a fast-moving stream.

"Still back there?" Jesse's voice was light, not a worry in the world.

"You feel that death grip around your body?" I loosened my hold just barely. We might have stopped moving, but I was still five feet from the ground on a horse.

"I'm feeling it," he said. "I'm feeling a lot more than

just a death grip around my body, though." Jesse's back did a little wiggle to prove his point. Hello, Jesse's back, meet Rowen's front.

"So much for all those sweet county boy manners I *thought* you had," I said, pinching his side.

"It's a tough act to keep up with you around." He looked over his shoulder and winked. In yet another super cowboy move, Jesse swung his leg up and over Sunny's neck before hopping off. "Are you planning on staying up there all day?"

"I'm thinking about it," I said, taking in the landscape. Nature as far as the eye could see was growing on me. "Why? Do you have any other suggestions?"

Jesse's eyes gleamed. "One or two."

"In that case . . ." I planted my foot in the stirrup and swung my other leg around Sunny's backside. By nothing short of a miracle, I managed to get off of that horse without falling on my duff.

"Impressive," Jesse said with a nod as I dusted off my hands. "You must have an amazing teacher."

I lifted a shoulder. "Maybe I'm just a really kick-ass student."

"Maybe," he said, coming toward me.

I didn't step back the way I knew I should. I didn't step forward the way I wanted to. I stayed where I was and waited for him.

"So, now that you've got me out here, wherever *here* is," I said, waving at the nameless landscape, "what did you have planned?"

I'd barely finished my question before Jesse's hand formed around the bend of my waist. With his other hand, he slid his straw hat off and lowered his face until it almost touched mine. Everything inside of me quickened. Jesse's skin hadn't touched mine yet, and my body was rushing like a runaway train.

His mouth was so close to mine, I felt his warm breath on my lips when he said, "This." His lips covered mine for such a brief moment it was more of a tease than a kiss. "And this." His mouth moved over mine long enough to be in the kissing category. "And this, too." He separated from me just long enough to get those words out before his lips settled back over mine. That kiss wasn't a tease; it wasn't anything close to a tease. It was the kind of kiss a girl would forever measure against. It set the bar for all future kisses. That kiss made me want to do nothing but keep my mouth firmly planted on Jesse's until the day I died.

The kiss made me moan when his tongue gently touched mine. Even with our mouths combined, I felt Jesse's smile move into position at my response. He was still smiling when we both came up for air.

"That good, huh?" he said, settling his hat back onto his head while I struggled to fill my lungs.

"That's some gloat you've got going on, Jesse," I said, circling my finger around his face. "And here I was under the impression you were humble."

"When a woman moans while a man's kissing her,"—he lifted an eyebrow—"that's grounds for a full-on gloat if ever there were grounds."

"Fine. Take it all in. Yes, your mad kissing skills made me moan. Soak it up and let's move on." I rolled my eyes.

"Oh, believe me, I'm soaking it up."

I crossed my arms and waited a few seconds. "Done

soaking?"

Jesse's dumb smile kept shining until he tapped his wrist where a watch might have been. "And done."

It was about time.

"What are we going to tell your parents?"

Jesse's face ironed out. "Wow. You really know how to kill a guy's soak."

I waited.

"Are you talking about us?"

"No, I'm talking about me and Sunny." I motioned toward the resting horse beside me while Jesse's forehead lined. "Yes," I said with exasperation. "Yes, I'm talking about us."

He shrugged. "What do you want to tell them?"

"Nothing yet," I said. "But we'll have to tell them eventually. We're sleeping together, after all."

"That's true. We *are* sleeping together," Jesse said. "I'm not usually that kind of guy."

"That's not what your exes say," I threw back.

His eyes rolled to the sky.

"No, really. In all seriousness, I like you, Jesse." I narrowed my eyes as I concentrated on finding the right words. Expressing myself, *truthfully*, had never come easy. "I don't want to feel like we're going behind your family's backs because I like them, too. But this is all so new to me. So totally different that I just want to take it slow until I figure it out." I almost gave myself a pat on the back for that whole soul-bearing bit.

"Different?" Jesse tilted his head.

Why did he have to ask every darn question I didn't want to answer?

I sucked in a deep breath. "You know . . . The whole

saying nice things to me, buying me gifts, looking after me, asking me on official dates . . . that's all very new to me." I knew how pathetic that sounded—an eighteen-year-old girl who'd "dated" dozens of guys wasn't used to hearing nice things or getting an occasional rose or something—but it was the truth. I wanted to try to be honest with Jesse. It was the only way, if there even was a way, that we would have a fighting chance. "It's going to take some getting used to."

"Is it something you want to get used to?" he asked, almost shyly.

"Yeah," I said, grabbing his hand. "I think it is."

"You look really nice, by the way," he said, examining me with a proud smile.

"You think so?" I gave a quick turn. "This guy I know picked my outfit out."

"He's got great taste." Jesse's eyes wandered to mine again. "*Great* taste."

I tapped my heels together Dorothy-style. "The boots are pretty fantastic, too. And I'm a girl who knows boots."

"Yes, you do," he said before grabbing Sunny's reins and leading him toward the stream. I followed and enjoyed the break in the conversation.

"So, there's this dance . . . thing." Jesse cleared his throat. So much for a break in the conversation. "It's next weekend, and I was thinking . . . Well, I wanted to ask you—"

"Jesse Walker," I said, coming up beside him, "are you asking me to the prom?" I clasped my hands together and batted my lashes.

"From the way my palms are sweating," Jesse wiped his hands off on his jeans, "you'd think I am."

"Well, I'd love to go with you, but I've already got a date."

His expression fell. "You do?"

"Yeah. Your ex-girlfriend," I said, nudging him.

Relief flashed over his face before it was promptly replaced with concern.

"Don't worry. I promise I'll save you a dance. Or two." I wondered if I'd just pulled a line from a classic movie or if people really said that kind of stuff. I didn't know. I'd never been to a dance. The closest I'd ever made it to one was the parking lot of my high school. After that not-so-pleasurable experience, I wrote off all future dances. I didn't want to go to all the trouble of getting dressed up when the only dance my date wanted was in the back seat of his car.

"Or three," Jesse added. "Or *all* of them."

"Greedy," I muttered to Sunny who continued to drink from the stream so deeply you'd think he was trying to drain it.

"Not greedy, just hopelessly optimistic."

"You know the definition of 'hopelessly,' right?" I lifted an eyebrow.

Jesse smiled into the stream and scratched the back of his head. "Well, then how 'bout this? We *have* shared a bed now, like you said. I think that kind of exclusivity goes with dance partners as well."

"Is it a waste of breath if I keep arguing with you?"

"Probably."

I shouldered him. "We'd better get back," I said, "before they miss us and the rumors start flying."

Jesse chuckled. "The rumors were flying the moment you and I were out of earshot." He grabbed my waist, and before the air had whooshed from my mouth, I was perched back on top of Sunny.

"Okay, Muscles," I said, grabbing hold of the saddle horn, "next time you decide to toss me on top of a giant beast, could you give me a moment's warning first?"

Just as quickly, Jesse's body slid into position behind me. He could literally mount and dismount a horse in the blink of an eye. He really was a cowboy.

"Moment's warning before putting you on top of a giant beast?" he repeated, bobbing his head beside mine. "Okay. Done." When his arms came around me to grab hold of the reins, I realized I'd been wrong. Riding behind Jesse wasn't as good as it got. Riding in front of him was. I was cocooned in his hold. Protected. Safe.

It didn't hurt that his legs were basically wrapped around me either.

"I'd loved to stay out here all day and talk, or bicker, or . . ." the inflection in his voice filled in the blanks, "but I've still got another eight hours of work in front of me today."

I threw a longing look at the sandy bank beside the stream. The bittersweet taste of what the day could have been . . .

"Yeah. And I've got about eight hours of egg collecting, porch sweeping, laundry washing, and meatloaf making in front of me."

Jesse made some clicking sound with his mouth, squeezed his legs, and we were off. Sunny seemed to only have two speeds: fast and holy-shit-fast. "Mom's keeping you busy?" Jesse had to holler a bit given the wind cutting over us from Sunny's take-no-prisoners sprint.

"A squirrel in the fall is busy. I'm something else

entirely," I yelled back.

"Ranch life's not exactly what you anticipated?" Jesse's mouth moved just outside my ear. I knew he'd likely done it so we didn't have to keep screaming back and forth, but like so many random exchanges between Jesse and me that were innocent on the surface, it felt oddly intimate. So intimate, my eyelids dropped and my mouth parted for a brief moment.

Then I realized Jesse was waiting for my response, and when I opened my eyes, he was watching me with a bit of amusement. That I didn't flush fire-engine red or become a stuttering idiot was a testament to how much practice I'd had overcoming those kinds of awkward situations. The embarrassment on my end part, not the smokin' hot cowboy staring at me with a melt-your-panties-right-off smile.

"No, it's not what I expected," I answered, twisting my head so I could return the mouth-just-outside-the-ear favor. "It's better."

I couldn't see Jesse's expression from the way my head was turned, but I felt it without having to see it. I felt it in the way his arms tightened around me. I felt it in the way the side of his face pressed into the side of mine. I felt it in the physical, but I felt it in the *something else*, too. In the something deeper that was just below the surface. It was staggering. It was purposeful.

It was a first.

Yet another of the many I'd experienced with Jesse. And the guy's hands and mouth hadn't even wandered into the PG-13 territory yet. That was saying something.

A whole bunch of something.

When Sunny tore up over a gentle hill, the tree, Old

Bessie, and the rest of the guys and their horses came into view. I wasn't exactly thrilled to be back to reality, but my emotions were more focused on those precious few minutes we'd escaped reality. I'd never been the glass-half-full girl, but I seemed in danger of becoming one.

Jesse pulled up on the reins when we were a couple hundred yards back, and Sunny slowed to a walk. Of course, it was a fast walk.

Neil stood in the bed of Old Bessie, closing the cooler back up, and gave us a wave when he saw us coming. No one else seemed all that interested in the two of us. Or else, like Jesse said about the whole rumors firing off the moment we left, they were just feigning disinterest.

Oh, well. Neil didn't seem to care that his son and I had ridden off into the lunchtime sunset, showed up fifteen minutes later with silly smiles on our faces, and Jesse's arms were cinched around me in such a way that wasn't necessary to keep me steady in the saddle.

"Why is it you don't look like a single person in your family?" I said lightly, taking in Neil. Other than the way they dressed, Jesse and he couldn't have looked more different. "Surely there's got to be a reason."

I waited for him to reply with something that had to do with consuming mass quantities of Wheaties or DNA took a day off when Jesse was conceived, but he shrugged. "There's a reason for everything, Rowen."

A person wouldn't have to be especially perceptive to catch the whole flood of meaning beneath Jesse's words. "Why, thank you, Aristotle," I teased. "And now I've seen it all. A cowboy philosopher."

His soft laugh vibrated against my back. "I'm much deeper than I look. I'm not the dumb hick you'd think I'd be."

It was my turn to laugh. "Jesse, I could tell after two words with you that you were not a dumb hick. Not in this life or any of your former or future lives."

"That is the sweetest, most strange compliment I've ever been given." He pulled up on the reins one more time, and Sunny came to a stop. We were back with the others, and I could tell from the sideways looks everyone threw our way that Jesse had been right. He and I just "slipping" away unnoticed had been a whole lot of wishful thinking. Then again, when their employer's son started paying attention to the new girl with a questionable past, I suppose rumors were an expected side effect.

"Jesse," Neil called over, "I need you to head out with Walt and Justin as soon as you get Rowen back on solid ground." Neil gave us both an amused smile. "A few of the cows have already crossed the river and the calves didn't feel so brave. They're making one heck of a raucous and are going to worry themselves into a fit if they don't get to their mamas soon." Neil's smile grew. "I hope you and Sunny weren't planning on staying dry today."

"I learned not to hope to stay wet, dry, hot, or cold a long time ago, Dad," Jesse replied. "I'm on it."

Neil nodded in acknowledgement before leaping out of the truck bed and heading over to his horse.

"You're going to swim the babies over to their moms?" I asked, trying to picture it. I couldn't.

"Well, Sunny's going to swim. I'm going to just throw the calf over my lap, hold on real tight, and hope the current doesn't whisk us away."

My face blanched. Now that, Jesse, Sunny, and some poor baby calf being tossed and rolled under the waves of a raging river, I could imagine.

"I'm just messing with you, Rowen," he said, pinching my side. "The river's deep, but the current's nice and slow. So slow it shouldn't even be called a river. I've done it hundreds of times. It's a piece of cake. There're a few calves every season that need a little help crossing."

"Okay," I said, feeling a little better. But only a little. It still sounded dangerous.

"I've got baby calves to save. So I'd better be on my way." His mouth came dangerously close to my ear again. "As much as I'd rather stay." He pulled back into the safe range when he spoke next. "Just swing your leg over Sunny's neck, and I'll make sure you land upright and not on your backside."

"I won't hold my breath," I said. I swung my left leg over Sunny's neck—thank goodness it was down since he was munching on some grass—and, sure enough, found myself landing on the ground on my feet a moment later. "You're good," I said, turning around.

From the gloat on his face, I guessed he already knew that. "I know my way around a horse."

I looked around before replying. "And me?"

The gloat was gone, but his smile became more pronounced. "I'm learning." Tilting his hat at me, he made that clicking sound again and turned Sunny around.

"Be safe," I called after him. "And don't forget to strap on a life jacket or something."

Even from where he was, I heard his laugh. "Hey, Rowen?" he called back. "Why did the calf cross the river?"

Really? What was next? Knock-knock jokes?

"To get away from you!" I yelled. That earned me a

few curious stares. Well, a few *more*.

Another laugh. That one was accompanied by a shake of his head as he and Sunny broke into a trot.

"What? Because you threw it on your saddle and swam it over? Because of Jesse Walker?" I yelled after him.

Both rider and horse came to a stop. Jesse reined Sunny around. Even from that distance, I saw the flash of intention in Jesse's eyes. It made my stomach drop. "Nope," he replied. "The calf crossed the river because that scared little thing wanted to." Jesse met my stare for another second before whipping around and charging up to the couple of riders ahead of him.

Even after he'd disappeared from view, I stared at the space where he'd been.

Jesse Walker was telling me something I wasn't so sure I was ready to hear.

CHAPTER ten

You can feel some people's presences before you even lay eyes on them. Some of those presences are peaceful and put you at ease. Like Jesse's. And some make you every shade of uncomfortable and disarm you. Like Garth's.

The trouble with me, or *one* of the troubles with me, was that my what-was-good-for-me compass was seriously screwed up. I'd always known that to a certain extent, but only after coming to Willow Springs did I really notice it in a big way. I didn't know what I wanted to do about it, if anything, but I was acknowledging it in a way I hadn't before.

A dark, few-noted chuckle sounded from behind me.

Speaking of presences . . .

"What are you doing still lurking around?" I said, spinning around. "All the guys left a few minutes ago." I hadn't stopped staring at the spot I'd last seen Jesse and Sunny until the man in black interfered.

Garth smiled that dark one of his that would have made me shiver had it been any cooler out. "I'm good at . . . *lurking*," he said in that deep, thick voice. "And yeah, the guys did leave a few minutes ago. One guy left even a few minutes before that." Garth walked toward me, his horse following him. His horse had a dark mane and tail. Like owner, like horse. "But that sure hasn't stopped you from staring at that same spot like you're hoping if you look long enough, Jesse fucking Walker will magically reappear."

My whole body tensed. I hadn't heard such a harsh word delivered in such a spiteful tone in so long that it caught me off guard.

"Where did you come from?" I asked, shoving the cooler farther into the truck bed. The sooner I got into the cab, the sooner I could get away from Garth Black. I still hadn't forgotten what he'd said to me at the rodeo or how he'd said the words with such cruelty. "I didn't see you earlier. Do you just decide to show up for work whenever the hell you please?"

I heard him and his horse move closer. I didn't flinch. I didn't shy away. I knew guys like Garth, people like him. They got off on knowing they intimidated others. I wouldn't give him that pleasure.

"I was here. I've been here all goddamned day, rounding up dumb cows and riding alongside dumber cowboys." I slammed the tailgate closed, and when I turned around, I found Garth not even two feet from me. I came close to squirming, so I crossed my arms and stood my ground. "But I guess it's no big surprise you didn't notice anyone else just now. Because you, my infatuated little girl,"—I bristled at the *little* part. He didn't mean my height.—"had eyes for no one but that golden boy atop his golden steed. Riding off to his golden tower and his golden family."

I rolled my eyes. "And your point to this whole 'golden' story?"

Garth's mouth lifted on one side. "Only that there's

no place for you in it."

My eyebrows came together. Was there no limit to Garth's cruelty?

"People like you, my tainted, deliciously flawed Rowen, are not and never will be anything close to golden."

Nope. There was no limit. The air rushed out of my lungs like he'd just punched me in the stomach. I knew if I stood in front of Garth any longer, he'd see how deep he'd cut me, so I shoved by him and marched for the driver's side door. My as-close-to-perfect-as-I'd-ever-experienced-afternoon had just been shattered by a few cutting words from a sharp-tongued guy. "If that's all you've got for me, I'm going to be on my very not-so-golden way," I snapped back.

"I didn't mean that as an insult, Rowen. I meant that as a compliment." Garth leaned into the side of the truck and ran his eyes down me before doing the same to himself. "From one very un-golden person to another, we will never be known as the ones to take the easy path. We will never be known as the ones to wag our tails and play fetch because that's what the world expects of us. You and me, Rowen,"—he flicked his finger between us—"we're a dying breed."

I wanted to spit nails right through that smug expression of his. He didn't know me any more than I wanted to get to know him. "No, Garth. *You're* a dying breed. And that's only because when you say shit like that to people, they start plotting a way to kill you."

Garth laughed as I fought to get the door open. "What do you think Mr. and Mrs. Walker are going to say when you and Jesse tell them you two have become a hot little item?"

Garth waited for me to respond. I had nothing to say because I didn't know. What would they say? I couldn't be sure. They were good people, but I'd be lying if I said I didn't have my doubts they might squirm in their accepting seats when they found out about Jesse and me.

"You think they're just going to smile and give you their blessing when they find out their precious son is dating the ranch freak?"

There was that word again. I'd heard it hundreds of times, and it had rolled off my back for the most part, but there on Willow Springs Ranch, where all my defense layers melted away, it sliced me in such a way I knew would leave a permanent scar.

"You think they're going to one day let him give you his great-grandmother's ring? A girl who's no doubt been in the back seat of so many cars The Guinness Book of World Records is leaving her messages?"

My fists balled. My eyes welled. I was angry. I was sad. I couldn't decide what I was more of, so I just stood there, silent and motionless.

"In case you never read the fairy tales when you were a little girl, here's a quick recap," he continued on. "The prince rides off into the sunset with the princess. Not the witch. In fact, the witch usually dies at the hands of the prince. In case you're wondering who you are in the fairy tale," Garth tilted his head and slid his thumbs under his belt buckle, "you're as much the princess as I am the prince."

My anger responded. "You're an asshole, Black," I snapped, glaring daggers at him.

He lifted a shoulder. "I am an asshole. But at least

I've accepted that about myself. I used to hate knowing I'd never end up with the princess. But now I've accepted it." His eyes went darker. "Once you accept who you are, Rowen, the pain will stop. I can guarantee that. Once you accept the Jesse Walkers of the world weren't meant for you, you'll be free." Why was I just standing there, letting him say those things to me? Why wasn't I arguing with him? "They pity us, when really, we should be pitying them. They live in a state of disillusionment. They live the lie, and what's worse, they don't want to find the truth when they realize they've been living a lie." A corner of his mouth curled into a menacing smile. "They're sheep, Rowen."

My silence finally came to an end. "What? And we're the shepherds?"

"No," Garth's smile twisted higher, "we're the *wolves*."

The hot summer day didn't matter—a chill ran down my back.

Jumping inside the truck, I fumbled to get the key into the ignition. "You know, Garth, just because your life sucks doesn't mean you have to take it out on everyone else."

"And just because your life sucks doesn't mean you *shouldn't* take it out on everyone else," he replied back in a cool voice. Maybe he had more to add, maybe he didn't, but the instant the engine fired to life, I slammed the door and hit the gas. I needed to leave Garth Black in the rearview.

By the time I pulled back into the driveway outside of the Walkers' house, I'd managed to calm myself down. At least half a notch. Garth had gotten under my skin. I wasn't sure what was more disturbing: that he'd gotten under it or that he'd known just what to say to get there. He'd somehow seen through my walls and knew my insecurities. He'd known just what to say to play upon my weaknesses. He knew that the core of my doubts when it came to Jesse and me was that I didn't deserve him. That I was the lack to his luster. That I was the coal to his diamond. That I was the nothing special to his everything special.

So I didn't deserve Jesse. That wasn't exactly a revelation. The revelation was in the light bulb going off that I never would. No matter what I did in the future, nothing could erase my past. Nothing could wash away the filth and dirt of my life before him. It was, to date, the most depressing thought I'd had.

For a girl who used to eat depression for breakfast, lunch, and dinner, that was saying something.

Rose waved at me from her flower garden while I sat in Jesse's truck contemplating what was next. What would tomorrow bring? Could I continue with Jesse for a while longer? How much longer? The end of the month? The end of the summer? How long could I keep the truth buried? How long before he woke up and saw it?

Those were crippling questions. Every last one of them. Questions I didn't want to think about and, what was more, questions I didn't want to have.

When I kept sitting in the car, Rose wove her way out of her flowers, closed the cyclone fence to keep all the wild animals from munching away on her garden, and headed my way.

Rose was just as perceptive as Jesse, and right then, I didn't want to be around anyone perceptive. I didn't want to give anyone a peek into my world.

So I rolled my shoulders back, wiped my expression clean, and shoved the door open.

"Did you find the guys okay?" Rose asked as she stopped outside the truck. She had her red hat on and carried a basket of bright, large-blossomed flowers. From where I stood, each one looked perfect. Everything around there, even the flowers, was on a perfect level I could only dream of.

I had to roll my shoulders back again. "The cooler's empty," I said, hitching my thumb over my shoulder. "So either I found the guys or ran into a pack of hungry bears."

Rose smiled. "Around these parts, they're one and the same, sweetie."

I swung around to the truck bed to pull the cooler out. Rose set down her basket of flowers and came over to help.

"Josie Gibson stopped by while you were gone." Rose grabbed hold of a handle on the cooler once I'd dropped the tailgate.

"Josie Gibson?" I said. "As in . . ." How did I put it? The drop-dead girl I'd love to hate but couldn't? The girl with a heart as big as the monster truck she drove? The Mother Teresa who gave me a ride home and practically begged me to hang out with her sometime? Or the girl who was—

"Jesse's ex-girlfriend?" Rose filled in.

Yep. That was the one.

I nodded once. "I met her at the rodeo but didn't catch her last name."

"That's the one. And she's a Gibson all right," Rose said as we carried the cooler up onto the back porch and settled it against the wall. "Those Gibsons have lived around these parts for so long, I'm not sure which came first—the Gibsons or Montana's statehood." She dropped into one of the porch swings, chuckling to herself. "When Jesse and her started getting pretty serious, I began to worry if they ever got married, she'd make him take her name instead of the other way around."

My stomach twisted over a few points in that inform-ation dump. *Pretty serious* and *married* being the big ones. I dropped into the rocking chair across from her and folded my arms over my stomach.

"Anyways," Rose waved her hand, "she stopped by to see you. She mentioned she'd somehow convinced you to go to the big ol' honky tonk next weekend and was just double checking to make sure you hadn't gotten cold feet."

"I doubt even if I tried to back out, Josie would let me," I replied, wondering why she'd showed up in person. There was a great invention, only about two hundred years old, known as the *telephone* she could have used. But I knew why she'd stopped by. Why she'd probably wasted fifty gallons of gas in that gas-chugging machine of hers to drive from her place to this place.

It was because she was driving to *his* place.

I wasn't a fool. Josie might have been the nicest girl I'd ever met, but she was still a young woman. That meant she was the most saint-like of sinners.

Jesse had been hers for a couple of years. I'd only spent a couple of weeks with him, and I knew he wasn't the type of guy a girl got over. He was the type of guy a girl spent her whole life asking herself, *What if?* He was the type of guy a woman thought about when she sat across the dinner table from her second husband.

All drama aside, Jesse was the guy a girl didn't get over. End of story. Truest story ever told.

I knew because I felt the same. I'd never get over Jesse Walker.

"You're probably right. Josie doesn't take no for an answer too often." Rose's expression changed. It eclipsed from carefree to worried. I'd rarely seen that shift on her face. "That's why I was so surprised when she took a no from Jesse when she tried to get back together with him. She didn't push back. She didn't fight. She didn't plead her case. She just . . . let him go." Rose's forehead lined as she studied the planks of the porch, like perhaps, within their cracks and crevasses, she could find the answers. "I don't know what happened between those two, lord knows Jesse's lips are sealed, but you don't go from all but walking down the aisle to not even wanting to say each other's name without something pretty big happening."

What happened between Jesse and Josie seemed to be the million dollar question. No one seemed to know.

"I tried to be strong for Jesse after they broke up. Even though he tried not to show how much he was hurting, I could tell. A mother always knows when one of her babies is in pain." I bit my tongue and kept my opinions on the matter to myself. "But I think my heart was just about as broken as his." Rose gave a sad smile and sniffled. "I was so sure Josie was going to be my daughter-in-law one day, I'd started treating her like a daughter without even realizing it."

"You miss her," I said. It was obvious from Rose's expression that she did.

"I do. I did a lot when they first broke up, but time, like anything, eases the hurt," Rose said, grabbing hold of the swing's armrest. "What I find I miss the most now, though, is the reassurance of knowing my baby had found himself a good person to spend his life with. When he was with Josie, I knew he'd be well taken care of and loved. At the end of the day, that's all a mother can ask for when her little birdies leave the nest." Rose exhaled slowly through her nose. "That they'll find another nest as loving and warm as the one they flew from."

My eyes closed. My heart dropped. My shoulders sagged.

I knew Rose wasn't saying any of that to hurt me—she didn't have a clue how I felt about Jesse—but her speech, coming hot on the heels of Garth's speech, was the tipping point. That last wooden block slid out of the tower and made it crumble.

I'd been living a dream. I'd gotten lost inside of it and mistaken it for reality.

And I'd just woken up.

I stood and found my legs were stronger than I would have thought. I guessed after waking up, I could accept my fate bravely. "Rose? Would you mind if I took the rest of the day off?"

Her face flickered with concern.

"I've had this nasty headache all day I can't seem to shake," I said, drilling my finger into my temple. The real pain ran a couple feet lower. "I'm just going to find a quiet place to park it under a tree and hope some fresh air and rest does the trick." I hated lying to Rose. I hated lying to her more than I'd hated lying to anyone else, but it had to be done. I couldn't make it another nine hours of holding myself together. She'd see right through my act, or I'd lose it in front of her, and I didn't want her to know about Jesse and me. I didn't want her to ever know. I didn't want to give her a reason to be ashamed of her son and awkward around me.

"Did you take some pain reliever, honey?" she asked, rising from the swing.

"Only about a hundred," I exaggerated, "but this thing's beyond medicine right now."

"You poor thing," she said, looking like she wanted to wrap me up in a giant hug. "Of course. Take the rest of the day off and just give a holler if you need anything."

Guilt made its debut when I saw how quickly she'd agreed. How easily I'd pulled the wool over her eyes. "Are you sure you and the girls will be all right? I can check back in around dinner time to see if you need a hand."

"Please," she said, waving me off, "the girls and I have been cooking meatloaf for so long we could do it in our sleep. Go find yourself a shade tree and get some rest." She pointed at the old trunk on the porch where she kept pillows and blankets. "Grab a blanket and pillow, and I'll check in on you later."

"Thanks," I said as I opened the trunk and grabbed the first blanket.

"You've got your phone with you?"

I patted my back pocket. "For your checking-in-on-me pleasure."

Rose shook her head. "Go get some rest, silly girl. You must have a headache. Your humor is off this afternoon."

I flashed Rose a wave before heading down the porch steps and bee lining for the field. My lungs weren't working right. Not since Garth's, and Rose's, words. I felt like I could barely fill them halfway up. I had a theory: the farther I got from Willow Springs, the better I could breathe again.

After hoofing it through a field of grass up past my shoulders for more than a half hour, I realized my theory was wrong. It didn't matter how far I got or how fast I walked. I still couldn't breathe quite right. My heart felt like it was shriveling to the size of a raisin, and my head felt like it might explode from everything running through it.

After another fifteen minutes of traipsing around some nameless field, I practically stumbled into something anything but organic. It was an old trailer, and *old* was putting it generously. It was basically a rat-infested looking, once-upon-a-time human dwelling so rusted out it made Old Bessie look shiny and new. More windows were covered by plastic sheeting than actual glass, and the front door—or was it the back?—looked as if a gentle breeze would blow right off its hinges.

Sweet pad.

Not.

Other than a run-down pickup that looked like it hadn't been started since Clinton was president, the place gave no indication any humans had ever lived there. Even in the trailer's prime, imagining people living in it was hard. It was so far gone, imagining it had been anything useful in its past was hard.

I tip-toed away until I realized I was tip-toeing when no one was around to hear me. After that, I continued to step away, but I didn't turn my back until the trailer was out of sight. It wasn't the kind of place a person turned their back on.

After I'd put a safe distance between me and the

trailer, I spread the blanket under the next closest tree, turned my phone off because I didn't want anyone checking up on me, laid down, and was lights out a few heartbeats later.

THERE WAS NOTHING quite like being woken up by the toe of a shoe tapping against your shoulder. It had happened to me a handful of times, and I remembered each one. I recalled each shoe that had nudged me awake since kneeling down and using a hand was apparently just too much work. That time, it wasn't a loafer, or a wedge, or a sneaker. It was a boot. A black one.

I groaned before I looked at the boot's owner. When I did, my groan deepened.

"What are you doing lurking around here?" Even in the dark, I made out Garth's twisted smile.

"You know me." I shoved his boot away and sat up. Stiff, stiff, and more stiff. "I'm good at lurking." I grabbed the corners of the blanket and wrapped it around my shoulders. If it was dark and cool enough to need a blanket, it was late.

That meant Rose was probably worried sick. That meant Jesse probably was, too. Jesse . . .

The reminders flooded my mind as the sleep cleared from it. I had no future with Jesse. In both the immediate and distant sense.

The pain had been bad that afternoon, but something about the night and being so close to the anti-Jesse brought on something else entirely. I almost reached for my chest, half-expecting to find the handle of a dagger protruding from it.

"What are you doing out here?" I asked, trying to distract myself. I didn't care. Not really. Some girls might freak out if a creeper like Garth Black stumbled upon them late at night in the middle of some random field, but I wasn't. I'd been around enough real creepers to know the difference. Garth was a creeper, make no mistake about it, but a harmless one.

Harmless save for the nasty comments he wielded like a damn samurai sword.

"I live here," he said, like it should have been obvious.

My eyebrows knitted together.

"What? Did you flatter yourself by thinking I'd come looking for you?"

I didn't like the way he looked down at me, so I stood and tucked the blanket tighter around me. "Of all the people who'd come searching for me if I needed to be found, your name wouldn't be anywhere on that list. Least of all *first* on that list."

Garth couldn't have looked anymore unfazed. "And who'd be first on that list?" From the curl of his smile alone, I knew who he would name before he did it. "Jesse? Your precious, infallible, ivory tower Jesse Walker, eh?" Garth extended his arms and did one slow turn. "Well, I hate to tell ya, honey, but that white knight of yours isn't here. He wasn't the one to come find you when you got yourself lost." His dark eyes shone. "Looks like you're stuck with me."

I glowered at him as hard as I'd ever glowered at anyone. "I. Am. Not. Lost."

Still the unfazed expression. I wanted to smack it right off of his face. "Rowen, you're so damn lost you've forgotten how you got there in the first place. It's just become who you are. Rowen the Lost."

Before I knew what I was doing, I shoved him. Hard. So hard he fell back a step. But even at that, he didn't look any more concerned than if he were dealing with a litter of mewing kittens.

"I'm not lost!" I balled my fists at my sides. "You are, you dickhead! You're the lost one—not me!"

"Yes," he said in a calm voice, "yes, I am. And so are you."

Giving him another shove for good measure, I spun around and marched away.

"I hate you!" I yelled over my shoulder, heading into a night so dark, I wasn't sure I could make my way back home.

Home . . .

Willow Springs wasn't my home. It was a mirage of one. A carrot dangled in front of me. A dream I'd let myself dream and one that would never be realized.

When Garth's next words came, I felt the first tear about to form in the corner of my eye. "You want a drink?"

I came to a stop. Sniffing, I turned slowly. "No," I said, the volume long gone from my voice. "I *need* one."

Garth inclined his head. "Me, too. And I hate to drink alone. Reminds me too much of my dad." He waited for me to cross the distance between us before adding, "Let's go drown our sorrows before we have to wake up and get back to our shitty lives."

Drinking alone with a guy like Garth Black wasn't the smartest thing to do. I knew that. Hell, I'd *lived* that. But right then, with the way I felt and the pain I wanted to forget, I just didn't care. I'd gone through a long period of turning to guys to make me forget, to temporarily ease the pain and sell me the illusion of being wanted and loved. The past couple years, I leaned more toward drowning the pain out with a bottle. Or I had, pre-Willow Springs. I hadn't had one drop of alcohol since arriving . . . but that was about to change.

I followed Garth for a few minutes. Long enough to wonder if he was leading me into the middle of nowhere. Until I remembered "middle of nowhere" was where I'd been since I'd stepped off of the bus. After another minute, Garth came to a halt. Sweeping his hand ceremoniously in front of him, he said, "Home sweet home."

Oh. My. God.

The trailer that made a person itch just by looking at it? Yeah, that was what we were standing in front of.

"Um . . ."

"Don't worry. I know what you're thinking." Garth moved around to the side where a couple of lounge chairs in the same ruin as the trailer were. "How can I live with myself living in the lap of luxury when there are little children dying of starvation."

I glanced over at Garth curiously. Was that a joke that had just slipped out of his cryptic mouth? Was that a bit of snark where I'd been so certain none could reside?

I didn't know how to respond to his unexpected slip of humor, so I stayed silent. After sweeping off the debris on one of the rundown chairs, he loped toward the trailer. "I'll be right back with whatever I can find that's the strongest."

I almost replied, *Don't touch anything,* but thought better of it. If that was Garth's home . . . well, that *was* his home. I wouldn't step a foot inside of it, ever, but that didn't mean I had to knock it.

A couple of windows had a bit of flashing light streaming from them, like maybe a TV was playing inside. I was just settling—*carefully*—into the lounge chair when I heard a couple of raised voices. So Garth didn't live alone and, judging from the deep voices, he lived with another man. A brother, maybe? A father?

Whoever else shared the dilapidated trailer with him, one thing was clear: they weren't on good terms at the moment. I couldn't make out individual words, just lots of shouting and curses thrown back and forth, but I was familiar with that "conversation." My mom and I had it at least once a week since I'd been brave enough to stand up to her.

When I heard the familiar sound of glass shattering, I popped up in my chair. I was about to break a solemn vow and actually enter that rust bucket when Garth practically lunged out of the door. What looked like a bottle exploded into tiny pieces behind him when it crashed into the doorway instead of . . . *his head*?

Garth glared at the ground for a couple seconds as he continued toward me, a bottle clutched in his hand, but when he lifted his face, his expression was almost as unfazed as it had been when I'd been the one yelling at him.

"What the hell was that?" I asked. I knew, as someone who'd dealt with it, if a person was within hearing or seeing distance, we hoped to hell they'd just keep their mouth shut and pretend they hadn't witnessed a thing. However, being on the other side of the equation, I understood why so many people couldn't stay silent.

"Well, let's see," Garth said as he stopped in front of me. "It's a weekday night, past ten o'clock, and all the liquor except for my secret stash"—he lifted the bottle—"ran out an hour ago. So that means he's still drunk enough to be pissed but not quite drunk enough to be passed out yet."

I jumped when I heard another breaking sound. "Who?" I asked, wondering if being within the same county line as that person, let alone their backyard, was safe.

Garth's expression ironed out. "My dad." His words were like ice again, and from that look on his face, I guessed he really did need that drink as badly as I did. "So? Bottoms up?" He shook the bottle in front of me, and even though I knew I shouldn't, I couldn't say no.

Not when relief from the pain was a few inches and drinks away.

"Bottoms up." I took the bottle from him and unscrewed the lid. "Tequila?" Judging from the label, it was cheap tequila.

"To-kill-ya?" Garth said as he dropped into one of the chairs. "Yep."

Since there weren't any cups to be found, I lifted the bottle straight to my lips. "Why do I have a feeling I'm going to regret this in the morning?"

"Because you will," he said as he slid his hat off and dropped it on the ground. Seeing those guys without their hats was always strange, at least when they weren't sitting around the Walker dining room table. "Me, however? I won't."

"You strike me as the kind of guy who doesn't regret much," I said before tipping the bottle back. Cool liquid entered my mouth and ran hot down my throat. I hadn't had a straight shot of alcohol in so long I almost made the pucker face and coughed, but I held it back. I passed the bottle to Garth.

"I don't," he replied, taking his own heavy swig. "And you shouldn't either." Garth kicked his legs up onto the lounge chair and stared at the stars. He took another drink before passing the bottle back.

"Regret's one of the few things I'm good at," I said, taking a shot-sized drink. "I'm not giving that up."

Yikes. The tequila was already getting to me. That's the only reason I'd let those vulnerable words slip through my mouth. I didn't like being vulnerable, but I *hated* seeming vulnerable in front of guys like Garth Black.

Time to change the conversation.

"So what's up with you and your dad? Always been this dysfunctional or did you recently decide to jump on that bandwagon?" I handed the bottle off to Garth. Too much, too fast, as my words proved.

Garth's eyes narrowed at the sky. "I don't want to talk about my past any more than you want to talk about yours," he said before taking a drink. Actually, it was more of a chug. "Don't ask me questions about my family unless you want me asking you the same ones about yours."

That got my attention.

"Like I said before, Rowen, you and me are so alike, if I had tits and got my head stuck in the clouds every now and again, I'd be you. And if you had a dick and were a bit meaner, you'd be me." Garth took another drink before passing me the bottle. It was halfway empty. That probably explained why the stars were swirling above my head.

"So." Just the way he said it, I was already wincing before he said anything else. "I take it, since I found you curled up asleep and alone a good couple miles from Willow Springs, that you took my Jesse warning to heart."

It wasn't a question. He knew I had.

The tequila had dulled the blow of hearing his name, but it hadn't made me immune. I knew it wouldn't matter if ten years down the road, I heard that name as I passed a stranger on the street. I would never be able to hear the name Jesse again without thinking about him.

"You don't want to talk about your dad, great. I don't want to talk about Jesse." When I took another drink, the tequila didn't burn. In fact, it drank more like water than alcohol. I'd experienced that enough times to know I was a few more drinks away from passing out. So I took one more drink and handed it back to Garth. I was officially cutting myself off.

"We can't talk about our families. We can't talk about our pasts. And we can't talk about Jesse, or I'm guessing any of the Walkers." He looked at me and waited. Like he was waiting for me to agree.

So I lifted my eyebrows and gave him a *Your point?* look.

"Then what will we talk about?" He seemed amused with himself. Or with me. Or with the situation. I couldn't tell, and the alcohol only made deciphering emotions more difficult.

"Why don't we just not talk?" I suggested. Partly because I didn't feel like talking, and partly because I was nearing the point where speech would be difficult. At least non-slurred speech. I burrowed down deeper in the chair and my blanket, closed my eyes, and let the alcohol do its job.

"That's my favorite kind of conversation to have," he replied, sounding like he was shifting in his seat.

So we agreed on something at last. "Mine, too," I said right before the haze took me over, and either I fell asleep or I passed out.

Whichever it was, I was pulled back to the surface when a hand molded over my cheek. The hand was warm, and rough, and strong. Another hand wove through my hair before a pair of lips settled just below my ear, at the pinnacle of my neck. The hands holding my head in place curled deeper when that mouth started traveling down my neck. When it stopped at the base and gently sucked at the sensitive skin, I moaned. The touch was familiar, yet foreign. The urgency in the touch, the gentle strength in the hands were familiar. The stubble I felt scratching against my neck and the spicy scent were foreign.

When that mouth made its return journey back up my neck, I arched for it to come closer and practically trembled when his tongue tasted my skin.

"Jesse . . ." I whispered, trying to push through the haze. I wanted to touch him back with the same kind of precision. I wanted to feel him, but my hands were numb and could barely function.

What happened next, I didn't expect. The hands and mouth pulled back as though I'd shocked them before I felt the whoosh of a body whisking away. Right before I fell back into my stupor, I heard what sounded like another bottle breaking against something.

CHAPTER eleven

I fell asleep to the sound of breaking glass and woke up to the sound of raised voices. They weren't really raised. They were more like exploding.

"Didn't expect to see you around this place ever again, Walker. Were you in the mood for slumming it?"

"So help me God, Garth! If you touched her . . . If you did *anything* to her, I will finish what I should have months ago."

I knew the voices were Jesse and Garth, and I could tell they were behind me, but I was incapable of anything else. I couldn't open my eyes, I couldn't open my mouth, and I certainly couldn't get up and go break up the on-the-horizon fight.

I was somewhat aware but totally immobile. The alcohol had been especially potent after my month of sobriety.

"You were a lot more fun to be around when you didn't treat me like I was some bottom feeder preying on girls. I've never touched anyone without them wanting it, asking for it, or in a case you're aware of . . . begging for it."

"You son of a bitch!" I heard some shuffling and a dull crack that sounded like a fist connecting with flesh and bone.

Garth's throaty laugh sounded next. "I like this whole anger thing you've got going on. You were boring when all you ever did was smile and play the part of Mr. Perfect."

I heard Jesse take a few slow breaths before replying. "What is Rowen doing here?"

"She came to see me. She wanted to shoot the shit with someone who wouldn't put her to sleep after thirty seconds of conversation."

Jesse made some sort of noise between a huff and a snort.

"I know it must blow your mind that a girl would prefer me to you, but it wouldn't exactly be the first time. Would it?" Garth's voice was cool and removed.

I knew it was coming before I heard the next crack. Garth chuckled again before spitting. Jesse must have nailed him in the jaw.

"Stay away from Rowen. And stay away from me." Jesse's voice quivered with emotion.

"I have no problem staying away from her. She's nothing but your regular, dime-per-dozen girl, but I can't promise she'll stay away from me." After a long pause, I heard footsteps heading up a couple metal stairs. "Oh, and one more thing," Garth said, his tone so overly innocent it sounded just the opposite. "If this trailer's arockin', don't come aknockin'. Oh wait, you already know that, don't you?" Another dark laugh sounded before a door screech-ed closed.

So much silence passed, I was almost passed out again when I heard a pair of footsteps shuffling my way. A moment later, two muscled arms glided beneath my body and lifted me out of the chair.

Jesse didn't say a word and I still couldn't, but even if I could have, I didn't know what to say. I was drunk. I'd messed up. Jesse had been the one to find me eyeballs deep in both. It was what needed to happen. He needed to see who I was because that made everything easier. I could only push him away for so long before I caved, but after he saw what I was, I didn't have to worry. His dimples wouldn't be waiting for me at the kitchen table anymore.

That was what I did. That was how I protected my-self. I pushed others away before they could do it to me. It was a self-preservation default, but as I nestled into Jesse's arms for the last time, I knew pushing him away was the opposite of self-preservation.

CHAPTER twelve

There are headaches. And then there's what I awoke to the next morning.

I was in my bed, and even though the curtains were drawn, the line of sunlight streaming through the middle made my head throb when I opened my eyes. I didn't know what time it was, I didn't know what *day* it was, but I knew I needed water and ibuprofen. STAT.

After prying myself up, I swung my legs over the edge of my bed. The motion hurt so badly, my stomach churned. I wasn't sure I could make it over to the waste-basket in time if my stomach decided to unleash on me.

My boots and socks were off, and on the nightstand was a tall glass of water, three brownish, round pills, and a note with my name penned across the front. I went for the water and pills first, guessing I'd need them inside of me before I read whatever was inside of that note.

I couldn't remember what had happened last night; I just remembered bits and pieces. Images, words, sensations. Garth's dark eyes, Jesse's heated voice, the burn of tequila trickling down my throat, stubble brushing across my neck.

Stubble . . .

Oh, shit.

One of the two men from last night always had a five

o'clock shadow. Another one's face was smooth as smooth could be. The one whose mouth had been on me last night was not the one I'd thought.

My stomach rolled again.

I tossed the pills into my mouth and swallowed them with a long drink of water. The coolness felt so good running down my throat, I finished the entire glass.

After dropping the glass back onto the nightstand, I went for the note. Jesse's handwriting made me eager to read it, but after last night and the piecemeal memories I had from it, I was just as apprehensive.

Before I over thought it for one more second, I unfolded the note and read. I didn't take long to finish. The note was short, concise, and heartbreaking.

What's up?

Damn. I almost would have preferred a novel's worth of rantings and ravings. What was up with me? I'd avoided that question most of my life. I knew the answers to that question, but I preferred to repress them because, really, the answers didn't heal anything. They couldn't erase the past. So what was the point of searching for the answers in the first place?

And why the hell was I still thinking about it?

I shoved the note inside of the nightstand drawer.

As I was deciding if I should just throw the blankets back over my head and forget about the world, or get up and get to it, a soft knock sounded on my door.

"Come in," I said a bit too loudly. I applied pressure at my temples and squeezed my eyes closed. "Come in," I whispered.

The door opened noiselessly—small mercies—and Lily slipped in carrying a tray. She smiled and headed my way.

"Hey, Lily," I whispered.

She set the tray down on the nightstand and whispered a quick *Hi* back.

"What's this?" I inspected the tray and sniffed the air.

"Breakfast," Lily replied so quietly I barely heard her.

I could see that. It wasn't what I usually went for, but that morning, it looked just right: a pile of thick-cut bacon, scrambled eggs coated in melted cheese, and a thick piece of bread with two large pats of butter melting on it. My usual breakfast consisted of oatmeal and fruit . . . Heart disease, you know? But I couldn't get a piece of bacon in my mouth quickly enough.

"Thank you, Lily," I said in between bites. I already felt the grease doing its work in my stomach. "You don't have any idea how much better I feel already." I didn't feel the need to get into the nitty-gritty of excessive alcohol use and its morning after effects with a sixteen-year-old who, I would bet a million bucks, had never drank a single drop of it.

"Jesse said it would help," she whispered just a hair louder so I didn't have to strain to hear her.

I stopped chewing. "Jesse told you to make this for me?"

Lily shook her head. "No, he made it. He just asked me to carry it up."

I dropped the remaining bit of bacon back on the plate. He'd come looking for me, carried me home in his arms—in his arms for *two* miles—tucked me into bed, left some water and ibuprofen on my nightstand, and had made me a greasy breakfast to ease my hangover suffering. I'd been so sure people like Jesse Walker didn't exist in real life. I'd been so, so sure.

I'd been wrong.

If I'd been wrong about that, what else had I been wrong about? Add that question to the mountain of others I wasn't ready to answer.

"Why didn't he bring it up himself?" I focused on the plate of food, a random act of kindness, and my vision started getting blurry.

"He and some of the guys are heading out for a week to keep a close watch on the cattle now that they've been moved higher up and farther away. They're always a bit finicky when they get to a new pasture, so some of the guys set up camp for the first week or so."

"Oh." I shifted on the bed. Note to self: don't wear tight jeans to bed. "When's he leaving?" I wasn't sure if he was ready to see me yet, or if I was ready to see him, but if he would be gone for a week, something needed to be said.

"He's already gone," Lily replied, lifting a shoulder. "He wasn't really himself this morning. He was . . . grumpy almost. He couldn't seem to get out of here soon enough."

I didn't need twenty guesses to know why Jesse couldn't get away soon enough. So he was upset, but not so much that it had stopped him from making me breakfast. I'd hurt him, but not so much he hadn't stopped himself from leaving water and pills on my nightstand. So much about the situation wasn't making sense.

The longer I thought about it, the more my head hurt, so I shelved the whole working-it-all-out thing and grabbed the buttered toast. "What time is it?" My phone was over on the charger, which meant Jesse had done that, too.

"Time for you to go back to bed and get some rest," Lily replied, sounding so much like Rose I checked the door to make sure she hadn't joined us. "Mom's orders."

Rose . . . I hadn't come home last night. I'd turned my phone off so no one could get ahold of me. Why wasn't she in there shouting at me I was grounded for the rest of the summer?

"Is everyone . . ." I swallowed and looked down into my lap. "Disappointed with me?" I didn't know why I bothered asking rhetorical questions, but I couldn't seem to kick the habit.

"Why would anyone be disappointed with you?" she asked, giving me an odd look. "Jesse told us you'd fallen asleep out in one of the fields and couldn't seem to shake that headache you told mom you had yesterday. It's a good thing he found you before it got too late. You wouldn't believe how many field mice are out there." Lily shudder-ed like one was scurrying down her back. "And don't get me started about the garter and bull snakes slithering around out there eating those mice." When she shuddered again, it was more of a violent shake.

A tongue gliding up my neck flashed to my mind. It was my turn to shake. "I think I might have run into one of those snakes." I popped the last bite of toast into my mouth. The grease and fat was doing its job, and the water and medicine was starting to work its way into my veins. I felt tired. Exhausted, really.

A guilty conscience had a way of tiring out a person. Jesse had covered for me. Lied to his family for me. Because I'd messed up the way I'd been born to do.

Dammit. The day couldn't get any worse, and I'd only woken up five minutes earlier.

"Thanks for breakfast, Lily," I said, burrowing back down into my blankets. "If you're sure it's all right with everyone, I think I will rest for a little while longer."

"That must be one nasty headache, Rowen," she said gently before heading toward the door.

"It's a nasty one, all right." I threw the covers over my head and tried to shut out the world.

CHAPTER thirteen

That next week, I tried not to think about Jesse, which was another way of saying I failed at not thinking about Jesse.

When I emerged from my monster "headache," no one asked me any questions or suspected anything. Rose gave me a hug, said she was glad I felt better, and we got on with the day. It was such an odd concept to me: being trusted. People in my life just assumed that when I opened my mouth, a lie was about to come out. My mom had been the first one to take away the trust card, followed by teachers, counselors, friends . . . you name it. Most people in the past five years had found some reason to not trust me.

I wasn't saying I was blameless in the whole denial of trust thing. Plenty of people had plenty of reasons to distrust me. What I'd grown tired of was everyone automatically assuming that because I'd done it before, I'd do it all the time. When people started expecting everything coming out of your mouth to be a lie, you just stopped trying.

But that's not the way it was at Willow Springs. I was given the benefit of the doubt. I wasn't labeled a liar because I'd been caught telling one. I wasn't labeled a good many of the names I'd been called before. I was given a fresh start.

Maybe that's why I made a vow to never tell another lie to another Walker. Or let one Walker lie to another Walker because of me. I wouldn't repay their faith in me by disappointing them.

I didn't know what the end of summer would bring, or what the kids at my new school would think of me when I showed up, but at Willow Springs, I was Rowen Sterling. Nothing else.

In one week's time, I'd kept that vow. I hadn't lied once to any of the Walkers, although I'd come close. Instead of answering Rose when she asked if I knew why Jesse had been so out of sorts the morning he'd left, I'd pretended my cell phone had just rung and dodged out the back door to take my imaginary call. Honesty through omission. It wasn't the best case scenario, but it was a far cry from the worst.

Between chores and sleep, I spent my free time drawing. Anything. And everything. Rose's hands as she kneaded bread dough in the morning, the hat wall beside the dining table, the girls picking strawberries, hell, I even sketched Old Bessie . . . I drew it all, but mostly, I drew Jesse. I never meant to, but halfway into my sketch, I'd realize his eyes were shining back at me, and even if I'd wanted to, I couldn't scrap it and start again. So I finished those sketches, and then I had a book full of Jesse. It made the week without him pass a little faster.

It was Saturday night, and I was anxious about that for several reasons. One, because it was the night of the big dance and barbecue everyone had been talking about nonstop. Two, because it was the night Jesse was scheduled to come home. And three, because I didn't want

Rose to freak out when she saw what I'd done to her three daughters who were the very definition of natural beauty.

We'd been stowed away in Lily's room for a couple of hours, spraying, swiping, and curling the heck out of each other. Well, I'd been doing the spraying, swiping, and curling. The girls, except for Clementine, had managed to sit still and endure it.

"Curly or straight?" I asked Lily once I finished powdering her nose and highlighting her brow bone.

Lily made a face as she considered it, trying not to smear her pale pink lipstick. She looked older but not offensively so. When Lily mentioned that morning she wasn't super excited to go to the dance, I of course asked her why. She said she felt ordinary and overlooked whenever she went to one of those things. She said she didn't feel like she fit in. After giving her a hug and telling her she should have her head examined, I suggested we turn her bedroom into a makeshift salon so I could give her a few makeup and hair tips.

Once Hyacinth and Clementine saw what we were up to, they refused to be left out. Clementine was easy, except for her bouncing around like a rabbit on speed. I curled her hair and let her slick on a coat of lip balm. Done. Hyacinth was a teenager, but just barely, so after doing her hair, I let her talk me into some mascara and lip gloss and prayed Rose or Neil wouldn't skin me.

Since Lily was sixteen, I took a little more time with her eyes and added a touch of blush. I found myself chuckling a few times as I anguished over using a light hand with the girls' makeup. I usually used the opposite with my own makeup.

Lily's face flattened as she finally made up her mind.

"Curly."

I almost sighed. The Walker girls had some long, thick hair that took forever to curl.

"Rowen!" Clementine called to me as I grabbed the curling iron. "Will you put some of that eyeliner stuff on me, too?"

"I most certainly will not," I replied as I wrapped the first chunk of Lily's hair around the iron. "If you keep bouncing like that, those curls are going to bounce right out of your hair." I tried to give her a stern look as she bounced on the end of Lily's bed, but it didn't work. Staring sternly at a little girl with perfect little ringlets bouncing up and down in a dress that was five sizes too big for her was impossible.

Her bouncing stopped immediately as she patted her hair to make sure those curls were still in place. "Lily!" We were less than ten feet away, but Clementine was big into shouting. "Can I pick out another dress to try on?"

Lily sighed. "Yes, just not the one I'm wearing tonight."

"Yippee!" Clementine dive-bombed from the bed and rushed toward Lily's closet where Hyacinth was looking for her own dress.

"Okay, I could smell the hairspray fumes and burning hair from the porch." The door swung open and in stepped someone I hadn't expected to see right that minute. The curling iron almost slipped from my hands.

"Jesse!" Clementine went from running to the closet to sprinting toward her brother. She tripped on the dress right as she made it to him, but he caught her before she crashed and burned.

After giving her a quick hug and greeting his other

sisters, his eyes shifted to me. Everything about him seemed hesitant, unsure. I knew I mirrored the feeling.

"Hey," he said, staying firmly planted in the doorway.

"Hey," I said. My heart thundered to life with two lame words exchanged between us.

"How was your week?" His voice wasn't quite cool, but it wasn't warm either. It was almost . . . conventional. Maybe that was worse than cool.

"All right," I said with a shrug. "How was your week?"

"All right."

We had that repeating each other thing down.

"Don't we look beee-u-teee-ful, Jesse?" Clementine asked, tugging on his hand to get his attention.

"Positively," he replied with a smile. So he could still form one, just not for me. "Did a fairy godmother come wave her wand your way or something?"

"No, silly," Clementine replied before her face wrinkled up. "Rowen? Are you a fairy godmother?"

"Definitely not," I said.

"I don't know about that," Lily said as I moved on to the next chunk of hair. Three down, three hundred to go. "I think you're working some magic in here."

I made a face at Lily in the mirror. She didn't need magic to make her any more beautiful than she already was.

"Are you going to the dance tonight?"

I had to look up to see who his question was directed at. Jesse was staring at me again.

I nodded. "Yep. I've got my dancing boots ready to go." Could our conversation get any lamer? I didn't want to answer that. "What about you?"

Jesse shrugged. "I don't know. It was a long week, and I'm pretty tired. I might just lay low and catch up on some sleep."

He got a trio of groans from the girls. I kept my own groan inside.

"Come on, Jesse. You always come to these things. If you don't come, all the single girls will revolt," Lily said.

"I'm sure the dance and everyone at it will get along just fine without me," he said, glancing my way once more before slipping back outside the door.

"Keep lying to yourself, Jesse!" Hyacinth shouted after him. "You're not fooling any of us!"

"He's been acting so strange lately," Lily mumbled.

"That's because Jesse's in love," Hyacinth announced.

I choked on . . . nothing. Yep, I just choked on nothing.

After the three girls gave me strange looks, I kept my head down and focused on Lily's hair, praying Jesse and love wouldn't be mentioned in the same sentence again.

"He is not in love," Lily said. "If he was, we'd know about it. Jesse can't keep a secret like that to himself."

"Just think about it, Lily," Hyacinth said, marching toward us. "He's acting strange, he's all moody, he gets this strange look on his face all the time, and I caught him checking out bouquets of flowers last week when he took me to the store and thought I wasn't looking. He's definitely in love with somebody."

Lily rolled her eyes. I was about to continue on with the lame conversation theme and ask about the weather when Hyacinth angled herself toward me.

"What about you, Rowen?" she said. "Do you know

who Jesse's in love with?"

That time, I did drop the curling iron. Thankfully, no skin or carpet was damaged.

"Oh, for crying out loud, Hyacinth. Quick acting like Nancy Drew and go get changed. There's no mystery here. Jesse isn't in love, and if he was, I'm sure you wouldn't be the first he'd tell."

Hyacinth wandered back over to the closet where Clementine had just emerged with yet another dress ten sizes too big. "Yeah, yeah, well, maybe he's in love but doesn't even know he is. You know?"

"You watch too many movies," Lily said.

"And you don't watch enough."

After that, the conversation was kept to a minimum as the girls changed and I finished Lily's hair. By then, Rose and Neil had already been hollering at them for the past ten minutes that the Suburban was leaving, so I helped Lily get zipped into her cotton summer dress, helped her pick out a pair of boots, and flew down the hall to my bedroom.

Josie was planning on picking me up, so I had a few minutes to spare but not many. I threw on one of my old dresses that wasn't black or especially dramatic, pulled on the boots Jesse had gotten me, and ripped a brush through my hair. Instead of throwing my hair into the side French braid I lived in at Willow Springs, I kept it down. I wasn't cooking or cleaning, so I could, literally, let my hair down.

I had just finished putting on my lipstick when I heard a truck pull into the driveway. I had the window open, and I would have been lying if I said it was to let the cool air in. I hoped it would let something else in. Even though I was just as confused as before about Jesse and me and what, if any, future we could have together, I did have some explaining to do. I had some apologizing to do as well.

I stuck my head out the window and waved at Josie so she wouldn't blast the horn in case Jesse was upstairs resting. Knowing he could be a floor above me, asleep in bed, didn't make me want to head downstairs and ride off with Josie, but I'd promised her.

She'd called again the night before to make sure I was still on for the dance, and a girl who went so far out of the way to be friends with me was someone I wouldn't ditch in the eleventh hour.

Josie waved back, then made a *Come on!* motion with her hands.

Coming I mouthed before ducking back inside. I grabbed my purse and jogged out the door. Neil and Rose had left with the girls, so the house was a rare quiet and I didn't even get ten seconds to enjoy it. Before I'd made it out of the living room, Josie's truck started thumping with music.

My ears were already bleeding before I'd closed and locked the front door. If there was a God, I knew one thing: He'd been on vacation the day someone invented country music.

"Hey, girl!" Josie shouted at me from the driver's side window.

"Hey, yourself!" I shouted back. Only because she wouldn't have heard me otherwise. "Did you know that every time a country song is played, a cute little puppy keels over dead?" Again, I had to shout because Josie was really blaring the honky tonk.

And we still had the actual honky tonk to get to.

"Aww, that's sweet," Josie said, cranking down the music to a level where I could be relatively certain my eardrums wouldn't burst. "Is our little girl making jokes about country music? I've never, ever heard one of those." She rolled her eyes at me.

"You know what they say about jokes," I said, bounding down the porch steps. "There's a kernel of truth in every one."

She gave me a look, then scanned my outfit. "Hot mama!" She was back to shouting again. "When you're not wearing pants or those shredded legging thingies, a person can actually see you've got some killer legs."

I stopped in the driveway, leaned over a bit, and scanned my legs. Nothing but a couple of knees and freckles.

"But, girl, do you have vampire in you or something? Because I've never seen skin that white."

"This is tan." I examined my arms. Yeah, they were at least a shade and a half darker than normal. I skirted around the front of her shiny truck and climbed up into the passenger seat.

"No, Rowen, this is tan." Josie held her bare arm against mine. Sure enough, I looked see-through compared to her golden goodness.

"Two words, Josie," I said, moving my arm from hers. "Skin. Cancer."

She laughed as she hit the gas. And by hit the gas, I meant we hit forty before we'd made it out of the driveway. "Two words, Rowen," she said, taking the corner the way she'd taken it last week. "Vitamin. D."

I double-checked my seat belt. "D isn't really a word. It's a letter."

"Oh, dear God!" Josie shouted out the window. "Get me to the honky tonk and get me there quick!"

"The way you drive . . ." I said, checking the speedometer. Yeah. We were going as fast as I felt we were. "You could be in Idaho 'quick.'"

"I knew there was a reason I was drawn to you, Rowen," Josie said as she skipped to the next song. The next one sounded exactly like the previous one that sounded like every single song ever sung in country music. "You have as wicked a sense of humor as me."

"And here I thought it was because you loved those shredded legging thingies of mine."

She tilted her head back and laughed loudly. Josie looked amazing, even more so than the night I'd met her at the rodeo. Some girls are pretty because they put a lot of work into it, and some girls are pretty when they wake up in the morning. Josie was in that second group. She had the glow that a beauty cream company would kill to replicate, and her hair was so shiny it looked like glass. She had on a short denim skirt, a floral sleeveless blouse, and a pair of candy-apple red boots. She'd be beating the guys away like flies.

Which made me wonder again what had happened between Jesse and Josie. Really, those two were the dream couple.

Before another song came to its twangy end, Josie pulled into a packed parking lot.

"The party's hopping tonight," she said, making her own parking spot in the front. Everywhere I looked, there were trucks. Big ones, little ones, old ones, new ones. Trucks, trucks, and more trucks. Maybe a few SUVs like the Walkers', but there was not a single car to be seen. I didn't know what those Montana people had against cars, but obviously gas mileage wasn't a concern around there.

"You ready for this?" Josie unfastened her seatbelt and examined herself in the mirror.

"Nope," I answered, swinging open my door. "But I promised you I'd let you be the one to pop my honky tonk cherry, so let's get this thing over with."

Josie shoved my arm before we leapt—I wondered if I should call for a footstool—out of her truck. "You city girls sure are crass."

"And you country girls aren't crass enough," I threw back before slamming the door.

The boys were already tipping their hats, and a few were brazen enough to whistle, as Josie and I made our way to the entrance. And when I say they were whistling at us, I mean they were whistling at Josie.

She smiled, made flirty eyes with a few of them, and walked with a sway in her step. In short, she was a pro at the man-eating game. I didn't sway, I more like clopped around, and I sure as heck didn't make flirty eyes. I would have looked like I had a nervous tic if I even tried, I'm sure.

Since I had no idea what to expect from a honky tonk, I was neither surprised nor unsurprised when we walked through the door. I guess it was normally more of a bar, band, and dancing sort of place, but a few nights every year, they turned it into more of a family place and served some good food, good music, and a good time. At least that's the way Rose had described it. I had yet to determine if there was a good time to be had or good food for that matter. I already knew the music would be a far cry from good.

"Josie Gibson! You'd better save me a dance, or I'm going home with a broken heart," a good looking guy in a flashy shirt called over to her as we walked in. He was also the type of guy that knew he was good looking. I looked at Josie and stuck my index finger in my mouth.

She snickered and elbowed me. "No promises, Ben," she said as we walked by. "And besides, don't you have a girlfriend down in Boise?" She lifted her eyebrows and waited for an answer.

A sheepish smile and a shrug was all the answer she received.

"Men," she groaned as she steered me through the crowd.

The place was bustling. People ranged in age from infancy to knocking-on-death's-door. Everyone was talking, eating, or dancing. Everyone had a smile. Everyone appeared to be having a good time. Just like Rose had said, and from the looks of the fried chicken, baked beans, and potato salad stacked high on plates, it looked like the food was pretty darn good.

The music, as predicted, blew big time. A live band was going to town up on stage, but really, how many times could they sing about could'a, should'a, would'a, and a dog before people's brains started to liquefy?

"You want something to eat?" Josie asked, motioning over to the food table.

My stomach grumbled. "We better before it's all gone." I'd learned at the ranch that if I didn't have my butt in a chair within the first five minutes of mealtime, I wasn't eating anything because nothing was left.

Josie and I made our way through the crowd toward the food. She seemed to know everybody and everybody

223

knew her. In a town like that, I doubted there were any quick trips to the grocery store. Not when you passed a person you knew on every aisle. Josie grabbed a couple of plates and handed me one before making her way down the table.

"Who do we pay?" I asked as she dropped a drumstick on her plate.

She looked over at me like I'd grown a second head. "Nobody."

I returned the two-headed look favor. "Wait. So the food's free, there's no entrance fee, and you don't have to pay to park?"

"Free, free, and free," she said, plopping a scoop of potato salad onto her plate. "This is a community deal, not a money-making venture."

Whoa. I wasn't in Kansas anymore. Or downtown Portland.

After I let that mental confusion bomb settle, I shook it off and helped myself to some home cooking. Some *free* home cooking.

We grabbed a couple of sodas from one of the big, ice-filled buckets then made our way toward what looked to be the only two free seats in the house. After saying hello to every single person we passed, Josie dropped into a chair. I plopped down beside her and cracked open my soda.

"Thanks for inviting me," I said. "I know I'm a snarky pain in the ass, but it was nice to be invited to something." I quickly took a sip of my soda and tried not to squirm.

"I like you, Rowen. You're different. You've got . . ." Josie's eyebrows came together for a moment. "Moxie.

That's it. You've got moxie."

My jaw dropped a little. "Wow. Really?"

She nodded her head emphatically. "Absolutely. Total, unadulterated moxie."

I didn't have to fake my smile. "That is the coolest thing anyone's ever said to me. Thank you."

She shot me a thumbs up before biting into her drumstick.

I was still too touched by Josie's unexpected compliment to eat, so when her eyes zeroed in on something across the room, I noticed right away. Whatever had caught her attention was also doing a good job of keeping it. She couldn't seem to look away. Following her gaze, I understood why.

A tall cowboy in a straw hat and a white undershirt was surrounded by a flock of females. Even from my seat, I made out every curve and bend of his lips and remembered the way they'd felt against mine. Jesse'd made it. I didn't know how long he'd been there, but once I knew he was there, I wasn't sure I could look away.

It seemed like Josie was having the same problem.

"I wish I knew what was going on with him," Josie said suddenly, sighing as she studied him. "I used to know everything going on in that head of his, but now I can't seem to figure out one single thing."

I cleared my throat and made myself look away from Jesse. It was hard to do, especially when one of those Jesse Walker fangirls rubbed her hand up and down his arm. "Why do you think something's going on with him?" Luckily, I sounded more innocent than my question was.

Josie huffed and waved her hand at him. "Because Jesse doesn't brood. He doesn't stand cross-armed and straight-faced on the sidelines when there's a dance floor in front of him. Jesse has never done that whole angsty, moody guy thing like he has been lately. Something's gotten under his skin." Her own eyes narrowed as fangirl number one made a double pass on Jesse's bicep. "Or *someone*."

I couldn't agree or disagree with her for fear of Josie seeing right through me. I wasn't sure how she'd take it if she knew Jesse and I'd had a few hot and heavy mouth-mashes. I didn't want to chance an impromptu cat fight if she didn't take it so well.

So what did I go with instead?

"What happened to you and Jesse? Why did you guys break up?" No points for steering the conversation into shallower water.

Josie sighed and looked away from him. Like it had suddenly become painful to look at him. "Cheating."

"What?" I twisted in my seat and scooted closer. "He slept with somebody else?" The idea was . . . earth shatter-ing.

"No." Josie whipped her head from side to side. "I did."

"What?" I repeated, stunned. The idea was, again, earth shattering.

A tear looked close to spilling from the corner of Josie's eye, so I grabbed one of her hands and gave it a squeeze. She looked like she needed it.

"You don't have to say anything else. I'm sorry I asked. I just . . . I never guessed that was what happened." Cheating had never crossed my mind when I'd wondered at the reasons for their break up.

"Jesse was leaving town for the weekend," she began,

shifting in her seat. "He was going to some cattleman's conference in Missoula the same weekend of my brother's twenty-first birthday party. Jesse was sorry he couldn't make it, but he asked one of his good friends to keep a close eye on me and make sure I didn't get into too much trouble." Josie paused and bit her lip. She was worrying the hell out of the hem of her denim skirt. The poor girl was a wreck. "I had a lot to drink that night, more than usual, but I knew Jesse's friend would make sure I didn't pass out on the bathroom floor or go home with some random guy." The first tear fell down her cheek. I felt so badly for Josie I wanted to hug her. "Turns out I just went home with him instead." She wiped her eyes and let her hair fall around her face. "When I woke up the next morning, I knew I'd ruined everything I had with Jesse. I couldn't lie to him about what had happened, but I couldn't find the courage to tell him either. So," Josie's head fell even more, "his friend told him."

I wasn't only hurting for Josie, but I was hurting for Jesse, too. He'd been betrayed by someone who loved him. I knew how that kind of pain felt. I knew how it left a scar behind. I knew how it changed a person.

"Oh, God, Josie," I breathed, letting her squeeze the hell out of my hand. I couldn't believe that there, at a honky tonk, I'd just had a girl pour her heart out to me about how she'd ripped out the heart of the man I cared for. It made the world seem very small. "Who was it? Which friend of Jesse's?" I'd only met a handful, most were ranch hands, but I wanted a name. The next time I saw him, he was getting hot coffee poured into his lap.

Her eyes flicked to mine, and I knew her answer before she said it. "Garth Black."

"Come again?" That was all I had. Garth Black and Josie Gibson. Getting it on. It just didn't equate.

"I had sex with Garth Black and have regretted it every single day since."

"And you lost Jesse." That was what I'd mourn the most.

She nodded, her eyes automatically drifting back to him.

"Do you miss him?"

Another nod, but that time she made herself look away from Jesse. "Every night when I find myself still anticipating his call to say goodnight. Every time I go to one of these things and I realize I'm not going with a date. God, Rowen. I miss him when I brush my teeth." Her gaze shifted from her lap to my eyes. They held a strength that hadn't been there just moments before. "But I know Jesse and I will never be together again. There's too much bad history between us now. So I can either spend the rest of my life missing him . . . or I can move on."

"Move on?" *From Jesse Walker?* I edited out because if she knew how to "move on" from him, mountains could be moved and pigs could fly.

"Maybe not today. Or tomorrow. But someday," she said. "I'm not going to waste my life longing for the guy-that-almost-was. I'm going to move on and find the guy-to-be."

I knew she made it sound about a thousand times easier than it was, but for a young woman who'd lost a Jesse because she'd slept with a Garth, she had a good head on her shoulders.

"Okay, you don't only give out life-changing moxie compliments, you also might be the most intelligent woman I've ever met," I said, still dumbfounded. "You are officially my hero."

Josie laughed, wiped the corners of her eyes one more time, and sat up straight. "Well, sometimes the lessons you learn remind you that you have to let your head run the show instead of your heart."

And sometimes the opposite was true, as I was learning.

"I'm going to run outside for a few minutes and get some fresh air. I promised myself I wouldn't cry tonight, and look at me." Josie waved her hands at her face. She still looked pretty damn perfect. "You going to be all right on your own for a few?"

"I'll be great," I assured her. "As soon as I'm done with this feast, I'm going to get out there and bust a move."

"Sure you are." Josie rolled her eyes as she stood up.

"Don't tempt me."

"I'm not tempting you," she said, propping a hand on her hip. Her eyes gleamed. "I'm *daring* you."

"What? Are we in sixth grade?" I called after her.

She waved over her shoulder. "See you on the dance floor, Move Buster."

I grumbled into my soda can before taking a drink. I'd never backed down from a dare, and I wouldn't start. I'd be on that dance floor before little Miss Sixth Grade got her daring butt back in there.

I was going in for my crispy chicken wing when I felt the air around me charge, like an electric storm was rolling in. The hair on my arms rose when I looked up. From across the room, Jesse's eyes had locked in on me and, from the tilt of his brow, I couldn't quite make out if that was pain or confusion lining his forehead. My wing dropped to my plate, and the air, the noise, the people, everything was sucked out of the room as he continued to stare at me.

It was the stuff people talked about. The love-at-first-sight mumbo jumbo I'd rolled my eyes at. That wasn't our "first sight," but I felt a lot of that other thing swirling around in places that had felt empty for so long, I'd forgotten I had them.

When that same little arm pawer dropped her hand on his other arm, Jesse's gaze shifted her way. Suddenly, I could breathe again. That was, until I watched her smile up at him, pop up on her tip toes to whisper in his ear, then raise her eyebrows at him. I was back to being unable to breathe. My claws were out that time.

I didn't know that girl from the one sitting across from me at the table, but I hated her. Like, raw, unadulterated hate. All because she was touching, whispering, and smiling at the guy I wanted to be touching, whispering to, and smiling at.

She was in my place because I'd let Garth Black pour poison in my ears. I couldn't even remember what he'd said, or why I'd been so sure I needed to stay away from Jesse. Right then, all I could think about was being close to Jesse.

I was out of my seat and weaving through the dance floor before I even knew I'd done it. He wasn't watching me anymore, but I was watching him. I couldn't look away, and the closer I got, the more impossible looking away became.

He noticed me right before I stopped in front of him. The tight circle of girls around him didn't budge, so I not-so-gently shouldered my way through them.

"Plenty of single guys around, ladies. No need to suffocate this one." Of course I knew what they knew: there were other guys, but there was only one Jesse Walker. I grunted when one of them threw an elbow into my side as I pushed by. Damn. Those chicks were out for blood. I should have worn my steel-toed boots. I would have if I'd known I'd be entering a combat zone.

Once I made it through the main swarm of girls, I squared myself in front of Jesse and the bicep petter. "Hey. You." She hadn't noticed me because she had eyes for nothing but Jesse's muscles. "You rub his arm any longer, you're going to wear the skin right off. Go find yourself another cowboy to pet. I need to talk to this one."

When she finally did look at me, I saw those county girls could make the same vicious expressions as the urban girls I was used to. Mental note made.

"Jesse," she said in a syrupy voice, "you know this . . ." her eyes ran down me, her nose wrinkling as she took me in, "this . . . *thing*?"

My fists balled at my sides. I reminded myself to take a slow breath. She wasn't saying anything I hadn't heard before. She wasn't saying anywhere close to the worst I'd heard before. I was winding up for my comeback when a white shirt angled in front of me.

"Bye, Shelby." Jesse's voice was cold and his shoulders were tensed. He was a tower in front of me, but when *Shelby* huffed, I couldn't resist peeking my head out from behind him.

"Bye, Shelby." I made my voice as syrupy as it would go and gave her an exaggerated wave.

Another vicious look, but she kept walking. For the

most part, the rest of her fellow Jesse worshippers followed her.

I almost smiled, but that brick wall of a back turned
around and those eyes of his made the whole inhaling and
exhaling thing difficult.

"You came," I said, stepping back because being so
close to Jesse made my head light. Logical thought process
became next to impossible to attain.

He lifted a shoulder, but that was the only response he
gave me. Was Jesse Walker giving me the silent treat-
ment?

"Are you having a good time?" I tried next, taking
another half step back because I could still smell that
soapy, shampooy scent of him, and that was messing with
my head, too.

He lifted the other shoulder.

So yeah. Jesse Walker was giving me the silent treat-
ment. I was probably the only person who could claim that
honor.

"Are you going to talk to me, Jesse? Or are you going
to communicate with me with shrugs the rest of the
summer?" Might as well get down to business. I didn't
know how long Josie would be gone, and I needed to talk
to Jesse. I had to clear the thick air between us.

He caught himself in the middle of another shrug.
With a sigh, he pinched the bridge of his nose and closed
his eyes. "What do you want me to say, Rowen?" he
asked, his voice tight. "I've been racking my head all
damn week trying to figure out what to say to you when I
saw you again, but I couldn't think of anything.
Obviously." He wiggled his shoulder and gave me a small
smile.

A small smile was a start. And he was communicating with me, real words and all. I'd take it. His gaze shifted, just over my shoulder, and those sky blue eyes went as black as they could go.

I didn't need to look behind me. I knew a black felt hat was back there somewhere.

Jesse lifted his chin. "Garth's over there if you want to dance with him." I stepped back again from the ice in his tone.

"And what if I want to dance with you?" I said, managing to sound braver than I felt. "What if you do?" Still the ice, but I wouldn't back down. I wouldn't let him push me away so easily. I owed him an explanation, and I wasn't leaving until he had it.

"Would you want to?" I asked. There was so much between the lines in that question, I almost winced just anticipating his answer.

"That depends." His eyes continued to glare holes into the back or front of Garth. I wasn't sure, and I wouldn't look over my shoulder to find out. "Are you planning on having a little campout at Garth Black's trailer tonight after you dance with me now?"

Bitter? Jealous? Those weren't words I'd use to describe Jesse, but tonight, he seemed to be a little of both.

"Jesse. I'm sorry," I said. "I let Garth get into my head. I let him remind me of all my fears and insecurities. I let him tell me what I deserved and what I didn't deserve." Shit. If I got any more vulnerable, I would turn into one gaping, bloody wound.

"Well, sorry, but I don't let Garth Black decide what I do and don't deserve. And you shouldn't either."

"I know," I replied quietly. I could have gone into all

233

the reasons I had. Why it was so easy to believe the Garth Blacks of the world. Why the bad was so much easier to believe than the good. Man, I could have gone into a day-long lecture on the special brand of screwed-up I was, but my apology wasn't about me. It was about Jesse. It was about me hurting him and needing to make amends.

Jesse studied my face, like he was trying to remain objective about the whole thing but he failed. A long sigh followed. "What were you doing at Garth's place that night anyways, Rowen? Why were you kissing the hell out of me that afternoon and snuggled into his lounge chair later that night?"

I could have cried from the pain in Jesse's voice alone. From knowing that my actions had caused that level of hurt in him. Everything inside of me wanted to edit the truth. Everything inside of me wanted to appease him with a surface answer. Everything inside of me wanted to protect myself.

I flipped everything inside of myself off and sucked in a deep breath. "Because Garth Black isn't able to break my heart." I bit my lip and pressed on. "You are." The ice in Jesse's expression melted. His eyes softened. The wrinkles in his forehead smoothed. "I never have to worry about Garth hurting me, because I know he will. I know what to expect with him. I know he'll screw up and leave me if I don't leave him first. I don't give him every piece of myself because I know what I'm getting into. I don't know what I'm getting into with you, and if I give all of myself to you, you could break everything." Was I really spilling my guts in a honky tonk with hundreds of people around? I took a quick scan of the area. Yeah. I sure was. "You make me feel too much, Jesse." I crossed those few steps I'd put between us. "It freaks me out."

There was almost a full minute of silence between us. Nothing but him studying me and me just letting him. A minute of silence after you drop that kind of deep stuff on a guy is basically an eternity.

Finally, Jesse's mouth parted. "When you open yourself up to people, you let the bad in with the good. I can't promise I won't ever hurt you, Rowen. But it won't be on purpose. I will never hurt you intentionally. I *can* promise you that." Jesse's hand dropped to my waist, but he didn't draw me to him. He drew himself to me. "But if this is something we're going to give a go, I need you to promise me the same. I need you to promise me you won't go out of your way to push me away, or hurt me, or fall asleep on Garth Black's lounge chair, *when*—not *if*—things get scary. I can tell you don't want to let people in, that it scares you, but you need to let me in if we're going to have a fighting chance. You can't shove me away the moment you let me inside, as much as I know you'll want to." His fingers curved into my waist, and the warmth and strength in them made my eyelids heavy. "Don't hurt me, Rowen," he whispered in a way that tugged at any and every feeling I had for Jesse.

I knew letting him in would be like going against a strong current. I knew it wouldn't feel natural, or be my first, second, or even third instinct, and I knew it would be a daily struggle to keep from running from Jesse when things got serious, when things got . . . scary, as he'd said.

But when I looked into those eyes of his that saw everything, those eyes that saw *me*, I knew the fight would be worth it. The struggle to let him in when I wanted to barricade the windows and lower the gates would be a battle I'd never regret fighting.

I inhaled. I exhaled. I wove my fingers through his where his hand still rested on my waist. I locked my gaze to his. "I won't."

It was a promise. A vow. A prayer. It thrilled me. It terrified me.

But what I noticed most was the warmth running through my body and into my veins. The feeling of peace that washed over me was nothing I'd ever felt before. The next thing that overwhelmed me?

The smile that lit up his face.

"I think you owe me a dance," he said, sliding his other hand around my waist. We weren't on the dance floor, nowhere close to it, but we could make our own little dance floor right there.

My hands settled over his chest, and I tried pressing closer. Apparently, we were as tight together as two people could get. "I owe you three." I winked up at him.

"After this past week, I think you owe me more than that." He tilted his hat back farther on his forehead.

"What did you have in mind?" I asked as we started swaying to the silence of one song ending and another beginning.

"I'll think of something." One corner of his mouth lifted higher than the other. "But why don't you kiss me while I'm thinking?"

It was one of those moments that felt like it was more a scene pulled from a movie or a book. Boy and girl moving in for a kiss as the band breaks into a slow song . . . girl glances for the briefest moment over boy's shoulder before she closes her eyes to taste his lips and sees . . .

The boy's ex-girlfriend.

"Crap," I whispered. Josie was watching the two of us with a blank expression. She didn't look over-the-moon pissed or irreversibly hurt. She looked more like she couldn't quite understand what she saw.

"What?" Jesse said, pulling back right before his mouth connected with mine. I could have been kissing him . . .

But I couldn't do that in front of Josie, not with her watching like she was the most confused person in the room. I owed her an explanation, too. I'd owed a lot of those lately.

"Hold that thought." I shot him a quick smile before winding around him.

"Rowen?" He grabbed my hand. "Did you just miss what I said a whole two minutes ago?"

I looked at him, confused.

"The whole you-can't-run-away-when-things-get-serious thing."

"Jesse, trust me, there's nothing I'd rather be doing right now than kissing the hell out of you, but Josie just walked in and saw the two of us together, and . . . Well, she looked a little . . . *shocked*."

Jesse's forehead lined as he checked behind me. He sighed when he saw her. "You want me to go with you? Talk with her together?"

I shook my head. "I think it would be a more productive discussion if you weren't present."

He lifted a brow.

"You distract me too much, and if I'm going to explain to Josie what I'm doing with her ex-boyfriend and come out on the other side with her not hating me, I'm going to need all my mental faculties."

He smirked at me.

"Wish me luck," I said, giving his hand a squeeze before slipping free.

"Good luck," I heard him say as I made my way to the still stunned Josie.

She didn't run off or glare at me as I approached; she just continued glancing between me and Jesse like she was trying to accept something impossible to accept.

When I stopped in front of her, she didn't look behind me again. I wasn't sure if that was because Jesse had moved on, or because she couldn't look at him anymore.

"You want to talk?" I glanced at the door.

She bobbed her head.

I led the way through the crowd, and she followed. The night had taken so many unexpected turns. Good ones, bad ones. Good, bad. Good with the bad. Just as Jesse had said. I had to accept the bad with the good because it's inevitable.

I didn't say anything until we were outside and out of range of anyone who would listen.

I spun around and couldn't get the words out fast enough. "Josie, I am so, so sorry you just saw that."

She stared at the ground and crossed her arms. "But you're not sorry for falling for my ex-boyfriend?" Her voice wasn't especially sharp, but the words hit me like it was.

I didn't want to lie to her, but I couldn't lie to myself. I couldn't make it seem like some shallow infatuation. "No, I'm not sorry for falling for Jesse," I said slowly. Josie's face lined. "But I am sorry for hurting you in the process. I'm very sorry for that."

She chewed something out on her lip for a moment.

"Why didn't you say anything to me?"

"Up until a few minutes ago, I didn't know what to say. I knew I liked Jesse. I knew he *used* to like me. I just wasn't sure if he still did."

Josie's eyes closed. "I saw the way he was looking at you, Rowen. The way he was touching you." She exhaled and leaned into the truck beside her. "If you're still not sure if he likes you or not, I can tell you with a hundred percent certainty that he does."

My heart burst at her words. It broke at her words. Damn, that was a hard discussion to have with the ex-girlfriend of the boy who made my heart go boom-boom.

"I'm sorry," I said, because I had nothing else. I'd say it all night long if that's what she needed to hear.

"No, I know, and honestly . . . I've had my suspicions that something's been going on between you two for a while now," she said. "It sucks, but it's like what I told you inside. I knew when Jesse and I split up, that was a permanent thing. I knew there was no chance of us making up and moving on together. I knew he'd wind up with someone else. I was surprised he wasn't seeing anyone sooner, given the parade the single girls practically had when they found out we'd split." She kicked the toe of her boot into the dirt and continued to stare holes into the ground. "I also knew it would break my heart when I saw him with another girl, no matter who that girl was." She glanced up at me and managed to form a small smile. "I guess at least I can say I like the girl he fell for."

Another heart breaking/bursting moment. Josie had just found Jesse and me an inch away from lip-locked, and there she was, two minutes later, admitting that it sucked to see, but at least I had her stamp of approval. Why did the first girl I'd wanted to be friends with in a long time have to be the ex-girlfriend of the boy I liked?

Ah, yes. Thank you, Fates, for the reminder: life was unfair. More times than it wasn't.

I did something totally out of character, *again*, and wrapped my arms around her to give her the most sincere, awkward hug in the history of hugs. "I'd understand if you wanted to hate my guts. I'd even say I deserved it."

Josie made a noise that sounded like part laugh, part sob, then hugged me back. Hard. We were talking the hardest hug in the history of hugs. "It would probably be easier if I hated your guts. It would be easier if I could hate Jesse's, too. But I can't."

I felt a couple of tears drop down my shoulder. "So you're saying you don't want to hate my guts? Because I'd fully support your decision if you did."

When she made that same noise again, it was more laugh than sob. "I'm sure. But if you break Jesse Walker's heart the way I did, I promise I will happily hate your guts then."

I'd hate my own guts, too.

"Deal," I said. "Any pointers on how to keep from breaking said heart?"

She leaned back to look me in the eyes. Hers were red and teary, but they were serious like nothing else. "Yeah. Stay away from Garth Black. As far as you can stay away. That guy doesn't have a soul."

I nodded, but I wasn't so sure I believed that last part. I was pretty sure Garth had a soul. He'd just chosen to bury it way down deep, the way I had for so long. The keeping my distance part I had no issue following. After what I had learned, I'd avoid Garth Black at all costs.

"Okay, so stay away from Garth," I said, lifting my index finger. "Anything else?"

"Yeah." She nodded. "Be good to him, Rowen. Jesse's been through a lot. Don't make him go through a lot more. He's been through more in his nineteen years than most of us will go through in our lifetime."

I pretended like I knew what she was talking about, but really, I didn't. Jesse had the most idealistic life I'd stumbled across. Of course, I knew what we saw on the surface was just that: the top layer. There was so much more we never knew of other people, so much kept hidden beneath the surface.

Whatever Jesse's past was, wherever his present led, one thing was certain: I wanted him in my future.

CHAPTER fourteen

I pulled into Willow Springs a good four hours later. And not because I'd been making out in the parking lot of a honky tonk with Jesse Walker until we were both blue in the face, as I *wished* I would have been.

After Josie and I worked out what we needed to, she asked me if I wanted to get out of there, drive to the closest Dairy Queen, and gorge ourselves into an ice cream coma. I said yeah. Not because I wanted to do exactly that right then, but it was the *right* thing to do. Josie had been a friend to me when I needed one, and from the lost expression on her face, I could tell she needed a friend.

So I texted Jesse, letting him know I was going with Josie and asking if he'd take a rain check on that dance. He'd promptly replied, *I'll take a rain check on *three* dances. But who's counting?* Then Josie broke every traffic law in the state of Montana as we made our way to the Queen of Dairy.

A few hours, a couple of cherry-dipped cones, and one shared banana split later, we'd closed the place down. We'd talked. And talked. And talked some more. Surprisingly, Jesse's name didn't come up again after we'd gotten it out of our systems in the parking lot. We just talked about the stuff girls talk about. It had been a while since I'd had an intense session of "girl talk", but it was . . . nice.

The Walkers' Suburban was in the driveway, and all the lights were off inside the house. All the lights except for one. My stomach dropped when I saw the light streaming through Jesse's window. Was he waiting up for me? Was he planning on "sneaking" back into my room? Was he still out and had just forgotten to turn out the light?

"The city girl and the country girl. B.F.F.s," Josie said, interrupting my endless stream of questions. "Who would have thunk it?"

I smiled over at her. Other than crying off most of her mascara, the girl looked as stunning as she had at the start of the night. "I sure as hell wouldn't have."

"Yeah, me neither," she said, "but I'm glad I gave the city girl a chance."

I huffed and tried to look insulted. "I'm glad I gave the country girl a chance."

"Yeah, yeah, get out of my truck already," she teased, leaning over the steering wheel and looking up at the house. "It looks like a light through yonder window breaks."

"Random Shakespeare pulls in everyday conversation?" I said, shooting her a thumbs up before climbing out of my seat. "I knew we were B.F.F.s for a reason."

"Sweet dreams, Rowen," she said, punching the accelerator the moment I closed the door.

I hurried up the stairs, and once I'd unlocked the door, I tried to open and close it as quietly as ancient-farmhouse-door possible. I really didn't want to wake up the entire house. I wanted to see Jesse too badly. I had it so bad, if he didn't climb his butt back down through my window within five minutes, I would climb my way up.

Once I was up the stairs, I knew I was almost in the clear. Just one long hallway to go, and I was golden. When I made it inside my room and closed the door, I did a mini-victory dance as I flicked the light on.

"Hi, Rowen."

Holy heart attack. "Shit!" I hissed, dropping my purse on the floor. "I mean, shoot. What are you doing in here, Lily? You scared the"—she lifted her eyebrows at me—"*poop* out of me." I lifted a hand to my chest to make sure my heart hadn't exploded through my ribcage.

"Sorry, I didn't mean to scare the *poop* out of you." She gave me the closest thing to a smirk Lily could make. "I heard you and Josie pull up, and I just wanted to tell you something real quick before you went to bed."

Lily was in her nightgown, the makeup washed from her face, but the soft curls still draped down her back. "What did you want to tell me?" I asked as I walked over to the window to make sure it was still closed. The last thing I needed was for a half-naked Jesse to catapult through the window while his little sister was in my room. There would be no way to explain that.

"I just wanted to say thank you," she said. "To say thank you for taking time to get me all dressed up and pretty this afternoon."

"Lily, you're pretty all the time. I just put some makeup on you and curled your hair."

"Yeah, but I felt different." She slid a chunk of curls behind her ear. "Almost like I was someone else."

Crossing the room, I kneeled beside her where she sat on the edge of my bed. "Lily, don't be someone else. Because I really like the person that you are." I smiled up at her. "Don't waste your time trying to be someone else. Just be the best *you* you can be."

I saw the wheels turning in that sixteen-year-old brain of hers. I wasn't much older than Lily, but I knew what wanting to be someone else was like. I knew what wanting to be anyone else was like. It was a huge waste. A person could try until they gave themselves an aneurism, but we can't escape the soul and flesh we were given when we were born. The key was accepting that and getting on with your life.

I'd learned that lesson, but I hadn't fully applied it yet. I was still working on the application part.

"I'm going to write that down in my journal," Lily said ceremoniously. "Just be the best you you can be."

"Sounds like a plan." I stood up when she did.

She paused on her way to the door. "Is that what you do?"

There was the million dollar question. "Working on it," I answered.

She nodded before heading out the door with a smile and a "Good night."

Once I heard her bedroom door close, I did the same. I kicked off my boots and hurried to the window. I couldn't get it open fast enough. Sticking my head out, I checked Jesse's window. It was open, and the light was still on. I was just about to open my mouth to say his name when I realized five sets of ears might hear if any of them were light sleepers. So calling to him was out.

Maybe it wasn't . . . My cell phone was a mere room length away. I could text him to get the heck down here, but then my eyes fell on the chimney. The one I'd been so sure he was certifiably insane to climb. Really, it wasn't so bad. The cobblestones were big, and there were plenty of good foot and hand holds for a person to use to climb.

I felt alive tonight. I wanted to feel my heart in my throat. I wanted to feel adrenaline trickling into my veins. I wanted to *be* as alive as I felt. Plus, I really wanted to see the look on his face when I returned the favor of leaping into his window unexpectedly in the middle of the night.

My short, shift dress would make for easy climbing, and my boots were already off. I was as set to climb as I'd ever be. After sucking in a deep breath, I slid through the window until my legs dangled over the edge. My heart was halfway up my throat, and I hadn't even set hand or foot to cobblestone.

Against every indication, I was a fairly practical girl. I knew that plan was not smart. I wasn't an experienced climber, nor was I athletic, but I was also past the point of caring about what was smart. I just wanted to get inside of Jesse's room.

If it wasn't already documented somewhere, it needed to be: hormones had to be the leading cause of teenage injury.

The chimney was so close to my window I could touch it from where I sat on the window ledge, but the next part was the hardest. Giving up what was safe for what could be dangerous. Letting go of the known for the unknown was the scary part.

I closed my eyes, exhaled, gave myself an internal pep talk, then swung my leg over to the chimney.

My foot slid into a deep crevasse. One limb down, a mere three to go.

I exhaled again and reached out until my hand grabbed hold of a small stone. By that point, I was sweating, but I was halfway there and wouldn't give up. I'd given up on so many things before; I wasn't giving up tonight.

The next part, though, would be the hardest part. My left hand and foot were in place, but I couldn't move my right hand or foot without moving both. Without leaving the safety of my perch. Before I could chicken out, I shook my right arm and leg to get the nerves out, then pivoted my core and swung both of them for the chimney.

I whimpered the next moment when I found myself hugging the chimney, all hands and feet in their own little nook or cranny. I'd done it. I'd taken the leap, and all that was left was the climb.

That part was easy. Hand, foot. Hand, foot. Slow and steady and, in what couldn't have been more than a minute's time, my head peeked into Jesse's window. There was no sight of him, but the room was strangely shaped. I could only see a small portion of it from the window.

I tried to be quiet as I grabbed the windowsill and, with some creative maneuvering, I managed to crawl inside of his window noiselessly.

So it wasn't exactly the grand entrance I'd wanted to make, but making it up that chimney without breaking my neck was the real performance. I took a few hesitant steps, still unable to see him. If I'd crawled up the whole way to find nothing but an empty room, I would not be a happy camper. The steep angles of the roof broke the attic up into a cluster of sharp angles and small spaces. The floors weren't carpeted, just weathered, plank boards, and the walls weren't drywalled, so insulation, wires, and cords were on display.

He might have only lived there for a few weeks, but

the room was already permeated with his smell. The room wasn't much, and I hadn't even seen a bed yet, but I liked it already. It was clean, had plenty of character, and housed the guy I liked. That had the makings of possibly the best room in existence.

Two more steps deeper inside the room, and I saw him. My throat went dry at the same time my heart leapt higher than it had while I'd been out on that chimney. He was pacing at the side of his bed in the same pajamas he'd worn the night we spent together—which was more like saying he wore no pajamas—and looked like he was swishing something around in his mouth.

As soon as I took a step toward him, his head snapped up. When his eyes landed on me, they went soft for one moment before they went as wide as eyes could go.

He raised his arms at his sides, obviously a bit frantic, but he wasn't saying much.

"I can't read crazy hand signals," I said, as he continued to wave at me, to the window, back to me. "Words are a safer bet."

He gave me an exasperated look, lifted his finger, and gave a final swish of whatever was in his mouth before turning around and grabbing a cup. After setting the cup back on his dresser, he turned around. I noticed the plastic bottle of bright blue liquid beside the cup.

"Mouthwash?" I said, trying not to smile. "Someone wanting fresh breath for any particular reason?"

Jesse rushed by me and bee lined for the window. "Someone *was* wanting fresh breath for a very particular reason until a certain someone pulled a stunt that could have killed her."

I was still smiling too much over the whole mouthwash thing to let his mood affect mine. "You mean the same stunt someone else performed a week ago that could have killed him?" I came up behind him and stopped when he was just out of arm's reach. Given that he was wearing nothing but a pair of cut-off sweats, I didn't trust myself to stop touching if I started.

"I've climbed that chimney a thousand different times, Rowen. That's totally different." He looked out the window again, and his body went more rigid.

"Well, I'm here now. Alive. In one piece." I couldn't pry my eyes from the deep seam running down his back. I wanted to trace it with my fingers. I wanted to taste it with my tongue . . .

I needed a sharp slap across the face and a cold shower. "So can we forget about how I got here and just enjoy that I am here?"

Jesse slipped his head back inside the window and turned to me slowly. His eyes were still anxious, but his mouth turned up just enough to let me know the worst of the storm had passed.

"You wouldn't want that mouthwash to go to waste, would you?" I gave him a suggestive smile, and he took my suggestion. He crossed the distance between us until his chest was nearly right against mine. His hands moved into their favorite spot: at the curve of my waist, just above my hips.

"No, I wouldn't want that," he said, his eyes now clear. It was amazing how, with the right distraction, a girl could talk a guy back from the ledge every time.

"Well?" I said a few moments later. "Are you waiting for an invitation?"

And since he wasn't moving fast enough, I clasped

my hands around the back of his neck, lifted up on my toes, and brought my mouth to his.

"Sorry. I was waiting for an invitation," he whispered in the space between our mouths.

I pressed my mouth to his. "Here it is," I said when I pulled back.

Jesse's eyes were still closed, but he smiled for a moment before he pulled me back to him. His hands tightened at my waist as our lips moved together. When our mouths parted and my tongue touched his, his hands tightened again. If he gripped me any harder, I'd pass out, so I gave him one last lingering kiss.

His eyes were still closed, and that smile had gone a little higher.

"Fresh mint?" I asked, still tasting the mint.

When he opened them, I saw how excited his eyes were. His pupils were dilated, and the irises were extra blue. "Spearmint."

"Well, I approve whatever it is." I couldn't just taste him; I almost felt him. It made me want to *actually* feel him again.

"It seemed like you might have," he said, looking smug.

"How was that for not 'pushing you away'?" I lifted an eyebrow and grabbed hold of one of his hands.

"You were most definitely not pushing me away just now," he said, staring at my mouth. "And I approve of that."

I laughed and pulled him away from the window. The way he continued to stare at my mouth made everything from my waist down constrict. "I'm glad you approve because *not* pushing you away when you're kissing me like that is really difficult for a girl to manage."

He let me pull him along. I loved the sound of his bare feet padding along the old wooden boards. It was comforting, somehow.

"Why do you push people away, Rowen?" His voice was gentle, but of course the question hit me in anything but a gentle way.

I knew if Jesse and I would make it with any kind of duration, I needed to be honest about the dark pieces of my past I kept locked away. I knew the sooner, the better. If anyone could handle the demons of my past, it was Jesse.

I also knew that if Jesse had asked me the same question just weeks ago, I would have told him to go screw himself and made avoiding him a top priority. But a lot had changed in a few weeks.

I was starting to be honest with myself. I'd give him the same.

I came to a stop a few feet in front of his bed, nothing more than a mattress laid out in the middle of his room and covered with a couple blankets. For some reason, my eyes locked on his pillow. The place his head rested every night as he dreamed.

"I push people away because I don't want them to see who I really am," I started. Jesse padded closer until his chest was against my back. His arms wound around my stomach, and he held me close. "Because if people know the real me and *still* choose to walk away, I'm not sure I could really take that." I focused on his pillow and the strong arms holding me tight. "So if anyone starts getting too close to figuring out that my act is a bunch of bullshit, I push them away before they can search for what's hiding behind the B.S." I paused to breathe and collect my next thought, but really, I'd just summed it all up. When that settled in—that I'd just bared my soul, my *real* soul, to Jesse Walker—I waited for the panic attack.

When he was quiet for a few more moments, I actually felt it coming on.

"I see the real you, Rowen," he said at last, tucking his chin over my shoulder, "and I like who you are."

I closed my eyes to keep the tears from forming. "I know you do, Jesse. Although I can't figure out why the hell you do like me. Sometimes I think if you watched a movie of my life . . . The drinking. The drugs. The guys." I swallowed the lump in my throat. I wouldn't let the honesty run dry. "You'd run away screaming like every-one else has. You'd give up on me, too."

After a moment, Jesse sighed. "I don't know what to be more sad about. That you feel this why about yourself, or that you have so little faith in me you think I'd leave if I knew every last detail about your past." His head shook against my shoulder. "Would you leave me if you were able to know everything about my past?" He didn't give me a chance to reply. "I know enough, Rowen. I know the woman you are now. I don't need to know every dirty secret to make up my mind."

The theory of keeping my eyes closed to keep tears from forming was nice. It just wasn't a factual theory. Jesse hadn't even flinched at what I'd just said. He hadn't run away screaming. He'd said some of the kindest things I'd heard. Words were just words, but not those ones. Jesse had proven those words before he'd said them. I'd just been blinded.

"I don't deserve you, Jesse," I whispered, never knowing anything more true. "There's nothing I ever could do to deserve you."

He bent his face into the curve of my neck. "We don't deserve anything, Rowen. We don't deserve punishment, we don't deserve happiness, life owes us nothing. Realize that." His voice wasn't gentle anymore; it was as strong as I'd ever heard it. "So we have to take what we want because life sure as shit isn't going to freely hand it over." He kissed the skin just above my collar bone. "And I want you."

I wasn't sure if his words or his touch affected me more, but everything inside of me, the ice, the walls, the fences, everything I'd built to protect myself crumbled. "I'm a huge failure. But I want to be better. You make me want to be better. I know you might disagree, but I *know* you deserve better." Oh, God. I was a runaway train. After years of keeping it all shut inside, it was flooding out of me. "But I love you." And there it was. Most vulnerable feeling ever. "I love you so much it scares me."

Jesse didn't move, and again, he didn't flinch. He just held me, almost like he knew I needed someone to help keep me together. "Are you done?"

It seemed the flood had come to an end, for the moment, so I nodded.

"Good," he said, his breath warm against my neck. "Because I love you, too."

The first tear I'd cried in a long, long time leaked out and rolled down my cheek. I'd associated crying with sadness, so I'd avoided it. I didn't need tears to remind me of pain. I hadn't expected them to come with happiness.

Happiness wasn't exactly the right word, though. No word in my vocabulary bank quite worked. Whatever that emotion was, it was the best damn feeling I'd ever had. I wanted his love more than anyone's . . . I *had* it.

I didn't know how to respond with words, so I used my actions. Twisting in his arms, I looked into the face of the guy I *loved.* I didn't wipe away my tears because, right then, I didn't mind being vulnerable.

"Do I need another invitation if I want to kiss you again?"

"No. You pretty much get to kiss me whenever you want now," I said, forming my hands over the grooves of his shoulders.

"Good to know."

Jesse might have been about to say something else, but he'd said everything he needed to. *Everything*.

He liked the real Rowen Sterling. He even liked the one I pretended to be. My past and all the dark parts of it didn't matter to him. He loved me.

Oh, yeah. I felt the exact same way about him. In all regards.

Nothing more needed to be said.

My mouth crashed into his and took him by surprise. His shoulders tensed for the shortest moment. It took all of one heartbeat for my lips to melt his. Before long, I was struggling to match Jesse's force and pace. He kissed me in long, hard pulls, literally leaving me breathless. His skin was hot and his shoulders rolled beneath my hands as his hands explored my body.

He kept to the "safe" areas: my arms, my back, my hips. After a minute of that, I wanted him touching me in the not-so-safe areas. I wanted it so bad, I grabbed his hand from the small of my back and slid it around to my stomach. Weaving my fingers through his, I guided his hand up. Past my navel, over my ribs, until it covered my breast.

Jesse's shoulders tensed again and his mouth slowed its pace against mine. He didn't seem uncomfortable, just unsure. His touch was hesitant at first as his hand moved over me. I left my hand over his, encouraging him as his exploration shifted away from hesitancy.

When he didn't obviously need any more help, my hand left his and wandered around his waist until my fingers slid over the deep groove running up the center of his back. It felt even better than it looked.

My other hand curved around him, joining the first in its careful inspection of his back. When Jesse's tongue journeyed into my mouth, twisting with mine, my touch instinctually deepened. My nails dug into his back, clawing their way down until they reached the hem of his sweats.

Jesse groaned and pulled back. His smile went right back into place as his chest rose and fell quickly. "Are you doing this because I told you I love you, or do you just think I'm smokin' hot and can't help yourself?" As he inspected my face, his smile stretched higher. Whatever expression I wore had made him downright cocky. From the way I felt, I didn't need to see a mirror to guess what my face looked like.

He had a right to be cocky. He unraveled the parts of me I was familiar with and the parts I'd never even known were there.

"Both," I answered, pulling back just enough to do what I wanted to do next. I reached for the thin straps of my dress and slid each one from my shoulders. The best part of undressing while wearing a shift dress? Two straps moved a few inches over the shoulders, and the entire dress was in a bunch at my feet.

Jesse swallowed.

That made me smile. My fingers trembled over the clasp of my bra, but a couple seconds later, my bra joined the pile of clothes at my feet.

My nipples were already hard from what we'd just been doing, but they hardened more still with the anticipation of what was to come.

Jesse gulped.

I smiled again. I was turning into a smiling fool around him. When my thumbs hitched beneath my lace panties, Jesse's mouth opened, but no words came out. Since I'd never known a guy yet to call "Uncle" at that point in the strip tease, I slid my panties down my hips and past my knees. Once they'd dropped to my ankles, I stepped out of them and away from the rest of my clothing.

Jesse's eyes moved over me like his hands had at first, keeping to the safe zones, until they couldn't seem to stay there any longer. His gaze lingered so long over certain areas, I almost started squirming. But I didn't. I focused on his face, the wrinkles lining his forehead, his parted mouth breathing short, fast breaths, his eyes exploring me almost like he was worshipping me.

It was the most intimate moment Jesse and I had shared. And he had yet to touch me.

After a few more seconds, I took another step toward him. "So?" I lifted my hands at my sides.

Jesse rubbed his forehead, staring at me like he was afraid to blink for fear of missing something. His mouth opened, but nothing came out. Again. He closed it and tried again. Still nothing.

I'd struck the man mute.

His mouth moved open again, and finally he managed, "Speechless," sounding as breathless as he looked. "Obviously."

That look of sheer and utter surprise left his face when his eyes returned to mine. "Have I mentioned that I love you, Rowen Sterling?"

"Yeah, you did." I needed him to touch me so badly it had become painful. "But you can say it as often as you like. I promise that I'll never get tired of hearing it."

"Noted," he said, moving toward me. His eyes never left mine, and between the emotion in them and the expression on his face, I was the one rendered speechless. When his hands curved over my lower back, they weren't shaky the way mine were. His touch had a confidence and strength that made the whole area south of my navel tighten even more. His hands slid lower until his large hands covered my backside.

My heart was beating so damn hard it vibrated my ear drums.

"You're so fucking beautiful," Jesse whispered just outside my ear.

I might have been in the heat of the moment, but his word choice still caught me by surprise. "Did you just say *fuck*?" I'd heard barely a handful of curses come out of Jesse's mouth and none of them had included the pinnacle of curse words.

"Yeah, that's how damn adamant and passionate I am about how beautiful you are." His expression was so serious I almost smiled.

"Well *thanks*," I said, running my hands down his stomach. "I'll take 'fucking beautiful' as the highest form of praise."

He kissed the corner of my mouth gently and squeezed my backside not so gently. My breath came out all ragged. "If there's a higher form of praise, I don't know it," he whispered, moving to the other corner of my mouth. A gentle kiss and a not-so-gentle squeeze.

Oh, dear God. Ying and Yang really had it right when it came to intimate touch. Gentle, hard. Soft, rough.

Since I knew I was nearing the point of being struck temporarily mute myself, I moved my hands down until they reached the top of his sweats. I was close enough to feel him *ready to go*, but one layer of fabric separated us.

Not for long.

He didn't say anything or try to stop me when I slid his shorts over his backside and let them drop to the ground.

Now Jesse's ass . . . that was fucking beautiful. I didn't have to see it sans clothes to know that; I could tell from touch alone.

I pressed closer until I felt him hard against me. Breathing was becoming such a chore I needed to get horizontal before I passed out.

Jesse's chest rose hard and fast against mine. "Just because I told you I loved you, Rowen, doesn't mean I expect sex two minutes after." He lifted his hand to my face and smoothed his thumb down my cheek. "I'm not one of those guys who expect sex in exchange for love."

I kissed his palm. "I know that. Believe me, I know that. Even if you were one of those guys who expected sex in exchange for love, I've known plenty of others who expect it for much less." The skin between his eyebrows came together, but his eyes stayed on mine. "I'm not going to have sex with you because I feel like I have to. I'm going to have sex with you because I *want* to." I ran a finger down the line between his eyebrows, trying to erase it. "I appreciate you checking, but if you're done playing the part of Mr. Chivalry, think you can hang up your moral high ground ways and rock my world?"

"I had to check," he replied before kissing my forehead. "I will most certainly try to . . . rock your world . . . but what I might lack in experience and skill, I can make up for with persistence and lots of practice." His smile curved up higher on one side. "*Lots* of practice."

"I'm sure you've got plenty of skill, but I'm totally committed to the lots and lots of practice thing. Sounds good." I winked at him, grabbed his hand, and led him to the mattress.

I loved how I was about to make love to the guy of my dreams on a mattress on the floor of a drafty old farmhouse attic. It wasn't exactly the stuff fairy tales were made of, but it was my tale. And I'd never envy that Cinderella chick again.

"Before we get too comfortable," I said, stopping at the edge of the mattress, "you better have your condoms handy. I won't be able to take much more foreplay. Really. I'm close to going cross-eyed if we keep it up for much longer."

Jesse's face went a little deer-in-the-headlights. I'd known plenty of guys who weren't big fans of condoms because they were Grade A Dickheads, but Jesse wasn't close to one of those guys. I knew that wasn't why he'd gone a little blank when I mentioned bagging his boy.

And then I realized another reason why his face might have dropped.

"Please tell me you've got a condom." Really, fate

wouldn't be that mean, right?

He rubbed the back of his neck. Oh, hell no.

I'd been on the pill since I turned thirteen. Mom was convinced that if I wasn't already, I would be getting it on soon. It was good to know that, at least once in my life, I'd lived up to her expectations. However, I adhered to the two forms of contraception rule for a lot of reasons. Even though Jesse was the closest by a landslide to the only exception, I couldn't. For his sake, for my sake, for the potential glimmer in our eyes' sake.

"Jesse?" I said slowly.

He lifted his index finger. He twisted around and inspected his room as if it was a black hole. "I've got a box in here . . . *somewhere*."

I exhaled my relief.

He bee lined for his dresser, so I made myself comfortable on his mattress and enjoyed the view. My God. That ass . . .

He tore through the contents of the top drawer. Socks and undershirts parachuted to the floor. Apparently finding nothing, he moved on to the next drawer. Same thing, except for the jeans being tossed out of the drawer. He was frantically searching and I only let myself grin at his panic because he couldn't see it.

One more drawer to go.

Jesse was the first guy I'd known who didn't know exactly where his condoms were. Guys lived by them and died without them. Or at least their penises did. For Jesse to have no clue where his were led me to believe he was either absurdly absent-minded or hadn't used them in a while.

Since he and Josie had broken up six months ago and

he had moved rooms for me, I supposed Jesse could have forgotten where he kept his stash.

Rummaging through the third and final drawer, Jesse gave a victory cheer as he threw his hand up in the air. A box of condoms was clutched in his fist.

I sighed again in relief.

He headed back toward the mattress, a victorious smile on his face. I had a full-on, frontal view, so my gaze didn't linger on his face.

"Exactly where I forgot I left them." He shook the box and opened it.

Like, opened it for the first time.

Something I'd never once considered entered my mind. "Jesse?" I said, sitting up. I felt a little deer-in-the-headlights.

"Yeah?" he replied as he fumbled with the box.

"You're not a"—I fumbled to get the word out—" . . . *virgin* . . . are you?" Please, please, please say he wasn't.

He stopped fumbling with the box. My stomach dropped.

"Define virgin," he said slowly.

My hand covered my mouth. No way. No. Way.

"But you and Josie were together for so long . . ." I was sure I was missing something. "I mean, the two of you never . . . like *never* . . ."

He shook his head once. "Nope. We never . . or *never* had sex."

There was only one question to ask. "Why?"

It wasn't because I was judging him because of it; I just couldn't conceive of it. The oldest virgin I'd ever met was a seventeen-year-old. Never would I have guessed the god in human form Jesse Walker, a nineteen-year-old all-man guy, would be one.

Jesse sat down on the edge of the mattress and dropped his hand over my knee. "Josie and I got together when we were young. In a small town where everyone knows everyone else, you don't sleep with a girl you're not intending to marry unless you want her dad coming after you with a shotgun. I wasn't sure I was ready to make either kind of commitment to Josie back then, and after that, we just sort of kept with the same kind of routine when it came to the physical part of our relationship." He lifted his shoulders. "I guess neither of us were ready to make that kind of commitment."

Commitment and love. Sex as the added bonus. I wasn't familiar with that equation. I had been so sure it was a bold-faced lie. Yet there it was, love, commitment, and the added bonus, sitting beside me.

Had anything I'd known of life up until that summer been true?

"Jesse,"—I rested my hand on his—"I'm not a virgin, you know. I haven't been one in a long time."

"I know." He nodded.

I bit my lip and looked him in the eyes. "Are you sure you want your first time to be with me?" If I could have gone back in time and changed everything—said no to all the boys and waited for a night with Jesse Walker—I would have done it. I wouldn't have needed a second to consider.

"Rowen—"

I shook my head. I didn't want to talk around the topic or have him sugar-coat anything. I wanted the truth, cold and hard if that's what it was.

"Are. You. Sure?"

Jesse scooted closer until his face was just a few inches from mine. Both of his hands moved to my face and those eyes of his blazed into mine. "I'm sure." If the conviction in his words didn't prove it, his expression did. "I love you, and I'm sure, Rowen. Now, why don't you help me figure out how that whole rocking-your-world thing works?"

I grinned again. Frowning was impossible when Jesse beamed at me that way. "There'll be a lot of hands-on coaching," I said, leaning closer until I almost tasted the salt on his skin. "But I promise to return the favor." When my mouth pressed into the base of his neck, Jesse's skin erupted with goosebumps.

"I'm fully committed to this whole endeavor," he said, his voice rough.

"Good," I whispered against his skin. Grabbing hold of his arms, I drew him closer. "Then get over here and make love to me."

Jesse shifted, and then he was pressing into me, laying me back onto the mattress. His arm wound around my back and the other traveled down my hip, winding around to my backside. His mouth covered mine as he lowered himself onto me. He didn't crush all of his weight against me. I saw the strain in his shoulders from holding his weight.

His tongue played with the seam of my mouth, although I didn't need much encouragement to grant him access. When my tongue touched his, he lowered the rest of himself on top of me, and the sigh I moaned into his mouth wasn't quiet or short. His erection pressed hard into my stomach, and even though I could barely breathe with it there, I wanted it pressed hard into something else.

My hand left his back and felt around the mattress, searching for that little box.

I kept pace with his kissing in the midst of my search and almost cried out with joy when my fingers touched that box. I grabbed what I needed and ripped one free of the strip. I needed both hands to tear the wrapper open, but it didn't take long. The whole time, Jesse's hands, mouth, and body continued their pursuits. Each kiss brought me closer, each touch lifted me higher. When his hips flexed against mine, I let out another moan.

"Damn, Jesse," I breathed, maneuvering my hands down where I needed them.

"What?"

"I need you to slow down and suit up or else I'm going to come before you even get a chance to lose your virginity."

He was breathing so hard he was almost panting and his face was flushed. "Am I doing something wrong?"

"No," I said instantly. "You're doing something very, very right."

That smug smile reappeared, and his hips flexed against mine again. Even if I'd wanted to, I couldn't hold in the sound that slipped from my mouth.

He said, "I've only waited twenty years for this moment. I've been playing this whole thing out in my head for a while, so it's good to know it's working in real life."

"It's working," I emphasized, right as my hand wrapped around him.

That smugness washed right off of his face. In fact, all emotion other than desire left his face.

I smoothed my hand down his entire length, then up, and repeated the process until I wasn't so sure he would be able to hold himself back if I did it one more time.

"How was that?" I asked, rolling the condom into place.

"Speechless," he panted, flexing into my hand as I finished with the condom.

I pressed a kiss into the bend of his neck as I guided him closer. Once he was right where he needed to be, I wrapped my legs around his hips and removed my hands.

A sheen of sweat covered his entire face and his chest was rising and falling so quickly, I wasn't sure how he managed to get out words, but he did. "I love you." He kissed me as sweetly as he'd ever kissed me before.

"I know," I replied, running my hands down his face.

His hips flexed, and he moved inside of me. I cried out and curled my hands into his hair. He moved so slowly and carefully inside of me, almost like I was the virgin. When he was as deep inside as he could go, he trembled and lowered his mouth to my ear. He didn't say anything. He just inhaled and exhaled, letting me keep pace with him.

"See?" I said, tightening my muscles around him. "Feels pretty damn great, doesn't it?"

Jesse groaned when I squeezed him again. "It's fucking beautiful," he breathed, and then he started moving inside of me.

I could tell he was trying to go slow, to take his time, but that wasn't a favor I needed. So I lifted my hips and rocked against him at a quicker tempo until he'd caught my pace.

"It's all right, Jesse," I said. "You can come if you're ready."

"I've been about to come ever since you took your

dress off. I'm just trying to live up to my end of the deal."

"Believe me," I said, fisting my hands deeper into his hair, "I'm there. I'm just waiting for you. *Please* don't make me wait any longer."

"Thank," he panted, moving deep inside of me, "God."

If I wasn't so close to my climax, I would have laughed at the relief flooding his expression. Instead, I lifted my hips and moved against him, bringing us both closer.

"Rowen," he sighed, and when he started groaning and moving inside of me like he couldn't move fast enough, I knew he'd found his release. I followed him one moment later, and as my body fell apart around him, all I could do was repeat his name. Over and over. Until the only word I knew was his name.

Even after his orgasm had ripped through his body, he held his weight carefully above me. He didn't collapse on top of me in a post-sex haze like I knew I would have if our positions had been reversed.

His breathing took a couple of minutes to even out and, as soon as it did, he lowered his mouth to my ear. "That was one hell of a dance."

CHAPTER fifteen

If I could spend the rest of my life naked and tangled up with Jesse Walker post-O, I'd never once feel like I was missing out on anything.

It had started to rain a few minutes earlier, and the droplets hitting the roof created a soothing song. The air coming in from the window had that fresh rain scent, and that, combined with the scent of Jesse's skin, was a powerful aphrodisiac. If we hadn't just finished doing it five minutes ago, we'd be doing it right now.

"How are you doing up there?" I asked, tilting my head back from where it rested on his chest. "You're awfully quiet."

Jesse's fingers continued their lazy pattern up and down my back as I lifted up onto an elbow beside him. "I'm still speechless," he said, grinning up at the ceiling.

"Pretty good, right?"

"Pretty good is an insult to what that just was," he said, shaking his head. "Speechless is really the best way to describe it."

"Was it as good as you were expecting?"

He grinned. "Better."

"I still can't believe you waited this long to have sex. What were you waiting for?" I teased, tickling my fingers down his sides. "Marriage?"

Jesse rolled onto his side so his face was level with mine. He skimmed his knuckles down my face. "No. I was waiting for you."

Those words earned him one hell of a passionate kiss. After we'd come up for air and I managed to somewhat recompose myself, I asked my next question in the how-could-Jesse-be-a-virgin file.

"So I get that you and Josie decided to wait, but what about after you two broke up? I'm sure you could have had your pick of whatever girl you wanted for a one-night, no-strings-attached roll in the hay."

"Maybe. Maybe not," he said with a shrug. "But it wasn't the physical part of the relationship I missed the most. It was the companionship. And a guy doesn't need a girl to . . ."

I stuck my tongue into my cheek to keep from laughing as Jesse fumbled for the right word. After a few more seconds, I came to the rescue. "Get off?"

Jesse shot me a sheepish smile. "I was going for something that didn't sound so dirty, but yeah, that's what I was getting at."

"And now?" I said. "Now that you've felt what sex with a woman and not your hand"—I arched my eyebrows—"is like, do you still think you wouldn't miss the physical part of the relationship as much as the companionship part?"

His eyes widened, followed by an emphatic shake of his head. "I'm in big trouble, because now I know what I'd be missing."

"I know, right? Those virgins are nuts enough"—I winked down at him—"but those born-again virgins are straight off the loony farm."

Jesse chuckled and pulled me closer. "Call me nuts all you want, but I'm glad Josie wasn't my first."

The mention of Josie and firsts reminded me of a conversation I'd had earlier. I cinched my arm tighter around him, almost like I was trying to protect him. "I'm sorry about what happened with Josie and Garth. She told me last night, and I can't imagine . . ."

The skin at the corners of Jesse's eyes creased.

"And then you found me at his place late at night." His anger that night made sense after I learned the history between him and Garth. "I'm sorry. I'll stay away from Garth from now on. I'll even mix some Mylanta into his eggs if you want me to."

The lines wrinkling Jesse's face slowly faded. "Tempting, but that's okay. Garth's life is punishment enough," he said, lying back down and pulling me with him.

A couple more minutes of silence, except for the rain pinging on the roof, passed. I should at least try to get some sleep because around here, we didn't really get days off. Cattle still needed fed, along with cowboys. I'd lost track of time, but I knew dawn couldn't be more than a few hours away.

"I think now that we've really slept together, we should tell my parents about us." I heard the smile in his voice. The smile on my own face disappeared.

"Are you sure?" I shifted against him, because I wasn't.

"I'm sure."

Of course he was.

I swallowed. "How are you going to tell them?" I couldn't think of an easy way to break the news to his parents. Would we tell them we were in love? No way would we tell them we'd had sex.

"Something really smooth," he said, scooting me closer until my head was just below his chin. I dangled my leg around his waist. "We'll totally ease them into it."

I didn't know how he planned to "ease" them into it, but Jesse was a smart guy. If he said he could ease them in, I'd believe him.

"Hopefully your dad and mom won't mind you dating a menace to society. Otherwise we're in trouble." I was mainly teasing, but when Jesse didn't reply right away, I knew he'd taken it differently.

"Why did you get into all of the drugs and drinking . . . and *stuff*, Rowen?" Jesse obviously didn't like to mention the guys from my past any more than I did.

"A lot of reasons."

Jesse exhaled slowly. "Why do you answer all my questions so vaguely?"

It was my turn to exhale slowly. Fine. Since we were apparently laying everything out on the table—girlfriends sleeping with good friends, confessions of love, the taking and losing of virginity, et cetera—I supposed I might as well dive right into the bottomless pit of my past.

"I've always been a little different, Jesse," I started, cuddling closer, "a little one-of-these-things-is-not-like-the-other. I grew up without knowing my dad. I don't think Mom even knows who my real father is, and the only parent I had was gone more than half the year traveling for work. I was pawned off on neighbors, acquaintances, and sometimes the random old friend passing through town." I studied the ceiling and focused on Jesse's body against mine. I was safe. I was loved. I wasn't that scared little girl anymore. "I really started getting out of control when I hit thirteen."

Jesse's knuckles skimmed up and down my back in slow circles. "Why?"

He asked all of the questions I didn't want him to ask. All of the questions I didn't even ask myself anymore.

I bit my lip. I could do it. "My mom was dating this one guy." I couldn't say his name. I hadn't said it since and I'd never say it again. "She dated a bunch of losers, but this guy really brought new meaning to the word. I'd find him staring at me when he didn't think I'd notice. He'd go out of his way to be close to me . . . he'd look for innocent ways to . . ." I swallowed, closed my eyes, and forced myself on, "to touch me. I didn't think much about it. I just wrote him off as a Grade A Creeper and tried to avoid him. My mom was gone for work one week, and she'd *responsibly* left me under the care and supervision of said Grade A Creeper." I felt Jesse's body stiffen beneath me. Or was that mine? "I'd just gotten home from school and headed to my bedroom. I didn't even know he was back from work yet. I was in the middle of changing, and he just opened the door and walked inside the room like he owned the place. I yelled at him to get out. He just smiled."

Jesse's hand stopped moving up and down my back.

"He said that because he took care of my mom, I needed to take care of him. He . . . he . . ." I swallowed, but getting the words out was harder and harder. It was the first time I'd told the story since the day after it had happened. "He said my mom would never have to know. He said it would be our secret. And he said if I ever told anyone, he'd suffocate me and my mom when we were

271

asleep."

Jesse's arms quivered around me. Then again, maybe that's just the way they felt since I was shaking, too.

"He came at me. I tried to run. He was faster. He grabbed me and I tried to fight, but he was a big guy and I was even smaller than I am now." When I closed my eyes, the entire scene played through my head, so instead, I opened them and focused on Jesse. I let him ground me. I let his eyes remind me I was safe. "He threw me on the floor, and I knew what was going to happen next. I knew no one was coming to save me. I knew I was alone."

Jesse's chest was rising and falling hard again. I hated taking him down the darkest road in my life. I hated that he had to know why I was such a goddamned mess. But I loved how not even a little bit did his hold on me loosen. He held me to him like he was trying to protect me from my own past.

"I looked around for something I could use as a weapon, and that's when I realized I had all the weapon I needed. You might have seen me in a certain pair of old black combat boots?" Everyone at Willow Springs had seen me in those a good dozen times. "They also happen to be steel-toed and, when kicked right into a man's balls, they can do some damage. I got out of the house as fast as I could and ran to a friend's house. I stayed there until mom got home the next day." The ball was back in my throat. I knew I was one of the lucky ones, my would-be rapist never finished what he'd started, but my ending was still devastating. In fact, the ending was the most heart breaking part of the story.

"I told Mom what had happened the moment I saw her. I told her everything." I paused because the tears had

272

started. I felt one drop fall onto Jesse's neck. His arms flexed around me. "And you know what she did after I finished telling my story?" Jesse shook his head against mine. "She grounded me for lying to her and said if I ever told her the same kind of lie again, she'd send me off to some all girls' reform school." My mom and I had never been close—I'd always known I was the mistake she wished she'd never made—but after that day, whatever frail bond we had was forever broken. "Her asshole boyfriend called later that night to break up with her. He thought it was for the best since I'd 'thrown myself at him' while she'd been away. She slapped me across the face, called me a little slut, and grounded me again."

If there was a way to curl deeper into Jesse's arms, I was trying.

"After that, I turned into the walking train-wreck that landed me here in the first place."

As hard as it was, retelling the story was easier than I'd expected. I guessed that was because of who I was telling, but as Jesse's silence continued, I wondered if giving him the "whole" story had been such a good idea.

"Rowen," he said at last. His voice was low and vibrated just enough that I knew he was trying to keep some emotions in check. "I love you."

I nodded my head beneath his chin.

"If there was any way for me to go back in time and protect you from that piece of shit, I would do it like that." He snapped his fingers. "If there was any way for me to go back and kick the shit out of him so he'd never even *think* about touching another girl again, I would."

The anger he restrained almost made me shiver. Other than that night with Garth when he'd come to get me, I hadn't heard Jesse sound like that.

"But since I can't travel back in time, I'm going to promise you this now. I will protect you. I will keep you safe." His mouth dropped to my forehead and he kissed it. "You *are* safe."

I was safe.

I. Was. *Safe*.

Those were three words I'd needed to hear from my mom five years ago. Jesse's arms wrapped around me the way I'd needed her arms to wrap around me then. He comforted me exactly the way I'd needed comforting as a terrified thirteen-year-old. He was healing the wound that had been opened so long ago, I'd almost forgotten it was still there. I'd distracted myself with things that numbed my mind and body just enough I could continue to forget.

I didn't need those things anymore. I'd never need them again. I wasn't healed—I wasn't naive enough to think some words and hugs would heal that kind of a wound—but I'd been *heard*. Finally, someone had heard me and believed me.

I could take my first step forward. Finally.

"Thank you for listening," I said. "And thank you for what you just said. I'm sorry my past is such a ginormous cluster-fuck."

Jesse's head shook.

"Please don't say you don't care about what I've done or what's been done to me," I said before he could. "*Please* don't say that."

"I wasn't going to say that." His lips brushed over my forehead. "I do care about your past, Rowen. It's made you who you are today, and that's the girl I'm in love with."

"Okay. Did you come with some sort of manual that

goes over the exact right thing to say to a girl?" I lifted my head so I could look at his face. After a moment, he mirrored my smile. "Because I swear to God, you say the *exact* perfect thing at the right time."

"I don't need a manual to tell the truth." He kissed the top of my head and pulled the blankets around me. "We'd better get to sleep. Or else you're going to fall asleep in the blueberry pancake batter in the morning."

Jesse was back. The anger was gone, his muscles had stop quivering, and his voice was back to normal. I'd just admitted my darkest secret, and he'd heard it, accepted it, comforted me, and moved on.

After five years of feeling like I was suffocating, I could breathe again.

"I don't want to go to sleep," I said.

"You've officially de-flowered me, and we've talked about so many serious things, my head's still spinning." I elbowed his side for the "de-flower" comment. "What else could you possibly have in mind?"

I rubbed my leg down his stomach. "You want to know the perk to the guy being the one losing his virginity?"

Jesse cleared his throat as my leg brushed over the part of him that was already hard again. "That he's not a virgin anymore?"

I laughed as I pivoted on top of him. "No," I said, running my hands up his chest. His eyes were excited, along with the rest of his body. No sleep for the weary. "That he can do it again right after."

CHAPTER sixteen

Jesse had been right. I did almost pass out into the pancake batter the next morning. Although it was huckleberry, not blueberry.

We did go to sleep. Eventually. But an hour of sleep didn't really cut it. I was waiting for the coffee to brew and almost counting the minutes until I could be with Jesse again.

It would be one long-ass day.

"Penny for your thoughts." Rose came up beside me holding a bowl and beating the eggs inside it with a wire whisk.

I didn't care if she offered me a million dollars for my thoughts. I would *not* admit having dirty thoughts to the mother of the boy I was having them about.

"It's too early for thoughts," I said, flipping a few pancakes. After my first pancake catastrophe, I hadn't burned another batch.

Knock on wood.

Or . . . ehem . . .

Shoot. I was blushing in front of Rose.

"Did you enjoy the dance last night?" she asked.

Focus on the pancakes and *try* not to sound like an imbecile. "I enjoyed myself." *Especially the after party.*

"I'm glad, sweetie," she said, heading back over to

the stove with her whipped eggs. "We all work so hard around here, it's nice to let your hair down and have a good time."

Mission accomplished, then.

I was about to check the pancakes when the back door swung open and a string of cowboys wandered in. They were all a little bleary-eyed, but one was especially so. Tired as he looked, Jesse had an I-just-got-laid grin on his face.

He hung his hat up and headed my way, making no qualms about it.

I'm pretty sure I flushed again as a few of the high, *high* points of last night ran through my mind. Our second time, I'd introduced Jesse to the cowgirl position—I thought he could especially appreciate it—and we'd taken our time. Well, we'd taken a bit more time. Not much.

"Good morning," I said with a bit of inflection as he stopped in front of me. He was close, a little too close for being in a kitchen of people who thought we were just friends.

Jesse snatched an apple from the copper bowl on the counter. "Why, yes. Yes, it is," he said, crunching into the apple. He managed to keep that grin on his face the whole time.

"How did you sleep?" I teased, smiling into the griddle.

He leaned in closer and whispered, "I didn't."

A shiver ran down my spine in the middle of a hot kitchen on a summer morning. The man had the art of inflection down.

"How do you feel this morning?" I asked, trying to sound like we were having the most ordinary of conversations.

He sunk his teeth into the apple again, his eyes gleaming. "Like I lost something," he said before chewing the chunk of apple in his mouth.

I snickered quietly.

"Oh, no, hun," Rose said, appearing out of nowhere. "What did you lose?"

Jesse's mouth stopped crunching as he did that whole deer-in-the-headlights thing again. He'd done a lot of that in the past twenty-four hours. "Uhhh . . . I don't know . . . what I lost?" He glanced at me like he was looking for some help.

I was still too frozen to talk.

Rose gave him an amused face. "Then what were you just saying you lost?"

Jesse gulped down what was left of the apple in his mouth. "I don't know. I won't remember what I lost until I find it."

I joined Rose in giving him an amused look. She lifted her hand to his forehead and ran it over his face. "Are you coming down with something, Jesse?"

"Nope," he said, sliding me a quick look. "I've never felt better. But I want to tell you and Dad something."

My mouth dropped open. He wouldn't do that yet. When he said he'd tell his parents, I thought I'd at least have a few days to get used to the idea. Apparently not. I mouthed *What?* at him.

His response? A wink and an *I've got this* mouthed back.

"Well?" Neil said, coming up behind Rose and resting his hands on her shoulders. "Tell away."

I was wincing before Jesse said one word.

"Rowen and I are dating," he said, all matter-of-fact. "We're together. We like each other. She rocks my world. I rock hers." He shot me a sideways look and tried to keep his smile contained.

My mouth fell open a bit more.

Jesse lifted a shoulder. "We just wanted you both to know so it didn't seem like we were sneaking around behind your backs."

If climbing up a chimney to get to his room so I could seduce their virginal son wasn't considered "sneaking," perhaps I needed to look that one up in the dictionary again.

Jesse wrapped his arm around me and pulled me close. He'd said it, so he was showing it.

Ground? Please open up and shallow me right now.

I chanced a look at Rose and Neil, certain they'd scowl at me like I was the wolf they'd let into their precious little flock of sheep. Instead, I found the opposite. Neil had a small smile on his face, and Rose's smile was tipped a little higher on one side.

"We appreciate you telling us, Jesse." Rose patted her son's cheek. "We kind of figured that out on our own." Neil and she exchanged a look. "But it was nice of you two to finally figure it out, too."

My mouth could only drop open. It certainly wasn't up to forming actual words.

"Yeah, well, Rowen kind of made me work hard for it," Jesse said, back to working on his apple. Neil just shook his head and smiled his way over to the table.

Rose glanced purposefully at me, standing beside Jesse, protected under his arm, and she winked. "As she should have." Then, like nothing especially profound had just been announced, Rose headed back to the stove and her eggs.

"See?" he said, kissing the top of my head. "Easy as that."

I rolled my eyes and smacked his butt as he wandered toward the table. A few of the guys who'd noticed gave him a thumbs up or lifted their cups of coffee my way. The embarrassment wouldn't end that morning.

"Yeah, that was the epitome of smooth," I said after him.

He spun around, his dimples on full display, and lifted his hands at his sides. "It was as smooth as I'm capable of," he said before sniffing the air. My shoulders went rigid before the next words came from his mouth. "The pancakes are burning."

CHAPTER seventeen

My days at Willow Springs were spent working, and my nights were spent with Jesse in some room, or field, or barn, or . . . whatever we could find. The summer flew by. July was ending before I knew the month had begun.

It had been the best month of my life.

That was no exaggeration, no form of the melodrama Jesse still liked to say I was partial to. It was the truth. I had found an adoptive family by most definitions of the word; I was in love with the kind of man who seemed too good to be true; I had found a handful of girlfriends with the Walker sisters and Josie; I'd managed to steer clear of Garth and he of me; and mom had thankfully delayed her grand scheme of flying herself and her new boyfriend out for a little get-together. My dreams, for the first time in years, were back to color. I'd even squeezed in enough drawing time to fill an entire sketchbook.

If months got better than that July did, I couldn't imagine it.

Plus, other than one night when Jesse had to camp out with the herd because one of the calves had gotten sick, we'd spent every night together. Some nights we did nothing more than talk until we fell asleep. Most nights we talked, then made love until we fell asleep. For being a virgin a month before, Jesse had meant it when he said he was committed to fine-tuning his sex skills. I'd be under-exaggerating if I said Jesse had mad skills in that department.

Neil and Rose might have given us the thumbs up in the dating department, but even Jesse hadn't worked up the courage to tell them about us sleeping together every night. Thanks to a lock on my door and the unspoken rule that no one ever went into his attic room, no one had walked in on us unexpectedly.

I didn't like omitting the truth with Neil and Rose, but I left that to Jesse. He knew his parents better than I did, and if he thought keeping our sleeping arrangements to ourselves for the time being was best, I was good with that.

After he'd described his parents as old-fashioned modernists, I couldn't look at Rose and Neil the same way. Jesse said they might realize we were sleeping together and they would support us because we were both consenting adults, but they didn't want to know it was happening a room or two above their bedrooms.

So July was legendary. The best on record.

And then August 1st rolled around.

I was busy in the garden picking early tomatoes when Rose came up to me with a stoic expression. Rose didn't do stoic, so my heart was already thumping before she'd said a word. My mom had called her, probably because I'd been ignoring her calls all summer, to tell Rose that she and boy-toy had a rare three-day-weekend coming up and would fly in that Friday night.

She didn't ask. Didn't wait for Rose to run it by me. She dictated. She steam-rolled. Like she'd been doing all eighteen years of my life.

From Rose's expression, I'd thought she'd come bearing the news of a loved one's death, so I was relieved for all of one second when I realized no one had died. My mom was just coming to dinner with her boyfriend. My moment of relief shifted to panic.

I knew it was silly, but Willow Springs felt like my something special. It was my world free of her and her toxicity. I didn't want to ruin things.

My mom wasn't the issue as much as the storm we created when we were together. We might have both been a bit unstable on our own, but together? Things got downright volatile. I didn't want Neil and Rose to witness that. I didn't want Jesse to witness that.

I didn't want to experience that either. Not anymore.

The summer had given me a new perspective. The lenses I'd been viewing life through for so long had been exchanged for a different set. A new lens that showed people as basically good and life as pretty damn great when I opened myself up to it.

I'd changed. Not entirely, but enough. A lot.

From Rose's description of Mom's call, I knew she hadn't changed. So I had and she hadn't. Would our relationship change? That was the question I couldn't answer and one I really didn't want to get to the bottom of over a steak dinner with the Walkers.

Too bad it was six o'clock on Friday night, minutes away from when Mom and Mr. Boyfriend would be pulling up. It was too late to call a time-out and cordon Mom and I off on our own little island so we could work out some serious shit I wasn't sure could be worked out.

Jesse snuck up behind me where I fretted over the fruit salad. "For the millionth time, relax." His hands lifted to my shoulders and his fingers pinched and rolled the muscles running down my neck and shoulders.

"For the millionth time," I replied, closing my eyes. Jesse's hands could work magic of all different kinds. "It's easy for you to say, but you've never met my mom. I don't think I've ever been relaxed around her."

"Yeah, but are you relaxed around me?"

I gave up trying to layer the blueberries on top of the kiwi just right, dropped my head, and let Jesse's fingers work. "Sometimes." I pressed back into him to further explain.

He chuckled. "Right *now* are you relaxed around me?"

It was impossible not to be when he was massaging my neck. "Yes."

"Good news then, Rowen. I'm going to be with you all night. I won't leave your side, so anytime your mom starts making you feel all panicky, just take a hit of my ultra-relaxing aura."

I smiled. "Ultra-relaxing aura, eh? And here I thought my boyfriend was a cowboy, not a hippie."

"Cowboy's in my blood, but my heart's all hippie." He kissed the back of my neck, right at my hairline, and wrapped his arms around me. "I love you. I'm here for you tonight. We're all here for you tonight. Everything will be all right. And if it isn't, I'll fix it. Okay?"

I nodded and tilted my head toward his. "Okay."

"Whatever happens tonight, it won't change us, Rowen. It won't change the way I feel about you." He planted a soft kiss on my mouth. I was already more relaxed. Then he moved in for another one; that one wasn't as soft or short.

What had I just been worried about?

"All right, you two. Rowen's mom will be here any second, and I don't want her to walk into the place and see you two lip-locked." Rose grabbed the fruit bowl and attempted to give us both a maternal warning look. It didn't really work because she capped her warning with a smile. "Let's give her a few minutes before we tell her about you two. I don't want her thinking the only thing you've been doing all summer is my son."

Jesse coughed. My eyes bugged out.

Rose inspected our reaction for one moment before it clicked. She flushed and suddenly couldn't make eye contact with either of us. "That came out wrong. *All* wrong."

"You think, Mom?" Jesse teased, his voice a couple notes high.

She swatted his arm affectionately as she headed for the table. "You know what I meant."

"I know what you meant, but you might not want to repeat those exact words when Rowen mom's here," Jesse said. "You know. In case she takes it the wrong way."

"Since you're so eager to hang out in the kitchen, why don't you go mash those potatoes?" Rose settled the fruit salad on the table, then stood back to inspect the table. She'd really gone all out.

She'd cut a few mini-bouquets of flowers from her garden and arranged them in mason jars. She'd set out the country rose china set passed down from her mom and she had polished up the silverware set, too. We'd spent a good half of the day making dinner. After making a dinner of cold meatloaf sandwiches and potato salad for the guys and dropping it off at the bunkhouse, we'd slaved away making pie pastry, picking green beans, and peeling, coring, and slicing apples. The menu was simple country fare, but it had been created in the Walker kitchen, so it would be delicious, too.

"I love this new dress," Jesse said, running his eyes down my body as he wandered over to the pot of potatoes. "Like *really* love it." The inflection in his voice almost made me shiver in anticipation. How many hours until bedtime?

"I might have had a little help picking it out." I shot him a smile as I went to the fridge to pull out some milk and butter. "I love that shirt of yours, too. Like *really* love it."

Jesse lifted his arms and did a spin. "I might have had a little help picking it out."

We'd gone into "town" shopping yesterday, and instead of picking out our own outfits, we decided to pick out each other's. Since Jesse lived in his white tees, I found a plaid button-down shirt with those pearly looking snaps. I got it one size smaller than he typically wore for the added eye candy. I didn't bother with picking out pants because Jesse's everyday jeans could not be improved upon. That was a fact of life I'd come to accept. Add his boots, straw hat, and belt, and BOOM! He was every girl's dream.

Once I'd grabbed the butter and milk, I headed over to where he was mashing away.

While I poured in the milk and dropped the stick of butter into the pot, he said, "No offense, Rowen, because this is one nice shirt, but I win in the picking clothes out for each other department. That dress is . . ." When Jesse's eyes traveled back to me, his mashing came to a stop. The corners of his mouth lifted as he skimmed my body.

286

"Well, that dress is something else. Something. Else."

I glanced over at Rose before sneaking a quick kiss on his cheek. "You really do know how to pick out a dress. But don't worry. I won't tell anyone."

"Thanks." He laughed as he got back to mashing. "My reputation as the strapping, manly cowboy that I am would be forever tarnished."

Jesse's selection had surprised me. Although maybe it shouldn't have. Instead of wandering the racks of one of the clothing stores specializing in western wear, Jesse had wandered into a funky consignment store. He claimed he got a contact high after being in there for only a half hour. He sifted through every last rack in the place before he found my dress. *The* dress.

It was a burgundy, no-frills dress that didn't scream *Look at me! Look at me!* It was eerie how Jesse had managed to find quite possibly the only dress in the history of dresses to blend both that punk, dark style I'd shown up in Willows Springs wearing with country flair. The dress was a little bipolar in the style department, but it worked.

I was pulling the salt down from the spice cabinet when the doorbell rang. I froze.

"They're here!" Clementine announced from the living room.

Rose pulled her apron off. "Ready?" she asked, wrapping her arm around me like she knew I needed the support.

Would it matter if I answered honestly? I just nodded my head.

Jesse grabbed a towel to wipe his hands, but Rose put the masher he'd abandoned back in his hands. "Get those potatoes on the table," she said. "Rowen and I can manage to open the door and escort a couple of guests inside the house by ourselves, I think."

Without another word, Rose pulled me along.

Jesse's eyebrows came together.

I'm okay, I mouthed. *Really*, I added when he didn't look convinced.

He nodded once, then started mashing like a maniac.

From the sounds coming from the foyer, Clementine was struggling to get the door opened. Lily and Hyacinth rushed down the stairs, smoothing their hair and adjusting their shirts. Neil was just finishing up in the barn, and Rose had warned him if he wasn't washed, presentable, and at the table by the time we sat down for dinner, he would sleep in the barn until winter.

Rose was one of the sweetest people out there, but I'd learned no one wanted to mess with her. The ranch hands listened to her better than they did Neil most of the time.

As we approached the door, I already felt Mom. I started worrying my eyebrow ring as I felt my steel gates and concrete walls begging to be raised. I felt my arms wanting to cross and my scowl wanting to form. I felt the little girl inside of me searching for the closest hiding spot.

Rose's arm tightened around me, and then Lily moved up beside me. She gave me a reassuring smile and, just like that, I was back at Willow Springs. Safe. Loved. Trusted.

The doorbell went off again. I heard my mom's drawn out sigh from the other side of the door.

Rose reached for the handle and pulled the door open.

There she was. Not a platinum strand of hair out of place. Not an article of clothing or accessory that wasn't designer. Not a hint of a smile.

"Kate," Rose greeted, opening her arms. "It's been too darn long, and you look too darn good after twenty years." When Rose's arms wrapped around her, Mom went stiff as a board and her expression twisted as though the hug was almost painful.

After a moment, Mom forced something meant to be a smile and patted Rose's back. "It's amazing what a good surgeon and money can do these days to erase a couple of decades," she said, practically breaking out of Rose's hug.

"Well, the only good surgeons we have in these parts are the ones that work on animals," Rose chuckled. "My beauty routine consists of a multi-vitamin and avoiding mirrors under overhead lighting."

Mom inspected Rose with that fake smile I'd grown up with. When her eyes trailed down to Rose's boots, I could tell it took everything inside of Mom to keep from cringing. For the millionth time that summer, I wondered what had brought those totally opposite people together in the first place. Or what had kept them connected, loosely as it might have been, for all of those years.

"And who are these lovely ladies?" Mom asked, moving on to the girls staggered around the door, after giving me a quick nod of acknowledgement.

"This is Lily, Hyacinth," Rose motioned at each girl, "and the little one here is Clementine. Jesse's in the kitchen finishing dinner, so you can meet him in a couple minutes."

Mom nodded her acknowledgement at each girl, keeping the plastered-on smile in place as she inspected them like they were last season's handbag.

Since she obviously wouldn't make the first move, I beat down the urge to cross my arms and said, "Hey,

Mom."

"Rowen," she said, the fake smile going faker. "I barely recognized you. It's been so long since it hasn't been dyed black, I'd forgotten what color your hair was." Yeah, I'm sure forgetting the color of her only child's hair was easy. "And, my oh my,"—her eyes skimmed down my dress to the boots Jesse had gotten me—"how lovely to see you in non-freak wear for once." One wall went up before I knew it. "I don't know how you managed it, Rose, but I owe you for showing my daughter the error of her fashion ways."

Rose took a step back and hung her arm around my waist again. The small comfort in that brought me close to crying with relief. "I love Rowen's sense of style. If I was younger and braver, I might sneak a couple things out of her dresser when she wasn't looking." Rose grinned over at me. "However, it's better to keep as much skin covered by no-fuss clothing when you're working on a ranch with a bunch of single men."

Mom gave that shrill, choppy laugh of hers. "When Rowen's concerned, it isn't *her* virtue you need to worry about."

Another wall went up and my arms crossed. I'd felt so strong, so sure of myself, just moments before she'd whisked through that door. She had me almost reverted back to that scared and confused girl I'd been weeks earlier.

Someone slid up beside me, grabbed my hand, and angled himself ever so slightly in front of me. "That's a joke, right?" Jesse asked, making his greeting.

Mom's eyes darted his way, and if a woman like her could get stars in her eyes, she got them. Her gaze drifted down his body in a way that made me feel territorial and icky all at once. "You can take it however you want." She flashed her charming smile—which was also fake—and lifted her eyebrows.

Since Jesse didn't look in the mood to make introductions, Rose stepped in. "Kate, this is my son Jesse."

"Wonderful to meet you, Jesse." Hearing her say his name made my stomach turn. Or was it the tone in which she said his name? Or was it the way her eyes dropped when she was done?

When she noticed my hand clasped in Jesse's, Mom's approving expression morphed into shock. "Oh, dear God. Rose, I am so sorry. If I had known Rowen would go after your boy, I would have never sent her here this summer." Mom's hand went to her chest and she shook her head. "I would have hoped she'd show better restraint when it came to hooking up with the son of one of my oldest and dearest friends."

I didn't need to hear anyone else talk about why I was all wrong for Jesse. I did enough of that on my own.

"Rowen didn't pursue me," Jesse said, his whole back going rigid. "I pursued her. And we are not 'hooking up.' We're in love."

"Oh, dear God," Mom said again, practically cringing. "I am so, *so* sorry, Rose."

Yeah, because a guy admitting he loved me was so much worse than one admitting he was just screwing me.

"What for?" Rose asked, resting a hand on Jesse's arm. It was a gesture of comfort and *stand down, I've got this*. "She challenges him. He challenges her. They love each other. As far as young relationships go, we couldn't be happier Jesse's with a girl like Rowen."

I doubted Mom would look so flabbergasted if she woke up the next day to find zombies stumbling down her driveway. "You're all right with this?"

"Yes," Rose replied. "These two have some good kismet. Don't you think, Kate?"

"They've got . . . *something*," Mom said, pursing her lips when she rechecked our connected hands.

"Where's your plus one?" Rose asked, shifting the conversation.

"He's still in the car on a business call," Mom replied, rolling her eyes. "Can you believe that when we checked in at the rental center, they didn't have a luxury option? The best they had was a mid-sized Dodge. I haven't been in a mid-sized anything since I was in college." Mom stepped inside and closed the door. Apparently "plus one" would be a while. "I don't know how you do it out here in the sticks, Rose. I don't think I could make it a day."

"I don't either," I muttered as we filed into the kitchen.

"I heard that, Rowen," she said over her shoulder. "Try to do something out-of-character and behave yourself tonight."

So my answer to my question? It didn't matter that I'd changed. She hadn't. Our relationship hadn't either.

"Out of respect for you, I'm going to try really hard to respect your mom," Jesse whispered over to me, keeping my hand in his. "But if she keeps saying stuff like that, I'm not going to stay quiet."

"Jesse—"

"No," he interrupted, "I don't care about her. I care about you. Because she's your mom, I will try to tolerate her, but I won't let her say those things to a person I love."

His words, his touch, his presence . . . all of it helped relax me some.

"Where were you five years ago?" I said.

"Right here," he answered, squeezing my hand. "I was right here."

A bit more of that relaxation thing trickled into my veins. I could handle one dinner.

"Dinner smells amazing, Rose," Mom announced as we entered the kitchen.

"Thank you. Rowen spent most of the day working on it," Rose replied.

Mom chuckled and patted Rose's back on her way to the table. "Getting in the way doesn't count."

Jesse was just opening his mouth and I was just getting ready to clamp my hand over it when Neil came through the back door.

"Washed up, cleaned up, and here a minute early," he announced, plunking his hat on one of the pegs. "No barn detention for me."

"Well if that isn't the bastard who moved my best friend out to the middle of nowhere."

Neil smiled his own version of her fake one. "So happy you were able to join us out here in the middle of nowhere, Kate."

I caught Rose giving him a *Watch it, buddy* face.

"After all you and Rose have done for Rowen this summer? Of course I had to pay you all a visit," Mom replied, sliding into a chair. "Rose swears up and down Rowen's been a huge help around here, so I had to come see it with my own eyes."

Neil took his time approaching the table, like he was putting it off for as long as he could. "I'm sorry to say it, but most of my hands don't work as hard as Rowen does. We've been lucky to have her."

The three girls sat on the opposite end of the table from my mom. Lily and Hyacinth just tried not to make eye contact with the swearing, blunt woman, but Clementine stared at her like Mom was a train wreck she couldn't look away from.

Jesse led me to the seat next to Lily and he took the one across from my mom. Mom gave Jesse a once over that made me blush from embarrassment and from anger.

My eyes shifted to my perfectly imperfect fruit salad. "Oops," I said, getting out of my chair. "I forgot the whipped cream."

I had just pulled the bowl of whipped cream I'd whipped my tail off making earlier out of the fridge when I heard heavy footsteps lumbering into the kitchen. Nice of the boy-toy to make it in time for dinner. As soon as I glanced at Mom's plus one, I froze. When his eyes slid my way and his mouth turned up into a familiar smile, the bowl slipped from my fingers.

Glass and whipped cream exploded at my feet, but that wasn't enough to break my frozen stare. Only when Jesse rushed over and blocked my view of the guy still smiling at me could I move and breathe again. Rose tossed Jesse a handful of paper towels.

"I'm so sorry," I said, inspecting the damage at my feet.

"Don't worry about it," Rose said. "Homemade whipped cream is my weak spot. My hips are thanking you right now, Rowen."

I kneeled down beside Jesse. He was busy collecting the glass shards.

"What's the matter?" he whispered, concerned.

What should I tell him? Should I tell him anything at all?

"I'm fine," I went with, mopping up the whipped cream with the towels.

"Rowen—"

"Here's a paper bag you can toss the glass and dirty towels into," Rose said, kneeling down beside us.

With Rose in earshot, it was decided. I couldn't say anything to Jesse.

Once we'd cleaned up the spill, Jesse picked up the bag and took it over to the garbage.

My mom had watched us clean up with a frown on her face. "Just let me know how much Rowen's damaged this summer, and I'll write you a check."

"Other than a couple batches of burnt pancakes, that's the only thing Rowen's broken the whole time." Neil grinned at me as I made my way back to the table. I avoided eye contact with mom's boyfriend as he introduced himself to Rose and Neil.

I slid into my seat and hunkered down. I even closed my eyes for a few seconds, sure I would open them to discover I'd just been seeing things.

When I finally did open them to find the same man who'd just walked in sitting in the chair across from me, I knew it hadn't been a hallucination.

"Hello there, Rowen," the man said, unfolding his napkin and dropping it into his lap. "It sure is wonderful to see you again after all of these years."

My hands trembled in my lap, and the only emotion I felt was helplessness.

"It's nice to have you back after all of these years,"

Mom said to him, leaning over and giving him a full on-the-lips kiss.

Neil cleared his throat. I wasn't sure if he could tell I was uncomfortable or if a couple of adults practically making out at his dinner table made *him* uncomfortable, but at least it made them come up for air.

Jesse was washing his hands at the sink, and I had the worst urge to get up and go to him. To have him wrap me in his arms like he did so well and shelter me.

"Oh, so you all already know each other?" Rose came back to the table with a basket of rolls.

"We've got quite a bit of history," *he* said. "Rowen, I must say you've turned into quite the young woman. When was the last time I saw you?" I couldn't take the way he leered at me. I couldn't take the way he smiled at me. I couldn't take the way Mom gazed at him like he was something to be celebrated. "Thirteen, wasn't it?" My legs trembled, too, as the string of memories played through my head. "I hope you can support your mom and me this time and not try to come between us." His eyes changed then. They went dark. Dark like that day in my bedroom when he'd cornered the scared girl I was again. "I'm really hoping we'll be able to pick up where we left off, Rowen. You and I always had a special kind of relationship." He winked at me.

I was out of my chair before I knew I would run. In fact, I shoved back so hard in it, the chair toppled to the floor.

"Rowen?" Jesse said, coming toward me.

I was past the point of being calmed. I was long past the point where his presence or his touch could relax me. I had to run.

Run the way I had the last time I'd seen that man staring down at me.

As I rushed out of the kitchen, a few more *Rowen!*s were called after me. I even made out my mom's irritated sigh over my mad dash for the front door.

I heard a heavy set of footsteps racing after me, and part of me wanted him to catch up. But another part of me wanted to get as far away from that kitchen as I could.

I'd just made it out the front door and was charging down the porch steps when a hand reached out and grabbed mine. A strong arm held my waist the next moment.

"Jesse, no!" I shouted, struggling against him. "Let me go! Just let me go!"

He pulled my body back into his and his face moved close to mine. "No," he said, just outside of my ear. "I will not let you go. I'm not going to let you shut me out of this. I'm not allowing you to push me away."

I slumped against him, sagging into his arms. I couldn't hold myself up, but Jesse wouldn't let me fall.

"Now tell me," he said, almost rocking me back and forth. "What happened in there? What made you run out of there like you were being chased by a demon? What am I missing?"

I shook my head against him. If I told him, I couldn't try to pretend the whole night had never happened. If I told him, I'd have to accept that my mom had done the unthinkable. And the unforgivable.

"Tell me," he said, his voice quiet, yet strong in my ear. "Trust me, Rowen. Prove to me you trust me the way I trust you."

Trust. *Trust.* What I'd lost, if I'd ever had it, from my own mother. What I'd found in the man holding me in such a way I could feel his love in his touch alone.

I couldn't show him I didn't trust him when he needed it most. We were at the place where trust was really made or broken.

"That man's the one," I said, my voice wavering. "He's the one who . . . the one who . . ."

"The one who tried to rape you." Jesse's arms still held me to him, but his body started to quiver. Mine did too when he said the word I'd never allowed myself to admit. I didn't apply the R word to what had happened to me because that was too much reality for me to handle. That was too much messed-up to repress.

It was the truth.

"Yes," I admitted at last. I admitted to the guy I loved that the man sitting inside his family's kitchen was the man who'd tried to rape me years ago.

Jesse's entire body tensed, but he managed to rub my arms and keep the rage I felt brewing beneath his surface contained. I started crying. "Shhh, I'm here. You're safe now. He can't hurt you, Rowen. I won't let him ever touch you again. It's all right." He kept repeating those words into my ear. Over and over until they started repeating in my head on their own.

After a minute of Jesse holding me and saying those words, I started to *feel* those words. I was safe. *He* wouldn't ever touch me again. It was all right.

I was just about to the point I could hold my own weight if Jesse's hold loosened when the screen door screeched open.

"Jesse?" Lily's voice was small and unsure. "What's going on?"

"Lily, I need you to do me a huge favor," he said,

setting me down onto the steps. "Grab one of those blankets up there and come hang out with Rowen for a few minutes, will you?"

I didn't want him to leave me, but he'd given me just enough of a boost to know I could manage without him. He'd talked me back from the cliff, and I could keep backing away from it on my own.

Lily walked down the steps and sat beside me after handing a blanket to Jesse. Her face was full of concern when she looked at me. "Is everything all right?"

I wiped my eyes and tried on a smile for her as Jesse wrapped the blanket tightly around me. "It's all right," I assured her.

Jesse grabbed my face in his hands, kissed my forehead, then bounded up the stairs. "It's about to be all right."

The tone of his voice put me on high alert. "Jesse?" I called after him as he stormed through the screen door. "What are you doing?"

"Putting a piece of shit in his place," he said, his voice murderous. "Lily, keep Rowen out here."

Oh, crap. I tried standing up, but Lily clamped her hands down on my shoulders and kept me where I was. For a sweet, little thing, she had some serious strength. She shook her head when I looked at her with exasperation. "I don't know what's going on, but let Jesse take care of it. He usually knows what's best."

"And that 'usually' part is supposed to reassure me?"

Lily wrapped an arm around me and looked like she was about to say something else when the sound of a familiar voice caught both of our attentions.

"Get out," Jesse demanded, his voice so loud it

sounded like he was just a few feet away, not back in the kitchen. A few seconds of silence passed. "Get out of our fucking house!"

I heard a few *Jesse*s called out from Neil and Rose before the sound of a serious brawl came through the open kitchen window.

I tried shooting up in my seat again. Lily caught me and pulled me back down. "Lily!" I said frantically. "Let me go. I'm not going to let Jesse get hurt over me when I could go break this up."

The sounds of glass breaking and things clattering to the floor, interlaced with the sounds of punches being thrown and followed by loud grunts, came next.

It sounded like everyone was shouting in the kitchen. Even Mom and the two youngest girls.

"Trust me. You don't have to worry about Jesse in a fight," she said, wincing when a particularly loud shattering sound came from the window. "I'd worry about the other guy."

I could never find one scrap of worry for the other guy. Not in this lifetime.

The clattering and shattering came to a sudden stop right before the back door off the kitchen busted open. Jesse had Pierce by the hair and arm, dragged him down the steps, and down the driveway. Neil and Rose charged out the door right after, followed by Mom and the girls. All Pierce could do was stumble along and try to stay upright. His suit was rumpled, his dress shirt stained with food and blood, and he'd be sporting a couple of black eyes for the next few weeks.

Other than enraged, Jesse didn't look like he'd just been in a fist fight. As they passed us, Jesse stopped and lifted Pierce's head so he looked my direction. "I want you to look her in the eyes. And I want you to apologize."

Pierce was scared. Frightened. Like he was the one who'd been thrown to the ground and hovered over. "I'm sorry."

I didn't say anything. I forced myself to look at him so I'd remember him that way: scared, beaten, and repentant.

"I want you to swear that you will never, ever come anywhere around her again," Jesse seethed. "Ever! Because if you thought the beating you took tonight was bad, just you come within a state of her again and I'll show you bad."

When Pierce stalled, Jesse drove a fist into his side. Lily and I covered our mouths. Neil moved closer, lifting his hands. "Easy, son. You've taught him a lesson. It doesn't need to go any further."

"It's going to go plenty further if he doesn't swear he'll never show his face around Rowen again!" Jesse shouted.

"I swear it," Pierce said instantly. "I swear I'll stay away from her. She'll never see my face again."

Jesse released him and shoved him down the driveway. "Now get the hell off of our ranch."

Once Pierce lifted himself from the ground, he fumbled in his pocket for the keys and hurried for the car. Mom broke away from Rose and the girls and marched up to Jesse like she was about to slap him.

That got me off of the steps. Lunging toward Jesse, I pivoted in front of Mom and caught her hand mid-air. Instead, she lifted her other hand and slapped me hard across the cheek. I whimpered, and Jesse pulled me out of reach and threw himself in front of me.

"Rose was wrong. You haven't changed. And you never will," Mom said.

The words hit me like another slap to the face.

"Neither will you," I replied, moving up beside Jesse. His arm pressed out in front of me, blocking my way. I wasn't sure if it was because he didn't trust what my mom would do to me or what I'd do to her.

Neil, Rose, and the girls huddled off to the side, watching the whole scene with confusion and sadness. They didn't need to know what was going on to realize something was extremely wrong.

By that time, Pierce had crawled inside the car and was blasting the horn.

"Rowen. Get in the car," Mom demanded, grabbing for my wrist. I swiped it away, and Jesse blocked my mom when she tried again. "You are leaving with us right now, young lady. I don't want you staying with these people another second longer."

My blood boiled when I realized my mom wanted to take away the one good thing I had going in my life: that place and those people. "These people?" I said, crossing my arms and glaring at her. "The kind of people who love me? You know, the unconditional kind? Oh, wait. Never mind, you're not familiar with that kind." I shook my head and stepped toward her. I wasn't backing away. I wasn't running away from her. I was standing up to her at last. "The kind of people who trust me? The kind of people who would actually believe their daughters if they ever told them they were almost molested?" From behind us, I heard Rose gasp. "The kind of people who wouldn't bring that same man back into their lives years later and expect everything to be all right? Are those the kind of people you're really so concerned about leaving me with? Because from my point of view, you and your *boyfriend* are the most concerning people I could ever be around."

I was venting years of baggage, years of frustration, and it felt freeing in a way I'd only dreamed of.

"You stay here," Mom replied, her face every shade of pissed, "kiss art school goodbye."

My dream. The whole reason I'd sucked it up and gone to Willow Springs in the first place. "Bye, mom."

Her eyes flashed onyx before she spun around and marched toward the car. As she swung the passenger side door open, she said, "Goodbye, Rowen. Have a nice life."

"I will," I whispered as they peeled out of the driveway. Mom never looked my way again.

Jesse draped his arms around me and pulled me close. "Rowen, I'm so sorry, baby. I'm so damn sorry you had to go through that."

I nodded into his shirt, feeling a couple of tears about to leak out. "Are you all right?" I pulled back so I could examine his face. His hair was a little rumpled, but that was the only sign he'd been in a fight.

"He never even landed a punch," he answered, running his thumbs under my eyes to wipe the tears away. "I'm just fine."

"Sweetheart," Rose said, tears streaming down her face as she approached us. "Oh, my sweet, sweet angel. I didn't know. I never would have let them come if I'd known—"

I shook my head. "I didn't even know until he walked into the kitchen. I'll be fine. Really." No one, least of all Jesse, looked convinced. "If you all don't mind, I just need a moment." I walked away. As Jesse started following me, I clarified, "Alone. To sort a few things out."

Jesse's forehead lined, and Rose looked like she was fighting her instinct to wrap me in her arms.

"I'm fine," I said before turning around and heading for the barn. I didn't want to go back into the house to witness the mess I'd inadvertently been responsible for, so the barn would have to do.

I jogged inside and checked once over my shoulder to make sure no one followed me. Everyone was filing back into the house. Except for Jesse. He camped out on the porch steps, watching me like he was fighting his instinct to come after me. But he did as I asked and stayed.

I wandered down the row of stalls until I found a clean, empty one with a few bales of straw. It looked like the perfect place to "have a moment" and let everything that had just happened catch up with me.

A few of the horses in the nearby stalls whinnied a welcome, but, other than that, the barn was silent. I dropped down on one of the bales and leaned my back into the stall wall. The thought that kept bursting to the forefront of my mind was how hard I'd worked all summer to make myself better, how I'd actually succeeded, and my mom saw nothing but the troubled juvenile delinquent she'd always seen in me. I knew I could never do anything that would impress her, never do anything to earn her unconditional love and respect.

I'd have to learn to accept that, but I wasn't sure if I could ever make peace with it. Could a person ever truly heal from that kind of a wound? Only time would tell.

The next thing that worked its way to the front of my mind had me lifting my legs up to my chest and curling into an upright ball. It was a thought, or a realization, or a damned epiphany that I didn't want to have, but I had it nonetheless. No matter how hard I worked to overcome that troubled girl I'd been, she'd always be hiding just below the surface, ready to pop out when something set her free.

That person I'd been for so long was not removable. She was a part of me. Forever. That girl could rise to the surface before I could stop her. She'd push people away before they got too close, hurt them before they could hurt me. I couldn't allow myself to be the toxic person to Jesse that my mom was to me. I couldn't poison his life the way she had mine.

I'd made myself into a better person, I knew that, but no matter how hard or long I worked, I couldn't risk that dark side of me striking out when I least expected it. I loved Jesse too much to put him through the pain or chaos of my life.

Who knows how much time had passed, but the longer I was alone, the darker my thoughts got. The farther down that trail they went. Only when a hesitant body slipped inside the stall did a ray of light cut through my blackness. Cut through, but didn't remove it.

"Did I give you a long enough moment?" Jesse asked, standing in the doorway of the stall like he was waiting for an invitation. "Because I can give you more time if you want." He hitched his thumb over his shoulder.

"Come on in," I said, patting the bale beside me and scooting over. "I've had more than enough moments to think."

"How are you doing?" he asked, taking a seat next to me. "Wait. That was a stupid question." Jesse shook his head and looked at a loss for words. "What's been going through your mind? Besides everything?"

I gave him a small smile. "Besides everything? I suppose realizing the worst part of the night wasn't Pierce showing up." I played with a piece of straw. Jesse shifted closer and draped his arm around my shoulders. "The worst part was that my mom invited him here." Jesse stared at the ground and nodded. "What Pierce did was not right, I'm not excusing that, but he was basically a stranger who had no interest in my life. My mom . . . She's my *mother*. She's the person who's supposed to love me first, and last, and best. She's the person who's supposed to fight with her life to keep scumbags like Pierce out of her child's life. She's supposed to . . ." I had to swallow to get the word out, "care."

"I'm sorry," he whispered, kissing my temple.

"I just don't get it, Jesse. It's so goddamned unfair. Why? Why does my mother hate me? Why do I feel like the biggest screw up when I'm around her? Why, after everything, do I still want her to look at me and say she's proud of me and give me a honest to goodness hug?" Another set of tears dripped their way down my face. "I've got so many 'whys' I'll never have answered, they'll probably drive me insane."

Jesse waited for me to catch my breath and dry my tears before he responded. I was so exhausted, I just sank into his arms and rested.

"We've all got questions. We've all got dark parts of us that we wonder how they got there," he said slowly. "We all, at times, feel like the positively most screwed up person to have ever walked the planet. But you know what, Rowen? We don't always need to know the answers.

We shouldn't get hung up on the questions we can't answer because life, by definition, is confusing. We're never going to have all the answers. Never. We should focus on the questions we can answer and make peace with the ones we can't."

It was a lovely thought and it would have looked great on an inspirational poster, but Jesse's life was so very different from mine. His questions he couldn't answer were easy to move past because they didn't consume him the way mine did me.

"Jesse, I love you and I love those things you just said, but how could you even think you could compare the questions I have from my fucked up life to the questions that have cropped up during your next-to-perfect life?" I knew Jesse had experienced pain and heartache, every human did, but there was pain and there was *PAIN*.

Jesse let out a long sigh. "I know my life seems idyllic, Rowen. I know you probably think I'm an idiot for drawing a parallel between your life and mine. But my life wasn't always so great." He paused and didn't say anything else for what seemed like forever. "My life didn't begin the way it is now. In fact, my life couldn't have been more different than it is now."

My brows came together. "What do you mean?" I looked up at him, and his eyes were somewhere else. Somewhere frightening.

"Neil and Rose are my dad and mom, Rowen. I want you to know that because that's one of the truest things I know. But they didn't become so until I was five years old."

"Wait." I shook my head, sure I was missing some-thing. "What are you saying, Jesse?"

"I was adopted."

I couldn't reply. At least not right away. Had I heard him wrong? Had he said it wrong? "You were . . . adopted?"

"Yes. I was taken out of my home when I was four by Child Protective Services. From there, I drifted around in the foster care system for about a year until Neil and Rose—my mom and dad—adopted me."

The stall spun a bit. Information was coming at me a little too fast. "C.P.S. took you away from your parents?"

Jesse cleared his throat. "They took me away from the people who conceived me."

I wasn't sure whose expression was more broken: his or mine. "Why?" It didn't make sense. Why hadn't I known? Why hadn't anyone told me?

Jesse's arm went rigid around me. "Because they lacked . . . parental skills." His words were flat and emotionless, but his face wasn't. His face gave away the pain running through him.

"What? I don't understand." In fact, I didn't have a clue. "Did they hurt you? What happened?"

"Yes, they hurt me. Yes, they didn't take care of me." Jesse shifted and dropped his head against the wall. "The point of me telling you this now is that I wanted you to know you're not alone, Rowen. I know what it's like to want to curl up and die rather than get up and face another day. I know what it's like to feel like not a single soul in the world would care if you died. I know what it's like to lose all of your faith in humanity."

I had a sudden and overwhelming urge to protect Jesse from both his past and future struggles. To drape my arms around him and hold him tight the way he did me when I needed comfort.

"God, Jesse," I said, wrapping my arm around his stomach. "I don't know what to say. *I'm sorry* seems like the worst possible thing I could say. But I can't think of anything else." What did a person say to that? How did a person comfort another after that kind of a reveal? I didn't know. I'd never had anyone show me the *loving* way to respond.

"*I'm sorry* works," he said. "I'm not telling you because I'm looking for sympathy, Rowen. I'm telling you so you know you're not alone. So you know you can walk away from a tragic past and live a peaceful life."

A peaceful life. What I wouldn't give to have one, but I was certain I'd never attain it. People like me, who'd lived the kind of life I had, didn't live peaceful lives.

"Why didn't you tell me sooner?" I sat up and twisted on the bale so I could look at him square on. Why hadn't he told me? We'd talked about seemingly everything else. I wasn't naive enough to think we didn't still have some secrets, but I didn't think they'd be those kinds of secrets. Monumental ones.

As I thought about all of the things I'd written off, it seemed so obvious, I should have figured it out. The lack of *any* physical similarities between Jesse and the rest of his family, the absence of his baby picture on Neil's office wall with the girls', people dropping hints about Jesse's life not always being so paved with gold. It was all so clear after I'd been given the last piece of the puzzle.

"I was going to, Rowen. Soon." Jesse turned so he looked me straight on as well. The skin between his eyebrows had been pinched together the entire conversation. "But it's not something I tell just anybody."

309

"Was it because you didn't trust me enough to want to tell me?" I worked to keep my voice level and my eyes on his.

"Of course not. I'd trust you with my life, Rowen. I trust you implicitly." His forehead wrinkled, too. "I didn't tell you right away so you could get to know me, who I am now, before I told you who I was then. I wanted you to know my present before you knew my past. I wanted to know that if you chose to be with me, it was because you loved me. Not because you pitied me."

I wiped my eyes before the tears forming could fall. "Are you ashamed of it?"

Jesse leaned forward. "No, just the opposite. I'm proud that Dad and Mom saw something in me I didn't, and they believed in me." He looked down at where our hands were entwined. He stared for so long, I wondered if he saw something in them I didn't. "I just don't see how it's relevant for every person I come in contact with to know I was adopted. It's my past. Yeah, I had a rough go of life. But I buried it six feet deep, made my peace with it, and moved on. I'm not going to let my past ruin my future."

He buried it, made peace with it, and moved on. Could I ever do the same?

Right then, after everything that had happened, it didn't seem so likely.

"And you had questions?" I asked.

He nodded and his eyes returned to mine. "I had so many damn questions I didn't know what to do with all of them, but I stopped looking for answers that never wanted to be found and moved on. When the Walkers walked into that adoption agency, they took a huge chance on a

310

troubled boy who likely would have turned into a violent teen. I wasn't going to repay them for taking that chance by living up to what everyone thought I'd turn into." He lifted our hands to his mouth and brushed his lips over my knuckles. "You and I are not so different, after all."

And that was where he was so very wrong.

"Jesse, don't you see?" I said, my voice high. "Our stories might have started out the same, but that's the only similarity. You took a bad situation and turned yourself into the person you are today." I paused just long enough to catch my breath. "I took a bad situation and let it define me."

Jesse combed his fingers through his hair and shook his head. "No, you took a bad situation, let it define you for a while, and then you decided to overcome it." He formed his hand over my cheek. "It just took you a little longer than me."

I wanted to believe that. God, I would have given anything to believe that. But I couldn't believe a lie. I couldn't betray myself by accepting a lie.

"That's the most sugar-coated version of a half-truth I've ever heard," I said, my voice elevating. "Beneath this 'reformed' girl you fell in love with is the screwed-up girl I've been my whole life. A girl who will always be, no matter how you try to put it, screwed up." I made myself look away from his eyes. It made what I had to do easier. "A girl with my past doesn't deserve a guy with your future, Jesse."

"Oh please," Jesse said, hanging his head back. "Get over the *I deserve this and I don't deserve this* crap and start choosing what's healthy for you. How about being honest with yourself as to what you want? Because maybe you can have it." Jesse's voice had gone up, too. We were both past the point of keeping our cool.

"Healthy? Honest?" I popped up because I couldn't stay seated any longer. "So easy for you to say. You're the one living a charmed life with a family who loves you, not the one who will have no one, *no one*, after this summer! So don't lecture me on what's healthy!"

Jesse inhaled slowly and exhaled slowly. "You're pushing me away again, Rowen. You're hurting me." Jesse waited for me to look at him. I couldn't. I shouldn't.

I did.

"Who does that sound like in your life? Who's pushed you away and hurt you? Who's done everything she can to keep you at arm's length?" he asked, his voice calm.

I had my answer instantly, but I sealed my lips and shook my head. I swiped a tear. I didn't like what he was getting at and I didn't like the comparison he was drawing.

Jesse nodded, accepting I wouldn't answer his question verbally. "What we've been denied is what we deny others. But why? Why do we fall into the same patterns of those people we always swore we'd never be like?"

"Haven't you heard?" I inserted, wiping my eyes with the back of my arm. "Life sucks."

Jesse kept going. "We will all, at some point in our lives, fall. Every single one of us." He hoisted himself up beside me and moved closer. "We shouldn't spend our time trying to avoid falling. We should spend it finding someone who will help us up."

When he lifted his hands toward my face, I backed away. "I just need to be alone right now." I crossed my arms and closed myself off.

312

"No, you don't," he said, coming toward me again. "You need to be with someone who loves you."

"Don't tell me what I need," I almost shouted. "You don't have any clue what I've been through."

"You're right. I don't." His calm and reassuring tone grated on me. I wanted him to get angry. I wanted him to enter into a screaming match with me to make it easier. "But I know I love you and I'm living proof that your past doesn't have to define you."

I sighed and headed for the stall door. "And I'm living proof that it generally does."

Jesse moved in front of me. "Don't do this, Rowen. Don't push me away."

"I'm not, Jesse," I said, giving him a cool look. "I'm walking away."

When I made another move toward the door, he let me by. Walking away from Jesse was the hardest thing I'd done. I also knew it would be the hardest thing I ever would do.

CHAPTER eighteen

It was raining, *storming*, when I rushed out of the barn. Big, fat raindrops drenched me by the time I'd sprinted into the house. When I shoved through the back door and into the kitchen, I found the dinner and whatever mess Jesse and Pierce's brawl had created.

Rose was at the sink, in her terry cloth bathrobe, drying the last dish.

I thought everyone would have been asleep. It was late, but I should have known Rose would stall, wait for me to finish with "my moment." I was cold and wet, but I was thankful for it. The rain coating my face disguised the tears.

I wanted to head to my room so badly. I couldn't talk anymore. A wound I'd been so sure was close to healing had been ripped open that night. Not only that, I knew I'd just given myself another one. Jesse Walker was the kind of wound a girl could never recover from.

Rose placed the platter she'd been drying on the counter and came toward me with her arms opened. I shot a quick glance at the stairs again, wishing I could escape up them.

Then Rose's tiny arms folded me up into a big hug, and there was nowhere else I'd rather have been.

"I love you, sweetheart," she said after a while. "We

all love you. You *are* loved." She smiled up at me through the tears trailing down her cheeks. "Don't let anyone else, most of all yourself, tell you you're not."

She was crying. I was crying. I'd never cried as much in my entire life as I'd cried that summer.

Giving me a moment to let that set in, she rubbed my arms, then let me go. Rose had a sixth sense about what I needed without having to even ask. She knew when I needed a hug, when I needed to be left alone, and when I just needed to think.

That sixth sense made sense. She'd been through it all before. She'd figured it out with Jesse first.

As much as I wanted to sprint up those stairs, I couldn't. I could barely put one foot in front of the other. I was exhausted, physically and mentally. Exhausted in the way that sleep wouldn't cure.

Once I was inside my room, I peeled my wet dress off and changed into a pair of leggings and that old tee of Jesse's that had become my favorite sleep shirt. I made sure my window was closed and locked before I tucked myself into bed.

It was the first night I'd kept my window closed since I'd climbed up into Jesse's room. I never thought I could cry as much as I did over a window, but my sobs ripped through me so long and so hard that, after a while, they rocked me to sleep.

A CLAP OF thunder shaking the farmhouse jolted me awake. It was still dark and my eyes still felt puffy, so I knew it couldn't have been all that long since I'd fallen asleep. After fumbling around for my phone, I saw it was just past midnight.

Another crack, that one shaking the house even more, and I instinctively reached for the space beside me on the bed.

I found . . . nothing. Just an empty space and a cool to the touch sheet.

Jesse wasn't lying beside me. He wasn't here to wrap me up in his arms, whisper in his sleepy voice that everything was all right, followed by a yawn, before we fell back asleep.

Jesse was gone because I'd pushed him away. Like I always knew I would. Like I knew I had to. For reasons I couldn't quite remember in my sleep stupor, but for reasons that had seemed important earlier.

I tried lying back down. That lasted for all of two seconds before it became clear I couldn't fall back asleep with the thoughts raging through my mind.

How could I let Jesse go? How could I let the Walkers go? How could I simply cut the best things in my life loose? Would I really walk away because things got hard? Would I really push the people who loved me away because they'd gotten too close? Would I really take the first healthy thing that had come into my life in a long time and throw it away?

The knowledge that I was strongly considering it made me realize I was, as Jesse said, trying to deny others what I'd been denied. I was becoming like my mom.

That was the thought that jolted me out of bed.

I moved silently down the hall and stairs and headed for the kitchen. I wasn't hungry, but I didn't know where else to go. All I knew was that I couldn't stay in my room and I couldn't climb up into the room I wanted to be in until I figured some shit out.

I knew I was facing one of those life-changing decisions. One of those defining moments. I was at a fork in the road. Would I continue down the same self-destructive, familiar path or would I choose to make a change, scary and unknown as that change would be?

A flashing sign with the answer in front of me would be really nice.

A light streaming from the living room caught my attention. The house was quiet except for my footsteps padding around the kitchen floor, so someone must have left a light on. I shuffled through the foyer, and when I entered the living room, I didn't find it empty like I thought I would.

Rose sat on the floor, a few photo albums spread out around her, along with a pot of tea still steaming on a tray.

My instinct was to back away before she noticed me. I went against my instinct.

"Couldn't sleep either?" I said, crossing the room toward her.

She didn't look surprised to see me. In fact, when I took a closer look at the tea tray, I saw two cups instead of one. She'd been expecting me, it would seem.

"No." She shook her head. "I never can when I know one of my babies is hurting. I suppose it's a mother's curse."

I stopped at the edge of albums. "You talked with Jesse?"

She reached for the teapot and poured some into the other cup. "I did. He let me know that he told you about his past. About his adoption."

I played with the hem of Jesse's shirt. "Did he tell

you about us?"

Rose set the teapot down and sighed. "He didn't need to, sweetie. I could see it all on his face."

I shifted and fought the urge to turn around and leave. "I didn't mean to hurt him, Rose. I just want what's best for him, you know?"

"Believe me, Rowen, as his mother, I know plenty about wanting what's best for him." She looked up at me with a serious expression. "I'm just hoping you're going to realize sooner rather than later that you *are* what's best for him."

"You don't mean that," I whispered.

"I wouldn't say it if I didn't. And neither would Jesse. Maybe one day, Rowen, you'll believe that, too."

I didn't reply. I wanted to believe that, but I wasn't sure if I ever could. "Is everyone else asleep?" I wanted to steer the conversation away from the current topic.

"The girls are, but Neil and Jesse headed out about an hour ago with a few of the other ranch hands to look for a missing calf."

I narrowed my eyes. "In the middle of the night? In the middle of this?" Another clap of thunder rocked the house to prove my point. "Couldn't it have waited until morning?"

"Well, it could have," Rose replied with a lift of her shoulders. "For anyone but Jesse or my husband." She smiled and shook her head. "I think Neil was eager to get out of the house after the . . . earlier events, and Jesse looked like he needed the distraction even more." I didn't need to wonder why or what he needed a distraction from. "It's probably for the best, anyways. There are plenty of predators out there, cliffs to tumble over, or fences to get tangled up in. A calf won't last long once it's separated from the herd."

It still seemed extreme, but that seemed to be the status quo when it came to ranching and cowboys. "I hope they find the little thing soon then."

"Me too," Rose said with a nod. "I was getting these out for you." Rose swept her hands over the photo albums. "When Jesse let me know he told you about the adoption, I figured you'd have questions and you know what they say . . ." she studied a photo of a young boy with white blond hair and smiled, "a picture says a thousand words."

I tip-toed around the half dozen albums she had spread around her and took a seat beside her.

"And then I started thumbing through one, and I just kept thumbing." She waved at the mass of albums.

I picked up the one closest to me and opened it to the first page. A young Neil and Rose stood with a young boy with sad eyes. He clung to Rose where she held him. Neil and Rose were smiling. Five-year-old Jesse was not. A note below the photo read, *The day we brought our baby home.*

A lump formed in my throat. I was so familiar with the hopeless, lost look on young Jesse's face I could have been looking in a mirror.

"I'm glad he told you." Rose leaned over and studied the picture. "It's something he doesn't like to relive, but it will always be a part of him." She was quiet for a few moments as she gazed at the photo. "What those people did to him was unthinkable. His own flesh and blood abused and neglected him in ways worst enemies wouldn't even conceive of doing to one another."

I polished my thumb over Jesse's sad face. I couldn't

comprehend how anyone could show anything but total love and adoration for the child in the photo.

"When the agency described what had happened to him . . . When we had to read through pages and pages of notes detailing the abuse he'd gone through . . ." Rose's voice trembled, but she cleared her throat and continued, "Neil and I couldn't not adopt him. We knew the risks. A young boy abused in the ways he had been had a high likelihood of becoming an extremely troubled young man. But you know what we said?" She chuckled and smiled down at the picture. "We told them to stick their 'likeli-hoods' where the sun doesn't shine and asked to take our son home."

I smiled with her and flipped the page. "And you all lived happily ever after."

"Well, I wouldn't go that far," she said, taking a sip of her tea, "but we didn't underestimate the power of a stable home and a loving family. We gave him that, and the rest was up to him."

The next page was his first day of kindergarten. Well, homeschool kindergarten, but he still had a backpack and a new pair of boots, and he posed in front of the Walkers' front door. His eyes were still sad, but he wore a smile.

The photo on the next page was Jesse up on a horse, maybe a couple years older. He had on a hat three sizes too big for him. He had another smile on his face, but in that one, his eyes matched his smile.

"He got better," I stated, flipping to the next page. "You and Neil fixed him."

"It took a lot of time and even more hard work, but yes, Jesse got better," Rose said, grabbing another album. "But he fixed himself. We gave him a hand up, but the only person who could fix Jesse was Jesse."

When her eyes shifted back to me, they softened. She might as well have just said *The only person who could fix Rowen was Rowen.*

A few pages later, I found a picture of the Jesse I knew. He was a few years younger, but he wore the same white tee, painted-on jeans, light hat, and brown boots. It was the first photo I'd seen where he'd been smiling big enough to notice his dimples. My heart hurt when I stared at that picture long enough.

I started to cry again.

"What is it, sweetheart?" Rose grabbed my hand and gave it a squeeze.

"My mom hates me, Rose," I said, wiping away the tears. "My mom brought that man back into her life. Back into *my* life. How could anyone who loved someone do that to them?"

"Your mother doesn't hate you. She just has a very poor way of showing her love." Rose scooted closer so she could wrap her arm around me. "I couldn't tell you what drew your mom and me together way back when. She was a lot like she is today, and I was a lot like I am today. But there was a chemistry between us. She never opened up to me, but I always sensed she'd lived a hard life. One she was running away from."

I grabbed my cup of tea and took a sip. I'd never known my grandparents. I'd never known any family other than my mom. I'd also guessed there must have been a lot of bad blood between them because I'd never once received a birthday card from my own grandparents. It was all I'd ever known though, so I'd never given it a lot of thought.

Could it be I didn't know a single blood relative, including my own *father* for crying out loud, because mom had pushed away everyone? The same way she'd pushed me away as much as a parent could an underage child in their home?

While I couldn't be certain, it seemed a very possible explanation.

"So what does that mean?" I said, taking another sip before setting my cup back down. "I forgive and forget?"

Rose shook her head. "No, Rowen. It means you let go." She brushed my hair behind my ear in a motherly way. "Sometimes we just have to cut off the dead branches in our life. Sometimes that's the only way we can keep the tree alive. It's hard and it hurts, but it's what's best." She paused to take a breath. "Don't let a dying branch take you down with it. Maybe one day she'll change, but don't go down with her, Rowen."

"But she's kind of taking me down no matter what I do," I said, unable to look away from Jesse's picture. "Art school was my ticket out of there. But now . . . the only place I have to go at the end of summer is back home. I tried following her rules this summer. I tried so hard to please her. But none of it mattered. I doubt she was even planning on paying my way through art school in the first place."

"Maybe she was, and maybe she wasn't, but don't let your mom decide your future."

I exhaled. "Kind of hard not to in this case." Another clap of thunder rocked the house. The lights flickered. "Art school's kind of expensive, and money isn't something I have a lot of."

"Have you ever thought about starting out at a community college with a good art program? Then transferring to a dedicated art school later?" Rose poured herself another cup of tea and topped mine off.

"Not really," I said. "But at this point, I'm willing to consider any and all options that have me doing something related to art. Unless it involves paint-by-numbers. Because that's the opposite of art."

Rose fought a losing battle to keep her smile contained. "Here's the way I see it. You'll have earned enough money this summer to pay for a year's tuition at a community college. If you want to come back next summer, we'd be happy to have you, and you could save enough for the following year." I wasn't sure if what I heard was real. Was the answer to my college dilemma so easily solved? "After that, you can apply for financial aid and scholarships and get into whatever art school you want. Doing it on your own, without being dependent on your mother."

"I was never coming here to work for pay, Rose. Mom sent me here so I could prove to her I could work hard and walk a line." The truck ride to Willow Springs, when Jesse played his favorite CD, popped to mind. Mr. Cash and his lyrics took on a very personal meaning.

"That may have been what your mom intended, but that's certainly never what Neil and I intended. You've worked hard this summer, Rowen. You've been an asset to us, sweetie, not a liability." Rose thumbed through the album in her lap. "I was just telling Neil I don't know what I'm going to do when you leave us for school in a few weeks."

A lot of information was coming at me. "You're going to pay me?" I asked, feeling yet another lump form in my throat.

"That is what one does in exchange for work, Rowen." She chuckled and rumpled my hair. "In the morning, we can start researching some community colleges with good art programs and late enrollment deadlines. Then we'll get you signed up."

I didn't know what to say. I was speechless, and I was grateful, and I was overwhelmed. Art school on my own, paying my own way, dependent on no one but me.

It sounded wonderful. Too good to be true.

Then something jumped to mind, and I realized it *was* too good to be true.

"What about Jesse?" I'd pushed him away just a few hours ago, I'd turned and run away from him, but he was the first thing I thought about when I considered leaving Willow Springs.

Rose opened the album in her lap to the last page. I took a double take.

It was Jesse and me, sitting in one of the porch swings. His arm was draped over my shoulders like it always was when we were together, and my arm was wound around his stomach. He was looking down at me and I was looking up at him and we were just . . . grinning at each other. Like we were the happiest fools in the whole world.

That was why I'd needed a double take. I wasn't used to the grinning, happy girl that had been caught on film. That wasn't me.

Yet it was. The photo was all the evidence I needed to know I could change, like Jesse had. I could move on. I could be happy. I could move on and be happy . . . with *him*.

You know all those people who talk about epiphanies and life-changing revelations? Yeah, I'd been positive every last one of them was full of shit up until right then.

My mind was in that state between boggled and blown when a loud rapping sounded at the front door.

Rose's eyebrows came together. "What in the world?" She rose and headed for the door. I rushed after her because part of me was worried my mom and Pierce were back for round two.

Rose glanced through the peephole before unlocking and swinging the door open.

"Justin," she said, motioning him inside, "what's the matter?" I'd seen some wet and dirty cowboys that summer, but not once had I seen one close to what Justin looked like. He was more mud than man.

"Sorry to burst in on you in the middle of the night, ma'am," he said, sliding his hat off and making sure he stayed on the door mat. "But there's been an accident." Justin glanced my way for a brief moment. "It's Jesse. He was out scouting the ridge, but when we all met back in the middle, Sunny showed up. Jesse wasn't on him."

I half gasped, half whimpered. Rose came up beside me and tried putting on a brave face. "Did he . . . do you think he might have fallen over the ridge?" Her voice wavered in places.

"We don't know, ma'am," Justin replied. "Neil and the rest of the boys are out searching for him right now, but he wanted me to let you know so you were . . . prepared for however we find him."

I couldn't decide if I was closer to passing out or having a heart attack. Either seemed probable.

"Listen here, Justin," Rose said, stepping forward with me in tow. "My boy is strong and he knows this land like the back of his hand. You *will* find him and we'll attend to whatever wounds he may have inflicted when you bring my boy back home. Bring. Him. Home." It was the closest I'd seen Rose to breaking, the weakest I'd ever seen her. "Do you understand me?"

"We will, Rose," he said, meeting her eyes. "We will."

"Thank you," she whispered.

"Neil asked me to grab one of the big first aid kits and some flares. Could you help me with that?"

"Of course. Come with me." Rose turned and rushed into the kitchen. "And don't worry about tracking in mud. Now's no time to be worried about dirtying the floors."

I put my hand out as Justin passed me. "Do you know where he is?"

"We know *about* where he is," he said. "The trouble with that ridge is that the trail's so narrow, if your horse takes one wrong step, you're free falling down a hundred feet of rock face. Jesse's a good rider and has traveled that ridge hundreds of times, but the rain's coming down so hard you can barely see more than ten feet in front of you out there, and the mud's up to our horses's knees in some places."

"Has anyone taken the ridge to look for him?" I stopped him again when he tried to pass.

"At night? In this weather? No, it's suicide unless you're Jesse Walker. Then it's just very, very dangerous."

"You're just going to leave him there? What if he's hurt? What if he's dying? Someone has to go look for him!" I felt frantic knowing he was out there somewhere, possibly injured, and I couldn't get to him.

"There's a way into that ravine. You just have to take the long way around if you don't want to or can't take the ridge. If he's down there, we'll find him, Rowen. We're not going to leave him alone."

"Yes, but you just said the long way around. How much time does that take?"

"A half a day—or night, in this case—on horseback," he answered.

"If he's hurt, he could be . . . he could be . . ." I couldn't get it out, so I clamped my mouth shut.

"Were doing our best, Rowen," Justin said quietly. "We all like Jesse. We'd all risk our necks for him, but going out on that ridge would be like throwing your life away. No one would make it to him before they fell over the side, too."

When Justin moved to pass by again, I let him.

I felt helpless. I *was* helpless.

Or was I?

With Rose and Justin preoccupied in the storage closet, I threw open the door and stared at the barn. A loud, almost frantic whinny came from it.

I could do it. I *would* do it.

I retrieved my ratty combat boots from the shoe basket beside the door, pulled them on, and raced for the barn. Justin was right. The rain was coming down so hard, I couldn't see too far in front of me.

Once I was inside the barn, I slowed just long enough to snag one of the rain coats and headlamps hanging just inside and made my way down the row of stalls. I didn't have long. Rose and Justin would have their supplies packed, and as soon as she knew I'd disappeared, Rose would figure out what I was up to. She wouldn't let me go and do what I was about to do. She'd throw me down and sit on me if she had to, but I wouldn't sit around when

Jesse needed me.

Most of the stalls were empty. Another loud whinny came from one of the stalls a bit farther down, and I almost cried when I saw who it was.

Sunny was as wet and muddy as Justin. He was in his stall, pacing around and rearing up onto his back legs every few paces. He acted as frantic as I felt. Justin must have led him back, and thankfully, he was still saddled and bridled.

Jesse had showed me how to both saddle and bridle a horse, but I wasn't especially quick at it. Right then, time was critical.

"Whoa, boy," I said, as calmly as I could. "Are you worried about Jesse, too?" After slipping into the rain coat, I reached for the gate and slowly slid it open. From the crazed look in Sunny's eyes, I worried he'd come barreling out of the stall as soon as I opened it.

Sunny flung his head about a few more times, then went as calm as a high-spirited horse like Sunny could go. I slid the gate the rest of the way open and grabbed ahold of Sunny's reins. He let me lead him out of the stall and even stood still for me when I lifted my foot up into the stirrup. In all the times Jesse and I had gone out for evening rides, I'd never ridden Sunny. I usually rode Lily's horse, Buttercup. The only time I rode Sunny was if Jesse was on him with me. Sunny didn't like any other riders except for Jesse. The couple ranch hand show-offs I'd seen try it had been thrown within five seconds.

And there I was, someone who'd never ridden a horse before that summer, about to ride a one-man horse into the worst possible riding conditions. My survival instincts apparently took a vacation when I knew Jesse was in trouble.

I shifted my weight into the stirrup and swung my other leg up and over. I grimaced the entire time, bracing my body for Sunny to throw me off as soon as I settled into the saddle. A few seconds later, I opened my eyes to make sure I was in the saddle, on top of Sunny.

Sure enough.

Buttercup never even stood so steady and she was a twenty-year-old mare who could barely manage a trot anymore.

"Okay, Sunny," I said, grabbing hold of the reins. "I'm going to need your help, buddy. I need you to help me find Jesse." I slid the rain coat hood over my head and squeezed Sunny's sides. He moved. He actually accepted a command from someone other than Jesse. "Take me to Jesse." We emerged from the barn into the same sheets of rain. Sunny whinnied, and I just barely made out a form looking out the kitchen window. So much for my head start.

Grabbing onto the saddle horn as well, I clucked my tongue, and Sunny sprang to life.

Other than holding on for dear life and trying not to fall out of the saddle, I let Sunny do the rest. He raced past the corrals, past the driveway, and turned without any prompting from me. He really was taking me to Jesse. Sunny charged down the dirt road I'd driven a few times when I had to take lunch out to the guys working in the upper fields.

It wasn't a dirt road anymore. It was a mud road. Sunny lost his footing a few times in the sludge, but I managed to stay in the saddle. Clumps of mud hit me from every angle, and the rain, at our speed, hurt my face until it finally went numb. It was the most rain I'd ever seen, and I'd grown up in Portland, Oregon.

Sunny charged ahead like he was the underdog in the Kentucky Derby. He did all the work, he blazed the trail; all I did was manage to hold on. So why did I feel so damn exhausted by the time Sunny's gallop slowed? Might have had something to do with being soaked to the bone and my lower half being all tingly and numb from bouncing around in the saddle.

We were long past the spot I'd dropped the guys' lunch off. I couldn't tell how far, but I knew it was miles farther. The rain was slowing, so the visibility had slightly improved, but when I saw where Sunny was heading, I kind of wished I couldn't see a thing again.

We were winding down a trail that continued to narrow. Where we were, the trail was wide enough for two riders to travel side by side, but every few feet, it got narrower and narrower until, finally, it seemed barely wide enough for Sunny and me.

To my left was a sheer rock face that went straight up a good twenty feet or so. To my right was a drop off. I couldn't tell how far down the ravine was, but I could tell it was pretty far away from how long the rocks Sunny's hoofs sent over the edge took to fall.

My heart pounded the farther down the ridge we traveled. Every survival instinct I possessed clawed at me to turn around and go back. Had turning around been possible on the narrow trail, I might have attempted it. I might have if any person but Jesse was down there.

That's what kept me going. That's what I knew kept Sunny going.

Jesse.

A moment later, I felt it. The oddest sensation I'd experienced to date. As though a slack rope I hadn't even known I'd been tied to went taut, I could go no farther. I pulled up on Sunny's reins, but it was a wasted effort. Sunny had stopped an instant before.

We'd found him. I knew it. It wasn't just the rope I could feel. It was him.

"Good boy, Sunny," I praised him, rubbing his neck. "You found him."

I slipped on the headlamp and clicked it on. It didn't cut through as much of the dark and the rain as I would have hoped, but I could make out that the drop off from that part of the trail was less treacherous looking. It was still steep but manageable with the proper equipment and experience. I happened to have neither.

I decided on which way I'd take down into the ravine before dismounting. Trying to climb off a horse on a trail that was maybe three feet wide was no easy task, but I managed it without causing permanent injury to human or horse.

I did one final check of my planned route before taking a deep breath. "I'm going to go get him, boy. I'm bringing Jesse back." I didn't know who I was trying to reassure, me or Sunny, but he replied with a low neighing sound.

I didn't stall any longer. Staring over the precipice wouldn't get me to Jesse any faster. I lowered my right foot, and when it felt stable, I lowered my left. The slope felt just as steep as it looked, but I was doing it. I was side-stepping, grabbing a hold of any branch, rock, or vine I could to give myself a bit more balance as I continued down.

I was in action, so my heart wasn't in my throat any longer and I didn't feel like I was on the verge of a panic attack. I'd jumped, quite literally, and there was no going back. Not without Jesse beside me.

My old boots didn't look anything like hiking boots, but they worked like champs on the muddy, steep, and uneven terrain. It was a bit surreal knowing a pair of black leather boots had saved me two different times in my life.

I was almost to the bottom of the ravine, not even a body length away, when I lost my foothold. The branch I'd been using as a support snapped, and I spent the last part of my descent rolling down the hill.

I groaned when I landed. The nice thing about the buckets of rain that had come down was that it had made the ground soft. Other than being a muddy mess and waking up to a few bruises in the morning, I was just fine.

I readjusted my headlamp and scanned the area. The ravine wasn't much more than some scraggly bushes and rock, but it was enough to conceal a body. So I'd check around every bush, rock, and cranny in the whole damn ravine if that's what it took. He was down there, I knew that. Just waiting for me to find him.

The thunder had died down almost entirely, so I held my head back and yelled his name over and over again as I searched.

No answer. No Jesse.

He was close, so close. I felt him, so why couldn't he hear me? Why wasn't he answering me? The only reason he wouldn't answer was if . . . My stomach twisted into a knot.

No. I wouldn't let myself think that. I *wouldn't* think that.

He was there. He was fine.

I started moving faster, searching more frantically. I had just rounded one of the bigger shrubs I'd seen in the ravine when I tripped over something. I flew to the ground again, followed by another groan.

Scratch that: I would wake up to more than "just a few" bruises in the morning.

"Rowen?"

My heart about burst right out of my chest. I rolled over and sat up to see what I'd tripped over. Well, *who* I'd tripped over.

"Jesse!" I cried, crawling toward him. He was laying on the ground, his back propped up against a level rock. He was as muddy and drenched as I was and looked so beat up, my breath caught in my lungs.

"What in the hell are you doing out here?" he said, struggling to sit up. He winced, grabbed his ribs, and collapsed back down into his prior position.

"Are you all right?" I crawled closer and scanned his body for visible signs of damage.

"I'm fine," he answered, shifting up again. That time, he made it, although from the look on his face, I would have thought someone just shoved a hot poker through his hand.

"Bull crap!" I said, noticing the way he favored his left arm. "What's hurt?"

"Pretty sure I broke my arm." He glanced at the arm he held carefully. "And a couple ribs." My eyes shifted to his chest. I couldn't see anything, but I could imagine the pain that came along with broken ribs. "And I'm going to need some stitches at the back of my head."

I scurried behind him to inspect his head. Sure

enough, dried blood matted his hair just below the crown. When I felt the stirrings of panic, I reminded myself I'd found him and that he was alive. Bones could be mended, wounds could be stitched. Jesse needed me. He needed me to be calm and clear headed for the both of us.

It went against everything I knew, but I fought the panic. Inspecting his head wound to make sure it wasn't leaking enough fresh blood to be concerning, I came around to his side again. His breathing was a little fast and his color was a couple shades lighter than normal, but otherwise, his injuries didn't seem life-threatening.

"What are you doing out here, Rowen?" he asked, inspecting my body like I'd just done his.

"I came to find you," I answered as I wiped the mud from his face with the back of my hand.

"How did you get down here?"

I swallowed and pointed up the cliff face.

His expression went pretty much exactly how I thought it would go: flabbergasted with a trace of out-raged. "You realize that's called Suicide Ridge for a reason, right?"

I crossed my arms and sat up on my heels. I wasn't there to argue with him. "Do you?"

"Yeah, I do. That's why I take it seriously when I travel it," he replied. I couldn't stop staring at the way his right arm cradled his left arm.

"And you call it 'taking it seriously' when you decided to travel it in the middle of the night during the storm of the century?" Why was I still arguing with him? Really, all I'd wanted to do since I'd stumbled over him was kiss him hard on the mouth and cuddle close until help came.

"It is when you see the calf everyone's been looking for at the bottom of the ravine." Jesse tilted his head toward the big shrub. I hadn't noticed at first, but a tiny black calf was laying under the shelter of the bush. She was as wet and muddy as the rest of us but resting as peacefully as I'd ever seen an animal sleep.

"You broke your arm, your ribs, and your damn head to save a baby cow?" I said, waving my hands at the calf.

"I wasn't planning on breaking *anything* when I climbed down to get her," he said. "But the mud, my balance, and my feet had other plans."

"What were you doing out here on your own in the first place? What were you thinking when you tried coming down that thing"—I waved at the steep wall in front of us—"in those boots?" I flailed at his feet next. "I have four-inch heels with better traction than those things!"

Jesse looked like he was fighting a grin. A second later, all humor left his face. "I am not answering another question until you tell me what *you* were thinking coming out here on your own. What you were thinking climbing down that thing in those things?" His pointed from the cliff to my boots. "And . . . and . . . how did you get here in the first place?"

I doubted my answer would put him any more at ease. "Sunny." I shrugged.

Nope, it definitely didn't put him at ease. It put him the opposite. "Sunny?!" He tried sitting up more, but he only made it a couple inches before grimacing.

"Would you lie back and take it easy?" I said. "Before you break or bust something else?"

He didn't right away, but Jesse eventually settled

335

back against the rock. I zipped out of the rain jacket and wadded it into a makeshift pillow.

"Rowen," he said, shaking his head, "put that back on right now. Don't be crazy."

"Jesse," I rolled my eyes and carefully stuffed it behind his head, "don't *you* be crazy. And don't tell me what to do." I rested my hand on the side of his neck, and even in the cold of the night and with the rain coating our skin, I felt the heat charging through our touch.

"Anything else?" he asked as he settled into the raincoat pillow.

"Yeah," I said, lowering my face over his. "Stop pretending like what I did was insane. Stop pretending you wouldn't have done the exact same thing if our roles were reversed."

Jesse's good arm lifted and his hand cradled my face. "That it?"

"No." I shook my head. "Stop pretending like you're mad at me because you suck at it."

A chuckle rushed out of his mouth. "I suppose I do." His thumb skimmed my cheek and, just like every other touch shared with Jesse, I melted into it. "But, Rowen, the guys would have found me. It wouldn't have taken them much longer. Why did you risk your life to find me first?"

A hundred reasons. A thousand explanations. I'd do it a million times over.

"I'm working on that whole healthy thing."

Jesse mirrored the smile on my face. "How is almost killing yourself healthy?"

I glanced over my shoulder, then back at him. "Because I'm here with you now."

"Is this the same girl who pushed me away, ran away,

and was so hung up on the deserve-don't-deserve thing?"

"It's the same girl. It's just the same girl who let a few wise words from a couple wise people set in. The same girl who let a few of her own realizations set in." I lowered my forehead to his, shielding us both from the storm. "Because I love you, Jesse. I know that I will love you more than any other person in the world ever could. Because you were right. Deserving has nothing to do with loving someone. I'm grabbing hold of what I want and not looking back."

Jesse's eyes stared into mine and they were as light as I'd seen them. "That sounds like a person who's gotten past her 'deserve' hang up."

I smiled. "Well, even if I haven't gotten *all* the way past it, I figured this whole saving your life thing was a step in the right direction." Jesse laughed, then winced. Apparently broken ribs and laughter didn't go well together. "So? Am I forgiven?"

"For being so careless with your life?" I felt his forehead wrinkle beneath mine. "No way."

I rocked my head back and forth against his. "No. For being careless with yours."

His eyes narrowed in contemplation as he murmured, "Hmm . . ."

Since he was working on making up his mind, I might as well help him. My lips dropped to his and rested in place. I wasn't sure I'd ever feel his lips again, for more than one reason, and I planned on enjoying the moment. When staying unmoving against him any longer was impossible, I sucked his lower lip into my mouth and tasted the rain coating it. I repeated the rain tasting with his upper lip.

By that point, Jesse's chest was rising and falling hard against me. As much as I wanted to kiss him until everything around us faded, the man all but panting below me had a couple of broken ribs. I pressed a final kiss to his mouth before leaning back.

"Okay," Jesse breathed, polishing his thumb over my lips. "You're forgiven."

If only everything were so easily fixed. But maybe, with Jesse, a lot of things could be so simple.

A light suddenly shone brightly down on us, startling me. I'd been so lost in the moment I'd almost forgotten the situation. I shielded my eyes and twisted around. The light came from a ways up, probably from the ridge.

"Am I breaking anything up?" a voice hollered down at us. "I can come back in twenty minutes or so if you want."

Jesse groaned and sat up again.

I stood up. "Garth? Is that you?"

The light shifted away from us. When it stopped, it shined on Garth's face.

"Convinced?" He flashed the light back down on us. "Maybe we can get you both out of there now."

"I'd rather spend the night out here than have Garth Black come save the day," Jesse muttered.

I was about to elbow him in the ribs when I caught myself.

"Jesse's arm and ribs are broken," I yelled up. "What's your brilliant plan for getting us up there from down here?"

"Thatta girl," Jesse said, tilting his chin at me. "Give it right back to him."

"Would you shush already?" I hissed back at him.

"You've got to be the only person alive who would turn away help from a guy because you don't like him."

Jesse shot me an exasperated look, then exhaled. "Garth?" he yelled. "There're three of us down here."

"You found the calf?" Garth circled the light around until it landed on the still sleeping calf.

Jesse lifted a brow. "I found her."

Garth's chuckle rolled down the ridge toward us. "No one could ever accuse you of not putting your heart, soul, and *body* into your work, Walker!"

"Why don't you stop talking and start working!" I shouted. "And your brilliant plan is . . .?"

I heard something swing through the air until it landed at my feet.

"A rope," Garth answered. That ego of his was dripping in two words.

"Did you find a good anchor up there, Garth?" Jesse asked.

"As good an anchor as I'll find. Now, I'm tired, I'm wet, and I'm ready to crawl into bed. So who's climbing up first?"

"Jesse!" I shouted.

"Rowen!" Jesse yelled at the same time.

Garth chuckled again. "Shit. I'm not getting any sleep tonight after all."

I spun around, my hands already on my hips. "I'm not arguing with you on this, Jesse. You're going up first."

"No, you need to go first, Rowen." He cut me off before I could interrupt. "You don't know how to tie a rope around that calf so we can get her up."

"And you can get a rope tied around a calf with one hand?" I stared at the arm he was cradling.

"I could tie a calf with no hands," he said. "I've been doing this for a while, you know?"

I exhaled my exasperation. He wasn't seeing reason.

"So we'll send the calf up first. Then you. *Then* me."

Jesse stayed so calm. He stayed as calm as I didn't. "And Garth's going to be able to wrangle a calf up there on his own while he pulls the two of us up?"

I opened my mouth, then clamped it shut.

"You need to go first so you can hang on to the calf while Garth gets me up. That's the only way we're all getting out of here."

"So we'll leave the calf. Your dad and the rest of the guys will be here in a few hours and can get her then." I couldn't just leave Jesse down there alone. I couldn't leave him.

Jesse's eyes landed on the calf. She really couldn't have looked more relaxed. She'd gotten separated from her mother, been lost in a storm, and had probably been terrified, but Jesse had found her. From the looks of it, that made everything all right.

"I can't just leave her, Rowen." His eyes shifted back to me. "I can't abandon her."

I knew I read more into those words than Jesse had intended, but I got it. I understood why he was the person he was. Why I'd fallen in love with him. Why he made me want to be the best person I could be. Jesse Walker didn't abandon a person, or in this case, an animal, when it needed him.

"Okay," I said. "We'll do it your way." The words were painful, but nonetheless, they were the right ones to say. "Are you sure you'll be able to get up that thing in your condition?"

"My condition?" Jesse smirked at me. "Rowen, I've had so many broken bones, I've spent as much time in casts and splints as I have without them."

I gave him an unamused look.

"I'm a cowboy, remember? I've got steel running through my veins."

"And hippie in your heart," I shot back.

"That's right," he said with a chuckle. "That's why I need the rope."

I was glad he thought the situation was amusing, because I sure as hell didn't.

"I just qualified for the senior discount up here!" Garth yelled down at us. "Is anyone planning on coming up? This decade?"

Jesse lifted his eyebrows and waited for me.

I sighed. "I am!"

"Ready when you are, princess!" Garth replied. "I've *been* ready."

Jesse hoisted himself up and came toward me. "Let's get that rope around you and get out of here." I grabbed the rope and handed it to him. "I'm ready to crawl into a warm bed with you."

Jesse was right. He really could tie a rope one handed. "In case you've forgotten you have bones inside your body that are broken," I said as he cinched the rope tight around my waist, "the only warm bed we'll be cuddling in is a hospital bed."

"Sounds perfect. Sign me up. You. Me. Bed. *Whatever* kind of bed." He gave the rope one final check. "She's ready, Garth!"

"It's about damn time," Garth said.

"Oh, and Black?" Jesse said, lifting his face up at the

light. "I'm putting Rowen in your hands. I'm *trusting* you." Jesse swallowed. "Take care of her, okay?"

Garth didn't snap back with his standard smartass remark. Eventually, it sounded like he was clearing his throat before he said, "I'll take care of her, Jess."

My mouth dropped open and I gave Jesse a look. "Did you guys just have a moment?"

Jesse looked as confused as I did. "I don't know. Maybe. I'll figure it out later. Right now, I want you to focus on getting to the top of that ridge safely."

"Hey," I said, "I've got a rope."

Jesse tried giving me a stern look. He sucked at that, too.

"See you at the top," he said, grabbing my face with one hand before pressing his mouth to my forehead.

"See you there," I replied. I turned to the muddy, rocky face I'd just come down and lifted a hand and foot to it.

"She's coming up, Garth!" Jesse hollered.

"For real this time?" Garth threw back sarcastically before the rope went taut.

Then with the help of the rope, and my hands and feet aiding in the journey, I made it up the wall. I glanced back once at Jesse. He watched me without blinking, almost without breathing. As I moved higher and the dark swallowed him up, I stopped breathing, too.

In at least a fourth of the time it had taken me to get down, I crested over the ridge. I curled over the edge and hoisted myself higher.

"Whoa, boy," Garth said, rushing around the side of his horse toward me. He kneeled in front of me and held out his hand. I took it and let him help me the rest of the way up.

We sat in the middle of the trail for a minute, catching our breaths. Garth tilted his head at me. "Good job, Rowen. Good job."

I nodded, too breathless to reply.

"She's up, Jess!" Garth shouted over the ridge. "She's safe."

He was a long way down, and there was a lot of space between us, but I could have sworn I heard him sigh in relief.

"Let's get this back down there." Garth worked the knot around my waist free before standing up and winding the rope between his elbow and hand. "Step back, Jess! The rope's on its way down!" Garth glanced over at me, a small smirk in place. "Not that it would do much damage if it did clock him in the head."

I swatted his arm and sighed. "Where's your flashlight?" I asked, looking around for it. "I'll hold it for you."

Garth smiled at me sheepishly. "The batteries died."

"The batteries died," I repeated and crossed my arms. "And you don't have any spares?"

He continued wrapping the rope around his arm. "I will next time."

The "next time" better not involve Jesse and broken bones.

I clicked my headlamp back on. It didn't produce near the amount of light Garth's flashlight had, but it was better than pitch black. After Garth had circled the rope back up, he heaved it behind him before tossing it out over the ridge.

"Got it!" Jesse called up.

While Jesse tied up the calf, or while I guessed he

was tying up the calf since I couldn't see since someone's batteries had died, I took a closer look at what Garth had rigged up. His big black horse was a little ways down the trail from us. The other end of the rope was tied to the saddle horn. From there, the rope was wrapped once around a young pine tree growing up the side of the ridge. It looked incredibly jimmy-rigged to me, but what did I know? For all I knew, that could be *the* way to pull both man and mammal up a steep dirt face.

"Where's Sunny?" I'd wandered a good ways down in the ravine before I'd found Jesse, but I wasn't sure if I'd wandered to the right or left of where I'd left Sunny.

Garth titled his head to the left. "A little that way," he said, "but don't worry. As soon as Jesse's up here, that horse will be right here, practically panting and waving his tail at him. That damn horse thinks it's a dog when it comes to Jesse."

I studied Garth toeing the ledge, adjusting the rope just so. If I didn't know better, I'd say he had a streak of hero running inside of him somewhere. "I have to say, you're pretty much the last person I would have thought would come save the day," I said.

Garth cracked his neck and continued examining the rope. "I've ridden this ridge dozens of times."

"So it isn't really *Suicide* Ridge?"

A corner of Garth's mouth twitched. "Only at night during a torrential downpour."

"Ah, fantastic," I muttered. "I feel so much better."

"Ready down here, Garth!" Jesse shouted.

"All right!" Garth headed toward his horse, then looked back at me. "You ever wondered if cows could fly?" He flashed a wink. "Well, you're about to see it with your own eyes."

"How about a little less talking and a little more working?" I called after him as I looked over the ledge. I couldn't tell how long I had taken to get up the face, but I wanted to be ready for that little thing whenever it got there. I already heard it crying its little calf cry.

"Gid' up, boy," Garth said, clucking his tongue. The rope starting moving up the face, around the tree, and down the trail. The calf was really giving her vocal chords a workout. I wasn't sure if she was bouncing her way along the side as the rope pulled her up, or if she was trying to climb, but either way, she didn't sound very happy about the entire situation.

"I can see her!" I shouted at Garth. "She's almost over the ledge."

"As soon as she is, give me a shout!" Garth yelled back.

The calf was making so much noise I wanted to cover my ears, but as soon as I grabbed her and pulled her up onto the trail, she calmed.

"Stop!" I yelled.

The rope went slack, and Garth rushed toward us.

The calf wasn't even struggling. Thank God, because she was a sturdy little thing, and I'd have my work cut out for me if she did decide to put up a fight.

"She's safe, Jesse! I've got her! She's safe!" And then, for reasons I wasn't sure I'd ever understand, I started crying. Almost sobbing.

Garth couldn't have looked more uncomfortable if he was wearing eyeliner and a tutu. After giving me a quick pat on the back and mumbling *good job*, he made quick work of untying the knots Jesse had fastened around the calf.

I sat in the trail, holding the calf, crying like the idiot I was, while Garth wrapped the rope around his arm again.

"All right. Two down. One more to go," Garth said before leaning over the edge. "Rope's coming down, Jess. If you don't make it to the top of this thing quicker than your girlfriend and a baby cow, I'm never going to let you live it down."

Jesse's chuckle rolled up toward us.

"His arm's broken, Garth. Not to mention his ribs, too," I said, giving him a small scowl.

"So?" he said before tossing the rope over the side again. "He can take a few pain relievers when he gets back to the ranch. You're not dealing with your wussy city boys, Rowen."

"That's right," I said, rolling my eyes even though he had his back to me. "I forgot you all are invincible gods."

Garth looked over his shoulder, "Nope, we've even better than that." I could see his smile gleam. "We're cow-boys."

"Set your timer!" Jesse hollered up. "Because I'm climbing!"

Garth gave another cluck of his tongue, and the rope snapped tight. I closed my eyes, held the calf tighter, and said a silent prayer. I'd never prayed before. I'd never known who to pray to. I didn't know who I was praying to now, but I sensed someone was listening.

"Get ready for him, Rowen!" Garth shouted at me. "That crazy S.O.B. really is going for some kind of a record."

My eyes snapped open and, sure enough, that rope was gliding up at least twice as fast as it had when the calf was coming up. I moved the once-again-asleep calf off of my lap, made sure she was tucked away from the ledge, then crawled toward it. Toward him.

Even in the dark, his white shirt cut right through the black. That, and his smile. He was climbing, using his legs and one arm in an odd looking but efficient way, toward me. His eyes locked on mine and his smile stretched.

A few seconds later, Jesse's hand dug into the dirt over the ledge. I grabbed it, dug my heels into the ground, and pulled. Working together, we pulled him onto the trail.

"I've got him!" I called out to Garth, cradling Jesse to me. "I've got you," I whispered before kissing the top of his head.

"Yeah," he said, winding his arm around my waist, "you sure do."

We rested that way for a minute, holding each other as we both regained our breaths.

"You found me, Rowen." He lifted his head. His eyes were shiny. "You came and found me."

I grabbed his hand and lifted it to my face. "Just returning the favor."

CHAPTER nineteen

We were back at the bus station. Back at the beginning.

Another month had gone by. Another month that was too good to be true. Another month with Jesse and the family I'd adopted as my own.

After making it back to the ranch the night of the storm, Jesse had been taken to the hospital to get splint up, cast up, and sewn up. He'd gotten his way, though. We'd crawled into a warm bed together later that night, although it was almost morning by then.

Jesse was released the next day, and everything went back to normal at Willow Springs. For the most part, at least. Climbing down a chimney wasn't an easy thing to do with one arm in a cast, so we improvised and learned to be really quiet tip-toeing into each other's rooms. I didn't believe we were fooling Neil and Rose, but neither of them said anything or seemed to care all that much.

After Garth and Jesse's "moment" that night, they seemed to make progress toward picking up their relationship. They weren't best buds like they might have been once, but they were getting closer. Once Garth stopped looking at me like I was a notch to be added to his belt, we were good, too. Pulling a person and a calf up over a steep wall had a way of forming a connection.

When I wasn't working or with Jesse, I hung out with Josie. In a short amount of time, we'd become the kind of friends I knew would last a lifetime. We were kindred spirits. The country girl and the city girl. I would miss her like crazy when I left for school.

After Rose and I had researched every community college with a good art school in the western half of the country, we struck gold when we found one that not only accepted late applicants but was in Seattle. It was almost too good to be true. I was winding up in Seattle, studying art, paying my own way. When my two years was up at community college, I could transfer to my dream school in the city if that's still what I wanted to do. After calling and explaining my situation to said dream school, they said they'd keep my application and acceptance letter on file and would "look forward" to seeing me in a couple years. So I was college bound, and that brought on so many emotions, I couldn't make up my mind what I felt most.

But right then, I was sad. I had on my brave face, but Jesse saw through it every time.

"Why aren't you letting me drive you to Seattle, again?" he asked, pulling me closer until his hat was also shielding my face from the sun.

I wouldn't cry. I hadn't cried earlier when I'd said my goodbyes to the Walkers. Not even when they'd given me the leather cuff bracelet I had on, with *Love is Organized Chaos* burnt on to the outside to serve as a daily reminder. Nor had I cried when I gave Neil and Rose a picture I'd sketched of their family rocking and swinging on the porch. I hadn't cried on the drive to the station either, so I wouldn't cry in the last five minutes.

"Because, one, your dad needs you on the ranch right

now." I wound my arms tighter around him, too. It would be the last time I'd have them around him for a while. "Two, because I'm positive Old Bessie would break down in the middle of North Idaho, which should really be considered its own country,"—Jesse rolled his eyes—"and three, because I'm kind of enjoying this full circle moment right now."

We glanced around the familiar place.

"I thought you hated the Greyhound." Jesse tilted his head at the bus behind me. The bus heading to Seattle.

"A couple hundred miles down the road, I probably will, but right now, I'm kind of loving it."

Jesse dropped his face into my hair and inhaled slowly. "How long until we get to see each other next?"

"I've told you, like, a million times."

"Is that melodrama I sense in your voice?" he teased. "This really is a full circle moment."

I swatted his backside. "Fall break. Six weeks from now."

"Six weeks?" His face twisted. "Crap. I'm going to forget you said that so I can pretend it's next weekend or something."

"We'll be all right."

"Easy for you to say. You're not the one who just lost his virginity a couple months ago and is eager to make up for lost time." His smile curved into place. The one that made my stomach drop and my thighs squeeze together.

"I'm sure we'll figure out some way to make it work." I arched an eyebrow.

"I'm sure we will." He kissed me for the thousandth time that morning. "What we have isn't the kind of thing that goes away when we're separated by time or distance.

It will suck not being able to kiss you every day, but that's a sacrifice I'm willing to make for you to be living your dreams."

If I wasn't already convinced Jesse Walker was a keeper, those words would have just convinced me. "And it's going to suck not being able to see your ass in those jeans every day, but that's a sacrifice I'm willing to make for you to be living your dreams."

He laughed as he held up the gift bag he'd been holding. "Mom made this for you, so don't blame me too much. I just supplied the material."

I gave him a curious look as I dug through the tissue paper until I found the present tucked inside. As soon as I pulled it out, I blushed and smiled. It was a shoulder purse Rose had sewn out of denim . . . Jesse's jeans to be exact. The worn material, complete with the *Wrangler* logo, was proudly displayed on the front of the purse. I slung it over my shoulder and couldn't pry my eyes from it.

"It's nice to know I can still grab your ass from a couple states away." I patted the outside of my purse.

"Yeah, yeah," he said, rubbing the back of his neck. "I wish I could do the same."

When I studied the denim purse against the rest of my outfit, I smiled even wider. I almost laughed. If I didn't look like I was positively nutso in the style department, no one did. I was in the burgundy dress Jesse had picked out for me, topped off with my favorite black hoodie, my cowgirl boots, and my new denim purse. It wasn't "freak" wear; it wasn't "country" wear. I was done with labels. I was done with letting them define me.

I was Rowen Sterling. I liked edgy clothing and kickass boots. I liked a pair of worn-in jeans and the boots my boyfriend had got me. I could be both. I could be whatever I wanted. The only person holding me back from doing that was me. I'd learned a lot of things that summer, a lot of lessons I'd take with me the rest of my life, but that was perhaps the one I'd hold closest to my heart. My future was wide open for the taking.

"I hate to break this up, kids, but the bus is leaving." A man cleared his throat behind me. Jesse and I sighed at the same time. We'd known it was coming, but it didn't matter how well we tried to prepare ourselves for it. It hurt like hell having to say goodbye. Even if it wasn't the permanent kind.

"Thank you, sir," Jesse said, tipping his head. "She's ready." But what I heard in his tone was *I'm ready*. So we were both ready, but that didn't make letting go of him any easier.

"Hey," the man said, "weren't you the guy looking for a young lady earlier this summer?"

I glanced over my shoulder and, sure enough, the same driver who'd driven me there was driving me out.

Jesse smiled at him. "That was me."

"Well?" the man asked, backing up toward the bus. "Did you find her?"

Jesse's eyes dropped to me. There was something in them I couldn't quite understand. It was something I wasn't sure I ever would. Whatever it was, I knew it was one thing: powerful.

"Yeah," he said. "I sure did."

I grinned at him, even though I felt the tears coming. I was too choked up for words, so I lifted up onto my toes and kissed him. It was a long, sweet kiss that wasn't nearly long enough, but I knew the driver was probably getting close to blasting the horn if I didn't get my butt on that bus.

"See you soon," I whispered, sweeping a quick kiss over his cheek. I turned and climbed onto the bus before I could throw myself back into Jesse's arms.

The driver nodded at me as I passed him. "I like that boy. He's just got something about him."

I smiled. "He certainly does," I replied, before climbing into an empty seat by the window.

Jesse was still smiling, a hand in his pocket and his casted arm in front of his stomach. Even through the dirty window of a Greyhound bus, he made me weak in the knees when he looked at me that way.

I waved, and he waved back. We were waving goodbye to each other.

I almost made it, but a tear dripped down the side of my cheek. As if Jesse had seen that tiny tear from where he was, he tipped his hat and mouthed those three words that had changed my life.

I'd come here one person, and I was leaving as that same person. Just that person who had let love into her life. The bus pulled away from the station, but I twisted in my seat and watched him until he disappeared. Way after I'd settled back into my seat and Jesse was long out of my sight, I still felt him. It didn't matter where I went or how far, I'd always carry him with me. What he'd done for me was something that didn't fade with time or distance.

Contrary to what I'd believed for a while, Jesse hadn't changed me. He just showed me the person I really was—the person I'd convinced myself didn't exist.

The rest was up to me.

ABOUT *the* author

Thank you for reading **LOST and FOUND** by bestselling
author, Nicole Williams.
Nicole loves to hear from her readers.

You can connect with her on Facebook: Nicole Williams
(Official Author Page)
Twitter: nwilliamsbooks
Blog: nicoleawilliams.blogspot.com

Other Works by Nicole:

CRASH, CLASH, and **CRUSH** (HarperCollins)
UP IN FLAMES (Simon & Schuster UK)
THE EDEN TRILOGY
THE PATRICK CHRONICLES

25254501R00209

Made in the USA
Lexington, KY
18 August 2013